TREEHOUSE

K.R. Mack

To: Forbes
I appreciate the support.
Hope you enjoy the tale.

Kevin

Dedicated to Haji, from my heart, for her unflagging faith

Thanks, Mary

PROLOGUE

Light and dark.

The mind makes the immediate connection to opposites. Stark contrasts in the strictest sense: such as man and woman, black and white, land and sea. The inherent qualities one possesses the other shall never have; and because of this, such disparate pairs remain eternally linked.

"Like night and day."

Sauter didn't mean to speak the words aloud and actually wasn't entirely certain whether or not he had. Not that it made any difference. Those around him were too preoccupied to have paid any notice. Besides, none of them were in on the running dialogue inside his head which led him to blurt out the words, if in fact he had.

"Whatever."

That was spoken aloud, albeit in a self-mocking voice not much louder than a whisper. Sauter repeated it with a shake of the head. He was willing to try anything to change the tracks on his train of thought. Maybe forcing himself to hear his own voice would do the trick.

"Sure, the same way I've learned to manipulate the old beltline to master those 'before and after' weight loss poses."

Sauter was talking inside of his own skull again and thinking it was a damn good thing. It was hopeless anyhow, he knew, because his thought processes had remained unchanged for the better part of the twenty-eight years he'd roamed the woodlands of northern Wisconsin. Fat chance changing now. Never willing to take something at face value or accept the obvious, Sauter preferred to delve deeper and peel back the veiled layers buried between the extremes.

It wasn't as if he fashioned himself to be a profound, complex thinker. An overthinker, maybe, but in essence Sauter believed he viewed things with an appreciation for subtlety and nuance. Take concepts as basic as light and dark, for instance. It's easy to grab hold of the fundamentals. Go into a *dark* room and turn on a *light*. One extreme to the other. There's no question where one ends and the other begins.

Yet, Sauter knew, nothing could be further from the truth. The forest was a constant reminder of that fact. Ever since he was a child Sauter had been helplessly enchanted beneath its canopy. Tracts of red pine, white pine and birch alternated with stands of oak and maple hardwoods; dense overhead growth broken by scattered open spaces.

Light and dark are equally at home in the forest, Sauter had come to appreciate, as is every shade in between. At sunrise and sunset the battles between light and dark rage with full force. If given the chance, Sauter took to the woods each day at dawn and again at dusk. He'd spent countless hours of his life huddled in a sleeping bag beneath the dew-soaked flaps of a canvas pole tent staring intently into the gray-black night, waiting patiently for the inevitable hints of an approaching sun. Or, conversely, hunkered down in a stand of pines as the last remnants of light flickered between the branches into a melancholy gloom, a precursor of the impending darkness lurking in the treetops.

In a purely aesthetic sense, Sauter drew immeasurable pleasure every time he bore witness to the sun's diurnal arrival and retreat. He coveted a certain satisfaction bordering on unabashed reverence in his knowledge that those two daily events never ceased to awe and inspire. Aside from that appreciation, a product no doubt of Sauter's so-called 'tree hugging' sensibilities, he never could shake a different take on daybreak and nightfall. This observation relentlessly coerced Sauter into drawing the inescapable comparisons with human nature, no matter how hard he fought against it. He couldn't think of a better way to spoil the simplicity of a sunrise than finding a way to connect it with the 'human condition'.

Leave it to me, Sauter thought. But the way the early morning sun infiltrated the woods, a virtual ebb and flow of shadow and light, it always seemed a great deal of effort was required to displace the darkness. The light seemed destined for the eternal struggle, although it certainly did give the appearance of winning the battle day in and day out. Sauter had come to accept the fact that this was just a ruse, a clever trick on the eyes if one was too lazy to look a little closer or change one's point of view.

Darkness never fully disappeared. Sauter exposed it tucked away beneath the thick, matted fronds of waist-high ferns. He found it lurking inside the rotting hulls of enormous white pine deadfalls or lazing beneath the outstretched arms of a mature oak. Darkness retreats into the low-lying cedar swamps, wrapping itself around the twisted trunks and clinging to the wet, spongy bog, holding the light at bay on the highground.

Come nightfall, it's a different story. Granted, there are similar gradations of tone, shade and color as the sun dips below the horizon, but darkness descends with little sign of struggle. And when the lunar cycle rotates to the new moon phase, darkness declares total victory. In Sauter's experience, there was no blackness like that found in the bowels of a forest on a new moon night.

The way Sauter had it figured, the same basic tenets hold true for people, only with a slightly more optimistic slant. There are a fortunate few who radiate light, their outlook and approach to life unburdened by a hidden, darker side waiting to shatter the calm surface. Then there are the less fortunate, those who wake up to face a daily struggle against the shadows lurking within their psyches. By Sauter's estimation the better percentage of humankind could be counted among the 'less fortunates'.

Lastly, and certainly not forgotten, are those who walk the face of the earth with blackened souls, trading in despair and evil as though forever trapped in a midnight woods. Shrouded in darkness, any redeeming light burns in incessant peril of being extinguished. Yet in Sauter's half-full, rose-colored glasses world, that would never happen. A ray would always find a place to hide even in the darkest of souls. Sauter tried to convince himself that this was true, but . . .

"What the hell, maybe I am a deep thinker," Sauter shrugged, reverting back to the spoken word. Deep thinker or not, it didn't take a genius to figure out that his way of thinking had brought him to this place on earth at this point in time. Barely past ten and the blackness of the late September night was oppressive, straining Sauter's eyesight until the trees loomed as hulking shadows and motion lapsed into a hazy, monochrome blur. Heavy clouds cloaked a moonless sky so the totality of the darkness came as no surprise; Sauter had pretty much expected that. He hadn't figured on coping with the distressing realization that a more malevolent, sinister gloom had cast its shadow over the forest.

On a normal night, this far back in the forest it would be dead quiet, save for the soft rustle of leaves in the breeze or animals in the underbrush. This certainly isn't a normal night, Sauter mused, trying desperately to shut out the chilling sobs and low, guttural moans rolling relentlessly out of the darkness. It was impossible. The mournful cries echoed off the trees and reverberated downward, pounding at Sauter until his skin turned cold and his knees fell weak.

The penetrating, high-pitched screeches of wood brushing wood tore into Sauter's ears as a weathered, ramshackle treehouse looming above his head rocked in the cradle of thick branches reaching out from the oak at his side. He steadied himself against the coarse, damp bark of its massive trunk, pinching his eyelids shut and clenching his fists. He stood that way for seconds at most, but to Sauter it felt like hours were slogging by.

He breathed deeply, filling his lungs with as much of the rich night air as possible. He forced his eyes open and pushed away from the tree. Sauter stepped beneath the thick, horizontal branch that bore the weight of the treehouse. He pushed upward with his right hand and lifted the small boy gently above his head, while at the same time loosening the coarse, blood-soaked rope that encircled and tore into the flesh of the tiny neck with his left. Sauter laid the lifeless, blue-gray body onto the forest floor and knelt beside it, the entire time wishing like hell that it was light.

*   *   *

Sauter stood back away from the others, his mind and spirit drained so that the only sensation was the sickness burning at the pit of his stomach. For the detectives still milling about, the night's work was over. All that was left now was the wait for the county coroner. A cup of coffee, a little bullshit, bag the body and call it a night. It wasn't that easy for Sauter, a rookie cop who had worn his blues two or three times max and then, boom, this hellish night. He was already trying to come to terms with the fact that this was going to stick with him for the rest of his life.

His eyes alternated between the blue cotton blanket shaped into the form of a little boy's frame at the base of the now menacing oak and the grim-faced, coffee-clubbing detectives milling about impatiently at the head of the trail leading out of the woods. Remorse, then disgust. And off on his own, sitting cross-legged and slump-shouldered beneath an over-sized police parka was another small boy. His vacant, bloodshot eyes stared unblinking at the lifeless form laid out on the bed of dead, brown pine needles that carpeted the forest floor. It was the victim's older brother, the tortured soul behind the haunting cries that had staggered Sauter earlier. Now quiet and statue-still, he sat abandoned by those who had supposedly come to their aid.

For Sauter, the whole eerie scene was more than he could bear. He wanted to go and comfort the child, but his temples were rocked by a mad pounding. Once again he felt his eyes squeezing shut and his fists rolling into balls. The ground rose fast and before he knew what happened he was on his hands and knees, swallowing hard to keep from filling the woods with cries of his own. Unlike earlier at the foot of the oak when the heart-stopping cries and tiny corpse swinging from the tree made time slow to a crawl, it now stood completely still, leaving Sauter to swing like a pendulum stuck in some horrific nightmare.

He didn't fight against it, either. Sauter found himself savoring the rocking sensation, an escape from the sickening reality the night had thrust upon him. Breathing gradually became less difficult, tense muscles slowly relaxed and frayed nerves grudgingly began to settle. Sauter shifted the bulk of his weight off his arms and crouched back against his heels in the sort of half-kneeling position favored by reluctant churchgoers. An awkward sense of serenity settled over him as his eyes stared half-focused into the smoky vapor swirling from his nostrils into the crisp, autumn air.

As the cold night overpowered his warm breath and the heavy mist from his lungs faded into the darkness Sauter's eyes snapped into focus. His entire body recoiled in rigid terror as he caught a glimpse of the young boy making a mad dash through the woods. A bone-chilling shriek of madness chased after the child as he careened through the trees in a dead sprint. Baby brother's dead body dangled like a rag doll from his arms, its lifeless head and limbs now animated and almost ridiculously alive, bouncing and waving in hideous time with each stride.

Sauter struggled to his feet but managed no more than a handful of stumbling steps before crashing back to his hands and knees. He groped along the forest floor, clutching fistfuls of dried leaves and dirt, helpless to prevent the abhorrent vision racing before his eyes from disappearing into the darkness.

CHAPTER ONE

Bright, blinding sunlight streamed into the room. The muted white walls were highlighted with bubblegum pink accents, a color scheme chosen deliberately to create a soothing, calming environment. The walls turned mirror-like instead and reflected the harsh glare with an intensity that contracted the muscles in the back of Dr. Amelia Devine's slender neck. She slipped her hand beneath the thick mass of black hair bunched about her collar and began to massage away the tenseness. No headaches now please, not on top of the stress already penciled into her schedule over the next couple of hours.

Devine had been a player in countless dramas similar to the one that was about to unfold over the course of the morning, but this particular story had transformed itself into the only personal crusade she could remember feeling so passionately about during her 15 years as a psychiatrist. Hell, probably the entire forty-two years of her life, she reflected, not sure if that held any meaning from a psycho-analytical standpoint or simply boiled down to the way life worked.

After all, growing up a Midwestern girl in the rural splendor of Wisconsin's rolling farm country didn't exactly provide the opportunity to latch on to many socially significant causes. Maybe there had been plenty of chances to totally submerge herself into something she believed in with all her heart and soul, but she had just been too naïve or self-centered to realize it.

As any good psychiatrist would, Devine always wondered if the dispassionate, emotionally introverted being she perceived herself to be could be attributed to some deeply rooted childhood trauma. Why not? That seemed to be the popular line of thought among her peers, as well as a reflection of society's way of thinking as a whole. Welcome to the new millennium, she mused, where personal and moral responsibility have taken a back seat to blaming your problems and shortcomings on someone or something else. Devine traced the origins of that cancerous way of dealing with life's setbacks to the self-absorbed seventies and eighties, placing a large part of the blame for its emergence on the scourge known as lawyers.

And what the heck, if she wanted to go that route herself, there was no problem recalling a general maladjusted upbringing spiked with one definitive moment that led to the stifling of her emotional development. Devine always started with her father. He was a short, barrel-chested man who deemed it his sacred responsibility to pound the same unrelenting work ethic into his children that enabled him to toil through a never-ending string of 12-hour days to keep his small dairy farm afloat.

There could only be one reason why any man worked as hard as her father did to provide food and shelter for his family, Devine figured, and it had to be out of love. Throw in his obvious love for the farm itself, his love for the animals under his care and his generational love of God and country, and old James Devine should have been bursting at the seams with love, by his daughter's reckoning. It wasn't a case of ever doubting his love. She bought into the whole 'actions speak louder than words' ideal; but Devine had always yearned to hear it spoken affectionately in her ear, or feel it through the soft caresses of a warm hug.

But that wasn't ever going to happen with her father. You could bet the farm on that. His voice never carried the slightest hint of affection and his touch was something to be avoided at all costs. The only time she felt the 'caress' of his hand was when it met her backside during one of the far too frequent reminders that laziness, uncleanliness, or any of the other numerous regressions she committed would not be tolerated.

That was just the way life worked, Devine presumed at the time, too young to worry about any future psychological consequences. But one childhood memory in particular left the scars which had grown into the barrier that formed the emotional cocoon she felt trapped inside.

She had nurtured a piglet that, under her care, had grown into a sow of elephantine proportions. She was rewarded for her hard work with a series of blue ribbons at the county and state fairs. Devine had named the pig Frenchy, dressing it up in a matching blue scarf and beret, an idea she stole from an episode of the old television show *'Green Acres'* in which Fred and Ethel Ziffel's pet pig Arnold wore the same outfit during an artistic phase he was going through. She treated Frenchy the same way the Ziffels treated Arnold, like another member of the family. In no uncertain terms, she loved that pig.

Then came the unforgettable, traumatic day when Devine jumped off the school bus and ran directly to Frenchy's stall in the barn, just like she did every other day. But on this particular day the stall was empty and the pig was nowhere to be found. That night, on the dinner table, nestled in among the mashed potatoes and peas, sat a steaming heap of pork chops. And to this day, some thirty-odd years later, Devine could still close her eyes and become that little girl clutching the back of an old wooden chair, her tears splashing off its wicker seat as she gaped in horror at the evening's meal. That's the precise moment Devine sealed herself off emotionally. She was certain of it; just like she knew from that moment forward she'd become a vegetarian.

Now, after all these years, she'd found herself another Frenchy. He stood just tall enough that the top of his head barely reached the shoulders of the two guards who flanked him. An oversized orange jump suit, crumpled and flashing neon in the bright sunlight, made him appear almost shapeless as he shuffled toward the solitary metal folding chair at the center of the room. His thin hair, tinged gray at the temples, and pallid, wrinkled skin drooped like a wet baggie from his skull. Couple that with his stoop shouldered, defeatist demeanor and Christopher Koenigs cut the profile of a man well beyond his thirty years. His dry, colorless lips formed a weak smile as he took his seat before Devine and three other doctors seated beside her at a long, rectangular table.

"Good morning Mr. Koenigs, thank you for coming," Devine began, realizing that everybody in the room knew he had no other choice. She pressed the record button and started the tape rolling on a miniature recorder before her on the table.

"It is 8:50 a.m. on Thursday, August 30, 2007 and this is case number 2502, the mental competency hearing of Christopher John Koenigs as administered by the medical examiners board of the Municipal Mental Health Center on behalf of the state of New York. My name is Dr. Amelia Devine, chairperson of the medical examiners board and the director of the psychiatric unit here at Municipal Mental. I'll let my colleagues and Mr. Koenigs identify themselves for the record and then we'll begin the hearing."

Dr. Sarah Perkins spoke next, just as Devine expected. Dr. Perkins was more or less the state's hired gun, in Devine's estimation, there to vigilantly wave the flag of caution when dealing with what she believed was a deranged criminal mind like Koenigs's. Perkins was a highly regarded and tenured professor at a respected private university who had made a splash in psychiatric circles a few years back with research into what she referred to as the "innate or genetic sociopath;" a naturally bad seed, so to speak.

In a nutshell, Perkins had set out to prove that unlike the average criminal who possesses the basic tools to reason between right and wrong, then opts for the latter, the genetic sociopath is born without the ability to make the distinction and therefore the choice. In her opinion, these are the inherently evil individuals who occasionally enthrall society by manifesting their deranged and antisocial behavior in extreme forms, such as murder, torture or rape; generally in early childhood.

The case studies she had presented to support her theory were a macabre group of sadistic prepubescent murderers, sodomists, rapists and complete moral degenerates who were incapable of expressing regret for the most heinous of acts. Definitely not your average little grade schoolers at play here.

Perkins had detailed the case of Karl Meriter, who, at the innocent age of nine, herded a half-dozen kids from his suburban St. Paul neighborhood into an ice shanty, locked them inside with a heavy steel chain, and proceeded to douse the tiny wooden hut with gas and set it ablaze. Paramedics who diverted his catatonic gaze from the twisted, acrid-smelling pile of charred flesh noted that Meriter 'like the flip of a switch' lost all interest in his handy work and bounded around with giddy excitement at the sight of the fire trucks.

Incomprehensible is the word Perkins always used to describe the particularly gruesome story of 11-year-old Nadine Kasten, who coupled her first babysitting job with a crack at a little in-home biology. Following the steps outlined in her older sister's high school textbook, the budding scientist meticulously dissected the neighbors nine-month old as he lay screaming in his crib. When the young parents arrived home from dinner and a show, they found Nadine at the kitchen table eating vanilla ice cream with chocolate syrup, her hands reddened by the infant's dried blood and his tiny organs arranged in a neat semicircle around her bowl.

Perkins's studies were replete with such ghastly scenarios. She had documented several cases, each a vignette of evil and mayhem cloaked by the innocence of youth, with one common thread that had tied them all together. The young children who had committed the soulless acts did so with impunity and afterwards had neither understood nor regretted what they had done. That, in Perkins's summation, ruled out mere imprisonment or any form of treatment as options for dealing with the demonic youngsters. Lock 'em up, she had no qualms with that; but she had also maintained that such severe cases should be the focus of rigorous testing and observation over a lifetime, with no hope of rehabilitation and release back into society.

"You gotta open that clock up to find out what makes it tick," became Perkins's favorite, albeit unoriginal, catch phrase during a highly anticipated speaking tour on the heels of the publication of her research. Professional and would-be psychiatrists had forked over one hundred and fifty bucks a pop to sit slack-jawed and aghast at the lurid tales of childhood depravity. It was high times for Perkins, whose long legs, cascading blond hair and warm smile may have accounted for some of those slack jaws in the audience; even though she was two years on the top side of fifty. In addition to the lecture series, which had been videotaped and ultimately broadcast during public television pledge drives, she hit the talk show circuit and hob-nobbed with the rich and famous enough to become both herself, if only to a modest extent.

At times, Devine couldn't help but wonder if part of the reason she clashed with Perkins was because she subconsciously envied her success and good looks. Probably not. Devine was happy with her rung on the ladder and had left a long trail of broken hearts as testament to a subdued, girl-next-door attractiveness. It wasn't exactly philosophical differences at the core of the rivalry either; not as far as the big picture was concerned, anyway. Devine had read all of Perkins's studies and had even coughed up the one-fifty to attend a lecture. From a professional standpoint she had felt compelled to endorse Perkins's work; and, although not the best of friends, had enjoyed her company in social circles as well.

That was all before Christopher John Koenigs came to roost in cell C- 28, Block 3, on the seventh floor of central New York state's gray and decrepit Municipal Mental Health Center. Koenigs's arrival a dozen years ago had been a much-heralded event. Two days removed from his eighteenth birthday, he had been honored by the esteemed Dr. Sarah Perkins as the latest addition to her steadily dwindling supply of "genetic sociopaths". In recognition of that honor, Koenigs had received a free one way trip to the East Coast, along with free meals and lodging for the better part of his early manhood.

In reality, he already had that deal, minus the trip to New York, having spent the last 10 years of his life enjoying the amenities of a typically depressing and dilapidated state mental health facility for the criminally insane in the Midwest. It had been, in fact, an anonymous tip from Koenigs's home state of Wisconsin, where he was incarcerated, which had piqued Perkins's interest in his case and pulled her halfway across the country to meet face-to-face with the prospective case study and his doctors.

The type-written letter had arrived in Perkins's office in a plain white business envelope with no return address, bearing the postmark of what she had come to learn was a former little logging town, by the name of Broadaxe, tucked away in the northern tip of the nation's dairy state.

"Dear Dr. Perkins," the letter had opened, its print barely legible from a typewriter ribbon nearly devoid of ink.

"I have to admit I had never heard of you, but now I can claim to be a big fan of yours after viewing your lecture series on our local public television station. The topic fascinated me greatly. I enjoyed watching you so much I pledged $200 to the station and in return received my own videotapes of the lectures, along with an autographed copy of your book.

The real reason I'm writing to you, however, involves a man by the name of Christopher Koenigs, who I believe fits your profile of a genetic sociopath as described in your lectures and book. To get right to the story, when he was eight years old Koenigs took his six-year-old brother out in the woods one night, dragged him up into a tree house, slipped a noose around his neck and pushed him out the door. From the information I have there is a slight variation from most of the cases you have cited because Koenigs was quite emotional when police arrived on the scene, crying wildly and even running off with his dead brother's body.

But I also know that his demeanor changed quickly and detectives on the scene testified at his trial that Koenigs's tantrum and crazed behavior appeared to be an act. He rarely speaks now, aside from occasional hallucinatory outbursts, and there is no record that he ever expressed any remorse over what he had done. He was convicted of murder nearly nine years ago, found criminally insane and placed in a central Wisconsin mental health facility for treatment and observation.

I have enclosed the address and the names of the physicians who are in charge of Koenigs's case on the chance that it may be of some interest to you. Thank you for your time, and good luck if you choose to pursue this further."

Perkins could hardly contain her excitement upon reading the letter, she had admitted later, and made arrangements that very same day to travel to the Midwest and meet with Koenigs and his doctors. She was already outlining methods for "cracking Koenigs's crystal and getting a glimpse of his inner gears" aboard the plane from New York to Wisconsin, she had recounted verbatim time and again during her lecture series; this before she had ever laid eyes on the patient or exchanged any correspondence with his attending physicians. At the time the drama had unfolded, and to this very day some 12-odd years later, Devine had viewed Koenigs as an unfortunate victim of timing and circumstance, thrust into Perkins's influential clutches at the precise moment her case study had desperately needed a new poster child.

While Devine viewed Koenigs with the same compassion she had nurtured for that prize pig as a child in Wisconsin so many years ago, she had come to realize with a certain amount of contempt that to Perkins he amounted to no more than a plate of pork chops.

"Christopher John Koenigs epitomizes the profile of the genetic sociopath and has therefore been selected for admission into my case study of this behavioral phenomenon. Effective immediately the patient will be transferred from Wisconsin to the Municipal Mental Health Center in New York state and placed under my direct supervision."

With those two sentences Perkins had made it abundantly clear just how far-reaching and powerful her influence had become within psychiatric circles. In less than 48 hours she had pulled all the right strings and twisted each appropriate arm necessary to change the course of one man's life. Koenigs had been two short weeks shy of his eighteenth birthday and his corresponding mandatory release date when the anonymous letter had crossed Perkins's desk and effectively ended any hope he had had of escaping institutional life for the foreseeable future.

Now, beaten down by twelve years of intense study and supervision, having been poked, prodded and manipulated until mind, body and soul withered and decayed, he sat mute and at the mercy of others once again. His hollow eyes and laconic gaze reflected the hopelessness trapped within the tormented being who had run this despairing gauntlet so many times before. He sat perfectly still and appeared uncomprehending, or merely uninterested, as the two remaining psychiatrists on the examining board identified themselves for the record.

Barry Karet and Ruth Welsch were two doctors caught in the middle of the tug-of-war over the fate of one man that their colleagues had struggled with for the better part of a decade. Whereas Devine and Perkins harbored impassioned and unflinching opinions in regard to Koenigs and their roles in his treatment and ultimate fate, their associates, in contrast, had divested themselves of any personal agendas; and had more or less relegated his case to just one more statistic among the seemingly endless parade of non-descript faces they dealt with on a daily basis. That had made it relatively easy for them to side with Perkins in both 1999 and 2003 when Koenigs's case had come before the examining board as required every four years. Perkins's high-profile, high-influence persona translated into big money and recognition for the institution and those associated with the case. The realities of Koenigs's situation and the impact their decisions had upon his fate appeared minuscule in comparison.

Devine was under no illusion that things would be any different this go-round, yet she remained steadfast in her conviction to once again allow Koenigs a proper hearing and a chance at a life outside the blinding white walls. Perkins had wielded her enormous influence to thwart Devine's efforts at every turn, lobbying hard for legislation to provide mandatory life sentences for individuals diagnosed as 'genetic sociopaths', regardless of the youthfulness of the individuals she had so labeled in her case studies.

"One needs to look no further than the unfortunate and unacceptable examples of the folly of past decisions for which we all can be held accountable," Perkins's voice boomed as she rallied support for the proposed legislation.

"Do the names and misdeeds of Karl Meriter and Nadine Kasten mean nothing? Does not the mere mention of those abominations against all that is moral and just, plus simple common sense, raise the bile of disgust and provoke a desperate need to ensure that such incomprehensible evil is never unleashed again?"

Devine could only nod in agreement at the time she had heard those words spoken, yet she knew in her heart that the proposed solution was unacceptable. Christopher John Koenigs was living proof. He had nothing in common with Karl Meriter and Nadine Kasten, she was certain of that; so much so that she had spent the last decade of her life trying to prove it. Her crusade had fallen on deaf ears thanks to Perkins, who had managed to irrevocably link Koenigs's name to those of ghouls like Meriter and Kasten.

And ghouls they were.

Karl Meriter and Nadine Kasten escaped the strict structure of the Perkins case studies thanks to mandatory release guidelines for juveniles under existing law at the time of their offenses. Born in the same year, the two were to be released within weeks of each other. Of course, Perkins vehemently opposed "the release of unreasoning, unforgiving evil back upon an unwitting society when the foundation for understanding from whence such evil originates has only recently been established. They have no remorse, no conscience to speak of and in my estimation no control over the dark forces in possession of their minds."

What they did have, however, was star power. Through a societal perversion not uncommon in such macabre cases, the two had obtained a certain celebrity which translated into money for the case study coffers and clout for Dr. Sarah Perkins. Meriter and Kasten were also among the first to earn the "genetic sociopath" label, and through several years of study Perkins had effectively proven that they had earned it. As if the heinous acts both committed at such tender young ages were not enough, their case study files bulged with the horrid bloat of twisted thoughts, emotional detachment and inherent evil which the rational mind is loathe to comprehend.

But those same files also contained the normal background information, such as birth dates; and, to Perkins's chagrin, the date each attained their eighteenth year and corresponding mandatory release had arrived before she could rally enough support to do anything about it. With their departures, the case studies she had dedicated herself to for so many years were on the verge of being relegated to the back shelf of current psychiatric thinking. If interest waned, the funding would disappear soon after; and Perkins feared that the theories and ideas she had so passionately espoused would inevitably fade into obscurity as well.

The initial media frenzy and public interest accompanying their releases had dwindled quickly, and months rolled by without a mention of the term "genetic sociopath" whenever the elite of psychiatric circles gathered socially or professionally. Yet the fates work in mysterious ways, and within the year events had transpired to bring the name of Dr. Sarah Perkins and the term she coined, "genetic sociopath", back to the lips of the collective psychiatric world.

Karl Meriter touched a match to the gasoline he had

carefully sprinkled throughout the halfway house he had been sent to, burning alive the five other residents and two counselors he had padlocked into a small pantry off the kitchen. He was arrested a short time later, eyes rolling wildly, white spittle covering his chin, laughing maniacally in the completely unsettled audience of a children's puppet show. A half-eaten apple, some chewing gum and enough matches and lighter fluid to burn down the theater were nestled in a small canvas gym bag at his feet.

Nadine Kasten removed an eight-month-old baby girl from a shopping cart at a local mall, tucked the sleeping infant in the flaps of her coat, and blended into the crowd. When authorities arrived at the home of Kasten's mother, they were sickened by the gruesome scene awaiting in the backyard. A metal shaft pierced the length of the infant's body, entering the swollen and bleeding rectum and exiting the gaping mouth, perched above a bed of coals as if prepared for some type of cannibalistic spanfarkle. The crime scene photos had reminded Devine of her long-lost pet pig in a perverse, nauseating way. Kasten sat straight-backed at a picnic table, eerily humming a familiar children's tune while interlacing the infant's eyes and vital organs onto a shish kebab between chunks of onion, tomato and pineapple.

There would be no case studies for the demented duo this time around; only scathing indictments, moral indignation, and the promise of a lethal injection under adult laws. And although Perkins had been vindicated in both general ideology and specific opposition to the pair's mandatory release, the hope of future case studies had still appeared bleak. In contrast to the early days of her work, "genetic sociopaths" had suddenly seemed to be in short supply.

Then, one fateful September day in 1995, the anonymous letter from a small Midwestern town had landed on the desk of Dr. Sarah Perkins. In a miraculous quirk of timing, Perkins had found her new poster child. Coupled with the insidious recidivism of Meriter and Kasten after their release, the introduction of Christopher John Koenigs had heralded a glorious rebirth for Perkins's nearly defunct genetic sociopath case studies. Medical professionals across the country had feverishly pointed to the example set by Meriter and Kasten as definitive proof of Perkins's theories, and had decried the unimaginable consequences lying in wait for society if future cases were not dealt with in the appropriate manner. Lost within the atmosphere of apprehension and self-flagellation over past mistakes had been the numerous instances of individuals who had obtained the Perkins moniker of incorrigible genetic sociopaths through horrible childhood transgressions, participated in the case studies, and upon their releases had become active members of society who had never offended again.

Under these circumstances, in a tumultuous environment rife with disillusion and remorse, Christopher John Koenigs became the instrument necessary to assuage the collective guilt and correct the egregious errors of the past. Correspondingly, there was little resistance to Perkins's proposal to make Koenigs the guinea pig for a new wrinkle in her rejuvenated case studies, an experimental program she referred to as Extensive Examination Beyond Mandatory Release.

Devine had represented the lone voice of caution and had opposed the idea as "an unqualified affront to civil liberties and a direct violation of an individual's rights to due process under the law." Just three years removed from completing her master's dissertation and then attaining her doctorate in psychiatry, her opposition had been duly noted and quickly dismissed, despite the fact that she was lauded as a rising star in the field and had recently been elevated to the directorship of the medical examining board of the state of New York.

Now, twelve years later, she found herself in the same position from both a professional and personal standpoint, although with one very important distinction as to why she held so fervently to her belief that Koenigs epitomized the picture of a man dealt a grave injustice by the system. Back when Koenigs had become an unwitting scapegoat for a society bent on revenge and seeking absolution for past mistakes, Devine had rallied to his defense based purely on the antiseptic belief that this faceless individual was being denied the basic rights granted each person within a democracy. It was shortly after she had met the man and familiarized herself with his case history that she had become convinced he had been wrongly accused and convicted in the first place.

A tragic childhood accident, in Devine's estimation, had resulted in the untimely death of Koenigs's younger brother Michael. The inevitable shock of such an awful experience accounted for the catatonic stare and emotional isolation Perkins had so convincingly attributed to an inherent evil that lurked within the tormented young child. Merely mentioning the names of Meriter and Kasten in conjunction with Koenigs had been enough to evoke horror and indignation, leading even the most rational of psychiatric minds to swear an oath that no one could accuse them of standing idle in the face of evil incarnate.

In the man sitting stoop-shouldered and defeated in the metal chair before her, Devine still saw the frightened little boy who had witnessed the death of his brother so many years ago. She knew Perkins would never be swayed to her way of thinking, nor convinced that the time had come to allow Koenigs the freedom which he had been unjustly denied for far too long. Yet, as she had each and every time Koenigs's case had been reviewed in the past, Devine hoped against all hope that her colleagues Karet and Welsch would finally see the light and act to correct the injustice that had festered beneath their watch.

"Christopher John Koenigs."

His colorless lips barely parted when he choked out the words, nearly inaudible in the funeral-parlor quiet that hung over the room, threatening to close in and crush all those trapped beneath its uncomfortable burden. As if on cue, papers shuffled, throats cleared, and a collective sigh of relief was almost palpable as the dictates of the competency hearing were finally set in motion. Each of the participants had walked this road before. None held any illusions that this latest incarnation of a well-worn script contained the promise of a surprise ending. That all changed with one sentence.

"I sit in judgment before you and ask that in your collective wisdom you see fit to grant me the release that I have long deserved and long been denied."

Devine could hear the rush of air past her ears as her head snapped to attention and unbelieving eyes focused on the pathetic figure slumped before her. When she regained her composure she glanced peripherally along the table at her colleagues, who stared at Koenigs with owl-wide eyes and mouths agape. Silence cloaked the stale air once again. The figures at the table sat back in rigid stillness, unable or unwilling to move as the suddenly animated eyes of the helpless creature before them darted back and forth, searching the fractured countenances of those before him.

Silence still.

Finally, struggling to remain composed and fighting to stifle an almost schoolgirl giddiness rising within her, Devine attempted to speak. Her mouth opened imperceptibly and her lungs unleashed the pent-up air, sounding as if an inner-tube lodged deep within her diaphragm had sprung a slow leak. Her teeth clicked audibly as she snapped her mouth shut and swallowed hard. Devine felt the collective stare of the others in the room bearing down upon her; and, in turn, she met each pair of eyes in an effort to capture the gravity of the moment.

"On behalf of the board, I'm here to promise you that we will do our best to grant you a fair and honest hearing," she finally answered after what seemed like an eternity since Koenigs had spoken. Straining to maintain a calm voice and demeanor, she turned and looked at Perkins as she continued.

"I'm well aware these assurances may have a hollow ring from your perspective, Mr. Koenigs, considering your past history before this board; and, for that matter, your entire history with regard to this institution in general." Perkins stared straight ahead, fists and jaw clenched, as Devine turned her attention back to Koenigs.

"As you are well aware, the grave responsibility involved with deciding your fate does indeed fall squarely upon our shoulders. It is true that in the past," she paused momentarily, glancing at her colleagues, "considerations outside of the sphere of matters pertinent to your case have greatly influenced the decision-making process. That is unacceptable and it is my intention to remedy that situation. It is also true, Mr. Koenigs, that part of the responsibility lies with you and the necessity on your part to help convince us that a decision to grant your release would be a correct decision. In that vein, it is very encouraging to note for the record that you have finally decided to speak on your own behalf; and quite eloquently I might add.

I do sincerely hope that it is indeed your intention to speak on your own behalf at this hearing."

Devine could still scarcely believe what was occurring. She was quite pleased with her own display of self-control under such shocking, emotionally-charged circumstances. For the first time ever Koenigs had entered a plea on his own behalf and had done so with a self-assured tone and rational demeanor. Since entering the institution in New York it was, in fact, the first time Koenigs had spoken more than his name or an occasional yes or no. His files contained no tangible evidence or documentation in support of the board's recurring decision that he remain institutionalized; he was in truth an ideal patient. Nor did it contain any compelling reasons to grant his release, other than the bewildering length of his incarceration. In Devine's estimation, simple common sense and human decency indicated that he had more than served his time.

In recent months there had been a growing sentiment among her peers in support of that opinion, but the lingering ghosts of Meriter and Kasten had scared away any desire to act upon those convictions. Devine had fervently maintained that if Koenigs could only tell his story, if he had the capacity to express himself by breaking through the emotional scars that shut him off from the outside world, it would become readily apparent that he was a far cry from the devil's seed Perkins had made him out to be.

Now, it appeared, that time had come.

"Yes, doctor, I do intend to speak on my own behalf. It is my contention that I am fit to return to society. I have held this belief for many years now, and have lived with the obviously misguided hope that others, such as yourselves, would share that opinion. I have done all that has been asked of me. I have served my sentence without incident and have been nothing less than entirely cooperative. It is true that it has been many years since I have spoken with anyone other than my God and myself. . ."

"Have you spoken with your brother lately?"

Perkins rose abruptly from her chair as she fired the question at Koenigs, as if she were the crusading district attorney center stage in an unfolding courtroom drama. She leaned forward over the table, resting the weight of her upper torso on the whitened knuckles of her clenched fists. She eyed Koenigs with a menacing stare and brooding posture that made Devine wonder if evil did not, in truth, lurk among them. Devine could not help but notice her colleagues Karet and Welsch squirming uncomfortably in their chairs as well, incredulous eyes scanning Perkins in search of some method behind her apparent madness.

Unlike those seated before him, Koenigs showed no visible reaction to the purposefully provocative question. If Perkins intended to trip some wire inside Koenigs's brain, send him into a demonic rage, or make him revert back to a helpless mute, she had failed miserably. With the same calm voice and placid expression, he picked up where he had left off as though Perkins's question had dissolved in midair before reaching his ears.

". . . and God has, many times I suspect, spoken back. This provided a great comfort to me, and is the sole reason why I sit before you today as sane a person as any in this room. I have never questioned my sanity at any moment during this long ordeal. I have endured the deepest, darkest chasms of depression. I have often questioned the very meaning of my existence; this I will not deny. In this regard, I suspect I am no different from most souls who inhabit this planet. If one could find any humor within this awful existence, it would be the insistence of certain individuals that I embody the essence of evil itself."

Devine found herself reveling in the words as they flowed effortlessly from Koenigs's dry, pursed lips and fell upon her ears as if all the heavenly angels had lifted their voices in celestial song. She wanted to let him continue speaking, unabated, ridding himself of the toxic thoughts and horrid memories which had festered inside this broken-down being for so many years. But she sensed another spiteful volley in the offing from Perkins, who appeared incapable of moving from the rigid pose she had struck when she sprang to her feet moments earlier. Devine decided not to give her the chance.

"Mr. Koenigs, do you think you could elaborate upon your bouts of depression, as well as the aforementioned questioning of your existence? Did suicidal thoughts ever enter in; and/or desires to inflict pain upon yourself or others?"

"Hurting myself or others? No . . . no. I admit that many times I wished that I were dead. I suppose in one sense that is what I meant by questioning my existence. Why my brother Michael and not me? Why should my lungs fill with air and my heart pump my lifeblood while Michael lay cold and rotting, robbed so prematurely of the cherished promise of many happy days? Coping with thoughts like these, locked for all these years within the walls of institutions, labeled as evil and the murderer of my own flesh and blood, do I really need to describe the inevitable onset of depression?"

Perkins had settled back into her seat and was about to pounce once again, but the raspy, cigarette-soaked voice of Dr. Barry Karet cut in. With caring, pale blue eyes set wide and twinkling in a pink, cherubic face, Karet had a childlike quality about him which made it hard to believe he was on the cusp of his sixtieth year. Thick black curls dangling unkempt above his brow furthered the youthful illusion. His outward appearance created a pleasant mask for the all-together unpleasant soul residing within.

"Insofar as being labeled evil and your brother's executioner, I admit to finding that scenario a little depressing myself. Yet did not your brother, in fact, die at your hands? Does your recollection of that day differ from the facts contained within the police report pertaining to the incident? Are you refuting those facts now, and if so, wouldn't it have been more prudent to do so twenty-two years ago?" Karet placed the pen he had been fidgeting with in the corner of his mouth, a poor replacement for the cigarette his lungs yearned for and hardly the placebo for his restless disposition.

Koenigs, head lowered, rocked slowly from side to side, his small frame absorbing the words like a ring-tempered boxer fighting off body blows. When he spoke, the calmness had deserted his voice and an odd mix of melancholy and desperation had taken control of his vocal chords.

"In all honesty, I have no recollection of that day. I wish I could remember, but there are times I think it's a blessing that I don't. We ran in those woods and climbed into that treehouse many times before that day. Recalling those times, good times, I have no problem at all." His voice trailed off to nearly a whisper. He cleared his throat and began again.

"Michael was two years younger than I was and a little bit smaller, but he was quick as a deer and could climb like a monkey. We had to cross a small field of lupines to get to the woods from our house, not more than a hundred yards from our back door, and every time Michael would race ahead and disappear into the maze of tall purple cones. Sometimes he'd lie in wait and jump out to scare me like some wild animal; or I'd break free of the flowers just in time to see him scramble up the trunk of an oak or dance like a howling madman on the dried leaves of the forest floor. Nine times out of ten I wouldn't lay eyes on him again until I climbed into the treehouse, panting and breathless after the quarter-mile run.

I can picture those days from so long ago as if they were yesterday, but that one particular day, the day that changed my life forever, as far as my memory is concerned it never happened. Those first few years when they put me away in Wisconsin, those amount to no more than a blur in my mind as well. Whatever happened that day, somehow I sealed it off and tucked it away in a corner of my mind that remains closed to this day. But even if all my memories were erased, there is one certainty that can never be taken from me. I loved my brother Michael with all my heart. I could never have taken away a life I held so dear."

"Is that what you'd tell Michael whenever he'd pay you a visit?" Perkins had bounced back to her feet again, the confidence of a poker player who had rigged the deck ringing in her voice. She had played her trump card and intended to savor the moment.

"Tell us, Mr. Koenigs, does Michael still come calling? Has he made the trip from Wisconsin to New York or is he waiting patiently back in the Midwest for the day his older brother returns? If you have visited with your brother lately, we'd most certainly be interested to hear all the details."

Devine knew that it was only a matter of time before Perkins broached that subject. The question had to be asked, and if her antagonistic colleague hadn't done so, she would have been remiss not to ask it herself. Over the course of the first few months of his incarceration in Wisconsin, there had been several instances where Koenigs fell into what his doctors at the time termed "depraved and hysterical rantings" purporting that his recently deceased sibling was appearing in his cell. The doctors did their best to disengage Koenigs from this torturous hallucination, but this would only elicit more frantic protestations:

"Michael touched me!" . . . "He talks through a hole in his neck!" . . . "Michael stares at me when I'm sleeping!" . . . "He's dead but he's not dead!"

Koenigs screamed those phrases, among others, repeatedly during the weeks immediately following his brother's death. His voice did not contain the frightened, high-pitched tremolos one would expect from an eight-year-old in such an agitated state. Quite the contrary in fact. The doctors noted a "deeply disturbing, hard-edged and throaty quality to the child's voice, highly incongruent with that of an eight-year-old." They also described it as "nerve-wracking" and "sinister".

And then, nearly a year to the day since his brother had died, Koenigs fell silent. He retreated into the empty-eyed, unspeaking shell of a being that would shape his character for the better part of the next decade. The indelible image that followed him into that introverted and isolated world was that of an unbalanced, maniacal murderer who had found his rightful home within the walls of an institution for the criminally insane.

Now, thirty years old and half-a-country removed from those tormented days of his lost childhood in Wisconsin, Christopher John Koenigs had rediscovered his voice. It was a far cry from the sinister and nerve-wracking intonation since he had last spoken. Instead, it carried a resonant, almost melodic quality that was both confident and self-assured, even beneath the withering glare and unrelenting inquisition of Dr. Sarah Perkins.

"Mr. Koenigs, have you conveniently lost the ability to speak yet again, or do you intend to respond to my question? Has your brother Michael kept in contact with you over the years?" Perkins's mocking tone sickened Amelia Devine to the point of embarrassment for herself and her two colleagues beside her. She could see that Drs. Karet and Welsch were on the verge of being overwhelmed by the spectacle unfolding before them, so she moved quickly to try and restore some sense of order and civility to the rapidly deteriorating proceedings.

"Take as much time as you need to answer Dr. Perkins's question Mr. Koenigs. It is very important that you do answer her question, and you should be warned that your response could weigh heavily on the outcome of this hearing. Rest assured that we are well aware of how difficult this must be for you, and of the pain inflicted by resurrecting these memories; so once again, take your time and answer Dr. Perkins's question regarding your brother Michael to the best of your ability."

Devine could sense the heat from Perkins's penetrating stare bearing down upon her. Her attempt to defuse the explosive environment Perkins was trying to create through her provocative style of questioning was guaranteed to enrage her egocentric colleague, but Devine cared little about that at this point. There might be hell to pay tomorrow, but today belonged to the little man in the oversized orange jumpsuit seated before them.

"That was a lifetime ago," Koenigs began softly, his tone and expression incomprehensibly calm, as if he sat within the eye of the storm as those around him battled against the raging hurricane.

"It was so long ago now that I often find myself questioning whether it all ever happened. Of course, we all know what my history holds. There are no secrets. And there are no magic words to change what happened in the past. There is a chance to change the future. That is the one hope that drives my bleak existence. I have lived in darkness. I yearn to see the light.

My brother Michael did indeed visit me many times when I was younger, just as I had claimed at the time, and in fact he still visits me to this day. But I realize now and have known for many years that Michael visits me in my mind, my memories, for that is all that I have left of him. When I was a child, dealing inadequately with the inevitable shock in the immediate aftermath of his death, I was incapable of separating fantasy from reality. I was so desperate in my desire to have my brother back, to once again run through the lupines and climb the trees of the forest, that those memories came to life and Michael came to life as well. When that happened, when my memories did come to life, there ensued nothing like the joy and rapture Michael and I shared when we were together. Far from it.

The result, instead, was pure and unabated horror. In my desperation and despair the Michael who I resurrected was not the carefree youngster who I had grown up with, rather it was the horrendous reincarnation of that pale blue and bloodied boy who had dangled like a ragdoll from a rope beneath that treehouse. I was haunted by that ghoul, that tormented spirit which my mind had conjured up from the netherworld. No matter how I tried I could not rid myself of that Godforsaken illusion, that illusion that had become so terribly real.

So I retreated within myself and shut myself off from the outside world, closing my mind to both fantasy and reality until there was no feeling at all. Only emptiness. Peace, quiet and blissful emptiness. Most importantly I had rid myself of the demons of my own creation, of the nightmarish existence that I had created for myself. Then and only then did I regain my capacity to distinguish fantasy from reality, but it was much, much too late. While I was withdrawn within myself others had created a new reality for me, a reality more disheartening than any of the fantastical nightmares that had haunted me before.

I had become the devil himself, the demon seed, evil incarnate. I had emerged from my self-imposed cocoon with a new-found hope that I could soar like the most beautiful of butterflies, only to fly headfirst into the flames of hell which I have endured for oh so many years. Facing that reality, that terrible reality not of my making but one thrust upon me by others, I found solace once again by hiding within myself. Yet unlike before I did not shut myself off completely. I only found it necessary to close my mind to those who threatened me, those who had transformed me into an evil entity, those who had crafted the most recent incarnation of my nightmarish existence.

Yet in my naivety I did not realize I was shutting out those who controlled my destiny as well. It was a lose-lose situation from my perspective. I could crawl back into my cocoon and allow the blissful emptiness to overwhelm me or I could emerge to face my demons. In the past I withdrew."

Koenigs paused and very slowly he met the eyes of the four doctors seated before him, finally locking his unblinking gaze with the steely-blue irises of Dr. Sarah Perkins.

"Today, I choose to face my demons."

CHAPTER TWO

"Demons? It takes him more than two decades to get up the nerve to speak and when he finally does he's got the balls to look us square in the eyes and call *us* demons?!"

The veins in Perkins's neck had turned a purplish-blue and bulged beneath her soft white skin, rising like the wrinkled ridges of mountainous areas on relief maps. Her nostrils flared wide as a raging bull's and she jabbed emphatically at the smoke-drunk air of the small, oval-shaped staff lounge. She spoke to the three doctors seated around her, each trying to find some measure of relaxation during a welcome break from the hearing, but her message was directed elsewhere. The words erupted from her throat and flowed down the corridors, resonating clearly through the open door of the board room four doors down where the pathetic figure in the oversized orange jumpsuit sat stoop-shouldered in the folding metal chair.

"I gathered the impression that Mr. Koenigs was in fact quite singular in his intent even though he spoke in the plural about confronting his demons," Karet interrupted through a veil of cigarette smoke that only partially hid the wry smile he flashed Perkins's way. Drawing hard on the third of a chain of cigarettes, he paused a moment as if he expected a retort from his irate colleague, then continued when there was none forthcoming.

"Dr. Devine? Dr. Welsch? Did either of you take it as a personal affront when Mr. Koenigs spoke of demons? I myself most certainly did not. Whatever or whoever those demons might be is known only to Mr. Koenigs and is merely conjecture on our part. What is reassuring is the fact that he has apparently come to terms with those so-called demons and has learned to deal with his problems in a constructive manner. Silent for two decades or two days, the voice that emerged today was reasonable, rational, and sane."

Devine would have been thunderstruck to hear one of her fellow doctors use any one of those three words in connection with Koenigs prior to the events of that morning. Attaching such an eloquent voice to the face that had been treated so unjustly for so many years made it very difficult to once again summarily reject Koenigs's release. Devine realized that; but she also knew from experience that her colleagues were capable of anything. Karet had provided her with an opening and she didn't hesitate to jump in.

"I understand that Mr. Koenigs's competency hearing is scheduled to begin again in fifteen minutes, but we've been over the facts of his case innumerable times and are all well aware of what is at stake. With that in mind, please indulge me while I reemphasize just what is at stake. One man's freedom. One man's life." Devine anticipated immediate and vehement opposition, but she plunged ahead without hesitation.

"Therefore, I put forth a motion to correct an injustice that has lingered for far too long by granting Christopher John Koenigs his immediate and unconditional release."

The metallic click of Karet's lighter forewarned of cigarette number four and of the additional smoke to be exhaled into the already polluted room. Beams of sunlight reached tentatively into the swirling vapors, extending and retracting like the tentacled arms of an octopus cautiously feeling its way across the ocean floor. The smoky light encircled the salon-styled head of Dr. Ruth Welsch, shrouding her dyed black hair with a wig of smog that blended perfectly with her graying temples. She consciously avoided eye contact by keeping her gaze on a stack of papers she shuffled with trembling hands.

Devine expected as much from her notoriously timid colleague. In her mid-sixties and closing in rapidly on retirement, Welsch was the senior member of the quartet in age and in tenure at Municipal Mental. Yet her proclivity to consistently defer to Perkins, coupled with an unwavering reluctance to add any input or original thought to the proceedings, cast an ineffectual shadow unwarranted for an individual who was so accomplished. She certainly wasn't going to stick her neck out and be the first to address the issue raised by Devine. Nor was Karet, perfectly content drawing hard on his cigarette with audible inhalations, much the same as a child trying to extract every last bit of juice out of the bottom of a glass through a straw.

That left Perkins, who stood in the doorway of the

small staff room and stared down the hallway toward the place where Koenigs sat patiently awaiting their return. Her expression gave the appearance that she was expecting a response to the words she had hurled down the corridor moments ago, or was anticipating the distant echo of her voice in some far off corner of the institution. The color of anger had retreated from her face, and her blood had cooled sufficiently to allow her veins to disappear beneath the slender curve of her neck. She shook her head slowly from side to side and chuckled softly through full lips, painted glossy pink to match the tailored coat and knee-length skirt clinging to her enviable figure.

"Just like that. It's that easy. All he needs to do is talk, string a few sentences together and assemble a few coherent thoughts and, voilà, he's cured." The words quivered with her laughter as she turned and walked back toward the center of the room. "Years of work and tangible progress toward understanding what makes a deranged individual like Koenigs tick and for what . . .? To throw it all away just when he displays an ability to finally communicate, a breakthrough that could be an immeasurable asset in the overall success of our case study?"

"Just like that?"

Devine was as stunned to hear the question explode from the perennially passive Welsch as she was by the incredulous and mocking tone of the question. Like a volcano come to life after lying dormant for ages, Welsch erupted and spewed out the emotions which had simmered deep inside for so many years.

"I wouldn't exactly call twenty-two years 'just like that'. Twenty-two years, Dr. Perkins, twenty-two years. We've crawled around inside that poor man's brain for so long now that if he wasn't truly crazy before it would be a miracle if we haven't driven him to it. What I saw before me today, despite all that he's endured, was in no way representative of the deranged, sociopathic, evil entity which we had conjured up to validate our recurrent and apparently improper decision to repeatedly block his release. We have the opportunity to make amends today, but Dr. Devine is putting the cart well ahead of the horse to suggest that we abandon all procedural guidelines and forego the required afternoon session by rendering a decision during a cigarette break!"

Karet took the reference to cigarettes as his cue and weighed in with his opinion, stubbing out number five in the ashtray before him as he cleared his throat with a forced phlegmatic cough.

"We are required to act under the restraints of strict procedural guidelines as Dr. Welsch has pointed out and, although admirable in her desire to bring this prolonged case to an accelerated and just conclusion, I also agree that Dr. Devine is outpacing herself in an attempt to resolve the matter right here and now. We need to return to Mr. Koenigs and fulfill the requirements of the competency hearing, and I think we should get back to it right now. Hell, I'm out of smokes anyway." He patted the pockets of his shirt and pants with open palms as he finished speaking.

After so many years of being the lone dissenting voice in Koenigs's behalf Devine was overcome by a strange mix of joy and apprehension at her apparently newfound position among the majority. For the first time she was confident that Karet and Welsch would finally cast their votes in accordance with hers and Koenigs would be released; but she couldn't shake the nagging fear that something would happen in the interim to change their minds. Perkins would do everything in her power to bring about that change, but Devine sensed an air of resignation and defeat overwhelming her rival as she trailed behind on the return trip down the corridor.

"So that's it, the decision has been made? What's the point of continuing this hearing if all we're doing is going through the motions?" At first Perkins's voice was weak and wavering, but she quickly recovered and spoke with a renewed sense of urgency. "You are reopening Pandora's Box and, mark my words; you will pay for this decision and rue the day it was made. I never dreamed I would have to remind anyone of this. I was certain that it was a sordid fact of our shared history that none could forget. The names Meriter and Kasten and the atrocities they visited upon innocent members of society surely could not have been forgotten, but if they have shame on you. You have my pity, but not my forgiveness for making the same mistake again!"

Perkins hit her target with the doomsday reference to Meriter and Kasten as Welsch visibly winced when she heard the names spoken aloud. While no one associated with the release of the two young sociopaths escaped the ensuing guilt when they departed the institution and proceeded to kill again, the incident took a particularly heavy toll on Welsch. She tumbled into a prolonged period of dark depression and intense self-loathing, teetering on professional and personal ruin as she tried to battle her way out through a disastrous combination of pills and alcohol. The downward spiral bottomed out with what was officially ruled an accidental overdose, an episode referred to in hushed tones and whispered conversations as a botched suicide attempt. To her credit and to the astonishment of her peers, Welsch emerged from months of physical and mental limbo and gradually fell back into the normal rhythm of life.

There was never any hesitation on Perkins's part to resurrect the unpleasant memory and hurl it wantonly at Welsch as a callous means to her desired end, and Devine despised her for it. At each of Koenigs's previous competency hearings the dreaded names of Meriter and Kasten and all the horrors implied therein eventually rose to the forefront of Perkins's impassioned pleas against release. Devine recognized the tactic as a direct attempt to sway Welsch's vote, but in the past she had viewed it as an unnecessary exercise since she had been certain Welsch's mind was set against release.

Now, Perkins's effort to invoke the demons of the past yet one more time seemed no more than an act of desperation. Welsch opened the door and locked eyes with Devine and Karet as they entered the conference room where Koenigs slumped patiently in the folding metal chair. She stared with steely resolve foreign to her normally timid nature, drawing battle lines with a stoical expression determined to keep Perkins out of her head.

Devine's lips parted into a thin smile as she slipped through the doorway and Perkins's pleading voice trailed off behind her. How unbelievable, she mused, that the dread she had felt for the impending day just hours before had been miraculously transformed into near euphoria. Her fatalistic approach to the competency hearing, though completely warranted by past experience, created an awkward sense of guilt that she had somehow let down her guard in her defense of Koenigs. Now that it appeared his release was probable, a type of twisted logic made her think that she was derelict in her duties for not approaching the hearing with a more optimistic attitude.

"Don't spoil the moment," she thought to herself, pushing the guilty feelings out of her mind with a conscious decision to enjoy the final chapter in the otherwise disheartening saga of Christopher John Koenigs. In the past, with the outcome inevitably decided against Koenigs's release before the competency hearing even commenced, the afternoon session became an agonizing exercise in compulsory drudgery which Devine dreaded. Now, she eagerly looked forward to completing the required review of Koenigs's entire case history, buoyed by the virginal hope that this time would be the last.

As Koenigs shifted restlessly in the uncomfortable metal chair in the center of the room, Devine sat waiting at the conference table with Drs. Karet and Welsch while Perkins lingered outside the door for several minutes. Devine suppressed a rising surge of panic at the thought of Perkins abandoning the hearing altogether and leaving Koenigs hanging in a state of limbo. She breathed an inaudible sigh of relief as Perkins finally reentered the room and took her place beside them. Koenigs sensed the air of defeat that hung over Perkins like a rain-soaked overcoat. A glint of hope sparkled in his normally dull eyes. His sloping, overburdened shoulders slowly drew back as he straightened his posture and sat erect with anticipation.

"It is 1:15 p.m., Thursday, August 30, 2007, and we are set to resume the competency hearing of Christopher John Koenigs, case number 2502, with the required review of the aforementioned's case history." Devine wasted no time getting started and was determined to dispense with the requisite formalities as rapidly as possible. She began by reading into the record the police report from the night of Michael Koenigs's hanging. At the two previous competency hearings Perkins repeatedly interrupted Devine as she read the police report, interjecting her own opinions or emphasizing a fact contained therein which she interpreted as support for denial of release. This time around she sat silent and unmoving throughout. Devine even paused at the appropriate times in anticipation of a Perkins outburst, then resumed once again, a bit surprised that there was none forthcoming.

The report detailed the discovery of six-year-old Michael hanging from a noose beneath a treehouse in an oak tree in the heart of a northern Wisconsin forest. Michael's tiny hands were tied loosely behind his back with a short length of coarse twine, a fact that Perkins viewed as evidence of premeditation in the boy's murder; yet she sat mute. There was no sign of any struggle. Perkins normally contended that this showed how the elder Koenigs took advantage of his younger brother's unquestioning trust to commit the murder. Devine paused, but Perkins said nothing. Christopher Koenigs wailed and cried when officers first arrived on the scene, then suddenly stopped and stared straight ahead with a calm and quiet disposition. A well-orchestrated act, Perkins usually suggested, citing the same interpretation of his actions from some of the officers at the scene as proof. Today, she sat in silence.

Devine continued to read from the report: "Upon arrival at the scene interviewed four eyewitnesses who claimed to have seen Christopher Koenigs, with a deliberate and stated intent to kill, put a rope around his younger brother Michael's neck and push him out of the treehouse beneath which his dead body was found. Each of the eyewitnesses, who identified themselves as neighborhood friends of the brothers, told similar stories of the elder Koenigs boasting that he was going to hang his younger brother and then laughing convulsively as he watched him dangle from the rope beneath the tree. All stated an overwhelming fear of Christopher Koenigs and were found waiting at the trailhead leading into the woods when we arrived at the scene."

"How do you explain the testimony of these four eyewitnesses, these neighborhood friends?" Welsch interrupted to pose the question, apparently emboldened by her earlier admonition of Perkins. "I'd like to hear your opinion of this now that you're on speaking terms with us."

"I wouldn't call them friends." Koenigs's response was immediate, but his slow and deliberate delivery conveyed the conviction behind his words. "I can't explain their testimony. I don't believe it, but I can't explain it, either. Nor can I dispute it. As I said before my memory of that day is incomplete, a shadedcorner of my mind where the details of that . . . stay just out of reach. Those four said what they did for a reason. As to what that reason is, you'd have to ask them."

There was a momentary pause after the exchange and for the first time Devine noted an irritated, almost angry tone in Koenigs's voice. A spasm of discomfort coursed through her body as she braced for an all-out assault by Perkins, who surely couldn't allow an opportunity to rattle the unsettled Koenigs slip away. Perkins maintained her silence, however, and by doing so made it explicitly clear that she was distancing herself from the competency hearing and its anticipated outcome.

"There is one other item in regard to the police reports pertaining to the events that transpired on September 20, 1985." Devine continued, more than happy to accommodate Perkins, reading from the only eyewitness account congruent, as she interpreted it, with her belief that the hanging was accidental: "Upon entering the woods I followed a trail for approximately one-half mile to a clearing which contained a lone, large oak tree near its center. I immediately noticed a young child's body, that of Michael Koenigs, hanging from a rope that exited the open door of an old, wooden treehouse suspended in the oak. It was obvious the child was dead. I also noted another young boy, Christopher Koenigs, struggling unsuccessfully to lift the boy hanging from the rope to safety. Christopher Koenigs was hysterical and appeared to be in shock, repeatedly crying 'No Michael, No Michael' as he tried in vain to save his brother. I forcefully disengaged Christopher Koenigs from his brother Michael's body, covered him with my police parka and attempted to calm him as best I could. Christopher Koenigs continued to cry uncontrollably as I returned to the tree, removed the rope from Michael's neck and lowered the dead child to the forest floor."

Each time Devine read the twenty-two year old words of then rookie police officer Henry Sauter, it reaffirmed her conviction that Christopher Koenigs did not purposely kill his brother. She harbored a secret desire to make Sauter's acquaintance and over the years had conjured up an idyllic fantasy of a chance meeting on one of her infrequent trips back home to Wisconsin. She had forged a powerful, imaginary alliance with a man she had never met who lived halfway across the country. It was Sauter's words she invoked whenever she made her impassioned plea for Koenigs's release, and she turned to them one last time, hoping that this time they would serve as confirmation for Karet and Welsch that the time had finally arrived and the decision they seemed to be leaning toward was the correct one.

"The first individual on the scene, police officer Henry Sauter, describes a Christopher Koenigs who in no way resembles a cold-blooded murderer. Would a cold-blooded murderer be 'struggling unsuccessfully to lift the boy hanging from the rope to safety'? Would a cold-blooded murderer repeatedly cry out his brother's name as he tried in vain to save him? Would he cling to his brother's dead body so tightly that a grown man twenty years his senior would have to forcefully remove him?" Devine didn't wait for an answer. She never did when she posed these questions.

"No, a cold-blooded murderer would not make an effort to save the intended victim. No, a cold-blooded murderer would not loiter about at the scene of the crime, clinging to his victim in grief and desperation. These are not the actions of a deranged killer, these are the actions of a devastated child trying desperately to save his brother's life. No, Christopher Koenigs is not a cold-blooded murderer. Sadly, he is the true victim in this case."

The speech was standard fare for Devine and she was grateful her colleagues indulged her one last time without interruption. When she finished, she quickly switched gears in an effort to bring the hearing to a rapid conclusion. Devine touched briefly on Koenigs's institutional life in Wisconsin and New York, once again revisiting some of the same episodes that had been discussed earlier that morning. She opened the floor to a final round of questions and closing remarks, an opportunity that the recently taciturn Perkins was unable to resist.

"The decision we are about to make can be influenced either by emotion or by fact. Our emotions tell us that this man seated before us, having spent the majority of his life behind institutional walls, deserves a chance at a so-called 'normal life'. The facts tell us that any chance this man ever had at a normal life evaporated in the crisp air of a fall night twenty-odd years ago in Wisconsin when he hung his little brother from that treehouse." Perkins walked to the front of the table where her fellow doctors were seated, turning her back on Koenigs as she spoke.

"We have learned a great deal and in all probability have saved a great many lives through our work here. There is so much more knowledge to be gained, knowledge that will only continue to save lives in the future. All of that promise walks out the door with Christopher Koenigs if we listen to our emotions and grant his release. Rather than saving lives we will be putting lives at risk if we return him to society. Tragically, history reminds us of that risk, a risk that I am as yet unwilling to assume. Whether we are guided by emotion or by fact, we all will have to live with the inevitable repercussions of the decision we make here today."

Perkins turned and stared at Koenigs when she finished, focusing intently on the pathetic figure before her as if she were trying to commit that exact moment in time to memory. She moved to the table and gathered up her belongings, then slowly retreated from the room without another word.

Devine nodded to the guard standing by the doorway, and a uniformed young woman, auburn hair cropped close beneath a baseball cap too large for her head, took Koenigs by the elbow and escorted him back to his cell. A look of total bewilderment covered his face as he shuffled slowly across the room and disappeared into the hallway. The fading afternoon sunlight pushed long patches of darkness across the floor and along the walls, fingers probing the interior of the room like the distorted digits of a shadow puppet. A hazy shaft of light crept between the shadows and illuminated the equally bewildered countenance of Dr. Ruth Welsch, who stared absently into the emptiness of the room before her. She spoke softly, either to herself or to the emptiness, but her words would echo in Devine's head for days to come.

"I pray to God that we're doing the right thing."

A small wooden writing desk, a beige upholstered chair, a brass lamp with an undersized shade, a painting on the wall, a twin bed with a dark blue felt blanket and a separate bathroom with a toilet, sink and shower. For the past twelve years, this was Christopher Koenigs's universe. It would have been the envy of an individual of modest means in search of shelter, save for the bars on the door and the less-than-ideal location on the seventh floor of a decrepit mental institution in central New York state.

Nonetheless, to Koenigs this was home and he was glad to be back. He trudged mindlessly to his bed and sat down hard, leaning back against the cool, gray concrete that walled him in. The events of the day swirled through his head in a frenzied jumble of words and images. It had been so long since he had reason to hope that he struggled to identify that elusive emotion now that it had crept back into his being. But what was there to hope for? Freedom? Freedom certainly didn't guarantee an escape from the nightmares and the dark thoughts that ran roughshod through his brain in unrelenting waves of terror and torment.

After so many years of silence he was genuinely amazed at how freely the words flowed earlier when he finally opened his mouth to speak. That made it easy to understand the look of astonishment on the doctors' faces. It wasn't what he said; merely speaking was enough to elicit the stunned silence and disbelief of those who sat in judgment before him. If they had listened, they might have realized that he was only telling them what he thought they wanted to hear. He certainly didn't tell them everything, far from it, but he realized there were some things they didn't need to know and other things they definitely would not understand. At times he was forced into blatant lies, but for this he held no remorse, only fleeting regret. He regretted that Dr. Amelia Devine would suffer the consequences of his evasiveness and deceit. He had little regard or little concern for the effect it would have on the other three. If he had told the truth and been completely straightforward there was no chance in hell that they would grant his release, he was certain of that.

The bombardment of thoughts and images boiled into a raging vortex, ripping through his head and twisting his mind until he lay dizzy and devoid of strength, unable to fight off the unrelenting onslaught. Desperate to escape, he struggled to focus on the purple cones of the lupines that burst forth from the painting that hung on the wall opposite his bunk. He lost himself in the soft lilac hues and rich lavender tints of the watercolor flowers that had magically carried him outside of the institution's walls so many times before. His eyelids hung heavy as he slowly slipped into a calm and peaceful world far removed from the reality of his dreary existence.

His childhood home loomed in the distance, a mirage in the desert of his youthful memories. The gray, peeling walls breathed in and out and the sunken, green-shingled roof rose and fell, as though viewed through heat waves rising in a great distorted curtain. With labored, deliberate steps he backed away from the vision and a sea of purple washed over him. The long spikes of the lupines towered over his head, swaying gently in a warm breeze that pushed the flowers' sweet, perfumed scent down upon him. The soft petals tickled his neck as the stems wrapped around his body, giant floral tentacles constricting movement and obstructing vision to the brink of suffocation.

The breeze grew to wind and the lupines eased their grip, caressing his upper torso as they withdrew. The wind roared and the flowers snapped wildly in the robust air, suddenly menacing as they lashed at his ears with a wicked whistle and thunderous rustle that built to a deafening crescendo. He closed his eyes and the commotion ceased abruptly, as though his blinking flipped some massive, meteorological switch. He opened his eyes to a silence and stillness unnerving in its totality. Unseen weights tugged downward at his arms as he struggled to lift the heavy limbs, which tingled and burned as if awakened from a deep slumber. He reached out and parted the statuesque lupines, which shattered upon his touch and fell to his feet like thousands of shards of tinkling, purple glass.

And there stood Michael, grinning from ear to ear and

signaling 'follow me' with a sweeping wave of his right arm. His straight, dark brown hair spiked from his scalp in an uncombed mess and his translucent blue eyes sparkled with all the mischief befitting a six-year-old. He wore his favorite tee-shirt, red with faded white lettering stenciled on the front. Cut-off blue jeans revealed a pair of dirty knees and equally dirty white socks peeked out from the top of his black high top tennis shoes.

The forest stretched endlessly behind him. Oak and maple hardwoods loomed above him with umbrellas of green leaves tinged yellow and red with the slightest hint of an early fall day. The massive trunks of old growth red pine and white pine disappeared into the hardwood canopy, busting through the ceiling to unveil cone-laden branches painted a rich green by their long, slender needles. Smaller conifers, balsam and spruce, sprouted in thick, random patches throughout the otherwise open forest floor.

Michael clicked the heels of his tennis shoes and his legs became animated with the steps of a queer little jig, an odd and comical variation of the traditional highland fling. Brown pine needles scattered with each footfall as he stomped spasmodically into the sandy duff. A hyperactive sprite set free within a magnificent arboreal landscape, he turned and danced away. Christopher tried to follow his little brother, but the weight which had encumbered his arms had now taken hold of his legs as well. He struggled in vain to move forward, yet with each labored step Michael and the trees of the forest seemed to fade farther into the distance. "Wait, Michael, wait!" he cried out with all his might, only to hear the words parting from his lips no louder than a whisper.

Just as Michael was about to disappear behind a thick, green curtain of balsam branches, the weight lifted and Christopher flew through the woods with the fleetness of Hermes. The forest around him dissolved into a blur as he raced toward his brother, a three dimensional figure standing in stark contrast against the nebulous background. In an instant they were face to face, estranged siblings reunited in the forest playground of their childhood dreams. Christopher felt Michael's hot breath upon his face, smelled the sweet scent of his favorite grape bubblegum and saw the unquestioning, carefree love they shared in his eyes. Great beams of sunlight bathed the brothers in warmth as the forest swirled about, placing them at the center of a giant carousel of trees. Christopher rejoiced in the feeling of complete and unadulterated bliss, surrendering himself to a happiness unattainable in the conscious world. He reached out to embrace his brother, to draw him close and swear to never let him go again, but Michael was gone.

The sunlight retreated into the treetops and dark, menacing shadows slowly snaked their way across the forest floor. The thick stand of balsam trees rustled in the icy wind that propelled the darkness deeper into the woods. *Christopher.* The windblown trees hissed his name; or was that Michael calling? *Christopher.* He heard it again and goose-bumps jumped from his flesh, stirred by the suddenly chilled air and the sinister whisper of his name. *Christopher.*

"Michael, is that you?" He dashed headlong into the dense tangle of evergreen branches, calling in desperation as the black of night cloaked the forest. The limbs tore into his skin, thorny obstacles impeding the frantic search for his little brother. A flash of Michael's red shirt just ahead, just out of reach, then just as quickly gone. The wind blew harder and the shadows grew blacker. *Christopher.* He pushed forward through the trees flailing wildly at the grasping branches, his cheeks stained by tears and sweat. His feet tangled and he somersaulted to the ground, coming to rest face down in the carpet of dead pine needles. Gradually and with intense foreboding he raised his head. He recoiled in abject horror at the haunting vision rising before him in the ebony sky.

A ramshackle treehouse loomed above him, eerily moaning and creaking in the cradle of an imposing oak tree's branches. The magnificent oak stood alone at the center of a clearing in the forest and Christopher could only watch hopelessly as Michael climbed up the trunk and disappeared into the treehouse. Paralyzed with fear and overwhelmed by terror, Christopher wanted desperately to run as far away from the menacing treehouse as his legs would carry him. Instead, he was dragged toward the oak by some unknown force, carried against his will up the rough bark of its trunk and pushed into the pitch black interior of the treehouse.

Pale light shone into the darkness through a door at the far side of the treehouse, silhouetting Michael's small frame and the noose that hung around his neck. Christopher groped his way blindly along the walls in the dark, searching desperately for an escape. Eyes suddenly glowed at him out of the darkness; vicious, horrid eyes, first one pair, then two, three and finally four pairs of horrific orbs that burned his flesh with their menacing stare. The eyes closed in upon him and he stumbled hopelessly toward Michael and the open door. Whispered voices whirled about his head and he slapped his hands across his ears to shut them out, but it did no good. *Push him! Go ahead, push him! Push him! Push him! Push, push, push, push, push* . . . The eyes surrounded him and the voices roared in his ears. He reeled backwards and lost his balance, tumbling into Michael and sending his little brother out the door. He watched in stupefied horror as the rope quickly unraveled and trailed out the door behind him, then snapped taut and swung like a pendulum before his horrified gaze.

"Christopher . . . Christopher."

The voice drew him back out of the treehouse, out of the forest and through the field of lupines. He blinked his eyes and looked at the purple-coned flowers in the painting on the wall. His hair was damp and his palms were clammy with sweat as he rose from his bunk. He turned and saw Dr. Amelia Devine peering through the bars on his door.

"Mr. Koenigs, I have some good news for you . . ."

Good news for one is bad news for another, Koenigs thought to himself, well aware that his freedom was at hand.

CHAPTER THREE

The early morning sun eclipsed the treetops and ripped the sleep from Margaret Schumacher's eyes. She squinted hard into the harsh glare, battling to bring the late summer day awakening outside of her window into focus. Heavy lids rose and fell slowly, unveiling tired orbs with bloodshot roadmaps converging upon the deep green irises at their centers. Scratching the scalp beneath a thick red mane misshapen by a restful night on the pillow, she surveyed the new day with a mounting sense of incredulity.

"Wake up, Tim. You are not going to believe this." She shook her husband by the shoulder and shook her head at the same time as she continued to gaze upon the world outside. Undeterred by his obvious displeasure at being rousted from his dreams, and unwilling to observe the sanctity of a Saturday morning, she raised her voice and once again nudged the motionless bulk in bed beside her. "Look at this for chrissakes! The sun is shining and it's snowing out. It's . . . what is it, September? It's the first of September and it's snowing out!"

"You've lived here, what, half your life now and you're still surprised by the weather? Gimme a break!" He spoke into the crook of his arm as he lay face down on the mattress, but the aggravated edge to Timothy Schumacher's voice was not lost in the muffled tones. The dry croak of a throat constricted from a night's sleep lent his words a soft crackle as he finished his thought. "It's like they always say about northern Wisconsin, Hon - if you don't like the weather, wait a few minutes and it'll change."

Margaret's fingers now ran through her husband's hair, soft and white as the snowflakes that danced in the air. The dark brown had gradually dissipated from his topside over the last few years, leaving a first-glance impression of a May-December relationship despite the fact he was only one year her senior. Entranced by the whirl of white offset by the rich, green hues of the pines outside her window, Margaret lost herself for a few moments; then made a feeble attempt at restating her contempt for the unseasonable weather.

"I don't care if it's northern Wisconsin or the North Pole; it's just not right, snow so soon," she insisted before grudgingly conceding the point.

"I'll admit it is pretty though, especially with the sun shining so brightly and the flakes sparkling like tiny diamonds. I've got to get Tony and Billy up and moving - Max is picking us up in about an hour." She slid out of bed and paused momentarily by the window. The light, misty snow had quickly trailed off, and the lone black cloud that carried the burst of precipitation drifted over the horizon.

"Good call, Mr. Smarty Pants. The snow is already gone and it looks like it's going to be a beauty day. Probably cold as a witch's you-know-what, though." Heavy, rhythmic breathing sounded from beneath the sheets, and she frowned with the realization that, for the past few moments, she had been conversing with herself.

The unseasonably cold night had turned the house into an icebox, so she reached into the back of her closet and pulled out a heavy robe normally reserved for the winter months. She pinched the soft flannel collar tightly around her neck and stepped into a worn pair of sheepskin moccasins. As she shuffled out of the room, she resisted the urge to prod her husband one more time just to spite him the extra few minutes of sleep she so coveted herself. Generosity of spirit overwhelmed her as she took great care to exit the room quietly and grant him the luxury she rarely, if ever, enjoyed.

There was a time when the well-worn footpath in the burnt orange carpet leading down the hallway to the bedroom shared by her two sons would inevitably ignite the smoldering flames of self-pity. The wish for new flooring would quickly coalesce with dreams of gleaming, freshly painted walls, updated furnishings, and a redesigned kitchen stocked with modern appliances. When her husband would accuse her of wallowing in "the short end of the stick syndrome," the natural fire in Margaret Schumacher's red locks burned brighter as the flush of anger darkened her countenance.

"Go to hell, Tim!" More often than not, that was the typical response she blurted whenever her husband called her out for feeling sorry for herself. With that, the conversation would come to an abrupt end, and she would wrestle with the regret of once again missing the opportunity to share her true feelings. What's wrong with wanting new carpeting? Are freshly painted walls and a few modern conveniences too much to ask? That's hardly feeling sorry for oneself, that's just a normal desire to create a better life.

It would always shake out that way, Margaret talking herself in circles without even speaking a word. The regret at keeping her mouth shut slowly faded to a genuine thankfulness for doing just that. A better life? If she ever uttered those words to her husband, he'd have every right to extend her an invitation to hell as well. Tim worked his ass off as a carpenter and was fortunate to have enough steady work that he could turn down jobs. Coupled with her position as the village librarian, she and Tim were able to provide a comfortable existence for their family.

"If we have our health, a roof over our heads and food on the table . . ." That was her husband's line of reasoning. Although Margaret nodded in agreement every time he expressed that long-held sentiment, she had never fully bought into it during the first years of their marriage. It took the better part of their baker's dozen worth of years together to fully appreciate where her husband was coming from, but now she couldn't imagine a time when she didn't equate happiness with the basic ingredients of life that most people – like herself at one time – take for granted.

Now, walking the upstairs hallway on this unseasonably chilly morning, a smile came easily to Margaret's lips as she pictured her two boys racing from one end of the house to the other in their footed pajamas, adding to the obvious wear and tear of the burnt orange carpet beneath her feet. This home had been lived in, that was plain to see, a tangible reminder of the love and growth the family shared within these walls. An array of photographs reached from floor to ceiling over Margaret's right shoulder; proud parents beaming with a newborn cradled in their arms, an excited face illuminated by the candles of his first birthday cake, those same two toddlers in their footed pajamas recalled moments before, here peaceful and cherubic, cuddled beneath the Christmas tree.

A pillar of sunshine tumbled into the hallway from an overhead skylight, animating the particles of dust that rose from the picture frames as Margaret gently ran her right index finger across the tops of the photographs. She lingered momentarily over the largest and most recent addition to her family's pictorial history, a group shot of the entire clan enjoying a backcountry camping trip earlier that summer. Tim had perched the camera on the edge of a large, chiseled boulder that jutted out above their campsite, then flailed his arms and legs in his best imitation of a girl on the run as he hustled back into position alongside the tent and canoe. Margaret could almost hear the familiar laughter jumping from the photo, her loved ones' grinning faces tanned and healthy from a week outdoors.

It had taken her oldest boy, Tony, just 12 years to shoot above her five-foot, five-inch frame. With a mop of blazing red hair, green eyes and a smattering of freckles across his up-turned nose and high cheekbones, the striking physical resemblance the boy shared with his mother belied a stubborn, analytical personality more befitting his father. Billy, by contrast, was short for a 10-year-old, yet possessed an uncanny strength and agility which virtually busted out of his wiry, compact body. He had inherited his father's dark brown hair, following his older brother's lead with a loose, shaggy cut which hung – irritatingly, in his mother's opinion – in a threadlike curtain over his placid blue eyes. Saddled with his mother's tender disposition, young Billy often battled to balance his inherent sensitivity against the stereotyped expectations of being a boy on the verge of manhood in the northwoods of Wisconsin.

Margaret's heart ached for her youngest during those all-too-frequent inner struggles, when Billy would find himself caught between a desire to follow his true nature and the understandable adolescent need to just fit in. The aberrant early morning snow hinted that the most painful time of year for the boy, autumn, was in the offing. For a young man who prefers to brush away – rather than swat and kill – the summers irritating, insatiable mosquitoes, the onset of northern Wisconsin's tradition-rich fall hunting season inevitably inflicted its share of shame and ridicule. It provided little solace to the boy, Margaret knew, that his mother found it admirable that his conscience wouldn't allow him to take the life of a Canada goose or dim the light behind the eyes of a whitetail deer. Not when his own brother and father, let alone all of his friends and their fathers, reveled in the camaraderie of the hunt and shared in the thrill of a successful kill.

Locked on her husband's blue eyes, tinted a shade lighter than the clear blue sky reflected in the river beyond the tent and canoe, Margaret braced against the warmth surging through her, the pace of her heart quickening with the silent acknowledgment that she loved the laughing man in the photograph, loved him to the bottom of her soul.

Tim was born and bred in Broadaxe – "a gen-yew-ine Northwoods native," he'd share with anyone kind enough to listen – and he was fiercely proud of his home's colorful past. In truth, the Ojibway Indian held title as the true native sons of this patch of northern Wisconsin, dubbing the region blessed with plentiful lakes and rivers *"Meskousing"* – "land where the waters gathered." The Ojibway, or Chippewa, were nomadic tribes that filtered into northern Wisconsin from Atlantic coastal regions thousands of years ago, reaping the area's rich natural bounty while sowing their own harvests of wild rice and corn.

The expansion of the European fur trade into the area in the late 1700s was a portent of the Chippewa's inexorably changing world. In a few short years, the north country's abundant beaver population was exploited to the brink of extinction. The victims of a rapidly evolving reality, in 1847 the Ojibway ceded the land of their forefathers to the United States. By the late 1800s, intensive clear-cut logging operations denuded the area of virgin stands of white pine in a misguided attempt to convert the sandy, rocky barrens into productive farmland. Following a rash of wildfires in the early 1900s, Broadaxe was gradually integrated into a cadre of small villages catering to a burgeoning tourist economy that sustained the town to this day.

Handed down from generation to generation, stories extolling the exploits of the early trappers and loggers – some supposedly occupying a distant branch on the family tree and tough sons-a-bitches one and all – perpetuated and ultimately embellished the type of character and personality necessary to carve out a niche "Up North." Tim came by his "pull yourself up by your own bootstraps" mentality honestly, Margaret had to admit, a philosophy shared by most of their northwoods neighbors. He could be as coarse as her fingernail file; she accepted that. His love for hunting and fishing was so ingrained he couldn't recall when those activities weren't a part of his life. Yet, much to his credit and with his wife's enduring gratitude; he never tried to force an obviously disinterested Billy into the hunting and fishing fold.

"Time to get up, Timmy!" Still basking in the glow of her rapidly coursing blood, her hot breath spreading a crescent of fog around her red-painted, right index finger as it pressed against her husband's lips beneath the framed glass, Margaret whispered the words and unconsciously covered her children's suddenly probing eyes with her left hand, shielding her offspring from the crude double entendre she planned to repeat back in the bedroom. Her fingers, moist with anticipation, trailed a greasy smudge as she slid them off the photograph, blurring the laughing, little faces beyond recognition.

A languid grunt was the only greeting Margaret received when she crawled back into bed and nestled into the crook of her husband's arm. Again, she stroked his snowy dome and placed her lips close to his ear, gently nibbling on the fleshy lobe as she repeated her prior invitation. "Time to get up, Timmy," the barely audible whisper and the intentional tickle of her sultry breath combined to convey her meaning. Sleep-heavy eyelids slowly drew open, unveiling watery blue irises holding the reflection of Margaret's disheveled red mane and paper-pale skin.

"Still snowing?" The small talk question, seemingly ill-timed as Margaret tugged off her husband's pajama bottoms – a pair of tattered gray gym trunks with faded Broadaxe Phy. Ed. Dept. lettering on the left leg – and roughly straddled his midsection, still taut and covered with a thick salt-and-pepper mat. "Just a quick flurry," she answered, still in a muted voice, her face directly above his as she brushed her pink, erect nipples along the hair on his chest. "Same as this is gonna be." Sliding her hips back down his stomach and settling back into his lap, it was obvious that he was willing to comply.

Treehouse   *49*

"Come on boys, rise and shine, let's go!" Margaret fumbled with the zipper on the emerald green corduroys as she bounced down the hallway and tried to finish dressing at the same time. The unexpected morning interlude, albeit highly enjoyable, had thrown off the day's schedule, leaving her flustered and frantic to make up time. The tails of a starched, white button-up shirt protruded from beneath a dark green sweater she had hastily pulled over her head. She kneed open the door to her boys' bedroom, releasing the long red locks that had been captured in the neck of her sweater at the same time. Hollering "Let's go" one more time as she entered the room, her brow furrowed as she found herself urging on a pair of empty beds.

"Jesus Christ . . . Jesus Christ . . ." the agitation in Margaret's tone was rising as she rushed down the stairs. It's Saturday morning, she reminded herself, which meant Tony and Billy were crashed on the basement sofas, passed out in front of the television after a Friday night spent watching movies, playing video games and stuffing themselves with junk food. In her stocking-footed race through the downstairs, Margaret careened through the dining room and slipped on the red oak floor, narrowly missing a collision with a sturdy wooden butcher block table. A small stack of papers – odd bills, receipts, coupons – fluttered off the corner and alighted on the floor in her wake. Evidence of the boys' previous night's rummaging littered the kitchen, so Margaret instinctively rounded up empty soda cans and snack bags on her way to the basement stairs.

"Don't make me come down there!" Normally that was the last resort in the never-ending struggle to roust the boys from their slumber, but there was no time today for the typical morning routine that started with gentle cajoling, escalated to impatient prodding, and culminated with an assortment of threats. "Max is going to be here shortly. Get up NOW!"

Among a long list of endearing qualities, Max Ferguson was reliably prompt. Less endearing to Margaret, more so because she had grown so fond of Max over the years, was his unwillingness to stand up for himself when people took advantage of his generous nature. In the mid six-foot range and a cheeseburger shy of 300 pounds, his sheer bulk alone offered reason to pause. A wild shock of black hair and equally unkempt beard framed a wind-leathered face, offering a first impression destined to be downright intimidating to most folks. Most folks aside from Margaret.

Max was the first person to approach Margaret when she arrived as a newcomer to North Lakes High School midway through her junior year. The school, a massive granite edifice of unremarkable architecture incongruously deposited in a gorgeous lakeside setting surrounded by towering red pine, drew in students from the area's several small tourist communities. Margaret's parents pulled the adolescent rug out from under her feet with the decision to pull up roots from the family home in central Illinois to chase a dream in northern Wisconsin. Yet, despite her best effort to convince herself that there would be nothing remotely worth living for in her new home, she couldn't help but fall under the spell cast by the clear blue lakes, rapid rivers, abundant wildlife, and never-ending forest.

"Girl, I love your redlocks, mon." No telling how long Max had practiced that line before he worked up the nerve to approach Margaret as she hid in a corner of the school library, immersed in an old paperback copy of "Madam Bovary." The stilted Bob Marley imitation, coming from the oversized teddy bear Max had already grown to resemble, instantly brought a smile to Margaret's face. Without thinking, "Ya, mon," slipped from her lips in an equally unconvincing Jamaican accent. The instantaneous relaxation of Max's body language evidenced his relief at somehow avoiding the "Get your fat Rasta ass away from me" reply he fully anticipated. "Friendship at first sight" is how they recalled that first meeting. Margaret knew Max had initially wished it could be more, but it was tacitly understood that the relationship would always remain amicable, at best.

"Pine Point Cabins" embodied the dream Margaret's parents had followed North, a rustic five-cottage resort situated along the shoreline of Cattail Lake, a gin-clear fisherman's paradise about 15 miles west of Broadaxe. Max was literally the only friend Margaret had made during her shortened junior year at North Lakes and he became a regular fixture at the resort once the ice thawed and fishing season opened in the spring. By the time summer rolled around he had finagled invitations for three of his buddies – with assurances to Margaret that each were good friends since kindergarten and therefore okay guys – to join him for a weekend of fishing at the resort.

"So Redlocks, what d'ya think?" Max had asked eagerly as he helped Margaret tie the boat to the dock. She had joined Max and his pals on the pontoon boat; and, at the close of a sunlit Saturday spent filling the live well with bluegills, Margaret thought the question smacked of a desperate, almost pathetic, search for her approval. "I'd say you've got it one-third right."

Why pull any punches? He asked, she had figured, but she wasn't prepared for his reaction as she passed judgment. His best friend, Timothy Schumacher, well she thought he was the most handsome boy she'd ever seen, and so polite, and so funny, and she'd love to see him again. As for the other two, Margaret pegged Richard – "Call me Dickey" – Mann as a smarmy, arrogant cheeseball who got off on telling other people what to do, while Jackson Kelly was an ass-kisser, plain and simple. Max had blinked hard and fast to stymie the tears welling in his deep-set brown eyes. Margaret was never quite sure if the hurt stemmed from her liking Tim too much; enough to marry him, in fact, or the other two not nearly enough.

"Hey Redlocks, got your shit together, or what?" Milk spurted out Tony's nostrils, triggered by Max's rude greeting. His mass blocked exit from or entry to the kitchen, but Margaret caught a glimpse of a freshly-showered Tim standing behind him in the dining room.

"Yeah, Maggie, are we about ready to get this show on the road, like Max said, or what? Wrestling tournament, remember?" Margaret couldn't see the smirk on her husband's face, but she could feel it. She also felt the familiar flush rising in her cheeks, her goddamn quick temper; but she wasn't going to take the bait. She wasn't going to give those two assholes the satisfaction of a reaction.

"Hey Max, thanks for picking us up. Ready in a second. Tony, Billy, finish up your breakfast and put your dishes in the sink." Margaret grinned as Max turned and headed out of the kitchen with an audible exhalation, shrugging his shoulders at Tim in an admission of defeat. "Meet you in the car," she chirped, adding "you dumb bastards" under her breath. It promised to be a long day, and Margaret was beginning to feel a bit slap-happy just thinking about it. To top it off, she'd have to deal with the cheeseball and the ass-kisser, as well.

Turning down the volume on the Johnny Horton CD he had cranked for the ride over, Max continued to absent-mindedly fidget with the stereo controls while casting occasional over-the-shoulder, agitated glances at the kids in the back of the minivan. He lived about a half-hour south, damn near the average distance to anywhere up in the woods, down County Highway B and west on pine-studded Bobcat Lake Road. Per usual, her husband was oblivious to the obvious, but Margaret sensed that something was picking at the behemoth behind the wheel. Alone on the bench seat near the sliding side door, she tapped Max on the arm, and, when he turned, gave him a shoulder shrug, hand gesture and look that silently asked the question, "What's up?"

"Dringama, drangama, dringama."

"What the hell are you talking about Max?" Not realizing one had actually commenced, Tim joined the conversation from the passenger seat.

"Dringama, drangama, dringama," Max repeated, at a slower cadence, as if he were trying to penetrate thick skulls with the words. "My grandpa always used to say that when the conversation turned a little too adult with kids around. Little pitchers have big ears. He said it, my dad said it, now I say it. That's how it works, alright?"

As he spoke, Max nodded his head toward the back of the minivan, where his son, Nicholas, was engrossed in a scissors-rock-paper death match with the Schumacher boys. Nick was the by-product of a short-lived, ill-fated romance – in all likelihood Max's one and only – with a buxom, bikini-clad member of the local water ski club, the Broadaxe Exadaorbs. The Exadaorbs (Broadaxe spelled backwards, someone's idea of clever) consisted of an obnoxious pack of college coeds wasting away the summer at the family's lakeside vacation home. Every Wednesday and Sunday night throughout the summer the Exadaorbs put on a ski show for the visiting tourists – pyramids, jumps, barefooters, clowns – and that's where Max first laid eyes on Elizabeth.

After ingesting a six-pack of Mickey's big mouths a piece, on a whim, Max, Tim, Dickey Mann and Jackson Kelly took in a Sunday night show. It was evolving into a beered-up local boys make fun of the spoiled rich kids falling on their asses kind of a night, until Max fell under the spell of Elizabeth Cantrell's water-soaked, skin-tight red bikini; or more aptly, the perfectly proportioned contents barely held therein. His gaze remained steadfastly in her direction for the remainder of the show, even when he had to elbow Tim in the ribs or reach over to cuff Dickey or Jackson in the back of the head to blunt their jeers. And, when Elizabeth stood close with her perfectly manicured hand on his shoulder as she moved through the crowd collecting donations, Max was thoroughly smitten.

Elizabeth was certainly smitten herself, but more with the persona Max presented than with the man himself. Although he was only in his early twenties, Max had already established himself as Broadaxe's premier hand-crafted log home builder. His own home, a two-story chalet pieced together from massive, hand-hewn western Douglas fir, sat tucked along a picturesque bend in the Rice River on property that had been in his family for four generations. Max lived off the grid, relying on a combination of solar-powered batteries and wood to light and heat his world. An idealized notion of his rustic lifestyle, coupled with Max's rugged lumberjack looks, left a naïve young Elizabeth wide-eyed and vulnerable. A summer romance blossomed, then withered quickly, but not before bearing fruit.

Four months before Nicholas entered the world, a prideful Max and a radiant Elizabeth exchanged vows in a simple ceremony along the banks of the Rice. Eight months later, to the day, Elizabeth abandoned her new husband and her newborn son, apparently disabused of the romanticized vision of a woodsman's wife soon after the realities of everyday living sunk in. Max, understandably devastated, never saw it coming. "Elizabitch," Tim took to calling the woman who tore his best friend's heart out. Even though it killed Margaret to see her dear friend Max battered down into a beaten shell of a man, she was still able to empathize with Elizabeth as a young, confused girl carried along much too quickly by the passions of the heart. Most importantly, there was a young baby to care for, and Margaret – new bride and new mother herself at the time – knew little Nicholas would be the savior of his father's spirit.

Little Nicholas didn't remain little for long. He was undeniably papa's boy, from his melon-sized head to his sausage toes. The unruly black mess sprouting from his head pulsated as he pumped his fist three times and straightened his fingers, whooping as he placed his "paper" over the close-fisted pair of "rocks" proffered by Tony and Billy. His single bulging paw swallowed up both hands and Margaret marveled at how, at 11 years old and sandwiched between her boys in age, he absolutely dwarfed them in size.

"I think the little pitchers are plenty preoccupied," Margaret had to raise her voice and leaned forward on the bench seat to be heard. Tim had notched the volume back up on Johnny Horton and was happily tapping his knee to the beat of "Sleepy-Eyed John."

"Sleepy-Eyed John, you'd better get your britches on, sleepy-eyed John better tie your shoes, sleepy-eyed John, you'd better get your britches on and try to get to heaven 'fore the devil gets to you . . ."

"Goddamm it Tim, turn that back down." Margaret knuckled Tim in the left shoulder and grimaced at the back of his bopping head.

"Ouch! What the hell . . ." he turned and gave her a puzzled look. "Look at your friend! Can't you tell something is obviously bothering him?" Margaret couldn't believe her husband, like most men, could be so utterly insensitive at times; especially when the people who mattered most were concerned.

Rubbing his shoulder as he readjusted the volume, Tim half-heartedly took his wife's blatant cue. "What's up, buddy? Got something on your mind?" Exasperated, Margaret rolled her eyes, the dopey grin on her husband's face confirming what she already knew – the man was incapable of taking anything seriously.

Max tightened his grip on the steering wheel and felt his palms growing slick against the hard plastic. Glancing to the back of the minivan, where Nicholas was in the midst of doling out simultaneous Dutch rubs to the scalps of his two helpless playmates, Max was satisfied that the boys' attention was adequately diverted. In an attempt to convey the gravity of what he was about to say, Max looked first into Margaret's eyes, then shifted his focus to Tim.

"Don't know if you heard, but Christopher Koenigs was released from that nut house out in New York." Margaret swallowed hard against the lump rising in her throat as she watched the grin evaporate from her husband's suddenly stoical face.

CHAPTER FOUR

North Lakes High School still loomed large and foreboding against the backdrop of red pine, many more of which had felt the bite of a chainsaw to make room for a modern, arched fieldhouse that housed an indoor track of red, vulcanized rubber, a fully stocked weight training room, and a trio of full-length basketball courts. The centermost court was emblazoned with the image of a crazed lumberjack wielding an oversized hatchet, the Monty Pythonesque-named team mascot, Ima. Wrestling mats hid the maniacal woodcutter from view, a patchwork of red and blue stretching from one end of the expansive gymnasium to the other.

Margaret normally dreaded the first whiff of group perspiration mingled with the greasy scent of the concessions being offered by the local Lions Club. Entering the gym today, however, she barely noticed the smell, which hung perceptively in the humidity generated by the teeming mass of bodies rolling around on the mats. The last twenty minutes of the drive to the school had proceeded in an uncomfortable silence after Max broached the subject of Christopher Koenigs. It was a part of local Broadaxe lore that had occurred a few years before Margaret's family moved north, but it still made her queasy just thinking about it.

"Christopher Koenigs sittin' in a tree, K-I-L-L-I-N-G. First comes a shove, then comes despairage, then comes Michael in a funeral carriage."

When Margaret first heard her own boys blithely singing that parochial variation of the childhood song, a tease to young sweethearts, her uncharacteristically harsh reprimand sent them both immediately to tears. After she recounted the incident to Tim, he responded with the same blank, unflinching stare she saw on his face earlier in the minivan. Watching Tony and Billy strip down to their doublets and join the other wrestlers warming up for the day's matches, she shuddered to think that either of her boys could be capable of maliciously hurting the other.

Besides, the librarian in Margaret concluded, the reconstructed children's ditty was patently stupid. Despairage? No such word! Artistic license aside, it still would have given her pleasure to place a couple knuckles behind the year of the person responsible. When she flew off the handle at Tony and Billy for reciting the melody, she chided them equally for the abuse of the English language and the unseemly contents of the song.

"Megs, your boys ready to whup some butt?" Margaret closed her eyes and took a deep breath to regain her composure. She knew it was Cheeseball, even before the cheap cologne he had taken a bath in washed over her, leaving her longing for the smell of fried food and sweat. Richard Mann was the only person who called her "Megs," persisting in the habit even after she made it abundantly clear she didn't care for the moniker. In retaliation, she refused to call him "Dickey," even though he had insisted, repeatedly, in the 16-odd years since he had shown up at her parent's resort with Max for a weekend of bluegill fishing. Margaret turned and put on her best face.

"Richard."

"So, did those two get a good night's sleep last night? We agreed on lights out by 9 p.m. It's a big tournament today, Megs, a big day. Billy should walk his way to a trophy. He's a machine out there. Tony's got a good shot too, if he uses his head and a couple of breaks go his way." He paused, anticipating a response, resuming when he realized there was none forthcoming. "Great, great. And please, Megs call me Dickey." He put his hand on her shoulder. She automatically recoiled.

The hand on Margaret's shoulder, pale and slender, appeared softer and more delicate than her own. It fit the entire package, nonetheless; for at a shade taller than six feet and no more than 165 pounds with a pocket full of rocks, Richard Mann exuded a subdued femininity incongruous with the "manly men of the northwoods" appearance shared by his contemporaries. With his shortcropped blond hair, penetrating blue eyes, vanishing lips and square jaw, "Aryan transvestite" popped into Margaret's head whenever she saw him. In the intervening years since Max's introduction, he had more than lived up to – more appropriately, down to – Margaret's less-than- flattering first impression.

Attired in a shiny, navy blue nylon sweat suit with a double row of white piping down the arms and legs, Richard did his best to dress in a manner befitting the "head coach" of the local youth wrestling club. In a community consumed by grappling – the championship banners hanging from the field-house rafters testament to a high school wrestling dynasty – it seemed a sacrilege to entrust the development of tomorrow's title contenders to a man who had never stepped on the mat himself. Many did consider the situation an abomination, including Tucker Donnelly, a burly four-time heavyweight state champion and current coach of the high school squad, who would have placed Richard in a permanent sleeper hold if given the opportunity. Most folks only shrugged and accepted it for what it was, just another example of Richard Mann's insidious ability to inveigle his way into positions of control.

No matter what angle she approached it from, Margaret could never figure out how one possessed of such obvious frailty of both mind and body was able to exert such influence over others. Much to her chagrin, Richard remained entrenched within her small circle of friends, an accustomed annoyance, like a wood tick trying to burrow under her skin. Tim was well aware of his wife's disdain for his childhood friend; she had never tried to hide it. But her husband's weak protestations that "Dickey's not so bad, you've just got to take him with a grain of salt," had long rung hollow in Margaret's ears. She had come to grudgingly accept the disconcerting fact that, for whatever improbable reason, the Cheeseball had an inexplicable hold on not only her husband, but her best friend, Max, as well.

"By the by, where's the old man? And where's Max? Didn't you guys hitch a ride over here with him? I need to have a quick chat with those boys." Richard's small, graying teeth poked out beneath his lipless grin like a row of rotting corn kernels. He was looking beyond Margaret, his eyes scanning the faces filing into the tiered, metal bleachers stacked against the walls, trying to pick Tim or Max out of the crowd.

Short, stout wrestlers paired off and strutted across the mats, stopping to tug at the long laces on their ankle-high boots, slapping their bare biceps and the hard plastic ear protectors strapped to their heads. Referees in crisp black trousers and vertically-striped black and white shirts, many cauliflower-eared former wrestlers themselves, motioned the young competitors toward the centers of the blue and red mats. Coaches shouted final instructions through cupped hands from matside as a volley of shrill whistles sent the wrestlers crashing together in a chorus of grunts.

"Say, coach, I don't know if you've noticed, but the matches have started." Richard's blue eyes flickered back in Margaret's direction momentarily, never really making contact or acknowledging the "hey, dumbshit" inflection in her voice.

"Never mind, Megs, never mind. Thanks anyway, but I see the guys over there." Keeping his eyes locked on Tim and Max, who were standing on the far side of the gym against the backdrop of the school fight song hand-painted on the wall in black, oversized script, Richard brushed Margaret's right side and knocked her back a step in his haste to join them.

"Okay, what the hell is going on here," Margaret mumbled to herself after taking note that the Ass-kisser, Jackson Kelly, had already wedged himself between Tim and Max. She couldn't hear the conversation from across the noisy gym, but as she started in that direction Margaret discerned that he was upset about something and adamant about making his point. Jackson Kelly was easily the shortest of the three, the tip of his pointed, bald pate nearly on a level with her husband's chin and, like most folks, he stood a mere munchkin next to Max. His bushy brow contorted into a triangular furrow which pointed downward between nondescript eyes pinched shut by the excess flesh of his reddened cheeks. He punched the air with his pudgy right index finger as he spoke.

Together, the three life-long friends accounted for seven individual state wrestling titles among them, and were contributing members of three championship teams. After placing second at state in his sophomore and junior years, Tim finally won a title as a senior, shortly after he and Margaret began dating. Max was undefeated, and virtually unchallenged, throughout his entire four-year career; while Jackson Kelly had two championships under his belt, and another all but assured, until he was caught drinking beer bongs in his underwear at a keg party two meets into his senior season.

All the more reason why Margaret was perpetually boggled by the unrelenting deference to Richard; pencil-thin, overbearing Richard, the fastidious student manager who fetched the wrestlers' water and collected their dirty towels and jockstraps after each practice. Once again, she watched disbelievingly as Richard immediately stepped in and took control of the animated conversation underway beneath the school fight song. Now it appeared not so much a group of buddies shooting the bull, but rather more like a strict headmaster lecturing to his wayward wards. Margaret wondered if it could be as simple as the fact that he was a full year older than the others; meaningless in their mid-thirties, perhaps, yet much more important as children, when the pecking order was ultimately being established.

"It's good to see you, Margaret." The high-pitched, birdish greeting detoured Margaret, purposely walking across the fieldhouse floor, about ten feet away from her husband. She tried in vain to make eye contact as he nodded like a bobble-head doll in agreement with whatever Richard was preaching. It had to be of grave importance, she reasoned, to distract the trio of state champions from the action on the nearby mats. She had been led to believe there was nothing more important than wrestling.

"Hey, Sally, you're looking great today," Margaret commented without really noticing, still straining, unsuccessfully, to catch a bite of Richard's monologue. It was a safe reply, at any rate. Sally Mann was blessed with a remarkable propensity for consistently cutting a stunning figure and sharing a honey-sweet disposition, despite being saddled with the onus of her daily existence as Mrs. Cheeseball. In truth, Margaret never judged Sally guilty by association, even though she had a hard time fathoming how such a lovely person could have hitched her wagon to such a low-life.

"Let's grab a seat. Terry's match starts in about five minutes." Sally physically grabbed her distracted friend's attention, hooking Margaret by the elbow and directing her toward the bleachers. Resistant at first, she eventually relented and fell in step with Sally's bouncy, tip-toed stride. With elbows still locked, long strands of Sally's soft, sandy-brown hair caught on Margaret's face as she turned and glanced back over her left shoulder. She stuck out her bottom lip and exhaled heavily, tickling her nose as Sally's hair – smelling vaguely like the forest after a springtime rain, Margaret decided – merely shifted and resettled on her face. Peering through the horizontal veil of hair, Margaret watched Richard place his outstretched arms around Tim and Max, both still nodding in silent assent.

Unsettled as she felt, Margaret did her best to settle into the hard, cramped bleachers. It was growing oppressively warm in the crowded fieldhouse, but the ribbed metal seats still chilled Margaret's cheeks right through her emerald green corduroys. "There's Terry, there's Terry," Sally trilled, proudly pointing to an anemic beanpole stumbling onto the mat, slump-shouldered beneath the weight of a gold elastic wrestling doublet that drooped to his knobby knees. "Go get 'em, Terry," Sally yelled, her elbow still locked around Margaret's, confiding in a whisper, "You know, he really didn't want to wrestle. He's more interested in his insect collection, and he loves to read. . . but you know Dickey. Dickey asked Terry 'How the hell do you think it'd look if the head coach's own kid doesn't join the team?' Terry didn't answer him. He just kept sticking pins in those little bugs; but I think his heart got in it a little more after Dickey brought home his new gold uniform."

Terry's shoulders were stuck to the mat within six seconds. "That has to be some sort of a record," Margaret heard a gravelly voice chuckle from higher up in the bleachers. "Should call that kid 'The Stickpin'," another suggested. Appropriate, Margaret conceded, considering Terry's twiggish frame and his inclination for impaling tiny, winged invertebrates. Still, she cringed empathetically for Sally, probing her moist, brown eyes for signs of the incomparable pain a mother endures when one of her offspring suffers. There was none to be found. From her prideful expression, one would have guessed that it was her spindly nine-year-old's hand, not his opponent's, being raised in victory at that moment.

"That a way, Terry! Good job, Terry!" Sally had finally unhooked her arm from Margaret's and was on her feet, clapping enthusiastically. Margaret rose and joined the small ovation, thinking the woman beside her must be a saint as her only son – Stickpin, the record-setter – wobbled teary-eyed from the mat and collapsed in a fit of exhaustion brought on by his six seconds of physical exertion.

"It's just not fair." Without meaning to, Margaret spoke aloud after mentally fanning through the cards that life had dealt her friend. Sally's 12-year-old daughter, Kaela, made the early jump into adolescent non-conformity, donning the black garb of the Goth and unconditionally disassociating herself from the outside world. Terry was a sweet little kid. Margaret loved the bookish nerd in the boy, but he seemed destined for a dim future under the parental tutelage of the insufferable Richard Mann.

"What's not fair, dear?" Sally had reattached herself to Margaret's arm. Margaret pulled free, relieved to see Tim and Max giving the defeated Terry a pep talk below the bleachers. Max gently rubbed the youngster's blond buzz cut, while Tim patiently demonstrated a favorite wrestling move to the disinterested boy.

"Terry's just so small and skinny, Sally, and the other boy was so much bigger and stronger. It isn't fair. He should be matched up against somebody his own size." Margaret knew that wasn't how it worked, but she was ducking for cover. Her own son, Billy, typically found himself pitted against bigger boys, but was able to overcome his smaller stature with quickness, strength, and what Tim proudly called "the mind of a wrestler."

Sally nodded in agreement. "It isn't fair," she ventured.

"No, it isn't," Margaret confirmed, shuddering to put herself in the shoes of Mrs. Cheeseball.

"What's all the mystery?" Joining her husband below the bleachers, the question jumped from Margaret in a tone a bit too hostile for her own liking. Max took the hint and excused himself, the promise of a treat at the concession stand raising a smile on Terry's tear-stained face. "You could easily answer that question too, you know." She called to the broad expanse of red and black flannel stretched across the departing Max's back. With his right hand on the tiny wrestler's shoulder and his left hand waving dismissively above his head, Max suggested "Some things are better left between husband and wife" as he lumbered hurriedly away.

"Mystery? No mystery. What the hell are you talking about?" Tim, sounding suspiciously defensive, turned and walked away through the symmetrical shafts of light reaching down between the metal bench seats overhead. "Billy's got his first match. Let's go," he added, trying to sound more conversational.

"The little huddle, the little conclave? You, and Max, and Jackson, and Richard. C'mon Tim, kids are wrestling and you guys decide to have a little chat instead of watching, instead of coaching from the sidelines? I never thought I'd see the day." Margaret, unwilling to let her husband off the hook that easily, fell in close behind and peppered the back of his head with her words.

Back out in the open expanse of the fieldhouse, Tim picked up his pace. Weaving through the milling crowd, which pinched down to a narrow aisle separating the aggressive little wrestlers on her right from the cheering parents to her left, Margaret fell several people behind her escaping husband. "You can run but you can't hide, Timothy," she actually called out, catching occasional glimpses of his snow-white head slaloming away. She was smiling now, well aware that even though her husband was running from her inquisition, he was conveniently in a rush to watch Billy wrestle, as well. No matter. She knew where to find him.

Crouched down on his haunches in front of Billy at the far corner of a worn wrestling mat, a red plastic surface blistering and peeling along the frayed, upturned edges, Tim held Billy behind the neck with interlaced fingers. Father and son stared solemnly into one another's eyes, their faces level. Tim was imparting some final words of wisdom, a pre-match ritual, the sanctity of which Margaret observed by remaining silent, three or four paces away. He was a great dad, loved unconditionally by both his boys, and as she watched him tighten Billy's laces and slap his rump in a final send-off, Margaret softened. Her husband could enjoy his son's wrestling match in peace. She could pick up the inquisition later.

A veritable Tasmanian Devil, Billy had been tagged as a potential state champion from the time he first took the mat as an eight-year-old. Now, two years later, those expectations had only increased. The normally taciturn Tucker Donnelly became effusive when talking about Billy's potential, telling a proud Tim that his boy had the makings to be one of the best in the long line of local wrestling heroes. Best of all, from a mother's point of view, Billy enjoyed everything about it; the hard work, the ceaseless practice, the competition and, of course, the enthusiastic encouragement. It was his ticket to the men's club, so to speak, and it soothed Margaret to know that the acceptance wrestling offered balanced the rejection he felt every autumn when his father and brother left for deer camp.

"Sweep, Billy, sweep!" Uncertain if he was heard, Tim raised his voice and stepped closer to the mat. "Sweep, Billy, sweep! Damn, why the hell doesn't he sweep?" He turned to Margaret, seated in the front row of the bleachers, and shrugged his shoulders, but she knew better than to attempt an answer when he was actually talking to himself. Well ahead on points near the end of the first period of the three-period match, Billy was having no trouble with his bigger, but athletically overmatched, competition. Tim constantly harped on Billy about his lack of killer instinct – the one chink in his wrestling armor, he told him – and apparently he was seeing it again today.

"Boy, Billy's really looking great Margaret, really great." Jackson Kelly's hot breath, punctuated by fine explosions of spittle, rolled down Margaret's neck as he leaned in precariously from the bench above. The stale blend of whiskey and cigarettes, insufficiently masked by spearmint gum, hung like a halo around her red tresses. "Man, I wish my kid could wrestle like that. You'se guys are lucky. Don't get me wrong, don't get me wrong. Jimmy's a great kid and all that. I ain't sayin' that, but he just don't got it, y'know, he just don't got it. I try to tell him what I know, I try to teach him, but he just up and looks at me like I got two heads, y'know?"

Other than squelching a strong desire to correct his speech, Margaret didn't know how to respond. She agreed wholeheartedly that Jimmy was, indeed, a great kid. Each time he strolled to the front row with a pillow under one arm and a stack of books under the other, eager anticipation for the start of another story hour down at the library written all over his face, Margaret couldn't resist the temptation to muss up a head of hair as red as her own, then slowly comb it back into place. Jimmy, entranced, basked in the personal attention, which came at a premium around the Kelly household. His father, a local beer-drinking legend, earned a reserved seat at the corner of the bar down at Tingle's Tap; while his mother, seldom-seen Dorothy, preferred to crawl into a bottle in the privacy of her own home.

In her left ear, Margaret could hear Jackson fidgeting with the zipper on the oil-stained, dull blue hooded sweatshirt he had stuffed himself into. His creased, blue mechanic's pants were also decorated with an assortment of synthetic blends, the orange residue of cheese curls fingered across the thighs. Everybody called him Jackie back in high school, until informed that he thought it too juvenile and wished to be called by his given name. Jackson it was then, for the few who were foolish enough to get on his wrong side bore the bruises, bumps and breaks he doled out in retaliation. He was short, but his barrel-chested, beast-like build and farm boy strength, fueled by a matchstick temper and a thirst for booze, rightly earned Jackson Kelly the reputation as the toughest son-of-a-bitch to walk the woods.

Age, and the alcohol, combined to soften Jackson in both body and spirit. His girth appeared to match his height, stretching his blotchy pink skin so tight one unconsciously guarded oneself against a spontaneous explosion of blood and guts. Thin, bright red lines spread upward from his bulging jowl, multi-pronged lightning bolts across his puffy cheeks, squeezing his eyes to slits. A fat, drunken Buddha, Margaret mused, none too thrilled to have the honor of the Ass-kisser's undivided attention. When her husband pulled out the same line in defense of Jackson that he used for Richard, the tired "He's not a bad guy, you just have to take it with a grain of salt," she had an easier time buying it. He worked hard at his garage and he tried hard around other folks, maybe too hard, giving credence to Margaret's claim – shared only with her husband – that "Jackson's kissed so much ass around here he needs his lips checked for butt-burn." She always cracked herself up with that line . . . Tim, less so.

"So that's some kind'a news about that Christopher Koenigs gettin' outta that looney bin out East, eh? You'se guys heard that?" Jackson looked down, laboring to see beyond his distended belly, picking at the blackened nails of his round, stumpy fingers with the tip of his coat's brass zipper. "Hearin' that news stirred up some memories, I'll tell ya. It got kinda crazy 'round these parts what with all the media and the shrinks . . ." he paused, splaying out his fingers to inspect his impromptu manicure. His speech was irregular, slurred. ". . . and what we all know'd about it."

"What *do* you all *know* about it?" Interest piqued, Margaret asked, stressing the words in a half-assed attempt to instill proper grammar in the rotund grease monkey. Jackson did little to suppress a guttural burp, and an unpleasant cloud of whiskey and cigarettes with a spearmint chaser washed over Margaret's face.

"Know about what?" The addition of Richard's cologne to the mix, let alone his untimely presence, proved adequate to turn Margaret's stomach. She felt the humid air of the fieldhouse pressing down upon her once again, and her stomach churned audibly during a momentary lull in the noise of the crowd. Remembering that she hadn't eaten a bite all day, Margaret took a deep breath and willfully suppressed the rising wave of nausea.

"Richard. Jackson and I were having a private discussion," she attempted, her voice wavering and thin in her weakened state. One glance at Jackson confirmed what Margaret suspected; with Richard present, he was done talking. She gave it a shot, anyway. "As I was saying, Jackson, what do you know about it?" He was back digging at his dirty nails; content, as always, to let Richard do the talking.

"Know about what, Megs?" Richard was insistent, placing one white tennis-shoed foot on the bench next to Margaret, craning in with his elbow on his knee. That left his package, postage-sized but plain to see, pressed against the folds of his shiny blue sweat suit, dangling uncomfortably at eye level. Margaret stood abruptly and bumped Richard backward onto both feet.

"You've no doubt heard the news, Richard," Margaret, feeling better upright – away from Jackson's distilled exhalations and Richard's shrunken assets – opted for the path of least resistance. If the Cheeseball wants to talk, let's hear what he has to say. "Christopher Koenigs? The little boy, from Broadaxe, who killed his little brother? He hung him, pushed him out of a treehouse, if I recall. When was it? Around 1985 or something like that, Richard? You've heard he's been released. I'm sure that was the topic of your guys' group hug earlier. Max and Tim seemed pretty upset by it, and Jackson here seemed to be implying . . ."

"Implying what?" Richard cut her off, moving a step closer and lowering his voice into a clipped, almost urgent cadence. "Don't stand there and presume to give me a history lesson about what happened to the Koenigs boys, Margaret. Remember, I lived here. Your husband lived here, so did Max and Jackson. You didn't. You couldn't possibly know what it was like. Christopher and Michael were younger than us, the 'little' kids in the neighborhood, but they were our playmates and our friends. Do you know what it's like to have something so horrible, unthinkable really, happen to someone you know?"

She didn't know. Her face reddened and she visibly squirmed, discomposed by her own blatant lack of sensitivity. Margaret had heard the oft-repeated tales, some factual and some distorted fiction, fashioning an almost mythical remembrance of an episode from the past that – for others, she realized belatedly – was all too real. The resurrected pain laid bare in Richard's voice and painted across his face prodded Margaret to reach out with words of comfort, but her years of antipathy toward the man left her at a loss.

"Richard . . ."

"Those are bad memories, Megs, for all of us." Unaware he had rescued Margaret from her floundering, Richard held up his right hand and continued, his voice now relaxed and conciliatory. He had called her Margaret for the first time ever moments before, but now, oddly, she welcomed his rapid reversion to the normally annoying nickname. "Just hearing Christopher's name stirs it all up again. Of course Tim and Max found the news upsetting. Hell, it upset me and I'm sure it did Jackson, as well. Right, Jackson?" Slack-jawed and bleary-eyed, Jackson nodded obediently from his perch in the bleachers.

"Megs, there were some folks around here, some folks who didn't even know Christopher and Michael, who took advantage of their misfortune to bask in the 15 minutes of fame, or infamy, the killing brought to our tight-knit community. Us neighborhood kids made a pact. We decided we weren't going to talk to anybody about it, nobody, except one another. We were just kids, and I guess that was our way of coping. It's been our way of coping ever since, I suppose. So there you go, Megs, mystery solved. Satisfied? Now, I've gotta see how my wrestlers are doing." Tilting his head, Richard motioned for Jackson to follow as he hiked up his already-too-high sweat pants and walked away.

"Sweep, Billy, sweep!" Her husband's shouts, vocal chords chafed and hoarse, snapped Margaret's attention back to the worn red mat. She turned just in time to see her sensitive son swing his legs under the feet of his tired, bewildered opponent, dropping the bigger boy on his back with the hollow thud of dead weight.

*   *   *

Margaret caught herself reading the same sentence over and over. It was a months old issue of one of Tim's do-it-yourself magazines, more a prop than anything, to give the appearance that she *wasn't* just waiting for her husband to come to bed. He had maintained a safe distance for the remainder of the wrestling tournament, save for a family photo with the boys and their respective trophies. After Richard's dress down, at least that's what it felt like to Margaret, she could understand why.

"Coming to bed, honey?" The door to Tim's office – in reality a closet with a desk and phone – was slightly cracked open. A sliver of light inched across the bedroom floor and crawled up the side of an antique leather and brass steamer chest, Margaret's grandmother's, pressed up against the foot of the bed. No response, but her question did trigger a brief rustling of papers and opening of drawers before the closet/office fell silent once again.

Margaret abandoned the façade and cast the magazine aside, catching the corner of the night stand and tearing the bungalow pictured on the back cover in two. Punching the center of her oversized down-filled pillow with a balled fist, she rolled on her back and settled her head into the depression she had beaten into the feathers. The delicately embroidered cotton pillow cases, also her grandmother's, enveloped her in a simple pleasure, clean and fresh from a day outdoors on the clothesline. After the cold morning start the day had warmed up nicely, still cool for late summer, but once the sun had set on a cloudless, star-filled sky, the temperatures plummeted once again.

Pulling the thick, pale yellow comforter close around her chin, Margaret resisted a sudden flash of melancholy as she lay alone in bed. A large black ant scurried across the ceiling. Like a lone motorist on the highway after dark, it followed a jagged crack that ran diagonally from corner to corner. The ant paused sporadically and raised its head, antennae flickering, as if in search of a missed exit ramp. She imagined herself in the ant's place, cruising the highway at night, alone, heading to an unknown destination, leaving Broadaxe in the rear view mirror. The thought unnerved her, sending a shiver down her spine that added goose bumps to her already chilled flesh.

Leave Broadaxe? Impossible now, Margaret knew, for the place was in her blood and her blood was in the place. It was home. She fell in love with her husband here, bore two beautiful children and raised them here, and she planned to die here. Margaret cherished the simplicity of her life. The changing seasons renewed her spirit, and she never failed to offer a word of thanks to the bald eagles that soared above her head.

A typical northern Wisconsin tourist town, there wasn't too much to Broadaxe. Jackson Kelly had his repair shop, a two-car garage offering the tourists gas, waterproof lake maps, minnows and worms, soda and beer, all at inflated prices. Jackson's shop was at the southern end of the town's main drag. To the north on the same stretch of road one would find: the post office, a cramped brick building with enviable working hours;

the Chamber of Commerce, an inviting log hut offering hot coffee and free information; the public library, where Margaret had assembled a respectable, if somewhat eclectic, selection of fiction and non-fiction; and St. Olaf's Community Church, an ivy-covered chapel that sat vacant for all but one hour each week.

One block east of the main road, a corrugated metal building housed the town office and community center. The volunteer fire department kept its trucks and equipment locked up in a tall garage complex just down the road. Maybe fifteen houses, some crumbling and unoccupied, were scattered about on a small network of side roads.

Of course, it wouldn't be Wisconsin without the taverns. There was Jackson's home away from home, Tingle's Tap, a dingy, smoky fire trap frequented by most of the locals. Cheap beer and shots, good burgers, and Tingle himself, a wizened old bar hand who squinted through coke bottle glasses and spouted off-color jokes, kept the stools full day and night. The upscale Grey Wolf Inn catered to the tourist crowd, while the Loon's Nest, Bill's Bar, and Lone Pine Lounge would serve anybody whose head reached the top of the rail. The Grey Wolf Inn was on the main highway, just north of St. Olaf's. The other taverns were tucked away in the woods off back roads, as were a handful of Ma and Pa restaurants that dished out affordable, mediocre fare in grotesque proportions.

Margaret sat back up in bed, wondering if Tim had fallen asleep at his desk. She pulled her knees to her chest, still chilled, and rubbed her arms to combat her goose flesh. Like most of the year-round residents, Margaret and Tim lived in a modest home tucked back in the woods surrounding 'downtown' Broadaxe. They purchased 10 acres from Tim's uncle shortly after they were married, and, with the aid of Max's expertise and effort, built a cozy two-story home with white pine harvested from the land. On the nightstand, the block numbers of a digital alarm clock glowed red against a birchbark-framed photo of a grinning Tim carrying Margaret over the threshold. She brushed back her hair and ran her fingertips down her temples, lingering near the corners of her eyes, the creeping crows feet a tactile reminder that she wasn't the young girl in the photograph any longer.

How did we get old so quickly, she wondered, reflecting upon her relationship rather than her age. Thirty-four was young, hell, she knew that; it seemed a lifetime ago since she and Tim had first sat alone together, huddled beneath a blanket before a dwindling, crackling bonfire. The beer had run out hours earlier and the temperature hovered near freezing, chasing drunken teenagers to their cars for life-and-death joy rides along the narrow, curvy backwoods byroads. Margaret and Tim had stayed behind, and the newly-crowned state wrestling champion had the confidence and liquid courage to awkwardly grope at her small, still developing chest. Margaret had managed to fend him off, not because her mother's oft-repeated "good girl" speech guided her conscience. She had already decided Tim was the one. She was just going to make him work for it.

Mellowed by his ebbing buzz and the flickering flames of the fire dancing on the pale green undersides of the pine boughs above his head, Tim had forfeited the carnal match to Margaret and contented himself with holding her close under the blanket. They had talked until the gray, morning light – teasingly, Margaret assumed – about a hypothetical future together; married young, children young, and a long, happy life nestled in their cabin in the woods. A self-fulfilling prophecy perhaps, Margaret conceded, finding herself hitched to Tim at twenty and the mother of his two boys at twenty-four. Most of their friends were already getting married and starting families themselves, and to Margaret, it had just felt right.

It still felt right. She never questioned the path she had chosen in life, although, at present, Margaret felt a tug of impatience. The digital clock's red block letters read 9:30 and she was in bed, alone, on a Saturday night without the boys, who were no doubt roughhousing right now at a post-tournament pizza party and sleepover. The day had turned out to be even longer than she had anticipated, but she wasn't prepared to pull the curtain just yet.

"Come on to bed, honey," Margaret, in her best pleading tone, sweetened the pot, "I promise I won't be a pain in the ass. C'mon!" She dropped her knees and sat cross-legged, considering her options. She could get out of bed and corner him in the closet/office, she could give it up and hit the sack, or . . . "Besides, Richard told me everything, honey, so I know what you guys were acting so weird about at the wrestling meet."

"You're shittin' me! Dickey told you everything? Dickey?" Tim was immediately standing in the doorway, barechested and clad only in his gray gym trunks. Christ, the man's a furnace, Margaret thought, bundling back up in the covers, chilled anew just looking at him. Almost giddy at first, Tim's mood quickly darkened. "What? What *exactly* did Dickey tell you?" A look of incredulity etched across his face.

"Not so quick. Show me that sweep move of Billy's, if you've got the guts." Margaret bounced up in the bed, posturing like the little wrestlers she had cheered for all day. "Bring it on, Mr. Champion. Winner decides what we'll do the rest of the night . . ." she winked for effect, shifting her weight from one foot to the other, ". . . and how we do it." She didn't think it was the sweep move as the ceiling and walls wheeled past. Tim slammed Margaret down on the mattress and landed astride her hips in one fluent motion. He pinned her shoulders back with the palms of his hands and tightened his legs in a vise around her thighs, immobilizing her beneath his weight.

"What the hell did Dickey tell you?" Tim wasn't just playing along with her game.

"Ouch, Tim, you're hurting me! Get the hell off me!"

"I'm not fucking around here, Margaret. Tell me what it is, exactly, that Dickey told you."

"Christ, Tim, you're spooking me out now, too. What's the matter with you? Dammit, get the hell off me!" He loosened his grip on her shoulders and shifted the bulk of his weight off her torso, easing her discomfort without letting her squirm out from under him. "Son of a bitch," she grunted in her futile bid for freedom. "I'll tell you what Richard said if you just get off me, alright?" The instant he let go Margaret punched Tim hard in the left bicep. He rolled to the mattress, leaving an arm draped across her breasts and a bent leg over her pelvis. "Bastard," she hissed, throwing his limbs off her body and pushing him to his back.

"You knew those boys, Tim. You knew Christopher

and Michael Koenigs. According to Richard, you all knew them pretty well. All these years you never said a word about it, not a word. How was I supposed to know? He said it got pretty crazy around here for a while. You were just a kid, Tim. You must have been so frightened. I can't imagine . . ."

"No, you can't imagine, Margaret, you can't. I pray that you and the boys will never have to imagine something so terrible, let alone live through it. I never wanted to burden you with it, never. What would've been the point of that? It was easier to just put it all behind me, best that I could, and let the past be just that, the past." Tim sounded distant, forlorn.

"Richard told me that you guys made a pact, that you wouldn't talk about it with anybody but each other. You want to talk about it now?" Margaret, still lying motionless on her back, didn't expect her husband to accept the invitation.

"What do you want to know?" He surprised her, but she didn't hesitate.

"What were they like, Tim, the Koenigs boys. You know I think of Tony and Billy . . ."

"They were a lot like Tony and Billy when they were that age," not what Margaret wanted to hear, "hell-raising, rambunctious little boys. We were all like 12, I guess, Richard was a year older, and Christopher Koenigs was something like eight when he . . ." Tim paused and Margaret heard him swallow hard before continuing. ". . . and Michael was just six years old, somewhere around there. They were always chasing us older kids around the woods, bugging us until we'd let them join in whatever it was we were doing. They got picked on a lot, being younger, but they were stubborn little cusses and kept coming back for more."

"Was Christopher . . . was he crazy? Was he, I mean could you tell before it happened, I mean, did it seem like he was evil, like everybody said, did it seem like he was capable of doing something like that?" Margaret was familiar with Christopher Koenigs's fate following his brother's hanging. The local newspaper dedicated three full pages to the story when he was transferred to a psychiatric hospital out east in the mid-1990s. The articles recounted the murder, outlined his history in juvenile detention and delved into the contributing factors that helped shape the pre-pubescent malefactor. Still, until now, it had always seemed like one of those dramatic things in life that happen to somebody else.

"And you know, honey, Jackson made it sound like there was more to it, like you guys knew something else, or knew something more," Margaret added before her husband could answer.

"Did you smell Jackson's breath today? Hell, I got a little tipsy just talking to him. The guy had a snoot-full, Margaret. When I talked to him he was hardly making any sense." Sounding a bit too defensive, Tim abruptly dismissed his wife's intuition. Jackson didn't seem all that drunk to Margaret, at least not by his elevated standards, and Margaret knew what she had heard. *". . . and what we all know'd about it,"* he had slurred before Richard interrupted. She didn't have an opportunity to protest, however, as Tim closed the conversation with an answer to her previous inquiry.

"Was Christopher a nut-job, was he evil?" He repeated the question. "Might of been, but not as far as I could tell. I thought he was just a regular kid, like anybody else. At least that's what it seemed like to me. I guess that's the scariest part. You think you know somebody, but what you see on the outside isn't always the same as what's inside."

"Yeah, that is scary," Margaret agreed, unable to shake the nagging feeling that there was still something murky lying just beneath the surface. She ran her gaze along the length of the jagged crack in the ceiling. The black ant had exited from the overhead highway, once again leaving Margaret alone on her imaginary nighttime cruise. Disquieted, she closed her eyes, and wondered where the road would take her.

CHAPTER FIVE

Sauter carefully folded the crisp white paper, slipped it back inside the envelope, and tossed it into the clutter on top of his desk. Swiveling in his chair, he pushed off with his heels and rolled across the hard plastic floor mat, slowing to a stop in front of a dented file cabinet. He tapped absent-mindedly on the cold gray metal with his right fingers and gripped the silver handle of the middle drawer with his left. Raindrops, big as quarters and driven sideways by a stiff northeast breeze, drummed a dull, irregular beat against the room's lone window.

Blackened thunderheads tumbled menacingly above the pointed crowns of swaying conifers, dimming the mid-morning sky and rattling the rain-streaked glass with each resonant clap. Through the shifting liquid curtain Sauter watched as a long-legged woman dashed through the downpour, trying in vain to hold both her wind-whipped, knee-length skirt and her red umbrella in place. Hesitating with the cabinet drawer pulled partially open, Sauter smiled, a blending of empathy and amusement prompted by the stranger's high-heeled romp through ankle-deep puddles.

"What a Monday," he mused, immediately catching his mistake. It was actually Tuesday, the typical start of the work week having been eaten up as part of summer's final hurrah, Labor Day weekend. "It sure as hell seems like a Monday," he assured himself, somewhat pleased that a few days spent pitching muskie plugs and drinking beer could temporarily displace time.

Sauter slid the drawer shut with nary a glance at the glut of alphabetically ordered case files. He leaned back and laced his fingers together behind his head. The inclement weather, coupled with the surprise he found waiting upon his return from the long-overdue weekend on the water, left the normally cramped confines of his second floor office feeling especially oppressive. What he wouldn't give to be running through the late summer thunderstorm himself right now, away from the Ojibway County Sheriff's Headquarters and the bureaucratic burden the municipal building embodied.

If it wouldn't have detracted from his ability to fish, Sauter would have considered surrendering his right arm to be back out at Buckthorn Lake. Fresh off a restful four days in pursuit of his home state's "official" fish, the mighty muskellunge, he despairingly realized the Labor Day weekend getaway failed to fully rejuvenate his enthusiasm for the daily grind of being Detective Henry Sauter. He had boated four fish ranging in length from three to four feet – toothy, beautifully-marked, deep green predators that ruled as the king of northern Wisconsin's freshwater lakes. The accompanying adrenalin rush, spiked by the ferocious strike and furious fight of the aggressive fish, contributed to Sauter's almost maniacal obsession with the never-ending search for ways to outwit his pea-brained quarry.

"No fishing today," he conceded with a deep sigh. Sauter stood and grabbed the back of his chair, pulling it behind him as he returned to his desk. Sitting down hard, he propped his elbows on the marred wood surface, pushing back disheveled stacks of manila file folders to make room. For the third time that morning, he retrieved the envelope that he had earlier cast aside. He flicked at the back flap with his thumbnail, reluctant to withdraw the missive – the morning's unsettling surprise – folded neatly inside.

Sauter had known the day would come, and, frankly, he was both amazed and chagrined that it had taken so long in arriving. Yet, like a boxer that sees a powerful left hook bearing down on his jaw, Sauter was nonetheless staggered by the expected blow. He pulled the letter from the envelope and snapped it open in one motion. It was dated just four days prior and in a remarkable display of postal promptness – particularly in light of the holiday – had landed in his mailbox sometime during the weekend. The postmark and return address were familiar, this being the latest in a series of similar letters he had received in the last dozen-odd years; each handwritten in purple ink on white unlined paper, in the same distinctive hand.

"Dear Detective Sauter,

This letter is to inform you that as of today, Friday, August 31, 2007, Christopher John Koenigs is no longer an in-

house patient at the Municipal Mental Health Center, State of New York. Per the ruling of the Center's accredited Medical Examiner's Board, Mr. Koenigs has been transferred to a state-operated halfway house to help facilitate his expected integration . . ."

Sauter, growing somewhat annoyed with himself, abruptly folded the letter and considered stuffing it back in the envelope, just as he had with the two previous aborted readings. He rubbed the doubled paper against itself, complementing the rain's gentle drumming with a soft, recurrent rasp. So many years ago, Sauter marveled, yet so starkly fresh in his mind, as fresh as the memory of the unfortunate stranger racing high-heeled through the storm. Whenever he closed his eyes, eventually, and inevitably, his mind would carry him back beneath that ramshackle treehouse, back to the base of that menacing oak, back into the shadows of that midnight woods, back nearly half a lifetime.

The decision to join the Broadaxe police force was prompted by common necessity, mainly a lack of money, rather than higher ideals. Sauter figured he had answered the call to service when, newly-graduated from high school, he had enlisted for what turned out to be an uneventful four-year stint in the army. His military background and his hometown-boy connections made him a shoe-in for a job he planned to hold until the proverbial "something better came along." Something worse cropped up first, however; an unwelcome quirk of fate that inexorably propelled Sauter down his lifetime path.

Still sluggish in his transition from fisherman back to Detective, Sauter exchanged the unnerving letter for his desktop calendar. He ripped away the month of August and tossed the crumpled, glossy paper into the trash. Tuesday, September 4. He stared at the date, trying to will himself back into the moment. Instead, Sauter didn't fight the overpowering urge to glance ahead. September 20. His eyes instinctively focused on the square, virtually indistinguishable from the surrounding numbered blocks, yet indelibly locked in Sauter's psyche since that fateful night more than twenty years distant. Twenty-two years ago this month, to be exact. Sauter blanched at the thought.

Twenty-two years! So many years, so much had changed, yet in many ways Sauter still felt like that overwhelmed rookie cop staring at death for the first time. He still had the same head of wavy brown hair and had managed to maintain his fit, muscular physique, projecting a deceptively youthful appearance for a man with a half-century in the books. Hardened by that faraway night in the forest, a night which would have left many rookies questioning their choice of careers, Sauter coped by immersing himself in his work. Following a mercurial climb through the ranks – he made detective by the time he hit thirty-five – Sauter heard, and ignored, all the small town talk. The sky was the limit for Henry Sauter who, it was assumed by many, would ride an illustrious law enforcement career off into a bright political sunset.

Sauter surprised them all, balking at every opportunity for advancement that came across his desk. He had unwittingly found his niche, content to work on solving crimes at the grassroots level. A detective for the past fifteen years, he had no intention of ever being anything else. It was a ceaseless, quixotic quest to comprehend the criminal mind. What triggered the collapse of conscience that manifested itself in theft, assault, or murder? Granted, the combined culprit behind the majority of the cases Sauter investigated was simply an excess of alcohol and a dearth of brains. A select few cases were driven by more sinister, less tangible motives spurred by the basest of human desire; hate, greed, envy, lust. Why? How? Twenty-two years since he had cradled Michael Koenigs's cold, limp, little body in his arms, Sauter ruefully acknowledged that he was no closer to the answers.

It was no use. He didn't even try to suppress the tide of emotions and memories washing over him. He had been here before, trapped in the undertow, dragged down to the bottom of his darkest thoughts. Sauter surfaced below the oak tree, its dry, brown leaves rustling unseen in the black night sky. The earthy autumn air filled his lungs, billowing out in tenuous white clouds with each heavy, amplified exhalation. Weathered, warped wood grated together, unleashing a shrill scream from the threatening treehouse rocking overhead. The mournful, disturbing wail of a young child echoed through the trees and Sauter turned slowly, desperately searching the shadows of the forest for its source. Coming full circle back to the oak, he nudged the small, suspended boy and sent the pallid body swaying back and forth beneath the treehouse. The coarse fiber of the noose dug deeper into the child's slender neck with each swing and Sauter reached out to stifle the hypnotic motion. Michael Koenigs's decaying, putrid flesh melted in his grasp and oozed between his fingers.

Mortified, Sauter dropped the calendar and gaped perplexedly at his hands.

"What's the matter boss? You look as if you've seen a ghost," Officer Seth Colins, standing tentatively in the hallway outside of Sauter's office, bore a look of genuine concern. "I wasn't sure if you'd be back in today or not. How was the fishing? Catch any of those huskies you've been telling me about?"

Sauter embraced the opportune diversion. He sincerely enjoyed the young patrolman's company, and he forced a smiled greeting in an attempt to mask his apparent discomfort.

"*Muskies*, Colins, the fish are called muskies. A husky is a dog, Colins, you know, the big furry kind that pull Eskimos around in their sleds? The dogs that run the Iditarod up in Alaska, from Nome to Fairbanks? You've heard of that even where you're from, I'm sure, Colins. Where is it you're from again?" Sauter was pimping the greenhorn, well aware that the scrawny Fife-alike hailed from Atlanta.

"Atlanta. Atlanta, Georgia, boss," Colins confirmed, without the least hint of the expected southern drawl.

Upon his arrival back in mid-August, the absence of an accent left Sauter doubtful of Colins's claim that he was a native Georgian, through and through. Quite earnestly, the newcomer laid bare his childhood dream of growing up to become a network television reporter or, better yet, an anchorman. And how often do you hear a network reporter or anchorman speaking with a thick Georgia twang? Never, Colins was quick to point out, which was the reason he had dedicated countless painstaking hours toward eliminating it from his speech.

"Muskies," he added, repeating it a second time, intent on committing the unfamiliar word, and fish, to memory. "Muskies. So, did you catch any of those muskies you were telling me about, boss?" The hallway's bright, fluorescent overhead lights reflected off Colins's too-small wire-rimmed glasses, silver mirrors hiding hazel eyes. He parted his gossamer hair down the middle. Most folks would call it red, only to be rebutted by Colins's adamant claim that it was, in reality, strawberry blond. Lithe and slump-shouldered, Sauter couldn't help but wonder if he was only allowed one bullet in his service revolver.

"Boated four of 'em, all legal, in four days. That's about as good as it gets muskie fishing . . . the fish of a thousand casts, that's what they say. I'll show you the pictures sometime." Sauter briefly considered inviting him along on a future trip but, preferring to fish alone, he always regretted having a second person in the boat. Instead, he asked Colins to join him on a little police business later that day.

"I've got some paperwork to catch up on here this morning, a ton of e-mails to sort through. It's unreal how much crap piles up when you're gone a couple of days." Sauter only had one piece of correspondence on his mind. "I'll grab you right after lunch, Colins, and we'll probably be out most of the afternoon. Hey, and Colins, I don't want to have to tell you again, no more 'boss', alright? It's Sauter."

Closing his office door on the copiously nodding newbie, Sauter hurried back to his desk. He hastily reopened the letter, suddenly anxious to read the remainder of its contents and get on with his day. The formal, antiseptic tone of the opening paragraph surrendered to a warmer, more personal approach.

    . . . I knew that you'd want to have this information as soon possible, and I wanted to extend you the courtesy of hearing it from me. I tried to phone with the news late last week, but was informed that you were away from the office until after Labor Day. I am loathe to correspond via the computer, much too impersonal and potentially none too private, so I sent this letter in the hope that you would receive it immediately upon your return.

    Along with a great deal of relief, I must admit to a nagging feeling of some trepidation. I suspect that you are being subjected to a wide range of emotions, as well. As I mentioned *earlier, Mr. Koenigs has been transferred to a state-sanctioned halfway house, with psychiatric and security staff on hand around the clock. I'll personally check on his progress at regular intervals and promise to keep you informed of any new developments.*

I hope this letter finds you well.

Fondly,

Dr. Amelia Devine

A wide range of emotions? Hell, you don't know the half of it, sister, Sauter rejoined, carefully placing the most recent letter in a folder containing the handful of other letters he had received from Devine over the years. Amelia Devine, a pretty name, Sauter had always thought, for some unknown reason suspecting that the woman was pretty herself, as well. He had never met her, never talked to her, never even seen her, not even a picture, quite a feat considering their lengthy acquaintance. An undeniable kinship had developed between the two, despite Sauter's thinly veiled attempts to maintain an impersonal, professional distance. He had unfailingly responded to her handwritten, personalized updates regarding the Koenigs case with terse, typed letters of appreciation.

Why was that so tough? Sauter wondered sheepishly. Devine's earlier letters, those were tough. He pulled the thin stack of envelopes back out of the folder, mildly surprised that today's mailing only brought the grand total to four. For some reason, it seemed like there should have been more. Sauter wasn't sure why, maybe because they were spread out over such a long period of time.

The first letter was dated 1995, the year Koenigs landed in Devine's lap out in New York. That ate away at Sauter's insides, still did to this day. Koenigs had already been under lock and key in Wisconsin for a decade at that point, since the hanging, and Sauter thought the kid had done his time. The state thought so too. Then that uppity East Coast psychiatrist, Perkins, had stuck her nose in, twisted some arms and pulled some strings. Sauter wouldn't have thought it possible to harbor such enmity for someone he had never even met. The next two letters followed his parole hearings before the medical examiners board, one arriving in 1999 and the next in 2003, sent by

Devine to inform Sauter that Koenigs's release had been denied. He couldn't comprehend it. By that point, he'd given up trying.

The anger remained, had actually intensified; a corrosive, almost debilitating anger born through the frustration of helplessness. The Koenigs case reeked of injustice heaped upon tragedy, and there was little, if anything, Sauter could do about it. He had never bought into the "Genetic Sociopath" bullshit that Perkins peddled, not just where Koenigs was concerned, but the whole pessimistic philosophy in general. There was always a ray of light, Sauter was certain of it, even in the darkest of souls.

Two little boys, a black September night twenty-two years ago, an ominous treehouse in an imposing oak. Sauter knew these were the rudiments of his being, the elements that shaped his very existence. Why would Christopher Koenigs want to kill his brother Michael? Why would he put a rope around his brother's neck and push him from a treehouse? Why? How could such a young child be capable of committing murder? How? The questions haunted Sauter, but not as much as the disheartening truth that he was still no closer to discovering the answers. With each passing year, the likelihood increased that he probably never would.

Strange, though, that he could always find solace in Dr. Amelia Devine's letters. Not so much in the content, which invariably proved frustrating and raised his ire, but more so in the flowing purple ink and feminine script. He liked how she hoped her letters "found him well," and was warmed when she signed each one "fondly." Sauter was indifferent to the cold truth that Devine's pathetically few letters accounted for the most intimate relationship he had ever shared with a female - aside from his dearly departed mother, rest her soul, and his hunting dog, Kizzie. "And she was a bitch," he noted wryly.

The sky was still dark, but the rain had subsided and shafts of sunlight broke through the thinning clouds. Sauter looked out the office window, fully expecting to see a rainbow.

 *   *   *

"Ready to roll, Peach?" Sauter immediately regretted the bungled attempt to bestow a nickname on the lad from Georgia. It came to him in the spur of the moment, and it came out sounding - weird. Noting the headphones protruding from Colins's ears, Sauter glanced thankfully to the heavens.

"Colins," he tried again, louder. "Peach?" Sauter silently derided himself, not wanting to know where *that* came from. The earphones were plugged into Colins's computer, and Sauter could just imagine the audio accompanying the blood-and-gut visuals spilling across the screen. Engrossed in the video game, Colins nearly leaped out of his pressed khaki uniform at the unexpected tap on the shoulder, much to Sauter's amusement.

"Little jumpy, wouldn't you say, son? You really should try and relax a bit. It's not good for someone your age to be so high strung. You should consider seeing a doctor about that." Sauter was enjoying himself. "Let's go, kid, time to hit the road." Colins snuck a sideways peek at the clock as he wrapped up the cord and placed the headphones in his desk drawer. 12:30 p.m. "I know, I know, I said after lunch," Sauter took the hint, nodding at the computer screen, "but it doesn't appear as if I'm interrupting anything important."

"Okay, boss." Colins, grinning, caught the brunt of Sauter's severe stare. "Alright, alright . . . Sauter. Geez, some people don't have any sense of humor. Hey, hold up!" Cleaning his glasses with a tissue, Colins had to rush to catch up with Sauter, already exiting the building. There was a lull in the day's on-again, off-again rainshowers, and the air was heavy with the inimitable aroma of pine and damp earth. Colins dodged between the chalky-gray puddles pockmarking the gravel parking lot, reaching Sauter as he opened the driver's side door on his rusting blue and white Ford Bronco.

"So anyway, unless its top secret and you'll have to kill me if you tell me, do you mind if I ask where we're going?" Sauter's sour expression indicated that yes, he did mind.

"Ever strike you as funny that there's not an oak tree to be found around here?" Sauter tipped his head toward the surrounding forest. Obligingly, Colins followed his nod and considered the trees, green needles glistening and bark darkened by the rain."You wouldn't know an oak tree if one was stuck up your ass and you started shitting acorns, would you?" Sauter interpreted Colins's meek shoulder-shrug as an affirmative. "Well, I'm just the man for you," he slammed the door shut on the Bronco and strolled toward the trees framing the parking lot, Colins close on his heels.

"These beauties are red pine; some folks prefer to call them Norway pine -*Pinus resinosa."* Sauter couldn't resist showing off his command of each tree's Latin translation. "I'd say these are about seventy feet tall, but Norway's can reach upwards of 100 feet. Trunks can get three feet around. There are a couple of easy ways to ID these guys. The bark's a dead giveaway." Sauter slapped the damp, large reddish-brown plates that girdled the tree. The trunk, ramrod straight, climbed high into a picturesque crown of branches. Sauter broke a needle cluster off a smaller tree in the understory and twisted it between his thumb and forefinger, dark green helicopter blades rotating back and forth. "See these needles? Well, there are always two needles in a red pine cluster – white pine have five – and check this out, if you bend the needles in two they'll snap. White pine needles won't do that. *Red pine, red snapper.* That's another way to remember."

The obvious lack of enthusiasm emanating from his captive audience didn't deter Sauter from plunging forward. He had spent his life in these woods and tried to impress the same reverence and respect he held for the majestic trees upon anyone willing to listen. Lacking any arboreal interest whatsoever, Colins couldn't help but be drawn in by Sauter's contagious zeal.

"*Pinus strobus*, the white pine." Sauter had ventured another fifty feet into the forest and had wrapped his arms around the massive trunk of a tree that towered a good forty feet above the rest of the canopy. Colins patted himself on the back for being a quick study, plucking and inspecting one of the bluish-green, five-needled clusters clinging to the branches. He traced the contours of the deep fissures in the tree's thick, grayish-brown bark, bending to pick up a cylindrical cone lying on the carpet of brown needles at his feet. Sticky white sap from the cone's resinous scales adhered to his fingers, and when he tried to wipe it off on the ground, dead needles collected in the natural glue.

"The smaller conifers – that's a cone bearing tree, Colins, an evergreen – most of the smaller conifers you see scattered around the understory are balsam fir." Sauter held his hands out, palms up, and looked into the treetops. Sporadic raindrops filtered through the web of branches, harbingers of the curtain of water rippling across the parking lot. "A few of them are spruce, but we'll have to pick up this lesson later," Sauter shouted as he raced headlong into the deluge, chased by an earthshaking peel of thunder.

Pea-sized hail mixed in with the rain, rattling the rusty Bronco like the inside of a dice cup. Sauter leaned back in the blue vinyl driver's seat, white stuffing peeking out of thin vertical cracks beneath the headrest. A bead of water dripped from his sloping nose as he leaned forward and flipped on the wipers. The windshield steamed and the outside world faded to gray. He sat back, waiting for the defroster to do its work.

"No oaks, though. None for a few miles around here, anyway." Sauter watched Colins wipe his glasses one more time, the lenses having fogged right along with the windshield. "An oak is a deciduous tree, Colins, a hardwood, same as a maple, or an aspen. Bunch of different kind of oaks, mostly red oak up here, *Quercus rubra*. Not in this soil, though, too sandy; but there's some real dandies where we're headed."

"And that is . . .?" Colins, struggling with his twisted seatbelt, gave it another try. Sauter jammed the Bronco into gear and punched the accelerator, careening through every rain-filled pothole and jostling his unbuckled passenger about.

"Broadaxe," he grunted, relatively certain that nothing much had changed since the last time he'd been there.

Turning left out of the gravel parking lot onto a narrow, macadam road snaking beneath an arch of pine boughs, Sauter reckoned it had been a good six years since he'd been back to his hometown. His mother had been the sole remaining reason for returning to Broadaxe, and, after she passed away, he never had the compulsion to go back. It wouldn't have taken much.

He lived and worked just forty-five minutes to the southeast, in Turtle Creek, the Ojibway County seat. But that was a long road to travel, he had convinced himself, to a place where bad memories and bad karma were all that remained. Besides, there was no denying it, he had worn out his welcome long ago.

Sauter could have swung right out of the parking lot and jumped on the main highway heading north to Broadaxe, the quickest route, but he was willing to sacrifice the extra fifteen minutes for a more leisurely, scenic ride on the back roads. Colins got to see a little bit more of the countryside this way; too, he further rationalized, as yet unwilling to acknowledge the voice in his head asking if this was such a good idea. Wise choice or not, there was no turning back. Christopher Koenigs had taken his first step back outside the walls, resurrecting a piece of Sauter that he'd long given up for dead, that he had buried in a subconscious crypt. He didn't know what he'd find there, didn't know what he wanted to find, he only knew it was time to go home.

To pass the time and assuage his apprehension, Sauter resumed his arboreal tutorial, unconcerned if his young sidekick was interested, or bored. Colins, for his part, was just happy that the veteran detective had asked for his rookie cop's assistance in . . . whatever it was they were doing. He listened patiently, nodding at what seemed like the appropriate times, as Sauter pointed out the densely packed, scraggly trees crowding a black spruce swamp. Almost wistfully, he explained how the adjacent tamarack's bright green needles turned an exquisite golden-yellow in the fall before dropping from the branches, the only Wisconsin conifer to shed its leaves.

"Black spruce, *Picea mariana*. Tamarack, *Larix laricina*." Sauter, suddenly aware he was monopolizing the conversation and sounding haughty at that, felt obliged to make amends.

"All that time you spent training your voice, Colins, to lose your southern accent, how the heck did you wind up as a cop? What happened with the news anchor, or the reporter gig you were hoping for?" Sauter was suddenly curious. He had just sort of ended up a cop, had never really wanted to *be* anything. This kid had a dream, had a goal in life, and he still ended up a cop.

Sauter's abrupt change of course caught Colins off guard. Flattered that the detective took an interest, it took him a moment to process the questions. Sensing the awkward silence, he plunged in.

"Sorry, I had my head up my ash," Colins, admonishing himself for the lame attempt at humor, was relieved to hear Sauter chortle.

"*Fraxinus,* you had your head up your *Fraxinus.* I take it you've heard enough about trees for one day. So, how did you end up in the noble profession of law enforcement?"

"Well, my daddy was a cop. That was a part of it, I guess, a big part, really. I had to do something after I was told flat out I had no future in television. I had a journalism degree from Georgia Tech and a stack of demo tapes, but my first three job interviews, the only interviews, as it turned out, lasted about five minutes. They all said I didn't have 'the look,' that I wasn't photogenic, that I should consider a career in radio."

Sauter had to agree, Colins was definitely behind the curve in the looks department, woefully so for the narcissistic microscope of television. "Why not radio, what's wrong with that?" he ventured.

"Radio, schmadio."

Realizing that was the extent of the explanation and able to recognize a sore subject when one slapped him in the face, Sauter tried a different tack. "So your old man was a cop, eh?"

"Yeah, still is, I guess. He's retired, but he always said, 'Once a cop, always a cop.' He's sort of a hero in the Atlanta P.D.; saved a couple lives, took a bullet for his partner. He pulled some strings to get me in the academy and could have got me a job in his old precinct with a telephone call, but I had to get the hell away from there, far away. That's how I ended up here. There's no way I could have lived up to the legend, not even close. I think he knew it, too, and was relieved to see me go."

It would have been a good time to say "Well, we're glad to have you here, son," or, "Everything happens for a reason," but the perceived burden of too much personal information caused Sauter to drop the subject cold. He noticed an island of oak along a ridge, up ahead on the right, but he didn't bother pointing them out to Colins, who, head bowed, was once again busy cleaning his glasses.

Sauter opened his window, and the hiss of water being channeled through the Bronco's oversized tires interrupted the quiet that had descended following Colins's abbreviated auto-biography. He sensed the kid's melancholy and callously re-gretted the decision to bring the ungainly rookie along. Why did I bring him along? Sauter wondered, anxiously analyzing his impetuous idea to make the trip in the first place.

"Welcome to Broadaxe, Where Mother Nature Raises Her Babies?" Colins's inflection suggested he was missing the intended message of the leaning roadside sign. Raised gold let-ters set against a blue background framed a pair of white-robed arms cradling a menagerie of exaggeratedly cute infant ani-mals. Sauter felt the cloying eyes of the baby deer, raccoons, porcupines, black bear and skunks turning in their dewy sock-ets as he passed, suspicious of his motives and far from wel-coming.

"Funny, but I don't see any city." Colins, his mood con-siderably lightened, blinked at the seemingly uninhabited ex-panse of forest swallowing the road ahead. Playfully, and with-out warning, he began to probe Sauter for information in the guise of his unfulfilled alter ego.

"This is Seth Colins reporting live, on-location in Northeast Ojibway County, where I'm joined by Detective Henry Sauter of the Ojibway County Sheriff's Department. De-tective Sauter is currently investigating the disappearance of the entire city of Broadaxe, which has vanished mysteriously from the coniferous and deciduous forest of northern Wiscon-sin. Detective Sauter, do you have any clues, any leads, where Broadaxe might be?" Colins thrust the mechanical pencil he had been speaking into toward Sauter's clenched jaw.

"You're kind of an odd little bird, aren't you, Colins." Sauter, speaking pointedly away from the improvised micro-phone, offered his opinion more as a statement of fact rather than a question. " 'The coniferous and deciduous forest of northern Wisconsin,' nice touch, I have to admit."

"Please, just answer the question, Detective," Colins insisted, repositioning the pink pencil eraser precariously close to Sauter's lips. Slightly agitated, Sauter snatched the pencil and threw it over his shoulder.

"In the first place, it's not a city, Colins. Back at the sign there, we just entered into the Township of Broadaxe; but the actual village itself is still a couple miles ahead. It's never been lost, never vanished. No such luck." Loose change rattled in the half-open ash tray as Sauter detoured from the pavement and headed north on a two- track, dirt road, softened and slick from the intermittent showers. Colins squeezed his armrests and pressed his body into his seat, bracing against the bumps and jolts accentuated by, in his estimation, Sauter's imprudent speed.

Cresting the rise of a verdant glacial drumlin, the dense trees parted into a small, circular opening and the road withered away beneath a shimmering carpet of knee-high grasses and ferns. Sauter barreled into the rain-soaked vegetation and cranked the steering wheel hard to the left, spinning the Bronco to a stop in a sharp, 180-degree arc. He looked beyond Colins – eyes pinched shut beneath his wire-rimmed glasses and hanging on for dear life – to an overgrown footpath leading into the cloud-shadowed forest. Sauter swung open his door, hinges squawking, and dropped his left foot into the wet grass before pausing half-in, half-out of the vehicle.

"The two biggest trees on the other side of the opening, those are oak trees, red oaks, *Quercus rubra*. Most of the oaks around here grow . . ."

"What are we doing here, Sauter? Why did you drag me out into the woods? Are you working on a case over here, in Broadaxe, or what? I'd appreciate being clued in, if you wouldn't mind." Making his plea to Sauter's back, Colins had dropped the intrepid reporter routine. Leaving the squeaky door ajar, Sauter pivoted back into his seat, satisfied that Colins's perspective was unsullied by any secondhand knowledge of Broadaxe's infamous past.

"Fair enough, fair enough. You've got a right to know what's going on," Sauter agreed, trying his best to sound conciliatory. "Long story short, twenty-two years ago this month an eight-year-old boy name of Christopher John Koenigs killed his six-year-old brother, Michael, right here in Broadaxe. Courts ruled that it was premeditated, cold-blooded murder. Christopher's been incarcerated ever since, ten years here in Wisconsin and another twelve years out East, New York state. Shrinks labeled him a genetic sociopath; unfeeling, incapable of reason or remorse, innately malevolent, you get the gist. The whole deal kind of blew this community apart at the time. Then folks made a conscious decision to bury it, pretend like it never happened. As of last Friday, Christopher John Koenigs is a free man, proving you can only keep old skeletons in the closet for so long."

"How did he do it? I mean, how'd the kid kill his little brother?" Colins interjected, eyes wide and Adam's apple bobbing in his throat, like a child listening to a ghost story around the campfire.

Pointing past Colins's nose, down the grassy trail cutting into the woods, Sauter struggled to maintain his composure. "He hung him, back in these woods. Christopher Koenigs tied a rope around his brother Michael's neck and pushed him out of a treehouse, an old, weathered treehouse built in the branches of one of the biggest oaks ever to grow around these parts. Not a red oak, though, a bur oak, *Quercus macrocarpa*. It's probably still there."

Sauter couldn't recall the last time he had made the pilgrimage to what had become a sort of self-flagellating shrine in the aftermath of the hanging. During those frequent visits to the oak, when he stood beneath its broad canopy of heavy, grasping branches, he invariably questioned just what it was that he expected to find there. Now, his lower pant legs soaked and clinging to his calves, he trudged reluctantly down the familiar trail, to the unyielding oak which offered no answers.

A shaft of sunlight pierced through a crack in the opaque, drifting clouds and bathed the open meadow in a hazy glow as Sauter stepped out of the trees. The light slowly crept across the forest floor, fading away just as it reached the base of the sprawling oak, a lone, formidable sentinel standing guard over the forest's secrets.

"That's not supposed to be here," he sputtered, knees

buckling and a dull roar rushing through his head, which he shook in disbelief. "I can't believe it. That shouldn't be here."

"I thought you expected it to be here. You said it probably would still be here." Colins stood a pace or two behind Sauter, assessing the oak. "Man, you weren't kidding, that is one humongous tree." He stepped forward, shoulder-to-shoulder with Sauter, and, for the second time that day, thought the detective looked as if he'd seen a ghost.

"Not the tree, the treehouse," Sauter moaned, pointing meekly at the rickety structure perched in the oak's branches, beads of moisture dripping from its gray, worn wood. "I tore that goddam monstrosity down and burned the son of a bitch myself, the day they put Christopher Koenigs away. It can't be, I tell you, it just can't be." He retreated down the footpath, backing slowly away at first, transfixed by the spectral vision before him, the oak and treehouse suddenly illuminated by a soft, golden aura.

Colins remained in the meadow, alone, after Sauter turned and plodded hastily through the greenery underfoot. Tentatively, he moved closer to the oak, careful not to trample the few remaining daisies and wildflowers peeking through the matted, coarse grasses blanketing the ground. Directly beneath the treehouse, Colins craned to see inside an opening, a portal of impenetrable blackness, hewed roughly from its warped flanks. A droplet of warm liquid spattered his forehead and trickled beneath his glasses, running between his eyes before forking into separate rivulets off the bridge of his nose. He pulled a neatly-folded handkerchief from his back pocket, but was rendered immobile by a faraway whisper, first from the darkness of the treehouse itself, then from the woods on his left, and finally from the treetops to his right. *Colins . . . Colins . . . Colins.* He tucked the unused handkerchief into his pocket, slowly and deliberately, trying to minimize his movements. A big city boy ill at ease in the gloomy, waterlogged forest, Colins kicked himself for not heading back to the truck with Sauter.

"Sauter," he breathed with a pent-up exhalation. "Shoot, that's Sauter." A smile, evoked by a mixture of relief and embarrassment, faded quickly to a look of concern as Colins hustled down the trail. A rookie cop keeping a detective waiting, never a good thing. Make it an obviously upset detective to boot? Colins braced himself for the wrath that awaited.

Sauter was livid, alright, and Colins launched into a preemptive apology as he jumped in the Bronco, cut short by the realization that the detective's ire was mercifully directed elsewhere.

"Who the hell would do something like that?" Sauter was beyond tense. Every tendon and vein was stretched taut or bulging beneath skin burnt red with anger. "After all this time, what kind of a twisted mind does it take to come up with that idea? To build a treehouse in that oak, any treehouse . . . but, my god, to build an exact replica of that old treehouse, the treehouse where Christopher Koenigs hung his brother and caused this community so much pain? That's one sick individual, one sick puppy."

"Maybe a litter, maybe one sick litter," Colins interjected. "Seems like a lot of work for one person, hauling all that wood out here and hammering that thing together, up in a tree, no less."

"I suppose you're probably right," Sauter nodded, "I just hate to think that there's more than one person around these parts capable of being so brutally callous, so insensitive, so . . . heartless."

"You're pretty riled up about this whole deal. You know those Koenigs boys, Sauter, or what?"

Sauter had known the family when he lived in Broadaxe; not well, just enough to give a friendly nod when they crossed paths. They kept to themselves and appeared to be ordinary, unassuming folks, transplants to the area from somewhere down south, Iowa or Ohio, it didn't really matter. It was a family fated to travel a tragic road. The distraught, young parents fled from Broadaxe following the loss of their two sons – one boy to prison and one boy to the afterlife – but were never able to outrun the haunting, unthinkable memories. After the hanging, both were dead within a handful of years; the guilt-ridden father from a self-inflicted shotgun blast to the back of his throat, and the inconsolable mother shortly after, the victim of unimaginable heartache and loss.

"I was there, the night of the hanging, a rookie cop a couple weeks on the job, just like yourself. I held that little boy in my arms, I took the blood-soaked noose from his neck, and I laid him down on the forest floor. I live with it, I relive it, every day of my life. You're goddam right I'm riled up." Sauter stomped on the gas and the tires momentarily spun on the wet ferns, catching with a jolt and sending the Bronco hurtling down the dirt road. "I know exactly where I can get some answers," Sauter muttered, barely easing up on the gas as he roared onto the slick pavement and accelerated down the highway, toward Broadaxe.

"Where we going now?" Colins asked, with trepidation, casting a sideways glance at his incensed chauffeur and wondering what the hell he had gotten himself into.

"The only place I'm still welcome around here," Sauter snarled, then tapped his finger to his forehead. "How the heck did you cut yourself, anyway?"

"What the . . ." Colins touched his brow and rubbed the congealed red fluid between his fingers in disbelief. He looked in the rearview mirror and again put his hand to the crimson stain that ran from the center of his forehead, down his nose, and across his cheeks. "You called me before, didn't you, when I was back in the woods? You called my name, right?" He removed his glasses and rubbed his face vigorously, coloring his folded white handkerchief with splotches of pale pink.

"Yeah, kid, right, whatever," Sauter was someplace else, distant and suddenly out of sync with the conversation. Colins didn't care. It was the response he was hoping for, so he willingly let it drop. He checked his scrubbed face in the mirror, then tucked his soiled handkerchief into his pocket. Unable to find a cut or a source for what appeared to be blood, disconcerted and a bit bewildered, he tried to shrug it off as just another odd twist in an increasingly strange day.

The plaintive strains of Patsy Cline belting out *I Fall to Pieces* serenaded Sauter and Colins as they stepped through the windowless door to Tingle's Tap. Smoke billowed out, as well, swirling away from long-ashed cigarettes abandoned in ashtrays or dangling from a drooping lower lip. The small, one-room tavern listed noticeably to the left, its low ceiling balanced on walls threatening to collapse like a house of cards. The bar was three-quarters full, typical at Tingle's, even on a weekday afternoon. Sauter squeezed between the beer-stained, red felt pool table and a disheveled row of barstools, most occupied, and if you kicked back to make room for a sot who had bellied up to the bar. Colins, self-conscious in his crisp new uniform, stayed in Sauter's back pocket as he worked his way toward a couple of open seats on the far corner.

"If it isn't the son of old Sammy Sauter
Who did lots of things that he shouldn't have oughta
But who'd ever have thought
That the one time he's caught
Is with his dick in the minister's daughter"

Limericks, that was Tingle's shtick, and he prided himself on his ability to personalize an off-color rhyme no matter the customer's name. Sauter's personal version always started with the same line, the middle stanzas varied over the years, and it always ended with his dick in the same place.

His first name was Donald, but Sauter figured even his wife called him Tingle, just like everybody else. Tingle had worked with Sauter's father, Samuel, over at the old paper mill in Turtle Creek, back when both were young men, and probably knew his old man better than he did. Samuel Sauter was killed by a drunk driver when his only son was just five years old, and Don Tingle had taken it upon himself to look after his dead friend's boy. He never became a father figure, nor did a close bond ever develop; but Tingle was always there for Sauter and stuck by his side, even in the dark years after the hanging, when he managed to alienate everyone else in Broadaxe.

"So, Tingle, how the hell have you been?" Sauter stuck his hand across the mahogany bar. Tingle responded with a firm grip, wiping the rich, reddish-brown surface with a damp rag at the same time. He flicked two circular drink coasters cut from a green rug onto the bar and tilted his head forward, peering over the thick-lensed, black-framed glasses pinched to the end of his bulbous nose. Slight of build with a stiff, graying crew cut, Tingle's popeye-large forearms and hands appeared powerfully incongruent with the rest of his withered frame.

"Damn good, Sauter, damn good. Every morning I wake up and take a breath, that's a good day. So what can I get for you and your friend . . . I didn't catch his name." Tingle extended his hand and Colins stood to shake, but Sauter purposely interrupted the introduction.

"I'll take a bottle of Bud, and get my friend here whatever he wants," Sauter smirked, certain that Tingle was chafing for the chance to impress the stranger with an improvised limerick.

"Here's your beer," Tingle set the perspiring long-neck bottle on the carpet coaster. Ignoring Sauter, he turned his attention back to Colins. "What can I get for you, mister . . ."

"Colins, Seth Colins. A root beer would be fine for me."

Reveling in the moment, Tingle popped the top on a can of root beer and emptied the contents into a frosted glass mug.

"There once was a fellow named Seth
Whose wife was a terrible meth
She was an uncomely lath
With a super-sized ath
But she had the most beautiful breathts"

On bended knee, Tingle threw his arms open and waved his hands, the old vaudeville finish, then popped up in front of Colins to gauge the first-timer's reaction. "I have to write that down," Colins laughed, reaching for a napkin. He patted his chest and slipped his fingers into his shirt pocket, a fruitless search for the discarded mechanical pencil/microphone. "You have something to write with, Sauter? I want to send that to my daddy, he'd think it's a hoot."

Tingle winked at Colins over the top of his glasses, using a knuckle to nudge the impervious lenses back over his nearly sightless, milky irises. Turning his attention to Sauter, Tingle grabbed a corncob pipe from an ashtray below the bar and tamped the aromatic, partially burned tobacco with his thumb.

"There's only one reason why you'd show your face back here in Broadaxe, Sauter," he lisped, the unlit pipe clenched between his large, yellow teeth. "Never could let sleeping dogs lie, that's what got you on the shit list around here in the first place. Shouldn't be surprised to see you, I guess. That Koenigs boy gets let loose from the looney bin, *in New York*, and here you are nosing around Broadaxe. Don't see you much anymore, but it's déjà vu for me and you, my friend. If you haven't let it go by now, I guess you're never going to. I'll tell you though, Sauter, things have been nice and peaceful in Broadaxe for many a year now, and we aim to keep it that way. What are you looking for, Sauter, what do you expect to find here? That was a long, long time ago, but not much has changed."

"News travels fast." Sauter tipped his bottle toward Tingle and took a long pull on his beer. He wasn't surprised that the old man had heard about Koenigs's release, just the opposite, that's why he made the trip. Not much happened in and around Broadaxe that Tingle didn't know about. This was his primary destination for the day. He wasn't sure what had possessed him to sidetrack to the oak, the site of the hanging, but now he was glad he did.

"I beg to differ with you though, Tingle. Things do change around here, that's a fact. I took a walk in the woods outside of town, back by that big old bur oak. Bur oaks are kind of rare this far north, you know, and the trees up here are usually smaller than the ones down south. Not this oak; this bur oak is majestic, a real specimen." Sauter took another swig of beer and bent closer to Tingle, both elbows on the bar. He didn't lower his voice; he hoped everyone in the bar heard what he had to say.

"Some peckerhead desecrated that beautiful bur oak. Somebody built a treehouse in that oak, Tingle, can you imagine that? A treehouse!" He paused, letting what he said sink in.

"You look a little shocked, Tingle. Well here's the kicker. It's a dead ringer for the treehouse that Michael Koenigs was pushed out of, to his death. I destroyed that old treehouse myself, so I was a little shocked, too, let me tell you. Apparently, I'm not the only one who can't let sleeping dogs lie. Now, tell me Tingle, any idea who the crazy bastard - crazy bastards," he said with a nod to a rapt Colins, "or who would pull a moronic stunt like that? Did you know that treehouse was out there?"

"Hell no, Sauter! How the hell would I know? I never go out to those woods anymore. Nobody around here does, that I know of, except maybe kids on a Halloween dare. Maybe that's who did it, kids, for a prank. The little shits around here still sing those songs about the Koenigs boys and most of them have heard the stories, so that's probably it." Tingle spoke in hushed tones, indicating to Sauter that he should do the same. "For chrissakes you're gonna stir up a hornet's nest around here Sauter. It's some damn delinquents' perverted idea of a joke; so for everybody's sake, don't blow it up into more than that."

Sauter finished the last of his Budweiser and pitched the empty bottle into a trashcan behind the bar. "One more thing, Tingle. How'd you find out about Christopher Koenigs so quickly? Hell, I just found out today, myself."

"Dickey Mann, who else? He told me the end of last week already. That fella, he's greasier than the hair on Bigfoot's ass, if you ask me, but he's the only one I know around here who's kept as close tabs on that Koenigs boy as you. Ain't that right Jackson? It was Dickey who come in here last Friday and told us." Tingle looked toward the far end of the bar, but the stool normally occupied by Jackson Kelly was vacant. Half a tap beer sat on the bar, and smoke spiraled from an Old Gold resting in the ashtray.

"That's funny, he was just sitting there. Never knew old Jackson to leave an unfinished drink on the bar. Anyway, you know Jackson Kelly."

Sauter had taken note of the rotund beer drinker at the end of the bar when he entered. The soliloquy about the treehouse was intended for his ears more than anyone else's, and his sudden departure signaled to Sauter that he probably got the message.

"Yeah, I know Jackson Kelly," he averred, tossing a handful of bills on the bar to cover the drinks.

CHAPTER SIX

The person on the other end of the phone line was an-noyingly persistent. Margaret, stark naked and soaking wet, tip-toed across the bathroom floor and wiped the moisture from the cabinet mirror with a green-striped washcloth. The tele-phone had been ringing since she stepped out of the shower, an irritating intrusion upon her morning routine. She squeezed a dab of mint toothpaste onto her brush and tried to block it out. No use, the repetitive ring was getting under her petal-soft, freshly washed skin.

"Will somebody please answer the phone?" Margaret stepped into the open bathroom door and hollered, rabid with white foam at the corners of her mouth and a toothbrush wedged in her cheek. "Somebody? Anybody?"

The house was silent, or would have been silent, she thought, if somebody would just answer the damn phone! She spit the toothpaste out in the sink and wrapped herself in a tow-el, her thick red hair dripping water on the bedroom floor as she moved to a window overlooking the backyard. Tim was in the crushed red granite driveway, loading two-by-fours into the bed of his pickup with the good- intentioned "help" of the boys. While dad toted three at a time on his shoulder, Tony and Billy struggled in their effort to move one of the long boards from the garage to the truck. Tim had to dodge and duck to avoid one wildly swinging board after another, and the boys stumbled and bumped into each other like a couple of drunken sailors.

It was a Three Stooges moment; the men in her life had plenty of those. "But those are my Three Stooges," Margaret said to herself, lovingly. Then, not so lovingly, "I'm coming, I'm coming! If this is a telemarketer . . ." She traded the towel for her robe and headed for the kitchen, where the obstinate caller continued to beckon.

"Good morning," Margaret, intent on sounding pissed off, grimaced at her cheerful greeting.

"Shtimm der?"

"Excuse me?" Margaret moved the receiver away from her ear, avoiding the brunt of the caller's obnoxious throat-clearing.

"S'Tim der?"

"Christ, Jackson, is that you? It's not even seven yet. How long did you plan on letting the phone ring?" Margaret didn't wait for a reply. She would rather it had been a telemarketer, after all.

"Tim, the phone's for you. It's Jackson," she called out the back door, lowering her voice when he neared the house, so the boys wouldn't hear. "It sounds like he's drunk."

"Jackson? No way," flashing an exaggerated look of disbelief, Tim squeezed his wife above the waist and kissed her forehead. "Hey, I told Tony and Billy I'd give them a ride to school today. That's how I bribed them for their help. I should have let them take the bus." Margaret easily shared a smile with Tim, who didn't know she had witnessed the slapstick loading operation.

"Tony, Billy, get in here and get some breakfast. Dad said he's taking you guys to school today. How do you rate?" Margaret, straining to eavesdrop on her husband's conversation, rubbed both her boys' heads as they bustled past her in the doorway.

"Would you just calm down, Jackson, you're freaking out for no reason." Tim cupped his hand over the receiver and hastily retreated from the kitchen, and the prying ears of his wife. Margaret took a carton of milk from the refrigerator and a box of cereal from the cupboard, wondering what *this* was all about. She had an idea, but there had been no further talk about Christopher Koenigs or the hanging since their disconcerting discussion following the wrestling tournament four nights prior.

"Sorry boys, sorry honey, but I can't take you guys to school today like I promised. Something's come up." Tim pulled on his work coat and grabbed his lunch box, but Margaret cut him off at the pass as he hurried toward the door.

"What do you mean, you can't take the boys to school, Tim? The bus already came and went. I'm not dressed and my hair is still wet, and it's Wednesday. If you recall, that means I don't have to go to work at the library until tonight." Without intending to, Margaret sounded pissed off now.

"I can't help it, honey, like I said, something's come up." Tim shrugged his shoulders, implying that the situation was out of his control.

"What's come up, Tim? What's come up that's so important that the . . ." she almost blurted Ass-kisser, but she remembered the boys and caught herself, ". . . that Jackson Kelly has to call here and let the phone ring interminably, at seven o'clock in the morning?"

Tim cocked his arm, and, with his thumb extended, pantomimed taking a drink. Margaret wasn't buying it. If it was an alcohol-related problem, Jackson Kelly would be ringing the phone off the hook every day of the week. Frowning, she continued to block his way, shaking her head slowly to convey her disappointment.

"What can I say, Margaret, he sounded pretty messed up. I can't just blow him off. I'm sorry, but I gotta go. I'll tell you all about it, later." He bent forward to kiss her, but she pulled back.

"I don't like secrets, Tim," she scowled, stepping aside to let her chided husband scurry by.

Even though the previous day's rains had long departed, sated plants and trees continued to shed their excess moisture, a timpani of drips and drops echoing through the forest. Tim angled his truck into the middle of the small clearing, parking out from under the weeping branches to keep the wood in the bed of his truck dry. He was alone. Jackson hadn't arrived yet, but he noticed the tracks of another vehicle that had spun a donut in the middle of the opening, leaving a swath of bent and uprooted ferns in its wake.

"Where the hell are you guys?" Tim heard the anxiety in his wavering voice, felt it in his contracted gut.

It was an irrational fear, he assured himself, yet he left the engine running and locked the doors of his truck. He glanced in the rearview mirror, hoping to see Jackson's tow truck lumbering up the dirt road. The oath he had sworn to himself many years ago to stay away from these woods, to never come back, was an exculpating pledge he never dreamed he would break. He was thankful for the ascending sun, just now eclipsing the treetops. He would never come back to this place at night, in the dark. Never.

Startled by a sudden blur of motion to his left, Tim hammered the truck into reverse just as a whitetail doe and her two fawns bounded into the clearing. Stopping abruptly in front of the truck, the skittish deer bobbed their heads and blinked the long lashes decorating their bulging, sentient eyes.

"Aren't you beautiful," Tim uttered, his heart still thudding in his chest. "If you weren't so tasty, I don't think I'd be able to shoot you." As if on cue, the three deer bolted back into the woods, their namesake white tails erect and waving goodbye. It wasn't the threat of ending up in the oven that sent the animals fleeing, however. It was Jackson Kelly's shamrock green tow truck, rumbling up the slope. Abashedly, Tim cut the ignition and unlocked the doors.

"That beast is a ball-buster," Richard jumped down from the driver's seat and walked around the front of the tow truck. He opened the passenger side door and Jackson, obviously inebriated, tumbled face-first into the dewy ferns. "No sign of Max yet?"

"Nobody here but me and the deer," Tim grunted, straining to help Richard get their fat, drunk friend to his feet. "Jackson's starting to worry me, Dickey. First he gets Margaret all worked up the other day at the wrestling tournament, then he calls this morning, babbling and nearly incoherent, insisting that I meet him out here, of all places. My wife thinks I'm hiding something from her, and she doesn't like to be kept out of the loop. Jackson's not helping. If he keeps this up, Margaret won't leave it be until she finds out what's going on."

"Nothings 'going on,' Tim." Richard crooked his fingers into quotation marks. "What's going on? You told her that we all knew the Koenigs boys, right, like we talked about? What is she, some kind of a royal bitch? Doesn't she . . ."

"Watch yourself, Dickey, Margaret's not a bitch." Thrusting a finger into Richard's chest, Tim pinned a weaving Jackson upright against the tow truck with his left forearm.

"Right, right, calm down. Megs is a great gal. I like Megs, I really do, but like I was saying, doesn't she understand how difficult that time was for all of us? We were just kids, for chrissakes." Richard rubbed his chest. "That hurt, you know."

Max pulled up in his minivan just in time to see Richard recoiling from Tim's forceful pokes to his breastbone. He rushed to position his bulk between the two of them, gently placing one of his big paws on each of their shoulders.

"What's happening, fellas, everything kosher here?"

"Ain't nothin' kosher around here. Actually, things is about as unkosher as they can get," Jackson slurred the words, but was surprisingly lucid as he knocked Tim's arm away and stood under his own power. Swaying back and forth from toe to heel, with eyes rolled back and a devilish grin, he looked to be possessed by more than just liquor. "Did 'ja tell 'em, Dickey, that I seen our old buddy Sauter yesterday? That ol' potlicker was over to Tingle's, and Tingle says to him, 'Why are you nosin' around here, Sauter,' cuz that's what he was doin', nosin' around. He knew'd Christopher Koenigs been let go, and Tingle told him you knew'd, too, Dickey, that's when I beat ass outta the bar."

"So what. You saw Sauter, the guy has the right to stop in a tavern for a drink just like anybody else," Max argued, unconvincingly. Sauter had been conspicuously absent from Broadaxe for a long time, and each of them knew it would take more than a cocktail to bring him back. Still, Max was adamant. "I really don't see what you're flippin' out about, Jackson, Sauter *was* born and raised here, after all. I don't like coming out here, Jackson. I don't like coming out to these woods. I don't think any of us does, so if that's what all the hullabaloo is about, excuse me, but I've got work to do."

"There's more, Max, believe me, there's more," Richard sighed. "Do you think I'd be out here, otherwise? Let's go, Jackson, spill it."

"Hullabaloo, hullabaloo, thank you sir, don't mind if I do," Jackson sang cheerfully, pulling a silver flask from an inside coat pocket. Max slapped the flask from his hand and the sticky, carmel-colored contents bubbled out onto the ground.

"Alcohol abuse," Jackson cried as he lunged to save whatever whiskey was left. Max placed a big, brown boot on Jackson's ample backside and sent him sprawling, one more time, into the damp vegetation.

"There's nothing funny about this," Max spewed,

"What's wrong with you, Jackson? Do us all a favor and try to sober up for a change. What about your boy, Jimmy? What do you think it's like for him, huh, to have a drunken slob for a father? Did you ever think about that?"

"Whoa, whoa," Richard stepped in, arms waving. "Jeepers, Max, was that really necessary? We all have to stick together, like we always have. We can't be at each other's throats. Man, help me out here. So Christopher Koenigs was released, big deal. You guys are hopping around like a bunch of scared rabbits. Just calm down, relax, there's no reason to get so worked up."

Richard extended a hand to Jackson, who sat cross-legged on the wet ground, his back against the tow truck.

"Bullshit. Bullshit. Bullshit!" Jackson, his distraught voice rising, angrily dismissed Richard's offer with a hard slap across the wrists.

"Owww, what gives here?" Richard whined, massaging his arms. "Between that goddam truck rearranging my insides, Tim cracking my sternum, and you bruising my wrists, I'm taking a real beating here. Sit there and get a wet ass then, see if I care."

A solitary tear dribbled on Jackson's shiny, flushed cheek. He caressed the empty flask, mourning the passing of its contents. Gently and slowly, at first, he thumped the back of his head against the door of the tow truck. He slammed his head, faster and harder, until the metal crumpled and the hand-painted lettering sprouted from his head like antlers; *Kelly's Service - You're in Luck, When You See This Truck!*

"Bullshit," he whimpered, eyes closed and head cradled in the dented door. "Don't tell me to calm down. Don't tell me to relax, Dickey. Yous don't know what it's like. None of yous do. I know it ain't funny, your goddam right I know it ain't funny! These last couple a days, I ain't been sleepin' and I get these voices whisperin' in my head. My name, I keeps hearin' my name, over and over, whisperin' in my head. And I gets this whistlin' in my ears," a second tear fell, faster than the first. "It comes and goes, a whistlin'. Know what else. Somebody's watchin' me. I can feel eyes on me and I knows somebody's there, but when I looks around ain't nobody."

"You know Max is probably right, Jackson, you should really think about laying off the sauce," Tim laughed, nervously, then moved quickly to help Jackson up when nobody joined in. "Come on, get up. Richard is right. It looks like you pissed your pants." He looked more closely to make sure that wasn't actually the case.

"You're goddam right I'm right," Max confirmed. He pushed Tim aside and grabbed the back of Jackson's coat, yanking him upright. "Get your drunken ass up and tell us why we're out here. You saw Sauter, big fucking deal. Dickey said that's not all, though." Max snatched the flask from Jackson's clutches and heaved it into the underbrush. "So quit dicking around and get to it. Like I said, I've got a lot of shit to do today."

Jackson brushed himself off and straightened his disheveled jacket, a modest attempt at regaining some of his diminished dignity. Using an oil-stained rag from his pocket, he wiped his glistening face and dabbed pitifully at his saturated trousers.

"Sauter says there's a treehouse back in that old oak, said he seen it 'fore he come into Tingle's." Aware of his words' impact, Jackson paused, allowing the hollow chorus of trickling water to fill the void. "Sauter says it's exactly the same as that old treehouse. Yous guys all knows what I'm talkin' about, that old treehouse that he tored up and burned, the one Michael Koenigs gots hung in . . . by his brother. Wanna go and have a look-see, Max, or now you thinkin' maybe you'd like to join me for a drink?"

Max, barely audible in his disbelief, stammered "holy shit" when he stepped from the brushy footpath into the small clearing. He stared unblinking at the big bur oak and joined his friends in their shocked silence. It was as if a haunting frame from each of their worst nightmares had been edited from their dreams and spliced eerily into reality. Tim's mouth watered profusely and he tasted the surge of bile rising to the back of his throat.

"What the fuck? What the fuck is this?" He broke the silence, high-pitched and sounding borderline hysterical. He convulsed, divesting himself of the cornflakes and orange juice he'd had for breakfast.

Max stood stone faced, oblivious to the vomit splattering his boots. "How do you explain this one, Dickey? That's the same goddam treehouse, from when we were kids. This is bizarre, totally bizarre. Do you think it's a coincidence, Christopher Koenigs getting out and then this, this treehouse? I'm getting bad vibes, man, bad vibes."

Richard laughed, derisively, sauntering across the clearing to the side of the oak. He leaned on the gnarled trunk, directly below the looming treehouse.

"Listen to yourselves, will you? A bunch of scared rabbits, I tell ya. What do you think, Max, that Koenigs was released Friday – what's that, four days ago – and he took a magic carpet ride across the country, here to Broadaxe, to build a treehouse that looks like the one he pushed his brother out of?" Richard was condescending, mocking in his tone.

"Seriously, give me a break. Like I said earlier, calm down, relax. Besides, Max, when was the last time you were out here? You just said yourself that you don't like to come out here, so what's it been, how many years? Who knows how long this treehouse has been here? By the looks of it, quite a long time. Do I think it's a coincidence? Damn right I do, a freaky coincidence, I'll grant you that, but nothing more."

"Tingle says to Sauter that maybe it was kids built it, you know, like on a prank." Jackson, sobering up, joined Richard under the treehouse. "That's probably who done it, hey Dickey? Some kids out thinkin' theys just havin' some fun. Maybe if we all talks to our boys, I'll talks to Jimmy, maybe one of them knew'd who done this."

"My Nicholas wouldn't come out to these woods, no way, no how." Max moved closer, stopping a few paces short of Richard and Jackson, and the treehouse. "I've never laid a hand on that boy, never, but he knows if I ever learned he'd been out here, I'd give him a whupping he'd never forget. I can't imagine Nick knowing anything about this, let alone being a part of it. I'll talk with him, anyway." He glanced at the treehouse. "You're right about one thing, Dickey, I haven't been out here myself since I was a kid, and when I leave here today, I don't plan on ever coming back."

Apologizing for his weak constitution, Tim sidled up behind Max, using his friend's enormous bulk as a shield between himself and the oak. Finally, he forced himself to look at the treehouse, to consider its disturbing presence with a rational mind, like Richard, instead of the distorted thinking of an emotional fool.

"I'm with Max. I'll have a chat with my boys, but I'd be real surprised if Tony or Billy knew anything about this at all. I haven't been out here in it seems like forever, just like Max. What about you guys?" Tim, emboldened by his own words, stepped around Max, coming face-to-face with Richard and Jackson beneath the treehouse.

"Who in the hell are we trying to kid?" Richard asked, emphatically. "None of us have been back out here since that night, we all know that. But I'll tell you what. I didn't stay away because I was afraid, because I was spooked by bad memories or because I had bad vibes." He held out his delicate hands and wiggled his slender fingers. "I never came back here because it would have served no useful purpose. We all know what happened here that night. It would have been stupid to come out here and wallow in it."

A gust of wind rustled the oaks broad, dark green leaves. The treehouse creaked and moaned in the swaying branches. Four sets of concerned eyes flashed upward, then dropped and met in a tittering of nervous laughter.

"This, too, shall pass, my friends," Richard continued, "so don't get your panties in a wad, ladies. Give me some credit, will ya? I've kept the hounds at bay this long, haven't I? After all these years, nobody cares anymore. Nobody really gives a flying fuck about Christopher Koenigs."

"'Cept Sauter," Jackson suggested, still unsettled by the chance encounter with the relentless detective at Tingle's the day before.

"Fuck Sauter!" Richard raged. "Fuck him! That pompous son of a bitch thought he was *so* smart, he thought he had it all figured out. Turned out he was damn near as crazy as Christopher Koenigs. It takes a big man to harass little kids, to fuck with their families, to try and make a name for himself off someone else's tragedy. Folks around here were damn near ready to string *his* sorry ass up in a tree, remember?"

"I never figured him for crazy," Max countered, "I always thought he was a man of strong convictions, who wasn't afraid to follow his instincts, to follow his gut. That's why he scared the hell out of me, still does. But at the same time, I always felt kind of sorry for him."

"Sorry for him! You have got to be shitting me." Richard threw his arms in the air and looked to the heavens, his inner drama queen unleashed. "I'll never forget how that bastard tormented us, and I can't believe that any of you have forgotten. For chrissakes, Max! Scared of him, sure, but sorry for him? I was afraid of what he could do to us, but that was back when I was a frightened little boy. He doesn't scare me anymore. Neither does Christopher Koenigs. Neither does this treehouse."

"This here treehouse don't scare me none neither, Dickey," Jackson volunteered, remaining taciturn about his lingering apprehension toward Sauter. "I don't know, the whisperin' in my head, the whistlin' in my ears, yous guys are probably right, I gots to think about layin' off the bottle, I guess. *That* thought right there scares the shit outta me, that ain't no lie." He shivered noticeably at the unpleasant prospect, then valiantly reasserted his flagging bravado. "I ain't just bullshittin', though. Christopher Koenigs don't scare me none and neither does this here treehouse. Too bad there ain't no way up in there. I'd be mighty curious to have myself a look."

A heavy, knotted rope silently slipped from the shadowy recesses of the treehouse door. It struck Jackson square on the top of his head, a startling surprise that sent him sprawling among the ferns for the third time that morning. He scrambled to his feet and snared the swinging rope to steady himself, short on breath from the combined shock and exertion.

"What's so goddam funny?" he bellowed, embarrassed at being the unwitting source of his friends' amusement.

"Now *that's* a freaky coincidence," Max, chuckling, grabbed the rope and yanked hard. It held fast, and he could only shake his head incredulously. "So big talker, you going up? I'd be willing to bet a ten-spot you don't have the balls, let alone the strength, to haul your lard-ass up there."

"You're on." Jackson took the bet, removing his coat and spitting on his hands. "I'll be back down in a minute to collect my dough."

Laboriously and sweating profusely, Jackson inched his way up the opportune rope. The treehouse protested noisily with every shift of his impressive heft. Three-quarters of the way home, he grinned victoriously at Max, dangling precariously overhead. "T'anks for the cash," he gloated, just as the taut rope mysteriously let loose. Jackson seemed to float weightlessly for a split-second, just like in the cartoons, long enough for the winning smile to fade from his face. He dropped like a big, round boulder, landing flat on his back and knocking the depleted wind from his lungs. The untethered rope spiraled downward and came to rest unceremoniously across his distended belly.

"It didn't break," Max confirmed upon his inspection of the thick, knotted cord. "That's weird. It's like it just let go."

From above, a scratching frenzy of clawed feet scurried across the treehouse floor, accompanied by an unnerving, high-pitched wheeze emanating from the inner blackness. The treehouse fell silent, abruptly, and an eerie stillness settled oppressively over the forest. Jackson, wheezing unhealthily himself, displayed some of the lost nimbleness from his bygone wrestling days, rolling from his back onto all fours and popping swiftly to a defensive crouch.

"Jiminy jumpers, for the chrissakes, what the hell do you'se guys s'pose is up there?" His wide eyes flashed toward his three friends, imploring them for a plausible explanation.

"By the sound of it, it's a good thing that rope let loose, Jackson, or else you might have stepped into a cage match against a cornered coon, or a porcupine," Richard rationalized, chuckling at the mental image. "I'd have paid to see that. Anyway, I don't know about you guys, but I've had enough excitement for one morning."

Tim and Max, enthusiastic in their agreement, eagerly led the exodus from the haunted meadow.

"Remember, relax, stay calm, everything is going to stay status quo," Richard, following behind, called out to their retreating backs and quickened his pace. "Are you coming,

Jackson, or what?"

Whispered voices chanted his name and a faint, raspy whistle caromed between his ears as Jackson hied from the flower-speckled clearing. Reaching the edge of the wood line, he stopped and rubbed the back of his head. His scalp tingled with an unsettling sensation, as if accusative eyes were boring into the back of his skull. He spun quickly and focused on the darkened treehouse door, uncertain if he'd actually seen the two yellow pinpricks of light slowly ebb into the shadows.

"I gots to quit drinkin'," he admonished, breaking into a rolypoly trot down the trampled trail.

*   *   *

Sauter winced with each sip of coffee, a tepid, bitter brew laced with a day-old, burnt aftertaste. A partially-eaten poppyseed muffin sat crumbling on the Bronco's dusty dashboard, which rattled and hummed with each static-filled inflection in the morning drive disc jockey's mindless patter.

"It's comin' up on half-past eight on what's shaping up to be a bee-yew-tee-ful Wednesday here in Ojibway County. Yesterday's rain, rain went away, leaving the north woods with nothing but sunshine, sunshine, sunshine. ."

Irritable from a lack of sleep, Sauter peevishly lowered the volume, then clicked the radio off completely. Yet again, his acknowledged obsession with the Koenigs case had gotten the better of him, and he had spent the entire night in his office poring over the oft-perused file. It was no use, but he couldn't help himself. Analyzing the antiseptic reports, he fully realized there was nothing within those pages capable of quelling his gut feeling that there was something askew, something just not right with the whole wretched affair.

"Are those the folks you were expecting to be here?" Colins piped up from the passenger seat, bringing Sauter's attention to the three-vehicle caravan exiting the dirt side road onto the highway.

Sauter traded his coffee for a compact pair of camouflaged binoculars, focusing in on the garish green tow truck, lumber-laden pickup, and accompanying minivan heading east, toward Broadaxe. An hour or so earlier he had parked the Bronco conspicuously alongside the saccharine baby animal faces adorning the tilting 'Welcome to Broadaxe' sign, unconcerned whether or not he was noticed.

"One and the same," he confirmed, "and they didn't waste any time at all. Good thing we got here as early as we did, otherwise we'd have missed them. So, did you enjoy your first stake-out, kid?"

"What, that's it? You mean we turned around and drove all the way back over here this morning just to watch some trucks drive away?" Colins snatched the binoculars from Sauter's hands and peered down the smoky blacktop, drying in the rising sun. "Kelly's . . . Service," reading the diagonal lettering on the tow truck's winch, he proceeded to deftly scribble each vehicle's license plate number onto the back of the notepad, never once taking his eyes off the road.

"Nicely done, but I won't be needing those tags. I know who those boys are. I know where to find them, if I ever need to," said Sauter, resigned to the transparent absurdity of his present circumstances. Why *would* I ever need to find them? He wondered, certain that they wouldn't talk to him even if he did. There was nothing to be gained, here in Broadaxe, nothing to be learned. Yet back in Broadaxe he was, "tilting at windmills" as his mother used to say, broken-hearted and confused by the singular obsession that consumed her son and alienated him from the town-folk she considered friends.

"Kelly's Service . . . Jackson Kelly, the guy who Tingle asked you if you knew, yesterday. Right?" Colins wasn't done sleuthing yet. "So, what about the other guy Tingle was telling you about, the guy who told him Koenigs was released, what was his name? Greasier than the hair on bigfoot's ass. Dickey, Dickey Mann. Was he driving the pickup, or the minivan? Who was driving the third vehicle? Do you think those three are the guys who built that treehouse? So what if they did, there's no law against building a treehouse, is there? And what about this whole Christopher Koenigs deal, the hanging, his release? What do these guys, Kelly, and Mann, and whoever the third one is, have to do with it?"

"Slow down, slow down. There's four of them, actually. Jackson Kelly, Richard Mann – a.k.a. Dickey – and two other fellas named Tim Schumacher and Max Ferguson. Those four were there that night, the night Michael Koenigs died. They were waiting out at the trailhead when I arrived at the scene. Little parrots who were much too eager to regurgitate the same exact story, it seemed to me." Sauter rolled down his window and pitched the dregs of his coffee into the bushes.

"I was present in the room with the detectives working the case when they brought the boys in to ask them some questions. The whole deal spooked the hell out of me and I was twice their age, so you'd expect them to be frightened. But that's just it, they didn't seem frightened. Oh, they were scared alright, but it struck me that they were afraid of getting in trouble themselves, like they knew more than they were letting on. The Mann kid did almost all the talking and his story seemed rehearsed. The other three just nodded or aped what he said."

"What was his story, what did Mann say happened?"

"Well, the Koenigs boys were a few years younger than these guys, but Mann claimed they were all running around those woods together. They played a game of kick the can, then climbed up into the treehouse, sort of a hideout where they'd get together after school, or on weekends. He said Christopher Koenigs all of a sudden just snapped, was wild-eyed, crazed, that sort of thing, threatening them all. They were all big enough to hold him off, but just barely because he seemed 'possessed with abnormal strength,' an exact quote from Mann. When Christopher lunged for his little brother, put the rope around his neck and pushed him out of the treehouse, Mann said they all jumped to the ground and took off running, never looking back."

"They were just kids. That'd be pretty frightening for anybody, like you said, so I could see why they'd high-tail it out of there, out of the meadow, scared and confused. You're probably right, they probably did think they were in trouble, big trouble. I guess I don't get it. Why are you so skeptical? Why didn't you buy it?" asked a puzzled Colins.

"The detectives bought it, lock, stock and barrel. Those boys told their tale and the detectives listened politely, but I don't think they really *listened*. It just confirmed what they were already thinking, that Christopher Koenigs intentionally murdered his younger brother. I've always trusted my instincts, Colins, my gut, and I'd bet a twenty to a turd that those boys were holding something back. I don't know, maybe it's only something inconsequential, but dammit, they know something. Why else would they come traipsing out here, just because Koenigs was released, just because someone built that treehouse?"

"You did the same, yourself, Sauter, and you brought me along, although I'm not sure why. Tell me, those boys and your suspicions, that's what Tingle was talking about when he said you couldn't let sleeping dogs lie. That's why you're on everybody's shit list." Colins felt the fog slowly starting to lift.

"You don't miss much, do you, son?"

"Hey, I was only drinking root beer, and remember, I'm a professionally-trained journalist crossed with a cop. When the facts hit, they stick." Colins grinned with self-satisfaction, then turned curious. "But, you know Sauter, with all respect, this all occurred a long time ago. I don't get it. What do you think you're going to find here, after all this time? What are you doing here?"

"I was just asking myself the same thing, son, I was just asking myself the same thing," Sauter admitted. He got out of the truck and stood next to the welcome sign. Unzipping his pants to relieve himself of the foul-tasting coffee, he modestly shielded himself from the prying eyes of Mother Nature's babies.

*   *   *

Margaret was delighted to discover a clean kitchen at the end of an excruciatingly long day, a day started by the wrong-foot fight with her husband and ending with a frustrating computer meltdown at the library. The mad scramble to save data and retrieve files wrenched every last bit of energy out of her tired muscles. It was ten-thirty, a good hour and a half later than her boys' school night bedtime, and she regretted missing out on their priceless goodnight hugs and kisses.

The house was quiet and dimly lit. Tim rarely made it up past ten on a work night, himself; but he left a small, seashell-shaped nightlight plugged in above the kitchen counter, and another burning in the hallway to illuminate his wife's walk up the stairs. Margaret longed for her soft pillow and warm sheets, so she chided herself for basking in the refrigerator's glow, habitually scavenging for a late night snack. After much deliberation, she selected a stalk of celery and a piece of smoked string cheese, congratulating herself on the healthy choice as she plodded off to bed.

Crunching on the last bite of celery, Margaret was glad to find Tim awake and reading when she entered the bedroom. He looked as tired as she felt, and she couldn't help but be warmed by his thoughtfulness.

"Honey, that was nice, but you didn't have to wait up for me," she crooned, shedding clothing until she was completely naked by the time she reached the closet. She squirmed into a knee-length flannel nightgown and crawled beneath the covers, snuggling up to her bare-chested husband. "So, how did your day go?"

"Oh, I've had better. How about you? You're awfully late. Did somebody shuffle up the card catalogue again?"

"Ah, the good old days. If it were only that simple. Modern technology, you know, makes life that much easier? Well, the damned computer fritzed-out again, second time it's done that. I managed to back everything up and I don't believe I lost anything, but I still have to call somebody first thing in the morning to come and look at it."

"I take it you got Tony and Billy to school alright," Tim broke the ice and made the first reference to the morning tiff. "Sorry if it screwed your morning up. It made for a mad rush, I'm sure. Like I said, though, it was just one of those things, you know? It couldn't be helped, really."

"Let's just say you owe me one, and you owe the boys one, too. They were a little disappointed, expecting a ride in dad's big, bad work truck and instead being pawned off on mom and her rusty little hatchback." Margaret giggled and poked Tim in the ribs. "So, how's Jackson doing, anyway?" she asked, trying to convey real concern even though she was still doubting her husband's alibi for leaving so abruptly following the phone call.

"As good as can be expected, I suppose, but it sounds like all his heavy drinking is finally catching up with him."

"What do you mean?" asked Margaret, as yet unwilling to extend Jackson any misplaced sympathy.

"The poor guy's hearing voices in his head, whispering his name, he said, and he's got a whistling in his ears, whatever that means. He's turning paranoid, too. Thinks somebody's watching him all the time. I feel sorry for the guy, I really do. It's obviously just the alcohol messing with his head and he's having delusions, or hallucinations, whatever you want to call it, but it's probably all real enough to him."

"So what's he going to do about it, anything? Did you talk him into getting any help?"

"Max and I both told him he needed to quit drinking, but that's a tall order for a guy who hasn't gone a day without a drop since who knows when. Max was pretty hard on him, basically told him he was a shitty father to Jimmy. It doesn't help that his wife's a lush, either." Tim set his book on the nightstand and flicked off the light.

"Max was there too, huh?" Margaret began to soften to the story.

"Yeah, Max and Dickey."

"Richard, as well, the whole motley crew, sounds like a regular intervention." Margaret regretted her tone immediately.

"You know, Margaret, I know you're not a big fan of Dickey or Jackson, but for . . . " the phone barked to life from the kitchen downstairs, cutting Tim off mid-sentence.

"It's damn near eleven o'clock, who the hell is calling at this hour?" he asked, apparently not curious enough to get out of bed to find out.

"I asked myself that same question early this morning, so I'll give you one guess," said Margaret, unwilling to make the trip back downstairs herself. "Tell me again why we don't have an answering machine?"

"There's no way it's Jackson, no way."

Margaret sat up and turned the light back on. "Goddam

it, Tim, I don't care who it is, get your ass out of bed and answer the phone before it wakes the boys!"

"Hold on, hold on, they'll hang up," he protested. The phone continued to ring, however, reminiscent of the day's wake-up call.

"For chrissakes Tim, it's Jackson. Would you please get up and take the call? Believe me, you don't want me talking to him right now."

"Alright, alright," Tim grumbled as he pulled back the sheets and trudged down the steps. Too agitated to sleep, Margaret had just started paging through an old Reader's Digest when she sensed Tim standing in the doorway.

"It was Jackson, right," she stated, adding spitefully, "What's the matter, did the voices in his head tell him to call you and wish you sweet dreams?" She kept her head bowed to the pages, blind to her husband's desolate, ashen expression.

"Yeah, that was Jackson," he whimpered, "His boy, Jimmy, Jimmy's gone missing."

JIMMY

It was dark, and Jimmy didn't like the dark. He knew there were wild animals that woke up at night and hunted in the forest. He felt tiny under the tall pines, and it scared him to think one of those animals might want to eat him. Bad people come out at night, too, his dad told him, bad people who might want to hurt little boys, just like himself. He didn't like the dark.

But he had forgotten to take the bowl of chopped carrots out to the small wooden bench tucked in a corner of the unmown backyard. He went there every night, usually when it was still light, and sat patiently at the edge of the trees, waiting for his adopted family of snowshoe hares to hop nervously from the underbrush. There were three of them, a mom and her two babies, Jimmy guessed, all with fuzzy, white, elongated back paws, alert, erect ears, and twitching noses. Their fur was brown now, but Jimmy knew it wouldn't be long until it got colder and snow covered the ground, and the snowshoes would magically turn all white, to help them hide.

Jimmy knew the bunnies were just like him, that they didn't like the dark, either. They were afraid of the other animals prowling the woods for dinner, same as he was, and they were normally afraid of people, no matter if it was dark or light. Jimmy was glad these snowshoes weren't afraid of him, that they trusted him and let him feed them. That's why he felt badly, they were probably hungry. He wondered, will they come out of the bushes tonight? Will they come out in the dark?

Jimmy spread the chopped carrots out on the cool surface of the low, moss-covered rock where his guests came to dine each night. He backed up slowly and plopped down on the bench, keeping his eyes peeled for any movement in the brush. Taking a bite from the carrot he had brought for himself, Jimmy didn't understand why kids teased him and called him carrot-top when his dark red hair looked nothing like the bright orange vegetable he held in his hand.

Cautiously, the hungry snowshoe family crawled into

the open, rotating their ears and sniffing the air for signs of danger. Jimmy sat rigid and quiet, like he always did, giving his friends time to get reacquainted, careful not to startle them. He shivered with a sudden chill. The snowshoe hare lifted their jittery heads in unison, then scattered in a frantic dash for cover just as Jimmy heard the odd, gurgling whistle closing in from behind.

Initially, the pain was excruciating. Jimmy opened his mouth to cry out, but his constricted vocal chords failed to produce a sound. Tiny bones cracked in his shoulder, pressed between the pinch of a crushing grip. Needle-sharp talons punctured his skin and tore into the sinew and muscle beneath his collarbone. The wooden bench teetered, then tipped over as Jimmy's wilted body jerked backwards and skidded across the ground into the concealing shadows of the forest.

The terrible pain subsided to a distant, dull ache and Jimmy felt his body tingle and fall numb, like his lips after a visit to the dentist. The harsh, repetitious whistle intensified, mingling with breathy grunts and nonsensical mutterings. He was being dragged; face up, with dizzying speed, along the forest floor. Exposed roots and groping branches shredded his pants, exposing the torn, abraded flesh on the back of his legs.

The enclosed canopy of tangled branches suddenly parted and Jimmy blinked at the ceiling of stars through terrorized, tear-filled eyes. He thought of his mom and dad, only for a fleeting moment, then shut them out. *Do they even know I'm gone? Do they even care?* He thought of his books, and the nice lady who read to him down at the library, the lady with hair just like his. Then, he tried not to think at all.

Swaying, purple flowers tickled his skin as he floated beneath the twinkling heavens. The ground and flowers fell rapidly away as Jimmy's battered, limp body rocketed skyward, scraping along the scaly, black bark of the ageless oak. He recoiled against the putrid, palpable stench that cloaked the impenetrable blackness of the treehouse, but his body ignored his mind's request to struggle, to fight.

The rope tightened around his slender neck and its coarse fibers scratched his youthful, tender skin. The paralyzing barbs buried in his shoulder retracted and warm blood trickled down his heaving chest, spurting from the unobstructed puncture wounds. He didn't rebel against the unrelenting approach of the gaping treehouse door. He couldn't. Plummeting downward toward the waving sea of purple flowers, the starlit sky spinning overhead, Jimmy heard the menacing giggle and saw the hateful yellow eyes following his descent. His frail neck snapped with the crack of a dry twig and darkness descended, but Jimmy was no longer afraid.

CHAPTER SEVEN

The house had fallen into disrepair and looked as if it hadn't been cleaned in years. The layer of dust coating the furnishings had congealed into a grimy black soot and the sagging drywall was tinged yellow by the same cigarette smoke that gave the depressing room its pervasive ashtray aroma. Dirty dishes overflowed the kitchen sink, spilling onto the countertop, where they battled for space against an army of empty beer and liquor bottles.

Margaret sat stoically on a wobbly, high-backed wooden chair, struggling to suppress her disgust with the filthy living conditions and ashamed at her pettiness. She stared blankly at the sole decoration adorning the dingy walls, an ornate gold cross entangled in a withered, brown palm frond. Resenting her husband's insistence that she accompany him, Margaret was certain that her presence was inconsequential, possibly even an intrusion, considering the circumstances. It was the first time she had stepped foot inside Jackson Kelly's uninviting home, and she assured herself that it would also be her last.

"Please, Margaret," Tim had implored. "It would do Dorothy a lot of good to have you there, another woman to talk to, a shoulder to cry on." Never close or a person she'd even remotely consider a friend, Margaret hadn't seen Jackson's reclusive, alcoholic wife for years. The passage of hard-time and the ravages of hard-drink were etched across her impassive, asymmetrical face.

Dorothy stood off by herself, leaning against the wall near a corner window, occasionally pulling back the drawn shade and peeking out into the moonless night. She held her right arm crooked, her trembling hand holding the latest in a chain of menthol cigarettes, never more than an inch away from her colorless lips. Ice cubes, melting slowly in a warm bath of brandy, tinkled together in the thick glass tub she clutched in her left hand, which hung languidly by her side. Leathery, careworn skin accentuated her severe facial features, and oily, thinning beige hair dangled like wet noodles from her white scalp. She appeared much older than her thirty-four years.

An oval clock designed to hang on the wall instead sat on the floor, propped up against the braided wooden spindles of an overstuffed magazine rack. Colorful songbirds represented the hours, and Margaret jumped with the distorted trill of the black-capped chickadee perched at one o'clock. It had been an achingly long two hours since Jackson had phoned, frantically searching for his missing child. Tim and Margaret rushed over and were the first to arrive, even before the police, and Dorothy had immediately retreated to her corner, alternating suspicious glances at the strangers invading her unkempt home with quick glimpses out the window. Leaning forward on the balls of her feet, heels raised, she tottered to the kitchen periodically to refresh her drink, avoiding any eye contact with a glazed, straight-ahead stare.

Margaret desperately wanted to escape, to return to her own clean home and check on her own two boys. She had tousled Tony's red hair and told her half-awake child that an emergency had come up, that she and his father had to run out for a bit, and that they'd probably be back within a couple of hours. Smiling groggily, Tony rewarded his mother with the bedtime hug she regretted missing earlier in the night. Now, Margaret tried in vain to gain her husband's attention without bringing any to herself, but Tim was too wrapped up in the unfolding drama to notice her raised eyebrows, head tilts and subtle waves. He was seated on the end of a shabby plaid couch, next to and above Jackson, who had sunk deep into the middle cushion, where he patiently repeated, for what seemed to Margaret like the sixth time, at least, how the evening had transpired.

"Like I was sayin', I gots busier than a three-peckered billy goat down to the garage, all day. I kinda lost track of the time, so I'm guessing it was somewheres around quarter to six when Jimmy shows up. I gots him a soda pop and a bag of chips, then he helps me clean up, yous know, put away my tools, empty the garage, close up shop. He asks me, am I comin' home to supper and I tell him no, I gots some things to do. He hops on his bike and rides away. That was six-thirty, I know'd cuz I seen the clock, right as I was lockin' up. That was the last time I seen him," Jackson choked up, swallowing a despairing sob as his eyes welled with tears.

"I know, Jackie, I know we've gone over this a couple of times here now, but I need you to stick with me here and tell me again, where did you go after you closed up the garage?" asked Bobby Kunick in a calm, soothing tone. Kunick was the chief of police for Broadaxe township's two person force, a civic duty he crafted into an unchallenged career for nearly three decades. Squatting on a plaid footstool facing the matching sofa, he squeezed Jackson's knee with one bony hand and held a pen poised above the notepad balanced on his own knee with the other.

"Somebody's got to talk to me," he turned and gave a lingering look to Dorothy, who dutifully continued her solitary vigil by the corner window. Rotating back to Jackson, "We don't want to miss anything here, something Jimmy might have said, someplace he might have gone tonight, anything. Tell me again Jackie, where did you go when you left work? Try hard to remember anything you might be forgetting."

Stiffly, Kunick arose from the low-slung stool, shaking the legs of his crumpled khaki pants, which were bunched up at the tops of his ankle-high, black patent leather slip-ons. He rested his right hand on his service revolver. Outside of the shooting range, he had never had occasion to shoot the weapon during his long tenure as chief of police. His crystalline blue eyes, set deep inside his disproportionately large, gray-stubbled noggin, shown comically undersized and unblinking above a flattened boxer's nose and a moist, fleshy mouth. Kunick gave a curt nod to Margaret, only just acknowledging her existence.

"Jackie?" He pressed for an answer, the only person left around Broadaxe who still used the forbidden childhood moniker.

Jackson buried his chin in his chest, pained by the prescience of Max's early morning rebuke that his boy, Jimmy, deserved better than a drunk for a father.

""Like I said, Bobby, after work I gone down to Tingle's, just like I do darn near every day. Hell, yous guys know'd that," he mumbled wearily, raising his pleading, guilt-ridden eyes. "I was just gonna have one or two, that's all, but yous know how it goes. I gots a couple a rounds buyed for me and I gots to playin' pool, and before I know'd it, it was 'bout nine-thirty. I gots home 'round quarter to ten, ain't that 'bout right, Dorothy?"

Jackson leaned to his left, looking around Kunick to his wife, still vigilantly standing her post by the window. Although Dorothy had drifted off into a tipsy world of her own, Jackson eagerly accepted the barely perceptible nod of her head as affirmation for his uncertain recollection.

"See there? That's right, 'bout quarter to ten I gots home. I looked 'round for Jimmy, but he ain't in his room readin' like usual, so's I asks Dorothy – she's in bed watchin' TV – so's I ask her where Jimmy's at. She says 'Ain't he in his room readin'?' just like I thought, but I says no, he ain't in there, I ain't findin' him nowhere. Dorothy says last she seen him, he was headin' out back to feed the snowshoes, feed 'em carrots like he done every night. I gone out there lookin' and sure 'nough he'd been back there. The carrots was gone, so was Jimmy. I picked up the bench he sits on when he feeds the hares, it gots knocked over, and I found this," Jackson caressed the blue, hard plastic bowl Jimmy used to carry the chopped carrots.

"Then I gots scared. It ain't like Jimmy to be outside after dark, not by hisself. So I come back in the house and called his name, mad-like, so in case he's hidin' he'd know'd I mean business and he'd come out. He don't, so I goes back outside and start yellin' for him out there. I looked in the woods and all up and down the highway, I looked for a good hour, but he ain't nowhere. I tried to call Dickey but he don't answer, so then I call Tim here, and I call Max, to see if they'd seen him, or if their boys know'd where Jimmy's at, and then I call you, Bobby."

Kunick hadn't written down a word Jackson had said, but he folded up his notebook and tucked it and his pen into his back pocket.

"Listen, Jackie, we've got plenty of town folk out scouring the woods and they won't leave a stone unturned in the whole township, I guarantee you that," his voice was measured, reassuring. "Jimmy's a smart little boy, if he got turned around out there in the forest, got himself lost, he'll be able to take care of himself until we find him . . . and we'll find him, don't you fret."

The rising river of despair finally breached Jackson's bravado levee and he slouched forward on the couch, slump-shouldered and shivering pitifully with sputtering sobs. Dorothy emptied her tumbler with one long, lingering sip of brandy, betraying no outward emotion as she stared blankly at her anguished husband. Savoring the alcohol's pleasing warmth, she closed her eyes and dragged greedily on her twitching cigarette, allowing the inhaled smoke to seep slowly from her flared, reddened nostrils.

Tim tentatively wrapped his arm around his friend's broad back and looked at Margaret with pleading eyes and a what-the-hell-am-I-supposed-to-do shrug of the shoulders. Holding her husband's attention at long last, Margaret resisted the urge to let him know how badly she wanted to go home. Instead, she nodded toward Jackson, mouthing the words "Just talk to him."

Tim took a deep breath, "Max got a bunch of folks from town together and they're all out looking for Jimmy right now too, Jackson. If there's anybody who knows these woods right around your house here better than yourself, it's Max. Listen to Chief Kunick, they'll find Jimmy and everything will be okay, he couldn't have gone far. Just pull yourself together buddy, alright?"

The heavy sobs dissipated and Jackson, now whimpering softly, wiped his damp cheeks and dripping nose with a sleeve sullied by the previous day's busy workload at the garage.

"But where's my boy at? He's only just nine. Your boys Billy and Tony just come to his birthday party, remember? Like I was sayin', Jimmy, he don't like the dark, Tim, he don't like it at all. I ain't gots no idea'r where he'd be at," he stammered.

"That's just it, Jackson, you have to think hard, really put your mind to it. There has to be a favorite place around here where Jimmy likes to play, where he and the other kids from the neighborhood go and hang out. You know, like when we were kids and we used to go . . . " Tim broke off, cheeks afire at the thought of how those idyllic afternoons spent out at the old treehouse came to such an appalling end. He cursed the stupidity, the insensitivity of the ill-timed example.

"Jesus, Tim, Jesus," Jackson moaned.

"Shit, Jackson, forget that. Forget that I even brought that up. I'm a complete dumbass," Tim conceded, hastening back to his original point. "You know what I mean, though, where's the most logical place to look? Think! Tony and Billy, they like to play down by that old tire swing over the bend in the river . . ." Tim blanched at the mental image of Jimmy's red head bobbing above the roiling surface of the river, his tiny body swept from site by the powerful current. He decided it would be a good idea to keep his misguided mouth shut.

"Ain't no place I can think of, and believe me, I been tryin' since he come up missin'. I just don't know what to do," Jackson whined.

"Well, I can help out there. How's about fillin' up my drink, honey," the heretofore mute Dorothy cooed, shaking the tinkling ice cubes in her glass as she sashayed over to her distraught husband on the sofa.

"Goddam it, woman!" Jackson thundered, jumping to his feet with uncanny agility, propelled by the metallic twang of the relieved sofa springs. He slapped the glass from her trembling hand, spraying the melted ice across the room and shattering the heavy tumbler into thick, jagged pieces.

"For the chrissakes, ain't you got no sense, Dorothy? Our boy Jimmy, he's done gone missin' and all you care 'bout is havin' another drink?" Jackson stormed into the kitchen and swept the dead soldiers from the counter, filling the small space with a resounding cacophony of breaking bottles. He snatched a half-empty bottle of Jack Daniels from the table and rushed back to his giggling wife.

"Here, have a drink you stupid bitch," Jackson grabbed the back of his wife's stringy scalp and cocked her head back. She drank hungrily as he emptied the contents of the bottle, gulping down as much as she could and licking at the sticky brown liquid running down her chin and neck.

Chief Kunick quickly interceded, forcibly pulling the

sparring couple apart and admonishing them for their lack of self-control. "Look at yourselves, both of you!" he yelled. "You're acting like idiots, like drunken animals. We're trying to find your son. We're trying to bring Jimmy home, safe and sound, and the best you two can do is drink and bicker? Is this what it's always like around here? Did it ever occur to you that maybe Jimmy's run off, run away from this?" Kunick waved a dismissive hand at the unpleasant surroundings.

The harsh rebuke and the disheartening plausibility that Jimmy had every reason to flee his dysfunctional home crashed into Jackson's conscience with debilitating impact. The drained bottle slipped from his flaccid fingers and he fell back onto the couch in a speechless, remorseful stupor. Unmoved, Dorothy glared apprehensively at Kunick as she sidled her way into the kitchen, where she groped blindly in the sink until she latched on to an unwashed glass. She slid open a drawer and withdrew another bottle of cheap brandy, poured a generous four fingers, and tapped a menthol cigarette from a previously opened pack. The broken glass and ice strewn about the floor crunched beneath her pink-slippered feet as she stalked back to the corner window in her doddering, forward-leaning gait.

"Unbelievable," said Kunick, plopping back down on the footstool in exasperation.

Margaret seized her dumbfounded husband by the shirt sleeve and pulled him aside. "Tim, I want to go home . . . I'm going home," she whispered, "I've got to get out of here, I'm just in the way. I shouldn't have come here in the first place."

"You're damn right you shouldn't oughta come here," Dorothy barked, "Just who the hell are y'all anyways? Who do you think you is, comin' into my home, tellin' me what to do, actin' like y'all gives a rat's ass 'bout us." She pointed the cigarettes glowing orange amber at her rigid, unblinking husband. "Y'all get the hell outta my home right now, you hear me? Get the hell out!"

Margaret escaped into the cool, clean embrace of the crisp night air, grateful for the opportunity to finally disentangle herself from the hellish drama she wanted no part of in the first place. Tim paused in the doorway, then reluctantly joined his wife only after Kunick provided assurances that he would stay behind to make sure the fragile combatants remained in neutral corners.

"Before you go off on me, I'm sorry, I'm truly sorry," Tim apologized sincerely, drawing Margaret close in a tight embrace. "I should have just let you stay home, like you wanted, but I was selfish. I wanted you here, I needed you here. This is scary as hell. It's every parent's nightmare. What if Tony, or Billy . . ." he trailed off, "Wherever Jimmy is right now, he must be so frightened."

Upset at being manipulated into a position that made her feel like a detached observer, a puerile voyeur of another's pain and misery, Margaret burrowed into her husband's smothering hug until the peevishness melted away. She didn't blame Dorothy for questioning her reason for being in her home and making it clear that she wanted her the hell out. Although Jackson remained a close friend of Tim's, to Margaret he was no more than a mere acquaintance, or annoyance, while Dorothy was in reality a complete stranger. Margaret had been so uncomfortable, so guarded during her impotent intrusion that the depressing reality of the situation had somehow failed to register – until now.

Jimmy's freckle-faced, red-headed visage flashed before her and the tears ran freely as Margaret contemplated the chilling possibility that he may never . . . No, no, no, she told herself, don't even think that. She would see the cute little boy she so adored again, toting his arm-load of books into the library.

"The library!" She pushed her husband away and blinked at him excitedly through watery eyes. "It's not so far-fetched that Jimmy ran away, Tim. I was in that, that sorry excuse of a home for five minutes and I wished I could run away. You asked Jackson if Jimmy had someplace special he liked to go, a favorite spot. Well, he loved the library; maybe he took his books and went down there, to get away from here. I'm going to swing by there and take a look around on my way home. It's worth a shot."

"Yeah, it's worth a shot," sounding unconvinced, Tim shielded his eyes from the glare of bright headlights arcing into the yard. "That looks like Max's minivan." He checked his watch, quarter to two, "so keep your fingers crossed, maybe they've already found him."

The headlights dimmed and Max literally jumped from behind the wheel. He stood like a monolith in the shadows of the yard and rubbed his temples feverishly, his mutterings unintelligible save for a few emphatic expletives.

"You doing all right there, buddy?" Tim called out, assuming that the hours spent searching a darkened woods for a friend's missing child had taken an understandable toll. Considering Max's demeanor he didn't expect good news, but still felt impelled to ask, "Any luck? Any sign of Jimmy?"

Apparently unaware that he had company, Max started at the sound of Tim's voice and self-consciously dropped his hands from the sides of his head. Bleary and distant, he appeared disoriented, agitated, and Margaret wondered if he had followed in Jackson's and Dorothy's inebriated footsteps. That would have been so unlike Max, who didn't drink much at all let alone at a time like this, yet she stepped closer and breathed in deeply, unable to detect the unmistakable aroma of alcohol.

"Has Jimmy turned up yet?" Max repeated Tim's question, which obviously hadn't registered in his preoccupied state.

"No, he hasn't," Margaret replied. "Are you sure you're okay, Max?"

"Oh, hey Redlocks, hey." He groped his way out of the mental fog, "What do you mean? I'm fine, fine. It's been a long-ass night, you know. How's Jackson holding up? And Dorothy?"

"They're doing as well as can be expected, I guess," Tim offered, "Jackson had been drinking over at Tingle's earlier in the night, but he seems to have sobered up. Dorothy? There's no telling with her. She's been pounding the brandy so hard that I'm not even sure it's hit her yet, that Jimmy's actually missing. They were at each other's throats a little bit ago, but Chief Kunick's still in there with them, trying to calm them down and get them to try and think of anything that might help narrow down the search."

"Shit, we've narrowed it down pretty good ourselves, at least in the woods right around the house here," Max waved his arm in an all-encompassing arc. "I managed to muster up a good twenty to thirty people and we walked an organized grid pattern, back and forth, shining flashlights and hollering his name. I even woke up Nicholas and brought him along, thinking he might have some ideas where to look." He pointed to his son, fast asleep in the front seat of the minivan.

"I imagine you've searched the town, as well," said Margaret.

"Sure, some folks were going to go look around down there. Why?" asked Max.

"Well, I don't know, I've felt like a helpless fool all night, but then it dawned on me. Jimmy loves story hour down at the library, and Chief Kunick suspects he may have run away. I thought maybe he headed there."

Max scratched his square, bearded chin and his thoughts drifted in another direction. "Have you seen Dickey? He said he was going to swing by here."

"Jackson said he tried to call him earlier, but couldn't get a hold of him," Tim looked at Margaret, who nodded her head in confirmation.

"It was kind of odd," Max continued, "Dickey showed up in the woods about an hour ago, out of nowhere. He was just standing there, in the dark. You know how he's always so neat and clean, his hair and clothes just so, almost like a woman? Well he was all sweaty and dirty, looked as if he'd been rolling around in the duff on the forest floor. I asked him what the hell happened to him and he got all defensive, said he was just out searching for Jimmy along with everybody else, said he tripped on some roots and fell on his ass a couple times, got tangled up in branches. He was a sight. When I left him, he said he was going to run home and clean up, then head over here to check on Jackson."

"I'm taking off. I want to get home and check on the boys." Margaret desperately wanted to avoid an encounter with Richard. "I am going to drive by the library on the way home, are you coming, honey?"

"Stick around, Tim, I'll give you a ride back to your place," Max interjected.

"I guess I'm sticking around," he shrugged, "I'll be home soon, hopefully with good news. Try and get some sleep, you look pooped." He kissed his wife tenderly on the forehead and walked her to his truck. As she drove away, a distant set of headlights flashed in her rearview mirror. "Cheeseball," she sighed, congratulating herself for departing in the nick of time. If she had been closer, she would have noticed the distinctive blue and red gumballs perched atop the Broadaxe patrol car.

Officer Megan Corcoran greeted Tim and Max with a look of grave consternation. Constituting one-half of the local police force, "Corky" Corcoran cut the stereotypical butch profile of a female cop. Her short black hair was pulled severely back and a thick unibrow jutted out like a hedge above her squinting brown eyes. A noticeable mustache graced her chapped upper lip and the deep cleft of her pointed chin separated a well-defined jawbone. She carried her squat, muscular frame with a confident, masculine swagger, one hand resting waisthigh on her service revolver and the other clasping a plastic evidence bag, cinched at the top.

"Boys," she nodded stiffly, "Chief Kunick's still inside, I take it?" She motioned to the police cruiser parked in the driveway. "Your search failed to yield any tangible results, is that correct Max?" Her syntax was measured, mechanical.

"Unfortunately, that is correct, Corky. How about you? Please tell me you have some good news," Max pleaded, but her solemn shake of the head indicated otherwise. "What's that in the bag then, is that something that might be important, maybe something belonging to Jimmy?"

"That's an affirmative. You had best follow me." She marched toward the house with Tim and Max, both tingling from a mixture of apprehension and curiosity, close on her heels.

The scene inside the untended home had changed little since Tim and Margaret had heeded Dorothy's adamant wishes and stepped outside. Jackson remained embedded in the sunken cushions of the sofa and his wife leaned listlessly against the wall by the corner window, her most recent drink and smoke both nearly depleted. Kunick sat erect on the footstool, flipping through the mostly blank pages of his notebook, eagerly awaiting an update from his officers in the field. When Corcoran entered the room ahead of Tim and Max, he vaulted to his feet with anticipation, fully expecting to hear that the precocious little runaway had been corralled.

"Chief, I have something here you need to take a look at." Corcoran hoisted the evidence bag above her head. "Mr. and Mrs. Kelly, I'm going to need the both of you to step this way, as well." She waited for Jackson to extricate himself from the depths of the couch, and, after realizing Dorothy had no intention of leaving her corner sanctuary, carefully opened the plastic pouch.

"We found a few snatches of cloth just like this, tangled in raspberry prickers and caught up in the branches of bushes and shrubs." Corcoran snapped on a rubber glove and opened the bag, extracting a frayed patch of denim, heavily stitched like a hem on a pant leg. Pointing with her baby blue latex finger, "Note here, and here, dark stains that appear to be dried blood."

"Lord Almighty, them could be Jimmy's jeans," Jackson blubbered, his pin-cushion face contorted in terror. "What happened to my boy? Where's my boy?" His panicked voice pitched upward and his lower lip quivered uncontrollably.

Corcoran carefully tucked the blood-stained cloth back into the evidence bag, out of sight, and maneuvered herself directly in front of Jackson. She placed her gloveless hand lightly on his shoulder, staring him down in silence until his darting, frantic eyes met her own.

"I know this is hard, Jackson, but we need your help right now. You have to be strong, for Jimmy, for your wife," Corcoran glanced at Dorothy standing wooden in the corner; amazed that any mother could be so heartless, so disinterested in the fate of her own flesh and blood. "We found one more item, Jackson, in the same general vicinity where we located the piece of cloth I just showed you. I told you, be strong. If this belongs to Jimmy that means we're headed in the right direction and we can refocus our search."

Jackson gasped at the sight of the small, black shoe, ankle-high with three raised, white stripes stitched into the sides. The ridges of the yellow rubber soul showed no signs of wear, but the canvas upper was mangled and torn. He began to weep.

"*Jackson* . . ." Corcoran prodded.

"I know, goddammit, I know! I gots to be strong!" Jackson snapped. "That there is one a Jimmy's new wrestlin' boots. He know'd he weren't supposed to be wearin' them new boots outside, I tol' him them's only for practices and matches. Now looky here, this here one's all tored up and ruin't. When I gets a hold a him, he gonna wish he were still lost out there in them woods." The callousness of his own overwrought words shocked Jackson back into the moment, causing his brave façade to crumble. "Oh, I ain't meanin' that," he convulsed, "I ain't meanin' that! Jimmy's my only boy, I just wants him back, that's all. I don't care 'bout no goddam boots, I just wants my boy back."

Tim arrived at Jackson's side just as he collapsed, summoning all his strength to save them both from crashing onto the floor. "Chief!" He grunted, casting a puzzled look at the inert Kunick, who belatedly came to his aid. Max grabbed a metal folding chair from the kitchen table and propped its cracked Naugahyde cushion behind Jackson's knees. Struggling to control his trembling, gelatinous mass, they haltingly lowered him into the seat. He hadn't passed out, rather, his flagging spirit seemed to have collapsed beneath the night's cumulative burden, taking his mind and body along with it. Hunched over in the chair, which had disappeared beneath his flabby girth, Jackson sat slack-jawed and stupefied, eyes glazed and lifeless.

Corcoran immediately shifted into high gear, reacting with the calm professionalism that the fluent situation demanded. She had organized the hastily assembled search party, orchestrating its movements with precision and efficiency, allowing Kunick to react to any new developments from his temporary base at the Kelly home. Now, unfolding a large, crumpled map on top of the junk mail and dirty dishes covering the kitchen table, she methodically updated Kunick on the as yet unsuccessful search for the missing little boy.

"This is an enlargement of Broadaxe township. The red dot, here, is where we are currently, the Kelly household, Jimmy's last known location. The search commenced here and progressed in a concentric grid pattern. The shaded areas represent ground that has already been covered. It doesn't look like much, but in the woods, in the dark, in just . . . what time is it now?" she checked her wristwatch, "Two-thirty, so we've been at it a little more than two and a half hours. We're making good progress. Note the smaller green dots. Those indicate the locations of the pieces of evidence we've discovered thus far. The first three locations, here, here and here, are where we found the pieces of torn cloth. The fourth location, here, is where the shoe was found."

"Excellent work so far, Corky, now what's the next step?" asked Kunick, who had gathered with Tim and Max in a tight semicircle around the map.

"I've re-established the center of the search at the location where the shoe was discovered and have set up a concentric grid pattern beginning from that point," she explained. "When I went to the squad to get the map, I put in a call to shift the remaining searchers to that site. Since it's all we have to go on, it makes sense to concentrate our efforts there."

Uncertain if it was his place to interrupt, Tim felt impelled to ask what everyone seemed to be avoiding. "I've got a question." He actually raised his hand. "Are you still thinking that Jimmy might have run away? I mean," he lowered his voice, shielding Jackson from what he was about to say, "what about those torn up pieces of blue jean, with blood on them? Or his boot, all chewed up like that? How the hell would that happen, if he was just running away? Do you think somebody might have snatched him?"

"I don't . . ." Corcoran started to answer until Kunick cleared his throat and cut her off.

"It's hard to consider things rationally under the stress of such irrational circumstances, and conjecture is never a good idea without weighing the facts." He joined his hands together at his chest, index fingers pointed towards his chin, like the church steeple in the childhood rhyme. "Jimmy was out back feeding carrots to snowshoe hares, presumably when he disappeared. Jackson said he did it every night. The bench he sat on was toppled and the carrot bowl was laying in the yard." Referring to the map, "Notice how the green dots where the articles of clothing were found proceed roughly in a northeast line away from the house, headed where? Deeper into the forest.

There isn't a road for a long ways in any direction from where that boot was found, so it just doesn't seem plausible, to me, that we have an abduction on our hands."

The progression of the green dots was not lost on Max, who traced the line with his finger and carried its trajectory out to the folded corner of the map. He didn't bother unfolding the crinkled page further, to see where the extension of the line of green dots would ultimately lead; he already knew. If Tim had been watching, he would have known as well, but he was too busy prodding Chief Kunick for his opinion on Jimmy's fate.

"So if he didn't run away, and he wasn't abducted, tell me what you think happened to Jimmy." Tim's tone had gravitated from pleading to slightly belligerent.

"First off, I'm not ready to say for certain that Jimmy didn't run away, or that he wasn't abducted. I just said I thought, considering the facts, that those two scenarios were no longer plausible – but implausible doesn't mean impossible." Kunick paused, graciously allowing time for that little nugget of wisdom to sink in. "What does seem plausible, again, considering the facts, is that Jimmy may have been attacked by an animal."

"Jimmy was attacked by an animal?!" Richard hovered in the doorway, freshly washed and nattily attired in a lime green leisure suit, orange silk shirt and white loafers, obviously abandoning his role in the search for his friend's child.

"I didn't say that," Kunick growled, "I said that seems like the most plausible explanation for what we're dealing with here. Don't forget, we live in the forest, and snowshoes aren't the only animals that get hungry out there. Jimmy could have stumbled across a black bear that didn't want to share those carrots with anybody else, and we all know how unpredictable a bear can be when food's involved. Maybe it was a sow trying to feed last spring's cubs. Now that's doubly dangerous. Attacks by black bear are more common than you might think. We've also got wolves, coyotes, possibly even cougar to consider. Be assured, though, at this point it's too early to rule anything out. We just have to keep searching, and keep praying that whatever's happened, we're able to bring that little boy home. But that's not going to happen if we stand around here jawing.

Corky, it's time to get back to work, but I need to talk with you, in private, before you head back out."

Kunick fell in behind Corcoran, who jumped at the informal order and obediently made a beeline for her squad car. Looking decidedly confused, Richard stepped aside to allow the police officers passage out of the house. He waited until they had crossed the yard and faded into the shadows before he closed the door.

"What makes him think that Jimmy was attacked by an animal?" Richard spun around on the tips of his white loafers as he posed the question. "They must have found something, huh, tell me, what the hell is going on?"

Max urgently waved Richard over to the kitchen table and the search map Corcoran had inadvertently left behind.

"Hurry up, hurry up." he pressed, "Corky's going to be coming back for this map any second, and there's something I have to show you guys. Tim, see if you can snap Jackson out of it and bring him over here, too. Jackson!" Max shouted, "Pull yourself together, this is your son we're talking about."

Jackson eyed Tim dreamily as he tried to roast him from his stupor. "An animal gots my Jimmy, is that what Bobby says? I don't think he runned off, neither, and I pray to the Lord he ain't been snatched up by no pree-vert." While he sat dazed, Jackson had obviously been absorbing Chief Kunick's theories. His words were only slightly slurred and in an instant he was astonishingly attentive. "We gets black bears out to the back all the time. More come 'round in the spring, when they just woke up and is hungry, but they come through pretty regular all year. I gots a book 'round here somewhere with pictures of folks been attacked by a black bear and Bobby's right, happens more than I'da thought. Killin' ain't typical of black bears so if that's what's done got Jimmy, he could still be alive, hurtin' out there in the woods. But if he run across a wolf, or a cougar . . ."

"Bullshit! I'm not buying that bullshit," Max raged, slamming his fist on the map and rattling the accumulated dirty plates stacked beneath it. "Look at those green dots. There's no way a black bear could have dragged Jimmy that far, that fast, let alone have the inclination. If a black bear grabbed him, it would have dragged him one hundred yards into the woods, tops, chewed on him a little bit, and lost interest."

"What if it was a black bear, and, like you said, lost interest," Tim offered, playing the devil's advocate in an attempt to consider every possibility. "Maybe it ripped off the pants and the shoe, chewed on those for a while, then spit them out where they were found?"

"Then where the hell is Jimmy? Corky's running the search like a drill sergeant, and that's a good thing, since she made sure somebody walked over every inch of the shaded area here on the map. He would have turned up. And wolves, or cougars? Give me a break. Find me a verified wolf attack of a human. It just doesn't happen. They've just been vilified because of blatant ignorance and irrational fear. Folks desperately want to believe cougars run wild here in northern Wisconsin, but there's not one shred of evidence to support their existence. Jimmy had a better chance of winning the lottery than crossing paths with a cougar, and he's too young to even play."

"Fine, Max, fine, we get the picture, you are not sold on Bobby's animal theory," said Richard, fairly dancing with nervous excitement. "I've got to tell you, I'm getting a little panicky here myself. I mean, what in god's name could have happened to Jimmy? I'm still kind of in the dark, you know? It could just as easily be my Terry missing, or Nicholas, or either of your boys, Tim. For chrissakes, we have to find him! Let's go Max, you're wasting time. You said you needed to show us something important on the map, before Corky or Chief Kunick come back."

Using an unopened business envelope he culled from the papers on the table as a straight edge, Max created an imaginary line through the four green dots.

"What's that, the green dots you were talking about, what are those? C'mon, I missed that, remember?" Richard whined in exasperation.

"Patches of bloody cloth, looked like bluejean material, were found at each of the first three dots," Max pointed them out hurriedly, "and one of Jimmy's wrestling boots, all torn up, was found at this last dot. Those dots are leading right away from this backyard, but look where they're leading."

Max extended the imaginary line out to the folded corner, just as he had done earlier, eliciting a collective gasp from Tim and Jackson.

"What? What?" Richard floundered. "What the hell am I missing?"

Slowly unfolding one more panel of the map, Max adjusted the envelope and looked at Richard, waiting for the light to go on. He just shook his head, utterly confused.

"Damn, you are a dim bulb," Max exclaimed, "Look at the map, Dickey, for chrissakes, look at the map."

Richard traced the spine of the envelope with his finger, slowing as he crossed the alternating black and white line of a highway. He stopped completely at the tip of a thin dashed line, a woods road, that intersected the pavement and extended a short distance into a green-shaded area marking county forest land.

"Is that where I think it is?" asked Richard in disbelief. "That's where we were, just this morning, yesterday morning now, I guess, back by the oak, the treehouse? What's your point, Max, what does this have to do with finding Jimmy?"

"Maybe nothing. I hope this doesn't have anything at all to do with finding Jimmy, but I'll tell you what, even before I connected those green dots there was a voice in my head telling me to go out there. Sounds weird, but it was like an actual voice, I shit you not." Max turned to Jackson, "Have you been hearing voices yet, and the whistling you were telling us about?"

Jackson tilted his head and frowned, devoting extra concentration to listening. "Funny thing," he smiled faintly, "It all kinda just went away, my head just up and cleared, right as I come home from down to Tingle's, just before I gots home to find Jimmy missin'. Why you askin', Max?"

"Nothing, no reason. I was just curious, just checking up on you," Max answered, diverting both his eyes, and the conversation. "Anyway, I don't know about you guys, but I'm going out there. I can't believe I'm saying that after I just promised myself that I'd never go back when we left there yesterday morning, swore I'd never go back. But, like I said, it feels like the choice has been made for me. I'm going back out there, and

I'm going right now."

Kunick walked in the door just as Max finished speaking. "Going back out where?" he asked pointedly as he walked briskly toward the intense huddle over the kitchen table. Max gathered up the search map quickly and folded it back into a small rectangle. He tapped the side of his head with the compact paper package.

"Back out to join the search, now that we have a better idea where to look. Corky's probably going to want this, don't you think," said Max, patronizingly, as he handed the map to Kunick. "What about you, chief, what's your next move?"

"I wish like hell that I could be out there walking the woods. That's killing me, but I have to hang back here for a bit yet," said Kunick, passing the map back to Max. "Give this to Corky on your way out. She's waiting for it."

"What's keeping you here?" asked Tim. "The more feet on the ground the better the odds of finding Jimmy, you said so yourself."

"When we have a missing child nowadays we put out what they call an Amber Alert, a nation-wide system set up after a little girl, name of Amber, was abducted down in Texas back in the mid-90s. Area law enforcement agencies – the county, adjoining townships – respond by sending personnel to assist in the search," Kunick explained, irked that his motives were being called into question. "Those folks should be arriving any time, and they're coming here. With any luck, we'll have found Jimmy by then. If not, I'll brief them on the situation and send them out in the field. Besides, if you three are going out," he motioned to Max and Tim, then eyed the inappropriately-clad Richard suspiciously, "that leaves Jackson and Dorothy here alone, and I don't think that's a good idea right now, for obvious reasons."

"Jackson's coming with us," Max asserted, "There's not much he can do to help his son holed up here in this house."

"You think that's a good idea, Jackson?" asked Kunick, casting a wary eye. "I'm going to shoot straight with you here, do you think you're prepared for what you might find, assuming it is an animal attack we're talking about?"

"I ain't worried 'bout no animal attack, Bobby. I'm just

worried 'bout my boy. We gonna go find him, bring him back home," Jackson vowed with determination. "I ain't sittin' 'round here no more, breakin' down like an ol' woman. Let's go, fellas, time's a wastin'."

Offering assurances to Kunick that he would keep a watchful eye over Jackson, Max ushered his small cadre out the door. Kunick joined the procession, reclaiming the search map and grumbling that he had to "have a couple more words with Officer Corcoran" before she departed. Tim lagged behind, catching a glimpse of Dorothy, a disturbing apparition standing still and erect in the corner of the room. Her dull, dreary eyes suddenly sparked to life and locked on Tim with a penetrating glare that sent chills racing down his spine.

"My babies dead, ain't he? My Jimmy's gone," she purred, her raspy voice drained of any emotion, "and it was you all done killed him, you all brung this on us, ain't that right? And the sins of the father shall be inherited by the son, so the bible say. My Jimmy's dead and you all done killed him, now get the hell out."

Tim, thoroughly unnerved, was still shaking when he reached the minivan. He crawled into the far back, passing between Jackson and Richard, perched anxiously at the edge of their seats. Max, turned sideways in the driver's seat with the engine running, faced his yawning and stretching son, who appeared uncertain of his surroundings in his semi-conscious state.

"Did they find Jimmy, Pa?" asked Nicholas, his voice soft and scratchy with sleep.

"No son, sorry," Max tousled his only child's shock of wild hair, lovingly, "but maybe you can be a big help. You awake now? I need you to think for me." Nicholas nodded his head attentively. "You know the block of county forest northeast of here, runs along the backroad that heads east out of town, toward Turtle Creek?"

"I know exactly where you're talking about, Pa, but I've *never* gone out there. You always told me big doesn't equal stupid, and you said you'd tan my hide if you ever found out I was out there. I may be big, but I'm not stupid," Nicholas grinned at his father, like a puppy wagging its tail in anticipation of praise for its obedience.

"What about other kids, friends, anybody you've ever heard about that's gone out there, or runs around out in those woods? Do you ever hear other kids talking about going out there? Do you know any kids who have a treehouse out there, or a fort?"

Nicholas scratched his head, puzzled, "Most of my friends' parents don't want them going out there, either, and I don't know anything about a treehouse, other than the stories. I know a little boy was killed out there a long time ago, in a treehouse, and I always figured that's why you didn't want me messing around in those woods, even though you never gave me a reason. If that's where you think Jimmy is, you're wrong Pa. Jimmy's afraid of the dark, isn't he Mr. Kelly, he wouldn't go all the way out there at night, by himself."

"No, no, you're probably right," said Max, agreeing that Jimmy wouldn't be out in those woods at night, *alone*. "We're just trying to think of anything that might help us find him. You've been a big help all night. I'm proud of you, but it's time for you to go home. You've got school in the morning."

"I want to stay and help, Pa. Jimmy's my friend," Nicholas pleaded.

Max checked the digital clock glowing green in the dashboard. "It's after three in the morning. Maybe I'll keep you home from school today, but you're going home right now to get some sleep - in your own bed. "

"Can you swing by my place too, Max?" Richard sniveled. "If we're going back out in the woods, I have to get out of this suit, and I don't want to ruin my loafers."

"Do you really think you have time for that, Mr. Mann?" Nicholas asked innocently.

"No," Max barked, "Mr. Mann does not have time for that." Richard sheepishly averted his eyes from Max's withering glare, instead focusing on his shoes and grimacing at the thought of grass and mud marring the glossy, white-patent leather.

It had taken just minutes to drop Nicholas off and drive the roughly five miles from Jackson's home to the forbidden woods. Max scanned the small opening at the crest of the hill, but the lush bed of ferns lay so broken and trampled from their previous visit that he was unable to discern if there had been any other traffic in the interim. He sat for a moment, vigorously massaging his temples, trying to evict the clambering voice from his mind. When he cut the headlights, the moonless night enshrouded the vehicle in an ebony cloak.

"Holy balls, I can't see my hand in front of my face," Richard nearly shrieked, "Do you have a flashlight in here, Max?"

"Here, take the goddam flashlight, we might need it. But for now, keep the fucking thing turned off. And quit your goddam whining! Keep your mouths shut, too, and walk quietly. No need to announce our arrival." Max doled out the orders and exited the minivan, gripping an aluminum baseball bat he had stashed beneath his seat. Richard and Jackson bailed out into the dark, but Tim didn't budge.

"Announce our arrival to who, Max? We are on a wild goose chase here, let me tell you. And what's that for?" asked Richard, pointing at the metallic silver bat resting on Max's shoulder.

"Tim, you coming? Get your ass out here," Max hissed, ignoring Richard's entreaties entirely. When Tim still didn't move, "That's fine, we're heading into the woods, you can wait out here in the dark, *by yourself*, until we get back."

"No need for all of us to go in there," Richard mewled. "Maybe I'll just wait back here with Tim." Max ground the lugged black rubber soul of his boot into the top of Richard's loafers, tattooing a muddy tread into the virgin white upper. "Hey! That was uncalled for," Richard cried.

Tim cowered in the back of the minivan, but the recollection of the anxious moments spent alone in his work truck, waiting for his friends in this same spot, when it was light no less, freed him from his terrified paralysis. He skittered into the night and sprinted wildly down the darkened, foreboding footpath, slamming into Richard at the rear of the silent, single file caravan marching through the menacing forest.

Suffocated by the pall of torturous memories and lost in limbo between the unearthly present and an eerily similar nightmare from his past, Sauter was unaware that he was no longer alone beneath the enduring oak until it was too late. He had just cradled the limp, lifeless body in a gentle bear hug and lifted the child above his head, straining to loosen the noose that had snapped the little boy's slender neck. He heard the whoosh of air and caught the glint of the silver aluminum bat out of the corner of his eye an instant before it crashed into his exposed side. His rib cage collapsed with the crackle of broken bones and he tasted the blood trickling from his mouth as he doubled over from the blow. The brown work boot swung upward like a pendulum at his bowed, exposed face, and Sauter blinked into unconsciousness when the unyielding steel toe introduced itself to his nose.

CHAPTER EIGHT

The dream had been pleasant, a fanciful flight above a lush green landscape bedecked with a plentitude of azure jewels. Sauter floated upon a billowing cushion of air, hovering above the placid waters of a lake lain transparent beneath a warming, radiant sun. Privy to its heretofore darkened depths, Sauter marveled at the glacial basin's undulating, underwater forests, the wispy golden-brown strands of its shallow sandbars and the submerged islands of jumbled rock. Tiny silver mirrors sparkled in the luxuriant, broad-leafed cabbage weeds, schools of baitfish chased from their hiding places by zebra-striped yellow perch and insatiable smallmouth bass. Marauding packs of walleye patrolled the deeper edges and open pockets in the vegetation, leaving themselves vulnerable to the razor-lined jaws of northern pike and muskellunge, solitary hunters spurred to instinctive hunger by the flashing flanks and aquatic echoes of the frenzied smaller fish.

Sauter tried to will himself back to sleep, back into that ethereal, unfettered dreamscape, but he was handcuffed to consciousness by the relentless ache ricocheting off the inside of his skull and the searing fire raging deep within his bowels. Breaking the seal of the salty crust coating his eyelashes, he blinked his swollen left lid and battled against the blinding, blurry brightness. Lying on his back, he reached up and gingerly probed his unresponsive right eye, wincing at the tenderness of the tumorous tissue. The familiar, sloping line of his nose was askew, crooked and compressed, and his torn upper lip burned with the sting of his fingertips.

Clarity crept in with the aggravating insistence of an uninvited guest, allowing Sauter to slowly assimilate his unfamiliar surroundings. The small room reminded him of the cramped, concrete bunkers he hunkered down in during live fire exercises back in basic training, other than the thick coating of clean whitewash glaring from the block walls and the low ceiling. The pain wracking his body caused Sauter to briefly entertain the illusory idea that he was cradled in the caring confines of a hospital, a comforting self-deception that evaporated with an oddly amusing revelation.

"I'll be damned, I'm in jail," he exclaimed in a laughing lisp that released a ripple of misery through his bruised and battered muscles.

Sauter's face fell into shadows as the overhead light, recessed into the ceiling behind a wire grate encased in clear plastic, was eclipsed by an inordinately large, indiscernible head.

"Nice work, Inspector Clouseau. I can see why you're making those big detective dollars with the county." Kunick poked Sauter in his broken, bandaged ribs, chuckling at the agonized convulsion provoked by the sadistic jab. "You certainly are a sorry looking son of a bitch, not that you were ever an Adonis in the first place, but those boys sure did a number on you."

Folding his arms in a protective shield over his susceptible midsection, Sauter's one functioning eye cautiously assessed the familiar face of his estranged old friend and mentor. He hadn't seen or corresponded with his old boss in years, their relationship just one in a long list of casualties Sauter accumulated in the divisive aftermath of Michael Koenigs's murder.

"Who are you talking about, Bobby? Who did this to me?" It hurt to even talk, but Sauter felt exposed and vulnerable on his back. He ingested the omnipresent pain and struggled to a sitting position on the edge of the wall-mounted cot.

"Hey, hold up there big shooter, you know how this works." Kunick placed a foot atop the thin mattress and rested an elbow on his bent knee, tugging up a pant leg and exposing his hairless lower calf. "The investigating officer, that being me, asks the questions, while the suspect, that being you, provides the answers."

"Suspect? What the hell are you talking about, Bobby?" snapped Sauter.

"You're just not catching on here, are you Sauter? That was another question, and that's not your role here, I just told you that," Kunick smiled weakly, then rapidly abandoned his feigned amusement. "Fine, I'll humor you and answer that one for you. You're a suspect in the murder of Jimmy Kelly, and you'll remain a suspect until I find out what in blue blazes is going on here."

Anticipating an outburst from the battered inmate, Kunick placed an index finger to his lips and shook his head slowly from side to side, eyes closed. Clinging to the cot like a kid on a carnival ride, peaked and woozy, Sauter tried in vain to derail the runaway roller coaster racing through his brain. His mind told him that he needed to remain upright and alert, but his exploited body rebelled and began a slow descent to the hard mattress.

"Wait a minute, wait a minute," said Kunick, clamping onto Sauter's clavicle and roughly halting his recline, "we're just getting started. We need to talk, Sauter, now. I gave you plenty of time to get your beauty sleep, for all the good it did you."

Digging deep to find the fountainhead of his intestinal fortitude, Sauter brushed away Kunick's supportive grip and wriggled defiantly from the cot. Steadying himself against the wall, he shuffled to the jail cell's small stainless steel sink and tripped the cold water. He splashed his lacerated face copiously, then filled his cupped palm and let the rejuvenating liquid run down the back of his neck. A highly-polished plate of stainless steel was bolted to the wall above the sink, but Sauter deliberately avoided the makeshift mirror, certain that he looked as horrible as he felt.

"Okay, Bobby, this is your gig. I'll play along, but humor me just one more time. What the hell time is it? What day is it, for that matter. The way my head feels, no telling how long I've been out," Sauter spoke into the silver basin below his bowed head, his back to Kunick in the center of the cell.

"It hasn't even been four hours. It's just after seven, Thursday morning." Kunick paused, expecting an acknowledgement, but Sauter remained hunched over the sink, shaking his head. "Thursday morning, September sixth? You turn up in Broadaxe a couple of days ago, after all those restful years, and lo and behold we've got a dead little boy on our hands less than thirty-six hours later. Any of this ringing a bell for you?"

"Jesus, Bobby, give me a break, you know I didn't have anything to do with that," Sauter protested the implication, turning weakly on his heels.

"The hell I do!" Kunick bellowed, "I'll tell you what I *do* know. I know you were here, in Broadaxe, Tuesday afternoon, poking around town until you ended up at Tingle's place. I know you graced us with your presence because Christopher Koenigs got his walking papers the end of last week. I know that there are certain people here in town who you've long suspected of knowing more than they're letting on about Michael Koenigs's murder. I know you badgered those folks relentlessly over the ensuing years – the actual charges were harassment and conduct unbecoming a police officer, if I remember correctly. I know that dead little boy, Jimmy Kelly, is the son of one of those folks, and I know last night's search ended when they found *you* holding his corpse in *your* arms. So you tell me, Sauter, what exactly do you expect me to think?"

The gnawing guilt that had long simmered just beneath the surface percolated to the core of Sauter's conscience, a persistent, familiar guilt spawned by the suffering others endured as the result of his well-intentioned actions. When he joined the Broadaxe police force as a twenty-eight year old rookie back in 1985, Kunick, only 10 years his senior, was already into the eighth year of what evolved into a lifetime appointment as chief. A familial bond developed almost immediately; Kunick the wiser, more experienced older brother to the impudent, eager to learn Sauter. That bond had never been severed, in Sauter's estimation, but it had been stretched so near the breaking point in the wake of Michael Koenigs's death that it could never revert to form.

"Who are 'they', Bobby, who came into that meadow and beat me when I was trying to get Jimmy down from that noose?" Sauter was persistent, unable to assume his assigned role of suspect in the informal interrogation. "That's what I was doing, you know, trying to get that goddam rope off his neck, same as I did with that Koenigs boys all those years ago. Jimmy was already hanging there, dead, when I arrived on the scene."

Kunick rubbed the silver-gray stubble on his prodigious dome and considered the injured man leaning on the sink before him with a grudging respect and admiration. Physically, Sauter was tough as a turtle shell, and Kunick had never known another man who was so adamant in his convictions, no matter how misplaced. Kunick had officially ordered, then personally begged Sauter to drop his relentless persecution of the four young boys who helped seal Christopher Koenigs's fate as the murderer of his younger brother. When Sauter persisted and incurred the wrath of some of the more influential citizens of Broadaxe, folks with the money and the means to make Kunick's life a living hell, the harried chief finagled a compromise that spared Sauter prosecution, and possibly jail time. Sauter, for his part, agreed to a forced transfer to the county sheriff's department with the implicit understanding that he would leave Broadaxe, and his four young antagonists, in peace.

"You know damn well who jumped you and put that licking on you, but you're going to make me say it, aren't you?" Kunick acquiesced, having neither the time nor the patience to deal with Sauter's obstinate nature. "It was Max Ferguson and Jackson Kelly, the dead boy's dad, who did most of the damage. It should come as no surprise to you that Tim Schumacher and Dickey, er, Richard, Mann were there, as well. I've got Ferguson and Kelly locked up as we speak."

"What are you holding them for? Do you think they might have something to do with that boy's hanging?" Sauter inquired.

"Do I think those two actually killed that boy? Hardly. Jimmy was Jackson's own flesh and blood, for chrissakes. Might they know a little more than they're letting on, maybe holding something back? That's a possibility. Lord, listen to me, I'm starting to sound like you now." Kunick allowed himself a halfhearted smile. "They haven't been able to give me a good reason why they went out to those woods when the search was nowhere near there, but that's not why I'm holding them. Last I checked, it's still illegal to take the law into your own hands and dole out corporal punishment with a Louisville Slugger. We particularly frown on it around here when it's another member of the law enforcement community."

"Let 'em go, Bobby. I'm not going to press charges," Sauter suggested innocently, but Kunick sensed that his authority was being impinged upon.

"Don't tell me how to run my goddam jail!" he thundered. "I'll hold those two as long as I damn well please. Same goes for your sorry ass. You know, they likely would have beaten you to death if those little hairs hadn't pricked up on the back of my neck." Kunick took two steps toward the cell door, which he had left slightly ajar. "Corky, if you can spare a minute . . ." he shouted down the empty corridor. Apparently eavesdropping just outside the cell, Corcoran abashedly stepped before the cold metal bars. Her uniform was impeccable, a starched light brown top accented by dark brown pocket flaps, tucked precisely into perfectly creased light brown trousers with dark brown piping down the legs. She stood with her thick-soled, buffed black oxfords splayed in a wide base, hands clasped behind her back and corseted chest thrust forward.

"Officer Megan Corcoran, Detective Henry Sauter, or should I say the infamous Detective Henry Sauter? of the Ojibway County Sheriff's Department." Kunick leaned back, opening a line of sight in the cramped quarters, allowing the exchange of curt nods. "You may want to thank Officer Corcoran. She probably saved your life. Isn't that right Corky?" She nodded at Kunick in affirmation, and Sauter obligingly bowed his head to her in appreciation. "If you'd be so kind, refresh our guest's memory. He's understandably a bit confused about what exactly occurred earlier this morning."

Corcoran narrowed her stance and cleared her throat, dutifully reconstructing the last few hours in her own hackneyed version of police jargon.

"At approximately three-oh-eight this morning Chief Kunick requested that I tail a late-model, gray minivan registered to, and being driven by, one Max Ferguson. Four other individuals were also present in the vehicle; Ferguson's eleven-year-old son, Nicholas, one Timothy Schumacher, one Richard Mann, and one Jackson Kelly. They proceeded first to the Ferguson residence, where I witnessed Nicholas Ferguson exit the van and enter the house. The vehicle then traveled approximately two miles east of town before turning north and coming to a stop at the end of an unmaintained woods road." She paused to see if Kunick had anything to add. He did.

"Corcoran was in charge of the field search for Jimmy

Kelly and she came by the boy's home, Jackson Kelly's place, where I'd set up the base of operations, to bring me up to speed. I pulled her off the search to follow those four because they were acting suspicious. As I said earlier, it seemed like they were hiding something from me, something they had discovered on Corky's search map. That's what raised my hackles," Kunick explained, indicating to Corcoran that the floor was once again hers.

"At that point, approximately three-twenty, I parked my patrol car on the shoulder of the paved highway and proceeded into the woods on foot. I observed four individuals exiting a gray minivan, the same four adults identified previously. Max Ferguson held what appeared to be an aluminum baseball bat. After a short discussion, they proceeded into the forest down a trail adjacent to the parked vehicle. I followed, maintaining an appropriate distance to avoid detection. Reaching an opening in the trees, I observed Ferguson beating an unidentified individual with said baseball bat, while Jackson Kelly repeatedly kicked the same. Schumacher and Mann watched but did not participate, nor did they intercede. I observed Jimmy Kelly, apparently dead, hanging below a treehouse from a rope. I identified myself as a police officer and ordered Ferguson and Kelly to cease and desist. Ignoring my command, they continued to beat the prone victim until I fired a warning shot and was able to bring the situation under control. Once the . . ."

Kunick cut Corcoran off, raising his hand like a traffic cop. He thanked her for her assistance and expressed a desire to speak with Sauter in private, telling her pointedly that her current workload didn't permit time to idle in the hallway. He gripped the bars of the cell door in his clenched fists and watched his chastised subordinate mope down the brightly-lit corridor until she disappeared around a corner. Kunick wheeled on Sauter, still perched feebly on the sink, slamming the heavy grate shut with a deafening clang.

"Those boys are under the impression that Jimmy Kelly died at your hands, Sauter. That's why they put that whupping on you. That, and possibly to vent some long pent-up hostility, settle some old scores," he mused, thrusting his hands into the bulging pockets of his pants. He fingered the loose change, tumbling the coins noisily as he crossed the concrete cell floor, reaching Sauter as he rose cautiously from his semi-seated repose. "I won't lie to you. Considering the circumstances, the history of this whole god-awful mess, that scenario doesn't seem all that far-fetched."

"What? That I actually killed that little boy? Are you kidding me?" Sauter was indignant, his flagging strength bolstered by a defensive surge of adrenalin. "Can we please cut the shit here, Bobby? I know you don't believe that for a second."

"Let's do that, let's cut the shit, shall we? You explain to me how I end up with a second dead child on my watch, two murders committed more than twenty years apart, yet, strangely enough, the manner of death and the crime scene itself are identical." Kunick shook with fury, his wide face shaded like a ripened, blue ribbon tomato. "Top that off with the same cast of familiar characters, and it all shapes up like some kind of morbid reunion. I consider myself a damn good cop, Sauter, but when that little boy turned up missing last night, I'll admit it, the thought never even crossed my mind. So tell me, what makes you so goddam smart?"

"About the crime scene, Bobby," Sauter asked submissively, testing Kunick's waning patience, "what was your reaction when you saw it, when you saw the treehouse, I mean."

"You know damn well what my reaction was," Kunick roared, angered by what he perceived to be blatant evasiveness on Sauter's part. "It was probably no different than your own. I nearly shit myself, that was my reaction." He slapped an open palm to his forehead and let gravity draw his hand downward, an unsuccessful attempt to wipe away the frustration. "Enough dancing around, no more changing the subject, you hear me? I want answers. What in the hell have you gotten yourself into? Give me a logical explanation for how you ended up back there, in *those* woods, with another dead boy in your arms. Straight up now, or else I might have to come take a look at those ribs of yours again."

Sauter reflexively shielded his sensitive side, not wanting to find out if Kunick would uncharacteristically carry out the coercive threat. He had to constantly rotate his head to see his interrogator, aggravated at Kunick's insistence on standing in the blind spot created by his swollen right eye. Shuffling to the seatless, undersized steel toilet bolted to the wall adjacent to the sink, Sauter addressed a sudden and urgent need to relieve himself. The simple act of urinating radiated currents of pain throughout his body, and his breathing restricted to short spasms, like exaggerated hiccups, as he fumbled clumsily with his zipper.

"I received the news about Christopher Koenigs when I returned to the office Tuesday morning," Sauter began, laboriously, "I wasn't in on Monday. I spent Labor Day weekend muskie fishing, over at Buckthorn Lake . . ."

"That's one of my favorite lakes to fish. Did you have any luck?" Kunick asked without hesitation.

There's a lure for every fish, Sauter always said, and he took great pride in his uncanny ability to pull the right bait from the tackle box. Getting Kunick to bite was easy, he assumed the old rowtroller hadn't been cured of what hard-core muskie anglers fondly refer to as "the disease." Raise the subject of muskie fishing, and, at least momentarily, those with the affliction are unable to think of anything else. And that's all Sauter was looking for, a few moments, a little time to tuck the pain into a manageable compartment, a chance to blow the carbon out of his brain. He had nothing to hide from Kunick, he just wanted to be sure all systems were functioning before he told his side of the story.

"I boated four fish, all of them nice, the biggest one just shy of forty-eight inches." Sauter set the hook, hoping to play Kunick for as much time as he could buy.

"That's the kind of weekend a guy dreams about!" Kunick gushed, rattling off the list of obligatory questions regarding weather conditions, water temperature and depth, bait selection, type of structure, the phase of the moon, and so on and so forth, until the subject was thoroughly, and regretfully, exhausted. Sauter addressed each inquiry with the appropriate gravity and added timely embellishments, as fishermen are wont to do, when he recounted the tale of each individual catch.

"Man oh man, that sounds fantastic. I wish I were out

there right now," Kunick droned, dispirited by the dawning realization that a murder investigation would seriously curtail his time on the water.

"Tell me about it," Sauter commiserated, with generous understatement.

"Right, right, enough fish talk," Kunick stammered, only just aware of Sauter's subterfuge and miffed at being so easily manipulated. "That is one hell of a weekend though, that's for sure, but you always were a lucky son of a bitch." He tried to sound nonchalant as he groped for a smooth segue back to the point of departure. "One hell of a weekend, but you were starting to tell me what you've been up to since. You were saying you heard about Christopher Koenigs, his being released, when you returned to work Tuesday morning."

Sauter thought of asking for a cigarette, maybe a cup of coffee, one more stall tactic to get Kunick's goat, then he thought of his ribs, and thought better of the idea. He had doggedly dragged himself back from the brink of physical collapse, the precipice of pain and agony that, once crossed, consumes the mind, body and spirit. There was no time for weakness, not when he was under suspicion for the murder of a young child. He needed to clear his name. To do that, he needed to track down the individual, or individuals, who actually did kill Jimmy Kelly. That wasn't going to happen when he was locked up in a jail cell. He needed out.

"Don't ask me why, Bobby, because I really can't give you a good reason, but as soon as I found out that Christopher Koenigs had been released, I just felt compelled to come back over here to Broadaxe." Sauter swiveled his head in search of Kunick, who had slunk back into his blind spot. He wondered how it was possible to lose sight of a head so large in a room so small. "I grabbed a young cop out of the office and we came across on the back roads, early afternoon, before one."

"What was his name again? Tingle told me, made me listen to the stupid limerick he made up. I remember his first name was . . . Seth?"

"Colins, Seth Colins, kid from Georgia who just hooked up with the county, his first job as a cop. I figured you would have talked to Tingle. I thought that limerick was actually kind of clever, 'beautiful breasthsts'," the newly formed scabs on Sauter's lips split back open when he smiled. "I brought the kid along because he's a blank slate, doesn't know anything about, well, much of anything. Besides, I thought I'd seem a lot less menacing to folks around here with a uniformed cop by my side. I told you we took the back roads over, so we came in from the east, right past the woods where I found Michael Koenigs. No coincidence, I guess. Same thing, like you said about the hair standing up on the back of your neck, there was this nagging sensation that I needed to stop. That's the first time I saw the treehouse. Did you know about that, Bobby?"

Disappointed that his visually impaired cellmate had spoiled the fun and given up on the irksome game of hide and seek, Kunick positioned himself within the limited line of sight afforded by Sauter's puffy left eye.

"Hell no I didn't know about that treehouse, not until Tingle told me you mentioned it in the bar, loud and clear so everybody could hear." Kunick was bobbing and weaving, un-sure if Sauter could see much of anything at all.

"I only cared if one person heard," Sauter clarified, "Jackson Kelly. As you're probably aware, he was at Tingle's when I was there. You might be surprised to know that Kelly and his three amigos were out in those woods, back to the treehouse, bright and early yesterday morning. Now, why do you think that is? Then Kelly's kid goes AWOL and he turns up dead, hanging from that same treehouse less than 24 hours later, and those four show up out there again, looking for the kid, on a hunch? What would possess those four, of all people, to go out to those woods? Something convinced them that boy might be out there."

"And round and round and round we go," Kunick raised an arm and twirled a finger above his head, "and we somehow end up right back on square one. I have to tell you, Sauter, you're really not helping your case much. You may even be digging yourself in deeper. I've been asking myself those very same questions, but with you in mind. Nobody around here knew about, or heard about, that treehouse until you broadcast its existence down at Tingle's. Tingle's! You know how word spreads like wildfire out of that place. You were out at the treehouse again yesterday morning yourself, had to be, otherwise how would you know those other fellows were out there? You beat them to the punch again this morning, remember? *They* found *you* with Jimmy Kelly in *your* arms, already dead. You seem to be one step ahead of the action, Sauter, on the wrong side of the ball, and that's not a good place to be when murder's the game."

Because the entire notion had seemed so outlandish to Sauter, that he would actually find himself as the primary suspect in a murder investigation, he had underestimated the gravity of his present circumstance. He couldn't fault Kunick's reasoning, he could only fault himself. He put himself in this unenviable situation, or allowed someone else to maneuver him there. Could it be possible? Was someone trying to frame him? He was loath to imagine that someone would actually sacrifice an innocent child as a conduit for revenge.

"You're pissin' in the wind here, Bobby. I didn't kill that boy." He opted for the direct approach. All he could do now was tell his tale, unembellished, and wait for the truth to shake out. "I'm giving you my word. I've given you a lot of headaches, been a thorn in your side, but I never lied to you, and I'm not lying now. I was in my office when the Amber Alert came across." Sauter saw Kunick raise a leery eyebrow. "I know, I know, it came across late, I think it was after midnight, but I don't have a life, okay? I don't sleep for shit, don't have any friends, so I pretty much work, and fish. Anyway, when I saw the child's name, saw that it was Jackson Kelly's kid, that kind of piqued my interest. I hemmed and hawed, trying to decide if I should drive over to Broadaxe, take a look around, but I figured it probably wouldn't be the smartest thing for me to do."

Kunick's laughter, a high-pitched *whee-hee-hee-hee*, reverberated sharply in the hollow acoustics of the concrete chamber. "By the looks of you, it would seem like you had that figured right. Still, here you are," he shook his ponderous pate with a *how-can-you-be-such-a-dumb-shit* smirk, "still not bright enough to listen to common sense, even when you're talking to yourself. Okay, excuse the interruption. So, you ignored your own best advice . . ."

"Not at first," Sauter continued. "I had actually decided that it would be in everybody's best interest for me to stay away. Then, a couple hours later, I hear through the grapevine that the kid's still missing, so I convince myself that nobody would be the wiser if I just snuck back to the meadow, checked out the treehouse, and snuck back out."

"Bingo! We're back to the million dollar question." Kunick clapped his hands once, loudly. "We just established the fact that you're no genius, so once and for all, tell me, please, what led you to believe you'd find Jimmy Kelly in the exact same spot where Michael Koenigs was killed. Enlighten me, if you'd be so kind, because for the life of me, I still don't see the connection."

It was futile, Sauter conceded to himself, to even attempt an explanation for actions which lacked any tangible rationale. There was no logic, no factual evidence that he could cite in defense of his questionable conduct over the past two days. There was only the persistent clamoring of the nebulous voice, calling him inexorably back to a distant place where long dormant demons lay in wait, demons resurrected only hours earlier beneath the homicidal branches of the familiar bur oak. He had no answer, no explanation, but he knew that was the last thing Kunick wanted to hear.

"You were talking about it earlier, about your reason for having Officer Corcoran tail Max Ferguson's minivan, so maybe you'll understand." He gave it his best shot. "This was the same kind of thing, one of those raised hackles, hair on the back of the neck kind of things. That's the best I can do for a reason, Bobby. I don't know what else to tell you. I was just kind of drawn there. It was more or less out of my control. I never even considered the potential consequences if I found that boy there – or if somebody found me, for that matter. I guess I should have."

Sauter expected that admission to elicit another of Kunick's carnival ride laughs, so the silence that settled over the cell came as an unexpected, albeit pleasant, surprise. It seemed no one was stirring in the entire jail, and Sauter marveled at a quiet that compared to the stillness he had encountered earlier that morning, in the forest, on his preordained pilgrimage to the treehouse. There was a dull throb banging on the base of his skull, the drum beat of a repressed enemy, reorganizing, threatening to unleash its armies of pain. He cringed at the prospect of another assault.

Rigid and mute, Kunick permitted the peaceful interlude to linger, until it became oppressive, coating Sauter in an apprehensive rime. He listened for the jingle of keys in a lock, the machine gun click of a typewriter, the shuffling of papers, any of the familiar, municipal sounds that would shatter the unsettling illusion that he was trapped in a bubble of suspended time. The sound of his own voice would have to suffice, would surely serve to break the spell, impelling Sauter to pick up his exculpatory narrative where he had left off.

"Bottom line, against my better judgment, I headed for Broadaxe. That was just before 2 a.m." He paused, offering Kunick an opportunity to back up, to comment on his vague, karmatic explanation for his prescient discovery of the dead child. Head bowed and pensive, Kunick stood steadfast in his unspeaking, unmoving repose.

Sauter, eager to finish speaking before his frayed senses and beaten body withered under the duress, continued, "I went directly to the meadow, to the treehouse. I parked my Bronco up the road, behind the welcome sign with the little babies, then I cut through the woods, to the meadow. It was so absolutely quiet that you could almost hear a hum, know what I mean, and it was pitch black. Seeing that little boy's limp body, suspended beneath that oak, hanging from the treehouse, it took me back to a dark corner of my past that I never dreamed I'd visit again, other than in my worst nightmares. From there on in, I was on automatic pilot, my mind detached, consumed by the moment, I guess, but my body still functioning. That boy was in my arms because I was trying to bring him to rest, bring him down from the noose that snuffed out his life. Hell, I didn't kill him. Those other fellows, I don't have any idea how long they were in that meadow with me, might have been there when I arrived, for all I know. One minute I'm alone, or so I thought, next thing, I'm getting pummeled. Then it was lights out."

Releasing a prolonged hiss of pent up air through unctuous, pursed lips, a reanimated Kunick turned and loped ponderously to the cell door. He reached through the bars and turned the burnished brass key, left trustingly in the lock, releasing the mechanism with a pronounced click. The portal to freedom swung open noisily, the intentionally neglected hinges rending an earsplitting, metallic screech, a built-in alarm that carried throughout the building. Corcoran materialized at the far end of the corridor, diligently responding to the sound of the cell door in a Pavlovian reflex. Just as quickly, she blended back into the walls, satisfied that Kunick was in control, that the crazy detective, Sauter, hadn't overpowered her beloved chief in an impulsive escape attempt.

Sensing the escalating depletion of his debilitated strength, Sauter ogled the measly, unappealing cot as if it were a voluptuous harem, where nurturing arms would massage away his misery. Wary of the oddly quiescent Kunick, poised indecisively on the threshold of the cell, Sauter shuffled back to the beckoning mattress as quickly as his faltering legs would allow. Too tired, too weak to counter the unyielding tug of gravity, he dropped to his seat in an unimpeded free fall, his defenses overrun by the swarming horde of agony. A shadowy balloon blotted out the light, and Sauter sensed the pitying presence of his long ago friend hovering overhead.

"When can I get out of here, Bobby?" He moaned, hunched over like a battered boxer between rounds, "You're either going to have to file charges, or let me go. I think I should go see a doctor," he lied. Kunick knew it. "And besides, you know where to find me, if you need me."

"Take a deep breath, Sauter. Maybe you haven't noticed, but you're a wreck," Kunick reclaimed his exasperated voice. "I've got paperwork to shuffle, folks I need to talk with, all that bureaucratic red tape, you know what it's like, so just sit tight for chrisssakes. If you *really* want to see a doctor, I'll bring one in, but the EMTs patched you up pretty good, actually wanted to take you to the hospital, but I put the kibosh on that. You weren't the most popular guy to begin with around here, you know, and I'm sure the smalltown rumor mill already has you pegged as the prime suspect in Jimmy Kelly's death. I figured you'd be safer here, and I need to know where you are, need to keep an eye on you for the time being. Here, take these, painkillers the medics left with me, said they'll help you rest, and believe you me, you're going to need it."

Kunick fished a multi-colored assortment of pills out of his breast pocket and deposited them in Sauter's quaking hand. The tablets were dusted with lint and pencil shavings, causing Kunick to fidget like an embarrassed host. "Hell, that won't kill you," he reasoned. "I'll just get you a cup of water to help wash those down." Sauter impulsively ingested the medicine before Kunick returned from the sink with an overflowing paper cup, yet he gratefully acknowledged the kindness and bathed his parched throat.

"I'm not so sure you should have taken all of those at once," said Kunick, warily, then turning skeptical, "You did take those, didn't you?" He opened Sauter's clenched fists and made a cursory inspection of the cot, patting down the sheets and stopping to scan the floor. Raising an eyebrow, "Listen to me, Sauter, I want to help you out, I want to believe you, but for chrissakes, meet me part way here. You were just *drawn* there? Guided to that dead child by some unseen force that had taken control of your actions? Your mind? I ask for an explanation and that's what I get, mystical mumbo-jumbo? You're telling me that you'd be comfortable feeding that story to a judge?"

"Are you telling me that I need a lawyer, Bobby? That you're seriously considering bringing me up on charges?"

"I'm telling you that I have a murder investigation to conduct, and, as of right now, you qualify as a person of interest, at the very least. Until I get some answers, some *real* answers, you're not going anywhere. The onus is on you, Sauter, it's up to *you* to convince *me* that there's a logical explanation for your involvement in this."

"What about my phone call, Bobby? I do get to make one call, correct?" Sauter slurred, drowsed by the heavy dose of medication rapidly moving through his system. He hoped the pain killers carried him back to the deep slumber he rarely enjoyed, back to the exhilarating, unfamiliar land of dreams, back to his birds-eye view of the enchanted, underwater world. Melting into the spare mattress, his muddled mind entertained the idea that he was already dreaming, that he would soon awaken to a body unbroken and a reality less harrowing.

"Who the hell are you going to call, Sauter? You just got done telling me you don't have any friends," Kunick droned from a distant corner of Sauter's waning consciousness. Sauter tried to respond, to ask Kunick if there was any chance, despite all that had passed between them, that their friendship had somehow survived, but he slipped away into the blissful embrace of sleep with the question left twisting in the ether, unspoken and unanswered.

Predator and prey swam side by side in an iridescent carousel, cruising just beneath the lake's glassy surface in a shifting whorl of marble eyes, gossamer fins and shimmering scales. Sauter floated above the circling jet stream of fish, a teeming vortex of minnows, bluegill, bass, perch, walleye, northern pike and muskie, all coalescing into a singular, undulant sea serpent. An opulent sun dappled the parabola of pine trees framing the water, and played delicately off the wisteria of weeds groping skyward from the shallows.

Basking in the idyllic familiarity of the subconscious realm to which he had longed to return, Sauter was ill-prepared for the sudden intrusion upon his insular reverie. Roiling, riotous clouds swallowed up the sun, breaking the entrancing, serpentine chain as thousands of individual fish froze, then scattered hectically, like shattered shards of glass. The swirling tempest churned the surface of the lake into a frothy black cauldron and the mists of menacing spindrifts licked Sauter's cold, clammy skin. The plummeting barometric pressure agonizingly sucked the air from his lungs and the clouds descended heavily, pushing his flaccid body down, into the watery maelstrom below.

Anticipating the impending baptism, Sauter closed his eyes and braced for the icy, imminent plunge. When the sinking weight lifted fortuitously, suspending Sauter just shy of submersion, he inhaled greedily as his deflated diaphragm decompressed and his racing heart returned to its customary beat. The buffeting winds bid a rapid retreat and the agitated waters lay down in a smooth, silver slate. When Sauter opened his eyes, he found himself ensconced in the thin envelope created by the now stationary bank of impenetrable clouds above and the eerily transformed lake basin below.

The healthy, aquatic ecosystem had been displaced by a barren, lifeless pool of murky shadows and brown, decaying vegetation. Almost imperceptibly, the rotting rafts of weeds morphed into the imposing, unmistakable canopy of a bur oak, its waterlogged branches gnarled and denuded. Ominously, Sauter sensed that the treehouse was there, as well, lurking somewhere in the depths, somewhere in the web of tangled limbs. He searched it out eagerly, just as susceptible to its powerful, inexplicable allure whether dreaming or awake. The treehouse materialized surreptitiously beneath the refracted prism of the water, rising like a distorted mirage in the desert heat. Two small figures wavered in the shadowy recesses of the rough-hewn door, bloated, blue corpses silhouetted against the yawning black backdrop. Starched with rigor mortis, the lifeless bodies tumbled headlong into the abyss and wafted toward the silted lake floor in lazy, pendulous arcs. Tethered to the treehouse, the rigid specters jolted to a stop with neckstretching abruptness and recoiled like rabid dogs rudely surprised by the end of the leash.

That's when Sauter saw the familiar faces, still distorted and discolored by the throes of death, staring defiantly through the turbid water with engorged eyes and impish grins. Dancing in their constricted nooses like fiendish little marionettes, the disturbing, ghostly visages of Michael Koenigs and Jimmy Kelly demanded Sauter's company, calling him to their gloomy catacomb at the bottom of the lake. The suspended clouds fell upon Sauter with the relentless force of an avalanche, mercilessly thrusting him beneath the surface in a terrifying, suffocating plunge toward the grasping tentacles of the tiny apparitions . . .

The damp chill of anxious perspiration clung to Sauter's skin and he shivered, momentarily addled by the startled departure from his dream-turned-nightmare. He wondered if he hadn't awakened, if he had slumbered long enough for those two deepwater demons to grab hold, would he have perished in his sleep, the purported fate awaiting those who dream of free-falling but fail to rouse before impact? The lingering effects of the painkillers further muddied his senses, and it took a moment for the location of his unfamiliar accommodations and the depressing reality of his current circumstance to sink back in.

"Everything okay in there? That must have been some dream. You were whimpering and whining like a puppy." Corcoran stood just outside the bars at the foot of Sauter's cot, sounding genuinely concerned for his well-being. He opened his left eye, pleased to find the swelling somewhat subsided and his vision less restricted.

"Yeah, sure, I'm fine, thanks," he croaked, swallowing hard to alleviate the dry scratch in his throat. He ignored her comment about the dream. "Could you please tell me what time it is? I'm a little out of sorts right now."

Corcoran checked the watch attached to her belt loop by a metallic blue caribiner, "The time is three-forty p.m.," she paused, trying to discern just how "out of sorts" the inmate was, then added, "the afternoon of Thursday, September sixth," just to be sure.

Eight hours! Sauter marveled at the unprecedented length of his repose. An electric jolt of anxiety coursed through his body when he considered all of the time that he had lost, never to be recovered. He sat up quickly, too quickly, and had to wait for the white flashes and dizziness of the ensuing head rush to subside. A notoriously quick healer, Sauter already felt much stronger than he had during his interview with Kunick earlier in the day. His ribs were not quite as tender, his facial features felt less distorted, and the pulsating drum beat at the back of his brain had disappeared.

Without another word, Corcoran started to retreat down the sterile corridor.

"Wait a minute, Corky?" Sauter called out after her, immediately regretting the untoward familiarity. He needed allies right now, right here, and to hear Kunick tell it, all he had was a surfeit of enemies.

"Excuse me?" She spun around in the hallway, her displeasure evident in the severely kinked furry caterpillar bunched upon her brow.

"I'm sorry, I beg your pardon, *Officer Corcoran,*"

Sauter corrected himself, hoping his contrition sounded genuine and not contrived. She remained resolute, staring daggers and standing tensely, hands on hips, unwilling to tolerate the blatant show of disrespect. "I do apologize, sincerely," he tried again, then let it go. "I still haven't had my one phone call, so if you'd be so kind, I'd like to make that call now, please. I've already talked to Bobby, I mean Chief Kunick, about this." She looked put out as she started down the corridor, and again Sauter raised his voice to her retreating back. "Oh, and I'll be needing my wallet, too. The number is in there."

Corcoran turned, shook her head in disgust, and tapped the name tag pinned to her battened down breast, a final unspoken admonition before she skulked away. Sauter gave himself a sarcastic pat on the back in recognition of his exemplary people skills, imagining that the prospect of being given access to a phone at any time in the near future was now dubious, at best. He couldn't disguise his surprise and gratitude, therefore, when Corcoran returned only moments later to silently escort her ill-mannered charge to a small alcove less than ten paces down the hallway from his cell.

"Dial a nine, wait for the tone, then punch in your number. You've got ten minutes." Corcoran was curt with her instructions, then stepped aside, feigning some semblance of privacy.

"My wallet?" Sauter asked sheepishly. She held it by a worn, brown leather corner, as if it were contaminated, and thrust it out at arm's length with her gaze fixed straight ahead. "You don't care for me much, do you?" he ventured rhetorically.

"You've got nine and a half minutes," she deadpanned, releasing the wallet from her fingertips.

Sauter caught the falling billfold clumsily with both hands and ducked into the alcove, a small nook cut from the concrete with a wall-mounted touchtone phone and metal folding chair for amenities. He opened his wallet and fished out a plain white business card, soft and crinkled from years of undisturbed hibernation, and resolutely tapped out the raised black numerals printed in the upper right-hand corner. It was a telephone number he never expected to dial, and he had only kept the card as a talisman, its mere possession evoking an indescribable insouciance. Taken aback by the unexpected swell of nervous excitement seduced by each successive ring and flustered by the adolescent butterflies flitting in his stomach, Sauter was reduced to a stammering fool when his call was finally answered.

"Good afternoon, this is Dr. Amelia Devine," the distant voice, strong, yet feminine, mimicked the flowing purple prose of her letters, in Sauter's instant estimation, and proved equally enchanting.

"Hello? Can I help you?" She added hastily, jumping into the awkward void created by Sauter's delayed reaction.

"Um, ah, yes, hello, Amelia? I'm sorry, ah, I mean, I meant to say, Dr. Devine," he stuttered, then fell silent once again, as if he'd forgotten who had initiated the call.

"Yes, this is Dr. Devine," she reiterated, impatience creeping in. "How can I help you? And who, may I ask, is calling?"

Sauter collected his wits, chiding himself for the idiotic first impression.

"I beg your pardon, Dr. Devine, this is Detective Henry Sauter, calling from out in Wisconsin?" He recovered, the inflection in his tone implying *Do you remember me?*, even though she had just written him regarding Christopher Koenigs within the past week. The line fell quiet once again.

"Yes, yes, Henry, how nice to finally hear your voice," Devine eventually blurted with a contrived casualness. "I must say, you were the last person I expected when I answered the phone, but this is an opportune coincidence. I just sat down to write you a letter and . . ."

Convinced that Corcoran would be a stickler regarding the ten minute limit she generously placed on the call, Sauter interrupted, failing to grasp the implication that Devine had news pertaining to Koenigs, the linchpin of their limited correspondence.

"Listen, Amelia – I hope you don't mind if I call you Amelia – I have to talk fast because I don't have much time here. This is probably going to come as a shock to you, but we've had another incident out here, in Broadaxe, the hanging of another little boy. I know it's been a long time since Michael Koenigs was murdered, but it appears we've got a copycat on our hands. This little boy, the child killed last night, his name was Jimmy Kelly. He was the son of one of the four kids who were out in the woods the night Michael was killed, and somebody went to a lot of trouble to recreate that crime scene from twenty-two years ago, right down to the treehouse. You have such a vested interest in the case, the Koenigs case, I guess I just thought you should know."

"My God, Henry, you're not going to believe . . ." Devine tried to break in herself, but Sauter talked her down.

"This is the kicker, Amelia, the irony of the whole incomprehensible situation, I'm sitting in jail right now, as we speak, the prime suspect – hell, the only suspect, as far as I know – in Jimmy Kelly's murder. I had nothing to do with it, of course, but there seems . . ."

"Henry! I have something I need to tell you," Devine pleaded with obvious urgency, determined to have her say, "There's been a breakdown in the system out here, a miscommunication or a misunderstanding. You're not going to believe this, but somehow Christopher Koenigs is unaccounted for and we're still not sure what's happened."

"What the hell do you mean, unaccounted for? You're telling me you don't know where he is?" Sauter was livid, incredulous. "What the hell kind of an operation do you people run out there? How do you go about *losing* an inmate, any inmate, let alone one who cuts such a high profile? Do you have *any* idea where he might be, or how long he's been gone?"

"No, unfortunately, we don't have a clue where he is, and we're not entirely sure how long he's been missing," Devine admitted, fraught with embarrassment by the confession. "It seems most likely that he's been unaccounted for since last Friday, almost a week. It appears as if there was some snafu in the transfer because he never made it to the halfway house, the staff there assumed we still had him and, well, vice versa. We're short on staff to begin with, what with budget cuts and all, and there was just a skeleton crew working the Labor Day weekend, so apparently he just . . . walked away. My god, Henry, do you think it's possible that Christopher, I mean, do you think he . . ." she heard the static clatter through the receiver when Sauter dropped the phone, "Henry? Henry?"

Sauter exploded into the corridor, an unsavory occupant regurgitated violently from the alcove, and raced toward the front of the jail, away from his cell, away from a wide-eyed Corcoran, who quickly gave chase.

"Where's Bobby? goddammit, I need to talk to Bobby, right now!" he shouted adamantly, opening doors and peeking in windows as he rampaged down the hallway. Sitting at his desk on the other side of the large plexiglass window separating the secured cell block from the main office, Kunick heard the commotion just in time to see Corcoran launch herself through the air. She drove her shoulder into the small of Sauter's back and wrapped her arms around his midsection, hammering his busted body into the cold linoleum floor with agonizing force.

CHAPTER NINE

The pool of blood was small, no bigger than a silver dollar, but since it was his own, Sauter took a strong interest in its origin. He was sprawled on his stomach, arms extended like airplane wings, his left cheek flattened against the cool, clean linoleum and his collagen lips pursed like a guppy. The little crimson puddle formed just below his puckered mouth, as if he were an old, broken down jalopy leaking oil on the shoulder of the road. He sputtered and gasped, reclaiming the wind that had forcefully been expelled from his lungs by Corcoran's take down and the ensuing impact with the unyielding floor.

Kunick's pull-on boots, still corralling the crumpled cuffs of his khaki trousers, dropped into the narrow slit of sight afforded by Sauter's lumpy left eye. Corcoran knelt on his back and pushed his head down, hard, giving Sauter his mushed, fish-out-of-water expression. She drilled her knee into the slight depression between his shoulder blades and he spewed a fine red mist, which dusted and dulled the black patent leather that Kunick diligently maintained with a military shine.

"That can't be good," Kunick surmised, but Sauter was unsure if he was referring to the blood or the boots. Corcoran cracked his spine with one more agonizing jab of her bony kneecap, and Sauter suddenly felt humiliated, like a shot-riddled mallard clenched in the jaws of a retriever at the adoring foot of its master.

"Goddamit Corky, would you ease up, that's no way to treat a guest! A strong, healthy woman like yourself should know better than to pick on the weak and defenseless," Kunick scolded instead of stroked, yet the admonition carried an undeniable undercurrent of mirth and tweaked Sauter's masculine pride. "Some folks might even construe that as police brutality, try and turn the tables, sic their lawyers on us, but you wouldn't do that, now would you, Sauter?"

Sauter supposed that Kunick wasn't really expecting a response and was certain that he wouldn't appreciate the one he had in mind. Corcoran obeyed her master's commands and released her captured prey, pushing heavily off of Sauter's head and lower back as she slowly leveraged herself to her feet. He remained prostrate, allowing his brain time to assess the barrage of injury reports being relayed through his system. Upon reflection, he realized the entire brouhaha could have been avoided if he had only handled Devine's shocking news with the proper constraint and decorum, but he conveniently blamed his weakened constitution for his indiscretion.

Kunick lowered himself to one knee and wiped the microscopic droplets of blood from one boot, repositioned himself, cleaned the other, and tossed the soiled white handkerchief into a nearby trash can with a disgusted grimace. Cautiously, Sauter rolled over and rocked to his seat, leaning his back against the wall and drawing his bent legs close to his chest.

"Needless to say, Sauter, I'm sincerely hoping you've got a damn good reason for disturbing the peace and quiet of my jail," Kunick condescended, remaining on a knee so he could address Sauter at eye level. Corcoran posed behind him, arms akimbo, but no doubt ready to pounce at the slightest provocation. "So, why all the excitement?" he pondered, then intuitively answered his own question, "Let me guess. You received some information, in your phone call, exonerating you of any culpability in Jimmy Kelly's death, information so critical to the case that you were willing to risk the wrath of Corky here."

Already regretting his rash response to Devine's incomprehensible revelation, Sauter's remorse was heightened by the realization that he had unceremoniously left her hanging on the line. There would be time to apologize for his impropriety later, he assured himself, certain that she would understand and titillated by the prospect of speaking with her once again. Cautiously, he alternated ulterior glances between Kunick and Corcoran.

"Give us a minute, would you, Corky?" Kunick correctly interpreted Sauter's unspoken wish for a private audience, but the overprotective officer balked at the chief's request. Flattered rather than insulted by her unaccustomed insolence, Kunick waited patiently, silently, until an unwilling Corcoran hesitantly exited the hallway. He immediately gave Sauter the nod to proceed.

"I have a connection out east, Bobby, inside the mental health facility where Christopher Koenigs has been incarcerated for the past twelve years, up until his parole last week." Sauter lit the fuse on the bombshell he was about to drop. "This may be hard to digest, but there was some kind of a mix-up – a royal fuck-up, really – when he was being transferred to a halfway house last Friday. Somehow, Koenigs got lost in the shuffle and his whereabouts are still unknown."

"So what are you trying to tell me, Sauter?" Kunick asked with admirable restraint considering the incendiary news.

"What the hell do you mean, what am I trying to tell you, what the hell do you think I'm trying to tell you?" Sauter gasped, infuriated by Kunick's calculated indifference. "Christopher Koenig's is gone, he's vanished!"

"And . . ." Kunick goaded.

"And within a week another little boy is murdered, here in Broadaxe, hung from the same oak where his little brother, Michael, was found dead. I told you, Bobby, I had nothing whatsoever to do with Jimmy Kelly's death, and, same as you, I've been scratching my head trying to come up with a list of logical suspects."

"Correct me if I'm wrong, Sauter, but are you implying that there's some kind of link between Christopher Koenigs's release and the killing of Jimmy Kelly?" Kunick queried in a tone dripping with exaggerated incredulity. "The same Christopher Koenigs who you defended so adamantly – at the expense of your job and your credibility, I might add – as a misunderstood innocent unjustly accused and convicted of his brother's murder?"

The implications of such an admission slammed into Sauter's psyche with a devastating mental impact equal to the physical blow delivered earlier by the baseball bat. He was staggered by the casual deterioration of such long-held beliefs and foundered like an aged edifice perched precariously atop a crumbling, poorly constructed foundation. It seemed frighteningly unfathomable and downright unconscionable that he could have been so wrong, for so long. He felt naked, exposed, and his body reflexively retracted into a protective fetal ball.

"I just thought you should know, Bobby, that's all," Sauter demurred, backtracking from his impulsive rush to judgment. "I'm not trying to imply anything, but the circumstances of Jimmy Kelly's death alone provide the connection to the Koenigs case. That would be true even if Christopher was still locked up, but since he's not, since he's been missing for nearly a week . . . well, that just seems like one hell of a coincidence, wouldn't you say? We need to locate Christopher Koenigs, that's imperative."

Kunick's stiffened joints popped in protest as he labored to his feet. He extended a hand to Sauter, who reluctantly accepted the offered assistance after Kunick rebuffed his initial refusal. Sauter inhaled deeply, crinkling his nose and shaking his head like a fighter sniffing smelling salts as bleach fumes from the recently scrubbed floor assaulted his sinuses. The hallway was wide enough to accommodate four people, shoulder to shoulder, but Kunick pressed in and sandwiched Sauter uncomfortably against the wall.

"*We* need to locate Koenigs," Kunick repeated sardonically, his warm, onion-tinged breath saturated with spittle. Sauter didn't bother to wipe the saliva from his smoldering cheeks. He knew the shower would resume when Kunick continued his close talk. "That's mighty kind of you, mighty kind, but at the risk of sounding immodest, I'm sure our little department here is more than capable of conducting this investigation without your help. Besides, you're really in no position . . ."

"What is my position exactly?" Sauter butted in, forcing his way past Kunick into the center of the corridor. "Am I being charged with anything, Bobby? I'd like to know, now. Either way, I think it's time to contact my attorney."

Kunick suspected Sauter was bluffing about the lawyer, just like he lied about wanting to see a doctor, but he also knew that he couldn't hold him any longer without just cause. He had no intention of charging Sauter with Jimmy Kelly's murder, and he wasn't surprised that the tactical threat failed to shake loose any helpful information. His instincts were conflicted, at once telling him that Sauter did not kill the boy, that murder wasn't part of his moral make-up, but at the same time pestering him with the nagging reality that, on some intangible level, his old friend was undeniably involved.

"I'm letting you go, Sauter, but I'm warning you, for your sake and mine, get the hell out of Broadaxe," Kunick demanded, adding the caveat, "but don't go too far. You're not out of the woods on this yet, not by a long shot, so rest assured that we'll be having another chat, real soon."

"What about Christopher Koenigs?" Sauter asked. "Please tell me you're going to follow up on that, Bobby."

Kunick took umbrage at the patronizing remark, "You're goddam right I'm going to check into that," he yelped. "It's going to be my first order of business, as a matter of fact. Remember, Sauter, I didn't buy into your whole cockamamie conspiracy theory. Hell, nobody did. I thought Christopher Koenigs killed his brother Michael, plain and simple, and I still believe that to this day. And I'll tell you another thing, if I had known last night what you just told me, that Christopher Koenig had escaped a week ago, I would have had a reason to go visit that meadow myself. A *reason*, Sauter, something you still haven't been able to supply to explain *your* presence there, with a dead child in your arms."

Sauter considered throwing caution to the wind, toyed with the idea of telling Kunick about the unrelenting, all-too-real inner voice that called him back to the base of the bur oak, dared him to find another deceased boy dangling beneath the treehouse, but he was well aware that his mental stability was already a point of contention. Kunick had, after all, derided his earlier attempt at an explanation as "mystical mumbo-jumbo." Sauter breathed a sigh of relief when he realized that he was apparently just emphasizing the point and wasn't actually anticipating a reply.

"Once a murderer, always a murderer. That's the way I look at it," Kunick continued, "so you can bet your sweet bippy I'm going to hunt down Christopher Koenigs. I'm guessing I won't have to go far to find him, either, because by the looks of things, our homicidal hometown boy has returned to Broadaxe. His escape, the killing of Jimmy Kelly, it's just *too* coincidental to be merely coincidence."

The muted peal of distant church bells chimed five

times, and Sauter noticed that a clock, centered between the transom of a door and an illuminated red exit sign, lagged nearly ten minutes behind. He tried to imagine where Christopher Koenigs might be, and, for admittedly selfish reasons, hoped he was nowhere near Broadaxe. The presumption that Koenigs had returned, had in fact murdered Jimmy Kelly, was in such discord with Sauter's normally infallible intuition – and the reputation he had staked upon it – that he found the possibility too painful to contemplate.

"What about my four pals, good old Richard and Max, Tim and Jackson? Did you get any satisfaction out of those guys? Could they explain how they wound up out in that meadow, pounding the crap out of yours truly?" Sauter asked, and Kunick answered with a somber shake of the head. "Do you still have the two who rearranged my face locked up?"

"Nope, I let Max and Jackson go. If you recall, you said you were unwilling to press charges, so I had no reason to hold them," Kunick explained. "I told them the same thing I'm telling you, stay the hell out of my way. I'm running this investigation, and I won't tolerate hooligans who take the law into their own hands. There's already a lynch mob mentality brewing in this town and they're no doubt fashioning a noose for your neck. Once word leaks out that Christopher Koenigs is on the loose, which it undoubtedly will, there's no telling what would happen if they got their hands on him before I did."

"Where exactly do you plan to look for Christopher Koenigs? I mean, where in the hell would you even start?" Sauter queried, hoping his relationship with Devine, his perennial umbilical cord to Koenigs, would provide an advantage in his own search.

"That's none of your concern, Sauter, but here's a suggestion I'm sure you'll ignore." Kunick softened his tone and smiled compassionately, "Lay low, keep your nose clean, give your body some time to heal. There's nothing left for you here in Broadaxe but trouble. For chrissakes, even a numbskull like yourself should have had that figured out long ago."

"Maybe I'll head back out to the lake, pitch some muskie plugs for a few days," Sauter contrived, hoping to get one more rise out of Kunick, who knew better.

"That would be considered a low blow, you son of a bitch, what with me stuck here with a murder that needs solving," Kunick snorted, "if only it were true. I know you, detective, I know you're not going to take my advice, I know you're going to start looking for Christopher Koenigs as soon as you walk out the door." He grimaced, the face of a man with a bad taste in his mouth. "I'll tell you what, if you find him before I do, you'll let me know immediately, and I'll extend the same courtesy to you, for old time's sake, deal?"

Those were old times indeed, Sauter reminisced, those halcyon days when he and Kunick had worked and fished together, catching small-time, backwoods criminals one day and muskie the next. It had been an all too brief interlude, so temporary, so fleeting, that Sauter sometimes found himself questioning whether it was a time of his life reflected in his memories, or in his dreams. In the end, it didn't really matter, for Sauter had relegated those memories, those dreams of a distant lifetime to a seldom visited corner of his consciousness.

"If I'm actually free to go, is there any chance I can get a ride out to my Bronco? I'm guessing it's still parked where I left it this morning, out by the welcome sign east of town?" Sauter asked evenly, blatantly ignoring his forgotten friend's plea for cooperation.

"Corky!" Kunick shouted impatiently, resisting the overwhelming urge to throttle Sauter himself.

*   *   *

The electric crackle of static poured from the police radio at a deafening pitch, threatening to strike up the marching band that had mercifully quit parading through Sauter's slowly healing head. He was able to pry open the yellowish-purple lid of his right eye, but it twitched sporadically and welled with tears, making it nearly as useless as when it was swollen shut. His broken ribs were still tender to the touch and the passages of his busted nose were caked with coagulated blood, but all things considered, Sauter felt remarkably well for a man supposedly on the brink of being beaten to death.

Corcoran captained her police cruiser with the dawdling

deliberation of a little old lady driving to Sunday morning mass. She clutched the steering wheel at the prescribed "ten and two" position and maintained her speed at a modest two miles below the thirty-five per hour limit. Her eyes were narrow slits, fixed responsibly on the road ahead, her countenance stern, and a slight spasm rippled across her cheek as she pensively clenched her teeth.

"Mind if I turn this down?" Sauter talked above the annoying fuzz as he tentatively reached for the squawking black box mounted beneath the dashboard. Without taking her eyes off the road, Corcoran unfurled a stinging backhand slap to his wrist, then graciously lowered the volume herself. "Thanks, I guess," he allowed, rubbing the pink finger imprints rising on his flesh. "If you don't mind my asking, *Officer Corcoran*, how come you've taken such an apparent disliking to me? We don't even know each other, after all."

The late-afternoon sun was still well above the treetops and the windshield magnified its warmth, raising the temperature inside the vehicle incrementally, like an oven set to preheat. Tiny beads of perspiration tickled Sauter's brow and the small of his back, but he resisted the urge to crack his window. Miserably off on the wrong foot, he nonetheless nurtured a dying hope that he might still win Corcoran over, cultivate a much needed ally in a town full of enemies. That wasn't going to happen if he continually drew her ire – she was visibly upset when he climbed into the front passenger seat rather than the back of the police cruiser as she requested – so he kept the window shut despite his discomfort. Corcoran never wavered, never betrayed the slightest hint that she had any intention of conversing, but Sauter was persistent.

"Is it because I called you Corky? Is that it?" he asked naïvely. "I meant no disrespect and I apologized once already, but if it helps, I have no problem saying I'm sorry again. I'm sorry." He paused, but there was still no reaction from his cheerless chauffeur, "Give a guy a break, I was understandably a little out of whack, a baseball bat will do that to you, and I must have heard Chief Kunick calling you . . ."

"You may not know me, Sauter, but I know you." The vehicle slowed noticeably as Corcoran turned to Sauter with unmitigated contempt. "I'm a big girl, detective, I know how the world works. I've had to put up with plenty of macho ya-hoos ever since I donned the uniform, cops no different than yourself. Like I said, I'm a big girl, I can handle the condescen-sion and the disrespect – when it's directed specifically at me. What I can't tolerate is a cop who shows no respect for the badge, no respect for his honor bound duty to protect the public and uphold the law."

"Can we back up a second, please? Macho yahoo? Just where in the hell did that come from?" Sauter was on the de-fensive, though he couldn't help but chuckle at the characteri-zation. "You may *think* you know me, although I admittedly don't know how since we only met this morning, but it's obvi-ous you don't, not in the least. No respect for the badge? No respect for my duty to protect and serve? I'd take offense to that, Corcoran, I truly would, if it wasn't such a load of bull-shit!"

Corcoran flipped on her blinker and coasted to a con-trolled stop on the gravel shoulder of the highway, apparently unable to converse and drive at the same time. A cloud of dust kicked up by the rotating wheels mushroomed above the hood, and beams of sunlight were delineated by the fine particles drifting lazily down to the ground.

"Everyone has a history, detective . . ." she began, her hands still gripping the wheel of the parked vehicle and her eyes now diverted.

"You can call me Sauter, everyone else does." He tried to bring a personal touch to the discourse.

"As I was saying, everyone has a history, detective," she repeated, preferring to maintain a professional distance, "and that history, good or bad, has a habit of following you around, like it or not. I know your history, that's how I know you. It's certainly no secret around here, and what I know, I don't like."

"And just what do you know, pray tell." Sauter had a pretty good idea what was coming, but he was curious to know how much fiction had padded the facts. Corcoran came pre-pared.

"Your trouble here in Broadaxe started shortly after you

joined the force and can be traced directly to a fratricidal incident involving two local children, date of 20 September, 1985." Corcoran delivered the biography in her typical terse, clipped cadence, "A young cop, overwhelmed by the stress and shock of the senseless murder, your mental stability quickly came into question as you became singularly obsessed with the case of Christopher and Michael Koenigs. That obsession manifested itself in the verbal harassment, physical intimidation, and slander of four young boys who testified that Christopher Koenigs did, in fact, intentionally kill his younger brother." She waited a beat, then swiveled her head toward Sauter, "Heard enough?"

"No please, do go on, this is fascinating," he implored.

Corcoran assessed Sauter quizzically, then continued per his request, "The harassment culminated with a physical confrontation between yourself and one Richard "Dickey" Mann, one of the aforementioned young boys present when Michael Koenigs was hung by his brother. Enraged and unstable, you beat the young boy until he was unconscious, nearly to death, save for the intervention of local citizens who witnessed the attack. You were brought up on charges, serious charges of misconduct and gross negligence, but, to put it bluntly, Chief Kunick stepped in and saved your ass, brokering a deal wherein the charges were dropped and you were kicked upstairs to a position with the county. Along with Richard Mann, the other children you harassed, all still residents of Broadaxe, were one Max Ferguson, one Timothy Schumacher, and one Jackson Kelly, the latter being the father of Jimmy Kelly, the young boy found hung early this morning. You, of course, were discovered holding the dead child in your arms. So, you see detective, I do know you, so you'll have to excuse me if I'm not one of your biggest fans."

There was no denying it, the young officer had been diligent in her research, but as Sauter suspected, some of the facts had been twisted and distorted with the passage of time. The terrible thrashing he supposedly doled out to Richard Mann actually amounted to no more than a hard pinch of his shoulders, a rough shakedown and a subsequent slam into his school locker. It was extremely poor judgment on his part, especially in light of his tenuous ties to an already distrusting community, and Sauter had immediately regretted his unacceptable lapse in self-control. It was the proverbial last straw and the charges were trumped up and overstated, designed to force Kunick's hand and rid Broadaxe of the disruptive thorn in its side.

"Can you take me to my Bronco now, Corky? Unlike some folks, I don't have time to sit around and chat," Sauter requested, abandoning his ill-fated attempt at making a new friend. He didn't care if she thought he was nuts, she was just one more name on the long list of people who held him in that regard. "Things aren't always what they seem on the surface, Corkster." Feeling oddly mischievous, he couldn't resist one more tweak. "Take yourself for instance, if I hadn't sensed the unbridled, animalistic attraction you have toward me, judging by your looks, I would have pegged you as . . . how can I put it tactfully? One who likes the ladies."

"Are you calling me a lesbian?"

"Hey, don't make it sound so bad," Sauter pimped, "I consider myself one – I love all the same things, Corky."

"It's Officer Corcoran," she growled, simultaneously stomping on the gas and shifting the transmission into drive, spraying gravel as the police cruiser fishtailed on the shoulder. The front tires bit into the pavement, chirping loudly, and a grim-faced Corcoran rocketed down the highway, now disregarding the speed limit in her rush to be rid of her aggravating, uncouth passenger.

Considering Kunick's dire warnings, Sauter feared that his Bronco may have turned into a convenient target for an unruly mob thirsting for instant retribution. He was relieved to find it unscathed, no slashed tires, no shattered windows, just the same array of familiar dents and deteriorating metal. Corcoran would have preferred to get Sauter out of her sight as soon as possible, but she stymied his equally eager bid for a quick escape from the police cruiser, punching down the automatic lock as he reached to open his door.

"Just can't get enough of me, can you?" he teased, forming his inflated lips into what he considered to be a flirtatious smile.

"Believe me, detective, I've had more than my fill of

you," she retorted, surprising Sauter with her own spontaneous grin. The smile, warm and natural, obliterated her accustomed severity of expression, softening her features and cratering her cheeks with deep, delicious dimples. It faded fast, "Chief Kunick wanted me to pass on this message, and I quote, 'Make sure that stubborn son of a bitch gets it through his thick skull that I want him out of Broadaxe.' Understood? There's really no ambiguity there, am I correct, detective?"

"You are correct, my dear, message received loud and clear," Sauter acknowledged with an emphatic salute, "Now, let me out of this vehicle, Officer Corky, before we do something that we'll both regret." He offered the same cheesy smirk, which collapsed into an affected pout when Corcoran, scowling, hastily unlocked his door.

"Get out, please!" She practically begged, and Sauter started to oblige before pausing part way out the door, one foot on the ground and one foot on the floorboard.

"One more thing, Corcoran, if you'll indulge me," he requested, continuing upon receipt of her impatient nod, "When you were out in the meadow last night, where Jimmy Kelly died, any chance that you happened to notice all the lupines?"

"Lupines?"

"Yeah, lupines, the plants with the long, flowery spikes? The petals can also be white or rose-colored, but these were a rich, exquisite purple. They're really quite beautiful, and the meadow was rife with them. Do you know what I'm talking about?"

"It was pretty dark back there this morning, detective, and I was a little preoccupied, if you know what I mean." Corcoran came off a bit defensive, like an ill-prepared pupil making excuses for not doing her homework. "Being a cop, I pride myself on my powers of observation, but I have to admit that no, I didn't notice any purple flowers. What's your point? Why do you ask?"

"Oh, no reason, really, it's just that they're pretty, not unlike yourself . . . when you smile," Sauter prevaricated, bringing an embarrassed blush to Corcoran's flustered face. In truth, he had completely forgotten about the riot of lupines carpeting the meadow until just now, and he was completely baffled by the flowers' sudden, inexplicable presence. The growing season for lupines had long since passed, yet even more perplexing, the flowers bloomed to full maturity in less than a day, like the fabled beanstalk bursting skyward overnight from magic seeds.

Sauter finally disembarked and wobbled cautiously toward his Bronco, making a mental inventory of the injuries that cried out with every arduous step. Reveling in the blissful solitude that had displaced the haunting voice which commandeered his thoughts throughout the previous day, he was startled when Corcoran called out, summoning him by name for the first time.

"Sauter? Be careful, okay? Don't do anything stupid. It's really not safe for you around here right now, and needless to say, you're obviously in no shape to defend yourself." She leaned across the center console between the front seats and spoke through the open passenger window. Sauter was ambushed by her genuine sincerity and concern, which resurrected the hope for an alliance he had only just given up for dead.

Pulling out onto the highway, he blew Corcoran an embellished kiss and turned his Bronco east, away from Broadaxe, as commanded. Flecks of yellow, orange, and red scintillated like colorful stars set within the green heavens of the leafy umbrella shading the road, pretty precursors of the impending seasonal shift. *Acer saccharum.* Sauter dutifully identified the sugar maple exhibiting the early autumn palette, a visual treat as sweet as the syrup that wept from the trees each spring. He bid a silent adieu to Corcoran as he rounded a southerly curve and watched her parked police cruiser disappear from the rearview mirror.

The deserted woods road was so overgrown with brush that it was barely discernible from the highway, but Sauter recalled its location, and, more importantly, he knew exactly where it went. It backtracked to the southwest, back to Broadaxe, so he plunged his Bronco into the camouflaging vegetation an defiantly trundled over the uneven terrain, as yet unwilling to leave his boyhood home behind.

The happy hour crowd at Tingle's harbored a decidedly

unhappy edge. The juke box was silent, as were the dismal diorama of drinkers swilling their cathartic elixirs in catatonic contemplation. The feeble light of an antiquated beer sign glowed dimly in the stagnant haze of second-hand smoke, and the gloomy darkness accentuated the prevailing mood.

Sauter strode into the funereal tavern with the impertinence of a mistress making an appearance at a paramour's wake. Migrating to the lone opening at the corner of the bar, he slid back the unoccupied stool and leaned listlessly on the rail. The adjoining seats were abandoned immediately, as if Sauter's infamy were contagious. The back bar was empty, Tingle having just ducked into the cooler to fetch a bucket of ice, and Sauter's skin prickled with the peripheral awareness that he was the focus of a collective, withering stare.

"Hey asshole, that seat is taken!" advised one of the two beefy, would-be bouncers who had stepped surreptitiously to his rear. Of course it was he who was being addressed, but Sauter refused to assume the mantle of "asshole" by answering to it, so he assiduously ignored the overture. "Do you hear me, buddy? I'm talking to you." A nudge in the small of his back for added emphasis caused Sauter to stiffen against a potential escalation in the verbal assault. "I'll tell you just one more time, that seat is taken."

Reflected unwittingly in the balustrade of booze bottles behind the bar, Sauter eyed the mirrored, scowling faces of his two antagonists, a pair of disembodied heads floating in the shadows beyond his shoulders. One of the Ziegelbauer boys was doing the talking and poking, although Sauter couldn't be certain which member of the prolific, Neanderthal clan of reprobates and poachers was currently at his back. They were a passel of hirsute, hard-headed scofflaws cultivated from the shallow end of the gene pool, destined to rebel against the monotony of their servile existence. Sauter also recognized the austere visage of Tucker Donnelly, the iconic high school wrestling coach, looking somewhat less than enthused with the role of barroom enforcer.

"I'll be more than happy to move when whoever it was that was sitting here returns," Sauter offered to the mirror images, hoping to defuse the potentially volatile situation, "Hell,

I'll even buy him a drink!"

"Maybe you don't understand, but this seat is taken, reserved, for somebody who's *welcome* in this bar, somebody who's a regular," the Neanderthal snarled. "This is where Jackson Kelly sits whenever he stops in for a drink, and I don't want him to have to see that you've taken his place if he comes by. Now get the hell out of there, you piece a shit."

"I think it's safe to say your friend is a little too preoccupied at present, wouldn't you agree?" Sauter didn't intend to offend, but he managed to all the same.

"Why you son of a bitch . . ." the Neanderthal grunted, struggling unsuccessfully to free himself from Tucker Donnelly's smothering bear hug.

"Goddammit, Ziggy, how many times do I have to tell you that I won't abide any rough stuff in my joint?" Tingle shouted as he emerged from the cooler and dumped a brimming bucket of ice into a stainless steel sink beneath the bar. The generic nickname for the Neanderthal failed to help Sauter figure out which Ziegelbauer he was confronted with, and he supposed it didn't really matter. "Thanks, Tuck," Tingle nodded at Donnelly, who eased his squeeze and escorted the Neanderthal to a seat at the far end of the bar. Belatedly, it dawned on Sauter that averting a confrontation, rather than fomenting one, was Donnelly's intent all along. "Somebody play the juke box, for chrissakes. It's like a goddam morgue in here." Tingle visibly cringed at his unfortunate comparison, but he hoped the music would afford some semblance of privacy for his unavoidable chat with Sauter.

A pair of rotund women, identically dressed in insulated flannel jackets and stiff bluejeans stuffed into unlaced pack boots, snatched the handful of bills Tingle waved in his hand and waddled off to plug in some tunes. Sauter recognized their first selection as an old Mason Proffitt number, and wondered if the choice was an innocent coincidence or the product of a warped sense of humor.

"Two hangmen hangin' from a tree, and that don't bother me . . ." Sauter assumed Tingle was going to eject the ill-timed number, but the old man merely shrugged his sloping shoulders and cranked the volume. He worked his way around

the bar, refreshing drinks and twisting the tops off longneck bottles of beer, never pausing to deliver one of his trademark limericks or to indulge in his renowned repartee.

"This one's on me." He presented Sauter with an ice-cold bottle of Budweiser, his rheumy eyes wrought with a confused, consuming sorrow. "I must say I'm surprised to see you, Sauter. Word around town was that those boys really knocked the snot out of you, damn near lined you up for a date with a dirt bath, if you catch my meaning. You look like you've been chewed up and spit out, no denying that, like you were a mobile home and those fellas were the tornado, like you were a log and they were the wood chipper, like . . ."

"Okay, Tingle, enough already, I get your point, I look like shit," Sauter belched the concession after greedily downing half the amber refreshment in a single gulp.

"That's only the half of it." Tingle cast a conspiratorial glance around the tavern, then returned to Sauter with a concerned countenance. "Rumor has it that you killed Jimmy Kelly, or at least that you were being held down at the jail as a suspect. I tell you what, I didn't believe it, not for a second, and it seems as though Bobby came to his senses, as well, otherwise you wouldn't be sitting here right now, am I correct?"

Doubting that anything had ever tasted so delicious, Sauter drained the bottom half of the sweating beer bottle. Without asking, Tingle popped the top on another and deliberately pushed away the crumpled wad of cash Sauter offered in payment.

"Thanks, Tingle." Sauter acknowledged the complimentary drinks and unsolicited show of support. He swallowed another healthy swig, surprised at how quickly the beer buzz began to tickle his subverted senses. "You know, I don't think Bobby ever seriously entertained the idea that I had anything to do with that boy's death. He locked me up because, well, circumstances didn't leave him much choice. Besides, he told me flat out that he did it for my own protection."

"I'm not going to sugarcoat it, Sauter, there most definitely are some fellas around here who would be more than happy to pick up pounding your ass where Max and Jackson left off," Tingle warned, tilting his head toward the Neanderthal to cite an example. "A smart man, a cautious man, would have gotten out of this unforgiving town when given the chance, but that's one of the things I always admired about you, Sauter. You were never one to run scared. You've got balls as big as church bells, I'll tell you what."

"There's no reason for me to run. Actually, I'd be crazy if I did. I'll tell you the same thing I told Bobby, and I'll swear it on my old man's grave." Sauter spoke louder, trying to be heard above the din of the pulsating music. "I did not kill Jimmy Kelly, but believe me, I'm going to find out who did." He lowered his voice. "That's where I was hoping you could be of some assistance, Tingle, since nothing happens around here that you don't know about. So tell me, what have you heard?"

Tingle raised a wait-one-minute finger and made the rounds behind the bar, distractedly tending to the line-up of locals who vociferously objected to Sauter's presence. In the silence between songs, Sauter smiled when he heard Tingle gruffly suggest that anyone uncomfortable with the company in his tavern should feel free to find someplace else to drink. No one accepted the offer. The juke box kicked back in – Carl Perkins's pre-Elvis version of *Hound Dog* – and the pair of portly disc jockeys stumbled about in their heavy boots, swiveling their hips in a drunken, rhythmless dance. The music modulated the melancholy, aided and abetted by the alcohol, and the gyrating women grinned and giggled. Heads pivoted toward the frivolity, drawing the heat of vengeful stares away from Sauter for the first time since he had walked in the door.

By the time Tingle returned, he had emptied the second bottle of beer. Although his unsated thirst begged otherwise, he prudently declined the offer of a third, figuring that was all it would take to turn the corner from tipsy to intoxicated.

"Anything? You heard anything at all that I should know about?" Sauter reminded Tingle where the conversation had left off, curious if the most recent news about Christopher Koenigs could possibly travel that fast.

"Hell, it only just happened last night, so I've only heard what I've already told you, about you getting beat up and arrested," Tingle deferred. "You know, the question everybody wants answered is, if you didn't kill Jimmy or have something to do with it, how is it you knew where to look for him when nobody else had a clue?"

"Give me some credit, Tingle, I am a detective, after all." Sauter, interested only in answers, avoided the question, "If that's all you've got for me, I suppose it's best if I do make myself scarce before I wear out my welcome around here." He stood as he delivered the sarcastic aside.

"Well, there are a couple of things you might be interested in," Tingle murmured with his back turned to the rest of the bar. He wanted to help his old friend, but not at the risk of alienating his paying customers. "This may or may not be important, that's for you to decide, but some folks who were out helping with the search, they told me about one strange incident. They said they were way back in the woods, out behind Jackson Kelly's place, and all of a sudden out of nowhere who comes tumbling into their search line, from the opposite direction, all disheveled and acting suspicious? – that's the way they put it – well, none other than your pal Richard Mann. Nobody had been able to get a hold of him all night, then bingo, he just appears. They just thought it was mighty odd, the way he was acting and what not, that's all."

"That's it?" Sauter wasn't sure what to make of it, either, imagining that it wouldn't take much for good old Dickey to lose his bearings in a midnight forest.

"One more thing," Tingle confided, "kind of a strange deal, as well. The last couple of days here, before his boy was killed, Jackson was constantly complaining about voices in his head, said his head was always humming, or whistling, something like that, and he was real paranoid-like, said it felt like somebody was spying on him. I felt bad for the guy. He was afraid he was losing his mind."

"Did he happen to mention what the voices in his head were saying?" Sauter probed with a curiosity piqued by his own experience, but he didn't feel the need to share the fact that his own mind had been infiltrated, as well.

"Yep, he said the voice just kept repeating his name, over and over, Jackson, Jackson, Jackson. He's a pretty hard-hitter to begin with, but he was drinking more than usual, said he was trying to drown it all out." Tingle's eyes widened with alarm. "Speak of the devil himself," the old-timer grunted, springing across the bar with the agility of a gymnast. He deftly positioned himself between Sauter and an obviously agitated Jackson Kelly, who lunged forward with menacing intent. Tucker Donnelly rushed into the breach, holding Jackson back and fervently motioning Sauter toward the door with his head.

"I'm truly sorry for your loss," Sauter offered as he sidestepped toward the exit, but the sincerity of his sympathy fell upon deaf ears.

"I'm sorry I didn't kill you when I had the chance," Jackson vituperated, his face red and contorted with spasms of undiluted hatred as Sauter slowly backed out the door.

Standing beneath the gloaming sky, expelling the stale, cancerous smog of the tavern and inhaling the rich, redolent air, Sauter weakened in mind and body, finally succumbing to the importunate emotional strain and physical duress of the past forty-eight hours. He closed his eyes and tried to conjure up enough energy to carry him home, certain that he would have no trouble capturing the unburdened sleep that so often eluded him. The inner mumblings of the tavern belched loudly upon his backside, then once again quieted as the door he had just exited opened and closed. Fearing yet another assault on a body already beaten nearly to the breaking point, Sauter's tired muscles tensed reflexively beneath a tingling flow of electric warmth. He kept his eyes closed and his back turned, hedging his bets against a coward's attack from the rear. A pair of intoxicated feet danced an indecisive shuffle before stumbling away down the gravel shoulder of the road.

Grateful for the reprieve, Sauter knew he needed to disappear before the next drunk, in all probability fueled with liquid courage and itching for revenge, joined him in the waning light. Still, he remained transfixed in his precarious position, rendered immobile by the unsettling realization that he was, in fact, not yet alone. He gathered a deep breath and tasted the acrid blend of booze and cigarettes churning through his nostrils. Fighting the tickle of trepidation, he slowly opened his lumpy lips and gasped at the ghastly visage hunched pitifully before him.

"You could've saved my boy, mister, but you're just as

guilty of killin' my Jimmy as the rest of 'em," the pathetic creature rasped, boring into Sauter with a pained, bloodshot glare. "You were onto 'em all along, but you lost your nerve and let 'em run you out of town, and now my boy's dead."

Could this really be her? Sauter wondered, recalling a younger Dorothy Kelly, untainted by time and tarnish. He pictured her pretty, fresh face, radiant smile, flowing hair and healthy figure, astonished that this wan, wasted woman could possibly be the same person. Awash in the alcoholic stench that oozed pestiferously from her pores, he understood the origins of the alarming transformation. She clutched the collar of a threadbare, floral-patterned housecoat tightly around the loose turkey-flesh of her scrawny neck. Opaque, white nodes of bone and bulging blue veins pressed against the taut skin of her clenched fist. Stringy, dirty strands of beige hair framed a face void of color, save for the dark black circles rimming her watery, lifeless eyes, and the rash of red surrounding her dripping nostrils. Her eyebrows and eyelashes had fallen out and her lips were indistinguishable from the leathery skin stretched tightly over severe features, lending her the eerie appearance of an animated cadaver.

Sauter tried to speak, wanted desperately to ask her to explain what she meant. How could he have saved her child? Why was he responsible for his death? What did she mean when she said he was "onto 'em all along?" He tried to speak, but there were no words, only an ineffectual croak, and he watched in frustration as she backpeddled haltingly across the road.

"The blood of my boy is on your hands, mister, and mark my words, the blood of more children will be spilt here in Broadaxe before all is said and done, blood that will further stain the hands of the sinners," she stood on the far side of the road and raised her withered, claw-like hand, her voice rising in an anguished tremolo. "And I will dash them one against another, even the fathers and sons together, saith the Lord: I will not pity, nor spare, nor have mercy, but destroy them." The haunting vision backed down into the roadside ditch and disappeared among the trees, leaving Sauter shaken, and hastening his long overdue retreat.

CHAPTER TEN

Fussing over a bouquet of fresh flowers, absent-mindedly rearranging the jumble of daisies and black-eyed susans soaking in her favorite vase, a fluted, cut-glass antiquity handed down from her grandmother, Margaret steadfastly averted her attention from the dour line-up of pouting faces perched upon her living room couch. Tim had surprised Margaret with the spray of simple, inexpensive flowers – also her favorites – when he returned from the florist after selecting a suitable arrangement for little, red-headed Jimmy Kelly's funeral. Peeking through the veil of white and golden petals, she choked back the bitter blend of sadness and anger evoked by the premature dissolution of childhood innocence.

The four forlorn figures were compressed at one end of the sofa, melded together in the hurt and confusion of youthful mourning, unprepared for the finality of death and the loss of a friend. There was also apprehension and uncertainty, but that had nothing to do with the vagaries of mortality. The boys had been billeted for an inquisition, and their limited experience had taught them that the exercise typically had one aim – the assignment of blame.

Nicholas, only 11 years old, already reminded Margaret of his sensitive, protective father, her old friend Max, back when they had first met in high school. Squashed against the arm of the couch, he was nearly as wide as the other three boys combined. His trenchant blue eyes dangled like ornaments from the cascade of black hair tumbling down his forehead, and the faint fuzz of a prepubescent mustache shaded his upper lip. Her elder boy, Tony, one year older than Nicholas yet so much smaller, kept his piercing green eyes focused on the floor. Margaret tried to catch a glimpse of his freckled-face, to let him know she shared his sorrow; but he only offered the riot of red hair sprouting from the top of his head. He and Nicholas book-ended the younger boys in the brood. Her other son, Billy, sat at his brother's side, his shaggy brown hair uncharacteristically pushed back from his brow and tears welling in his tender blue eyes. Richard Mann's fragile little fellow, Terry, leaned his slender torso trustingly into Nicholas, who affectionately scratched his undersized companion's fuzzy blond pate. Both boys, Billy at ten years and Terry at nine, were tiny compared to not only Nicholas, but Tony as well.

"Did we do something wrong, Mrs. Schumacher?" Nicholas mewled.

Margaret, half-expecting the miniature Max to call her "Redlocks," just like his father always had, abandoned the ruse of fiddling with the flowers and joined the quiescent quartet on the sofa. She sat next to Tony and tenderly caressed the back of his bowed head, agonizing over her helplessness, her inability to free the boys from the frightening grip of inconsolable grief.

"No, no, not at all. You boys didn't do anything wrong, don't even think like that," she comforted. "Your fathers just want to talk with you, that's all, just to make sure you're all okay. You've had quite a shock. You're probably scared, feeling all mixed-up inside, and it's alright to feel that way."

"But how long do they expect us to sit here? When are they coming back in?" His limited supply of youthful patience running short, Nicholas sprang to his feet defiantly and stomped to the living room window. His eyes widened and his lips parted with the involuntary drop of his jaw. "Are . . . are you sure we're not in trouble," he stammered, "they sure look awful mad."

Huddled in a heated exchange beneath the ascending branches and narrow, rounded crown of a pin cherry, Tim and Max had Richard backed up against the trunk of the tree, its reddish-brown, papery bark catching on the back of his shiny green track suit. Margaret and Tim had planted the pin cherry to mark Tony's arrival in the world, regarding the tree's robust health and lusty growth as a reflection of their own good fortune. The child and the tree each brought immeasurable pleasure to their lives. Margaret often lost herself completely in one or the other, either reveling in the miracle of her child at play or delighting in the cedar waxwings and evening grosbeaks that plucked at the pin cherry's ripened fruit.

The branches were without birds at present, the truculent bickering having scared off even the normally unflappable red squirrels that relentlessly raided their feeders. "Go on, sit back down. They're not mad at you." Margaret placed her hands on Nicholas's shoulders and directed him back to the couch. She studied the intense confrontation from the window and wondered with exasperation, "What now?" Her own patience was being put to the test, and she resented it; hated feeling like the lone adult stranded on an island of immaturity. The argument ended abruptly when she opened the door and stepped into the yard.

"What the hell is the matter with you guys? You're worse than the kids, for chrissakes!" Margaret scolded as she arrived beneath the pin cherry. "How long did you plan on leaving those poor boys sitting there? It's bad enough that they're sad and confused about Jimmy's death. Now they're scared silly that they're in trouble, that they've somehow done something wrong."

"We all know what that feels like, don't we, Dickey?" Max growled with unmasked enmity.

"And what the hell is that supposed to mean?" Margaret demanded, but Max dropped his head and fell silent rather than face Richard's withering glare.

"We were just having a disagreement among friends, that's all. Isn't that right, boys?" Richard sniveled, fixing Margaret with a smug smile when Max and Tim nodded enthusiastically.

"Your boys are in there suffering and you're out here like idiots, fighting with each other? What's the deal, Tim, why the *disagreement*?" Margaret hissed at her husband.

"It was merely a difference of opinion," Richard interjected, anointing himself group spokesman, as he always did. "We were discussing possible suspects in Jimmy's murder and the boys here simply disagreed with my theory. So it really wasn't a fight, you see. It was more of a lively debate."

The cloying, condescending tone of Richard's voice made Margaret bristle. She suppressed the urge to slap the puerile smirk off his delicate face, ashamed that she, too, was being goaded toward hostility. Tim and Max danced uncomfortably, the familiar kowtow shuffle in unfathomable deference to Richard, and Margaret felt ashamed for them, as well. She knew from experience that the only answers forthcoming, no matter how deceitful, would be those offered by The Cheeseball.

"Fine, Richard, let's hear your theory, the one that sparked this so-called lively debate. Tell me, who killed Jimmy?" She relented, her curiosity winning out.

"Dickey, Megs, feel free to call me Dickey," Richard predictably suggested as a preface to his explanation, "I don't believe Jimmy was actually murdered, I think his death was an accident, a case of childhood mischief gone horribly awry. That's why we've brought the boys together at your place, Megs, if you'll recall; to get some answers, to get to the bottom of this. We should go in and have that talk right now." He headed for the house.

"Not so fast." Margaret held up a hand and blocked his path, sorry that her desire for information left the boys twisting in the wind a little longer. "What are you talking about, Richard? Where do you come up with that? You know as well as the rest of us that Jimmy was beat up pretty bad, so how do you conclude it was an accident? The police think he was murdered, and so does everyone else in town. So what, exactly, are you basing this theory on? What do you know that nobody else does?"

Richard appeared flustered, as if he didn't anticipate the need to explain himself further. "Call it a hunch," was the best he could do for his rationale. "I just think we need to discuss this with the boys, find out what they know, if they heard about any kids fooling around out in that treehouse, or if they were out there themselves. Hey, if it turns out I'm wrong, I'll be the first one to admit it; but maybe there's a *reason* the boys are afraid they might be in trouble."

Fooled by the relative quiet following the argumentative storm, an evening grosbeak on the wing flashed its bright yellow flanks and alit momentarily atop the pin cherry. It cocked its head and assessed the earth-bound intruders with beady eyes set between its blackened brow and bulky beak, careening off into the woods just as quickly in search of a more peaceful meal. Margaret envied the bird's flight and the freedom it afforded, and was rueful of her own inability to fly away from the lies and deceit.

"That's what set you guys at each other's throats? Richard's preposterous theory? Is that the story you want to stick to?" She turned again to Tim and Max, but her incredulity was met with silence. "So let's pretend for one minute that that's what you were actually arguing about. Who do you two think killed Jimmy?"

Less practiced at the art of deception, Tim and Max shifted uneasily and pathetically looked to Richard, who was more than willing to fabricate their side of the story, as well.

"Sauter, who else?" he deigned. "He is suspect number one around town, you know, and a lot of folks would like to see him get his comeuppance, guilty or not. He'd make a convenient scapegoat, there's no denying it; and I wouldn't shed any tears if he was locked up, I'll admit that. Still, it's a huge leap from an asshole, which he is, to a murderer, which he is not."

Cupping his bearded face in the deep bowl of his beefy hands, Max expelled a guttural, aggravated groan. He slid his hands back along his brow, rubbing his temples and shaking his head. He surveyed the surrounding woods with a wild-eyed intensity and brusquely dismissed Margaret's overtures of concern.

"Back off, Redlocks, goddammit, I'm fine! Make yourself useful for a change, will you? Go back in the house and tell the boys we'll be right there," he commanded gruffly, shocking Margaret with an unpleasant side of his personality, a side that she had never seen. Max had always been a confidant, an ally, and she felt betrayed and hurt by the sudden reversal. Chastised and choking back tears, she scurried away in distraught subservience.

"Nicely done, Max, I was beginning to think that we'd never get rid of her," Richard cajoled, but Max vehemently rejected the unwarranted pat on the back.

"Fuck you, Dickey, you son of a bitch," he seethed through clenched teeth. "We should have told her, she has a right to know. She's going to find out soon enough anyway. Now we've got her all upset for no reason."

"*We've* got her all upset," Richard repeated with mocking laughter. "You're the one who nearly bit her head off! She looked like someone punched her in the stomach when you lit into her. What the hell's gotten into you? Have you finally tired of fawning over your best friend's wife?"

Expecting a violent response to the unseemly remark, Tim considered stepping between his two friends, but he laid back, hoping to derive vicarious pleasure through Max's well-placed fist. Instead, Max slumped over and once again squeezed the sides of his head. "Are you sure you're okay, buddy?" Tim prodded, his concern for Max incongruent with the spiteful stare he fixed upon Richard.

"I told you there's nothing wrong with me," he said softly, but his distressed, defeated demeanor suggested otherwise, "At least I don't think there is, other than the nagging suspicion that I'm slowly going crazy." He smiled weakly. "Remember when I busted Jackson's chops, when he was whining about hearing voices, and whistling in his head? Maybe I'm being taught a lesson, a lesson in tolerance; you know, learn to keep your mouth shut until you walk in somebody else's shoes."

"What are you trying to say, Max?" Tim inquired.

"Funny thing about it – what is today, anyway, Friday? Yeah, Friday. Well, a couple nights back, when we were leaving Jackson's to go out to, you know, to go out and look for Jimmy, I asked Jackson if he was still hearing things, if he still felt like he was being watched. He told me that the voices, the whistling, the eyes on his back, he told me it all disappeared that night, just up and left him. He said he didn't know where it all went, he was just glad it was gone. Well, I'll tell you where it all went," his eyes rolled back and he grinned demonically, tapping the side of his possessed head with a shaky index finger.

Tim and Richard backed away, a half-step at most, enough to reveal their fear that the *madness* might actually be contagious. It had, after all, jumped from Jackson to Max, or so it seemed, lending an unsettling afterthought to Jimmy Kelly's death. The moment was fleeting, but each friend, in turn, saw their own thoughts reflected in the brooding faces of the others – the stifling onus of inevitable atonement.

"We should have told her," Max reiterated his regret.

"You saw the way she looked at us. She knew you were handing her a straight line of bullshit, Dickey. It would have been better to just tell her, instead of adding on to all of the lies."

"Just tell her what, Max? That Christopher Koenigs is back in Broadaxe? That he killed Jackson's boy?" Richard was riled, but he delivered his message with restraint. "We don't know that. He could be anywhere, but I find it hard to believe that he'd come back here. I told you, all I've been able to find out is that he walked away from his halfway house out in New York, probably a week ago, last Friday; so let's hold off on the hysterics until I can gather more information."

"It's him, I know it," Tim said in monotone resignation. "Max is right. There's no reason Margaret has to be kept in the dark. Like he said, she's bound to find out soon enough. I'd rather she heard it from us, from *me*. Christ, she's my wife, and I'm afraid to even look her in the eye."

"And what are you going to tell her when she asks why, Tim? Why Christopher Koenigs would come back to Broadaxe to hang Jimmy Kelly? Have you thought of that?" Richard fumed. "No, you haven't, of course not, I have to do all the thinking for you guys."

"And look at how well that's working out for us," Max derided. "Christopher Koenigs was a crazy child. That's always been your story, Dickey, remember, or have you told so many tales over the years that you can no longer keep track of the truth yourself? Crazy child grows up to become crazy man, that's all the explanation that would be needed. I agree with Tim. Christopher Koenigs is back, and we better figure out what we're going to do about it. Sauter didn't kill Jimmy, and it wasn't some accident." He paused and glanced at the house. "I'm going in to talk to the boys now. The sooner we get this charade over, the better."

The boys were still clenched together on the couch and bore the foreboding expressions of little death row inmates awaiting execution Margaret had once again busied herself with the bouquet, which she had separated into two smaller vases. The daisies were destined for the living room and the black-eyed susans were to be relegated to the kitchen. She refused to meet Max's sorrowful, apologetic eyes, the sting of his harsh rebuke as fresh as the flowers she clutched in her hands. Reluctantly, he turned his attention to Nicholas, who immediately perked up in the warmth of his father's doting affection.

"You're coming home today, son. You'll sleep in your own bed tonight. How does that sound?" Max purred to the boy who stood at the adoring center of his universe. Margaret had picked Nicholas up the night of Jimmy's death, after Max had been thrown in jail for beating Sauter with the baseball bat. Max had come to retrieve his son when he was released the day prior, but Margaret had convinced him to let Nicholas stay with her boys one more night. Richard had brought his boy over that morning, and Terry warily eyed his father from the security of Nicholas's embrace.

"Before we head home, I just want to ask you a couple questions, Nicholas, okay?" Max commenced the farcical interview immediately. "We talked about this the other night, when you were helping us look for Jimmy, but I need to ask you one more time. You can tell me the truth, don't be afraid, I'm not going to punish you. The woods we talked about, out where Jimmy was found, the meadow with the treehouse, do you know anything at all about that? Have you gone out there? Do you know of any other boys who've talked about going out there, about the treehouse?"

Puzzled and hurt that his father would be asking the same questions, as if he had some reason to doubt the veracity of the answers he'd already given, Nicholas paused, trying to discern if there was something that he was missing, if he was expected to say something else. In the end, he realized there was nothing else he could say.

"I told you, dad, I *never* went out there. I don't know anything about a treehouse, or anybody who does. Don't you believe me?" Nicholas was upset, unaccustomed to the distrust implied by his father's repetitious inquiry.

Max swallowed the bitter pill of self-contempt, thoroughly disgusted by his callous mistreatment of the two people he held closest to his heart. Both deserved better. Margaret always knew when something was amiss, and what did she get for that kindred insight, her loving concern? Belittled, her head bit off. And poor Nicholas, prideful of the trust and respect he had rightfully earned from his demanding father, now left to wonder if their special bond had been betrayed.

The voices clamored inside of Max's head, calling his name in a sinister cadence broken only by the whistle that wheezed intermittently in his ears. He felt the noose tightening on his neck, the suffocation of panic accompanying the prospective dissipation of both mind and soul.

"I'm sorry, son, I believe you. I never doubted you," he said humbly, gathering his wits, determined to set things right. "I want to apologize to you also, Redlocks." He offered Margaret a daisy from the living room vase, which she graciously accepted. "It takes some kind of an ass to snap at somebody who's only trying to help. I could never hide anything from you. I am a bit off-kilter, mixed-up in the head; but I think everybody is, under the circumstances. I just want to take Nicholas home now, spend some time together, talk things out. I could use some rest. I'm so tired."

"When was the last time you got some sleep?" Margaret asked, worried by his gaunt expression and the dark, wrinkled bags sagging down his cheeks.

"Not for a couple nights," he admitted. "I couldn't sleep in the jail cell, and I couldn't sleep last night, so I guess it was Tuesday, Tuesday night."

"My goodness, you must be running on fumes," Margaret fretted. "Leave your minivan here and let Tim give you and Nicholas a ride home. You're in no shape to drive, and you need to get to bed. No wonder you're not yourself!" She was relieved to discover a logical explanation for Max's discordant behavior. Eager to end his boys' confinement on the couch and happy to delay the unavoidable confrontation with his wife, Tim moved toward the door, shaking his truck keys.

"Hold on, not so fast. We're not done here." Richard raised his hand and the sleeves of his track suit slid down his spindly arms, bunching up below the bony knobs of his elbows. "I haven't talked to my son yet; and Tim, you still haven't asked your boys if they know anything about that treehouse. We're trying to find out what happened to Jimmy here, remember? Max can get his beauty sleep anytime."

The palpable essence of futility permeated the room.

Margaret wished her husband could walk away from Richard's pertinacious influence once and for all, achingly sensed his repressed desire to do just that; but she harbored no illusions about such an actuality. Water dripped from the scalloped lip of the vase as she swept up the black-eyed susans and slipped off to the sanctuary of the kitchen, unable to watch Tim spinelessly bend in servile obedience to the Cheeseball's bidding. Singed with the shame of his wife's calculated departure, Tim was determined to meet Richard's demand on his own terms.

"Tony? Billy?" His interview was intentionally succinct, and he gladly accepted his sons' somber head shakes as truthful denials of any pertinent knowledge. He turned the children loose, into the yard, then wheeled on Richard with unreserved rancor. "Satisfied Dickey? Our boys don't have anything to do with this. They don't know anything about it. You knew that, we all knew that, yet you insisted on dragging them into it, making them a part of your deception."

"But . . ." Richard tried to mount a defense, but Tim wasn't finished.

"But what? There are no buts, Dickey. Maybe our time would have been better spent asking *you* some questions, like where you were the other night, when Jimmy went missing. The folks out searching the woods that night, Max included, found it a bit strange when you appeared out of nowhere, looking pretty rough around the edges. Isn't that right Max?" Tim had ventured out on a limb, unsure of his intentions and disheartened to find that he was, for all intents, completely alone. Max nodded dutifully, but his eyes shone vacant, reflecting a mind absorbed in a fatalistic fight to free itself from the throes of insanity.

Richard pounced. "What are you insinuating, Tim? Your tone sounds somewhat accusatory, and, I must say, I'm more than slightly offended," he huffed self-righteously. "I don't have to explain myself, not to you or to anyone else."

"What about me, Dickey? I'd like to hear where you was." Jackson, strikingly clean and sober, emerged unexpectedly from the kitchen. Margaret peered over his shoulder, baffled by the emerging rift between the friends at a time when they should be pulling together. "How come it is I can't gets a hold of you, nobody knew where you was that night, but you end up out there in the woods? I hear tell down at Tingle's that you was comin' from the other direction, comin' from the direction out there where my Jimmy was found. How is that, Dickey? Or are you still thinkin' you don't have to explain yourself?"

"Jackson . . . I . . . I," Richard groped for words, his eyes flashing with the panic and fear of a cornered animal. He tugged at the glossy green sleeves of his track suit in nervous agitation, befuddled because he had somehow lost the control which he so ardently coveted.

"Calm yourself, Dickey, for the chrissakes; quit dancin' round like you gonna piss yourself," Jackson rejoined, his speech atypically unblemished by the slurring effects of alcohol. "There ain't no reason for you to get all flustered, eh, less'n yous gots somethin' to hide. Is there somethin' yous ain't tellin' us? Somethin' more 'bout my Jimmy's death than yous lettin' on? Why was you in the woods that night, Dickey?" Jackson moved into the living room. Margaret, intrigued, followed.

Richard responded with a manufactured, self-assured smile. Heeding Jackson's advice, he allowed himself a moment to regain his disheveled composure. He walked slowly to the living room window and stood beside Max, who gazed blankly beyond the resilient youngsters racing around the yard, oblivious to the happenings outside of his haunted head.

"Look at this lummox," he snorted, tipping his head toward the giant zombie frozen before the window, "Our friend Max here is a complete mess." Richard tried to focus the attention away from himself. "I think maybe he's following in your footsteps, Jackson, looking for answers at the bottom of a bottle."

"I ain't touched a drop since the night Jimmy done disappeared," Jackson vowed, momentarily sidetracked by Richard's diversionary ploy. "I even went down to Tingle's last night, just to see if'n I could goes in there without havin' one, but it just ain't the same. Folks down there done treated me like a leper; not Tingle so much, just all them losers at the bar. Shoulda seen 'em gawkin' at me when I up and ordered a soda pop. You'da thunk my head done fell off. Tingle's the only one offered me his sympathies. The rest of 'em were too busy drownin' their own sorrows, I guess."

Margaret was stunned by Jackson's amazing transformation, all the more unbelievable under the stress and heartbreak he had to be enduring since the tragic loss of his only child. Clean shaven, he had scrubbed away the accumulated grime of the garage, erasing the acrid cologne of stale smoke and booze that normally heralded his arrival. The greasy work clothes that Margaret figured had been fused to his flesh were gone, replaced by unstained, stone-washed bluejeans and a pressed polo shirt. His brown hair bounced soft and fluffy, a shade lighter when washed, and his feet were clad in a pair of hand-stitched leather moccasins. She couldn't help but wonder how long this improbable turnabout could possibly last.

"How are you holding up, Jackson?" she offered meekly, aware of the stilted appearance of her belated concern. "And Dorothy? Please let her know she's in our prayers." Tim blanched at the mention of Dorothy's name, recalling the cryptic accusations and biblical admonitions she hurled at him as he left her house that night, destined to find the child she had already given up for dead.

"I'm doin' as well as can be expected, Margaret. I do appreciate yous askin', and I'll be darn sure to pass the kind words on to the missus." He thanked Margaret with genuine gratitude, then surprised her by having the presence of mind to resume his waylaid interview with Richard. "Max ain't on the drink, Dickey. Believe you me, I'd know if he were, and he ain't. He gots bigger problems." Jackson tapped a finger to the side of his head, unwittingly mimicking the motion Max had made earlier in the yard. "I ain't stupid, I ain't forgot what we was talkin' about, 'fore yous changed the subject. What was it brung yous out into the woods that night? What is it yous tryin' to hide, Dickey?"

Richard, taken aback by Jackson's brash persistence, rocked uneasily from heel to toe. Irked by the irrepressible gumption flagrantly displayed by his longstanding lap dog, he masqueraded as a misunderstood martyr.

"After all I've done for you, Jackson, this is the thanks I

I get; the implication of complicity on my part in your son's death," he blustered, pounding his fist to his chest for emphasis. "I've always thought of you as a brother, Jackson, and I loved your boy Jimmy like he was my own son. I don't know what to say, other than I'm deeply offended and hurt by your obvious lack of trust – trust that I believe I have earned many times over, I might add."

"Quit bein' so goddam melodramatic. It ain't very becomin' and it don't hardly answer my question," Jackson scolded. "I ain't accusin' you of nothin'. I was just askin' how come you was where you was that night. Seems strange you'd be out there, seein' how you didn't even know'd that Jimmy'd gone missin'."

"Who says I didn't know Jimmy was missing?" Richard asked rhetorically. "Of course I knew he was missing, why on earth would I have been out in those woods otherwise? I don't generally take a midnight stroll in the woods, Jackson, and I'm not much for the outdoors, day or night, you know that! It's humiliating having to defend myself like this, but if you insist, there *is* a logical explanation."

Richard timed the dramatic pause to provide Jackson the opportunity to spare him further embarrassment, to mercifully end the offensive inquest. Jackson wasn't interested, fixing his old friend with a resolute stare that sent the message "Yes, I do insist." Imagining that icicles were hanging from the eaves of the houses in hell, Margaret delighted in the unprecedented role reversal. Richard the control freak had always given out orders to his submissive underlings, and he was obviously perturbed to find himself, for once, on the receiving end.

"Because you're my dear friend, Jackson, because you are most certainly not yourself right now, I will suffer this indignity and swear I will not hold it against you," he puffed with bloated magnanimity, a self-effacing preface to his pending tale. "I had to go to Turtle Creek that evening, some personal matters to attend to, and I was held up there much later than I anticipated. When I returned to Broadaxe that night, well after dark, I noticed the searchers' cars along the highway and stopped to see what was happening. Somebody was out at the road, a woman, I can't remember who it was," he hesitated, as if he were trying to recall an elusive name, or face, "but she's the one who told me Jimmy was missing and that folks were out in the woods searching, as we spoke. Well, of course I rushed home, changed, and returned to join the search."

"Why didn't you'se call me, Dickey, or come by to the house?" Jackson inquired.

"How was I to know that's where you were? I just assumed you, and everybody *else* for that matter," Richard glanced at Tim, "were out in the woods looking for Jimmy! I was shocked, upset, I was just trying to do what I thought was best."

"What was you'se doin' in Turtle Creek so late on a Wednesday night?" Jackson pried.

"I *told* you, it was personal business." Richard declined to elaborate.

"Who was this woman, the one done told you'se Jimmy'd gone missin?"

"I can't remember who it was! Why is that important?" Richard's voice jumped an octave. "The point is, that's how I found out about Jimmy, and that's how I ended up in the woods. And before you ask, I stumbled into the searchers from the opposite direction because I got turned around in the dark and I walked around in circles in those damn trees. I got lost, plain and simple. Are you surprised? Everything looked the same, for chrissakes." He modulated his tone to express the gravity of what he was about to share. "I haven't mentioned this to anyone else, but I saw something out there in the woods that night, something that scared the living shit out of me – I'm not ashamed to admit it. God knows exactly where I was, somewhere out in that forest," he waved his arm expansively, "but I heard this grunting, a heavy wheezing, like an animal panting or something. I only caught a glimpse of it, off a ways and it was really dark, but it was some kind of animal I've never seen before. It wasn't that big, all skin and bones, like it had the mange, and it was clutching a smaller animal in its claws and dragging it through the woods. When I saw that, I just took off running, tripping over roots and breaking through the brush and branches. That's how I got so mussed up. There! Are we all satisfied now?"

The story, although entirely plausible, was greeted with an unspoken skepticism by the assembled audience. Richard sensed the collective doubt and took additional umbrage at the unmitigated assault upon his character. Max, however, remained indifferent, staring out the living room window with his back turned on a conversation he didn't even hear.

"Who's that kid?" he asked quietly, pointing to the small stranger who had joined their children in the yard.

The child, back turned to the house and partially obscured by the cone-laden branches of a balsam fir, appeared to be a boy. He was smaller than the other children, maybe six or seven years old judging by his size, with tufts of dark brown hair augmenting his short stature. Dressed in a faded red tee-shirt, cut off bluejeans and black high-top tennis shoes, the mother in Margaret couldn't help worrying that the child must be chilled in the cool autumn air.

"Can't say I recognize that little guy," she admitted, hoping that he would turn so she could get a look at his face. The other boys formed a semicircle around the newcomer, Max and Tony once again the bookends, with Billy and Terry stuck in the middle. The child stood erect, his arms straight down at his sides, almost inanimate, motionless, as if he were a statue. He held the rapt attention of the other children, struck speechless and oddly entranced, like pawns at the mesmerizing hands of a hypnotist. Margaret went to grab one of Billy's coats to offer the boy, intending to use it as a pretense to meet the child and find out who his parents were; but when she returned, he had disappeared.

"Where'd he go?" she asked, not waiting for an answer as she dashed out the door to see if she could catch him. "Which way did that little guy head?" she called to the boys, still locked in their semicircle, not amused when they pointed her in four different directions. "C'mon you guys, quit goofing around, which way did he go?" she pleaded, but they continued with their vexing game. She hurried to the road and looked both ways down the long, straight stretch of pavement, but the child had vanished. "Who was that boy?" She directed the question toward Tony, who shrugged his shoulders in response. "He didn't say his name? Tell you where he lived? Who his parents were? Nothing?" She addressed all four boys now, but their blank expressions told her that her curiosity would not be satisfied.

"He said he wanted to be our friend." Nicholas finally surrendered some information. "He didn't say who he was, but he knew all of us by name, didn't he?" His three friends nodded in agreement. "You'll probably get to meet him sometime. He promised that he'd come back soon. He said he couldn't wait to come back and play with each of us. He had funny eyes."

"What do you mean by that?" Margaret suspected the boy was cross-eyed or had bulging sockets, something fairly innocuous, so she was a bit bewildered by Nicholas's description.

"I dunno, they were like telescopes, or magnifying glasses, like he could see everything or they sucked everything in, kind of like the black holes we've been learning about in science," he explained matter-of-factly, the school reference prompting a question of his own. "Do you think we'll have to go back to classes on Monday, Mrs. Schumacher?" he asked with the innocence of a child wondering how many days off were merited by a friend's death.

"I'm guessing you probably will, Nicholas, but don't worry about that right now, you've still got the whole weekend ahead of you." Margaret heard the door open behind her, and the boys rushed past to greet their fathers as they exited the house. She was left to ponder the enigmatic description of the unknown child's "funny eyes".

"We're going to take Max and Nicholas home now." Tim met her halfway across the yard and wrapped her in a lazy hug. "Dickey's going to take the two of them in the minivan so Max has his vehicle. Jackson and I are going to follow them over and bring Dickey back. It'll give me a chance to chat with Jackson, see how he's doing, if he needs anything." He gently kissed her forehead. "It's Friday. If you don't feel like cooking, maybe we can take the boys out for a fish fry. Think about it. I'll be back in a little while."

Richard, Max, and Nicholas were in the minivan and gone before she had a chance to say goodbye. Tony and Billy begged their father to ride along in the bed of the truck, but Tim had arranged things so he could spend some time with Jackson alone, so the boys were sent sulking back to their mother with their scrawny friend Terry in tow.

Tim rolled down the window of the truck, venting the astringent lemon-lime aftershave Jackson had slathered over his clean-cut face. He drove slowly, trying to stretch the trip beyond its normal half-hour length, hoping there would be enough time for Jackson to answer a question that had been haunting him since the night of Jimmy's death.

"How have you been holding up, Jackson? I must say, you seem to be doing remarkably well," he plunged right in, offering his concern out of sincerity and as a ploy to conceal his ulterior motives, as well.

"I ain't gone off'n the deep end or cracked my nut, so's I guess I ain't doin' none too bad. I ain't on the drink no more. I weren't bullshittin' 'bout that, but ain't no tellin' when my weakness will get the better of me," Jackson confided.

"How about the voices and the rest of that? Max said you told him that all went away. Has any of that come back, or what?"

"My head up and cleared that night, yous know when I mean, when Jimmy . . ." his voice trailed away, but he recovered quickly. "That's the same night I done quit the drink. I ain't superstitious, but I took that as a sign, figurin' maybe if'n I stayed sober my head wouldn't be so dad-burned muddled all the time. I ain't foolin' myself. I know'd I shoulda got off the bottle long time ago, for Jimmy's sake if'n nothin' else." His shoulders wilted with guilt. "It's too late for the boy now, I know'd that, but I'm hopin' it ain't too late for me."

"I don't know if he told you, but Max says he's hearing voices now, the whistling in his ears, just like you described. I'm worried about the big guy," Tim confided.

"Yous should be. What do yous think I meant when I done said I know'd he got bigger problems. Somthin' strange is in the air, Tim ol' friend, somethin' beyond our understandin', I'm fearin'," Jackson portended.

"What about Dorothy, how's she coping," Tim proceeded to the crux of his inquiry.

"I ain't holdin' out much hope for the old girl," Jackson admitted cold-heartedly. "You fellas all thunk I could pack away the sauce, well let me tell yous, old Dorothy done puts me to shame. She got me worried somethin' fierce. The crazy woman done crawled even further into the bottle, lookin' to escape. She's always babblin', quotin' the bible, rantin' and ravin' 'bout how everybody gotta pay for their sins."

"It's funny you should mention that." Tim had the opening he was looking for. "That night, when we were all leaving your place to go out to the meadow, to look for Jimmy at the treehouse, Dorothy confronted me at the front door and said some things that have had me spooked ever since. The words keep playing over and over in my head, like a record skipping, but in her voice, exactly how she said it that night. It's been so incessant that I can repeat what she said, word for word."

"Let's hear it," Jackson urged. "I'm doubtin' that woman can spook me any more than she done already. I *am* the one been married to the hag all these years."

"Okay, here goes. She said, and I quote, 'My baby's dead, ain't he, my Jimmy's gone, and it was you all done killed him, you all brung this on us, ain't that right?' Remember this is before Jimmy had been found," Tim cautioned. "Then she raised her voice and said 'And the sins of the father shall be inherited by the son, so the bible say. My Jimmy's dead and you all done killed him, now get the hell out.' That's exactly what she said. What did she mean, Jackson, when she said we all killed Jimmy, that we brought this on ourselves?"

Jackson let the desperate question hang for what seemed like an eternity, long enough so Tim wondered with a hint of panic whether or not he would get an answer before arriving at Max's house. The truck crept along, pine cones popping like firecrackers beneath the grinding tires. Jackson hung his head dolefully, submissive as a sinner sitting in the confessional.

"It means she know'd what happened, Tim. It means she know'd all along, has know'd everything for all these years. I'm sorry, oh so sorry, can yous ever forgive me?" he pled with Tim for absolution.

"What are you talking about?" Tim feigned ignorance, but Jackson called his bluff.

"Yous know what I'm talkin' 'bout, but if I gotta say it, fine, I ain't fearin' the consequences no more, Dickey be damned!" he asserted defiantly, adding mischievously, "It was fun to see ol' Dickey squirm back there, though, weren't it? I know'd he ain't got nothin' to do with Jimmy's death, not directly no how, but Dorothy was right, we all got his blood on our hands sure as I'm sittin' here. Like I says, she know'd all there is to know 'bout Christopher and Michael Koenigs, what happened out in that meadow when we was kids. I done told her everything so there weren't no secrets between us when we got married."

"You told her *everything*?" Tim gasped, astonished to learn that someone outside their circle of accomplices was privy to the unspeakable secret of their past.

"Everything," Jackson reiterated, relieved to unburden himself of the festering betrayal. Tim sat in stunned silence, ashamed that he had never had the guts nor the decency to come clean with his own wife, a woman deserving of nothing less than the truth, yet forced unknowingly to exist within the shadows of deception.

"I envy you, Jackson. I envy your honesty and I envy your integrity," Tim moaned, awash in self-loathing. "I've always wanted to come clean with Margaret. I know she would have understood, but it's too late now. I've lived the lie for so long, I'm afraid the truth would tear us apart."

"Listen to yourself. *Yous* envy *me*? Don't insult me, and don't sell yourself short. A good lookin' guy like yous, with a beauty of a wife and two healthy boys, envying me? A drunken slob saddled with an alcoholic crone, my only child done killed and 'bout to be laid in his grave? Quit beatin' yourself up." Jackson reached out and clutched Tim's wrist. "Besides, that's the only thing I done told Dorothy the truth about," he chuckled softly, his clear eyes twinkling. "I done lied to her 'bout near everything else."

The blinding cloud of denial suddenly lifted and Tim understood the downward spiral of Jackson Kelly's moribund existence with devastating clarity. He coasted to a stop at the end of Max's driveway, his body gripped by the cold, foreboding fear that Dorothy's ominous warning would come to fruition and the sins of his past would indeed be visited upon his innocent sons.

CHAPTER ELEVEN

It had been a lazy day, quiet and restful, marred only by an unremitting undercurrent of malaise. Margaret intended to tackle the endless accretion of mundane household chores, but instead she idled away the afternoon hours watching her boys frolic in the yard. In truth, she was powerless to do otherwise, her overprotective nature ratcheted into overdrive by raw, instinctual fear. A young child had been murdered and the killer was still on the loose, a monster that posed no threat to her children as long as she diligently stood guard. She thought the little boy with the "funny eyes" might return as well, and she hoped to meet him if he did.

Tony and Billy were currently playing catch with a football along the side of the garage, where her husband had been holed up since he returned from dropping off Max earlier that afternoon. Tim was visibly upset by his talk with Jackson, but when she approached and tried to console him, he shunned her advances and asked apologetically to be left alone. Margaret understood, imagining the emotional strain of comforting a bereaved friend, and she respectfully granted his request. Now, with dinner time near and two hungry boys to feed, she decided to intrude upon his self-imposed isolation.

The garage door was open, exposing the accumulated clutter that kept both of their vehicles parked in the yard. A small aluminum fishing boat mounted aslant a rickety trailer occupied one stall, surrounded by the disorganized jumble of toys and tools that filled the remaining space.

"Head's up Mom!" Tony yelled, and Margaret ducked in the nick of time, barely avoiding being struck in the head by her son's errant pass. Billy scrambled past her to retrieve the football and she chased after him, assuming the role of would-be defender, much to the amusement of her giggling, much faster little boy.

"Touchdown!" he squealed as he ran away, breaking into an impromptu end zone dance as Margaret raised her hands above her head and ducked into the safety of the garage.

Tim sat hunched over on a stool in an unlit corner, his

elbows resting on the waist-high workbench that ran the length of the back wall. His chin rested heavily on the heels of his palms and his clenched fists pinched his face, pursing his lips and pushing the loose flesh of his cheeks upward in wrinkled furrows. He had a pencil behind one ear and a crossword puzzle book lay open on the sawdust covered bench, but his eyes were closed and Margaret wondered if he had nodded off. She crept up beside him and scribbled "I love you!" in the sawdust with her fingers, careful not to rouse him.

"I love you too," he mumbled, awake after all and ruining her planned surprise. He grabbed her by the waist, lacing his fingers through the belt loops of her jeans and pulling her close between his open legs, pressing their torsos together. She felt his excitement growing against her belly, bemused by her man's ability to become sexually aroused regardless of the circumstances. He nuzzled her ear and cupped her breast in his hand, making her wriggle uncomfortably with Tony and Billy so nearby.

"It's almost supper time, honey, and the boys are getting hungry. I was wondering if you still wanted to go out and grab a fish fry." She pushed away and he pulled her back, indicating he had an appetite for other things.

"We could have dessert first, right out here in the garage," he teased playfully, squeezing her bottom and nibbling the soft, erogenous skin of her neck.

"The boys are right outside." She broke his grip and backed off from his enticing seduction, fighting the warm spread of her own sensual stirrings. "There'll be time for that later," she promised, deliberately offering an indeterminate time frame. "What d'ya say, fish? Or do you have something else in mind?"

"You know what I have in mind," he whispered one final flirtation before succumbing to Margaret's demurrage, "but I guess food will have to do. I know it was my idea, but I'd rather not go out tonight. How about pizza? You order it, I'll fly. Deal?"

"Deal." Margaret agreed to the offer and they clasped hands to seal the bargain. Tim drew her near once more, his eyes no longer clouded by the dreamy fog of lust. He ran his fingers through her tangled red tresses, and, without warning, began to weep. "It's okay honey, it's okay, you've had a long couple of days, just let it all out." Margaret laid his head on her shoulder and tenderly applied her lips to his feverish forehead. "Holy cow, Tim, you're really warm. Are you feeling okay?" She placed a hand upon his brow to gauge his temperature, not knowing that he was flush with the heat of anxiety rather than illness.

"Christopher Koenigs escaped!" Tim gasped, regurgitating the ort of deception festering in his bowels and tearing at his conscience throughout the day. "I'm sorry, I should have told you earlier . . . I don't know why I didn't."

Margaret withdrew her hug and folded her arms across her chest. She noted the purgative effect the seemingly benign admission had upon her husband. Confused, she cocked her head to one side. "What do you mean escaped? Last weekend, at the wrestling tournament, I thought you guys were all in a tizzy because he had been paroled. If he was released, how could he escape? What am I missing here, Tim?"

"He was released from the mental institution, but he was supposed to be transferred to a halfway house, out in New York, not just *let go*," he explained. "There was some screw up or something, and I guess he just walked away, a week ago to the day supposedly – last Friday."

"Where did you hear all this?" Margaret suspected she knew the answer.

"Dickey told us this morning," he admitted sheepishly, confirming her suspicion that it had to be the Cheeseball. "That's what Max and I were so upset about. Dickey, too, I guess. We were all pretty shocked by the news, especially, you know, what with Jimmy's murder the other night and all."

Only semi-enlightened, Margaret still didn't make the connection. "So Christopher Koenigs escaped, so what?" she asked with genuine naiveté, involuntarily blinded by her in-grained ignorance.

"So what? What do you think?" he asked in a tone that suggested Margaret was simple-minded, forgetting for the moment that she was, at no fault of her own, only partially informed. "So Christopher Koenigs is back in Broadaxe. He's the one who killed Jimmy!" Tim alleged with a certainty that Margaret found difficult to comprehend.

"How can you be so sure that he's the one who killed Jimmy? Why would Christopher Koenigs come back to Broadaxe and hang that innocent child?" Margaret posed the logical question, just as Richard had predicted, sending Tim into a quandary as he considered the ramifications of the dichotomous explanations he had to offer.

There would be no better time to share the secret of his past with his wife, he recognized that, regretting that he hadn't done so long ago, as Jackson had with Dorothy. Yet, he couldn't help but wonder if the shared burden of the conspiratorial concealment had manifested itself through their dysfunctional, debilitating descent into alcoholism. Would a similar fate have befallen him and Margaret? Might it still? *Could* he tell Margaret, now, after all these years? Would she understand? How could she be expected to accept the lifelong betrayal without losing faith in the basic presumption of trust that sustained their relationship? Ashamed by his cowardice, he knew he couldn't take that risk. What little resolve he'd had to finally set things right quickly melted away, just as it had so many times in the past.

"Christopher Koenigs was certifiably crazy as a child, Margaret, and he proved it when he hung his little brother Michael. They called him a genetic sociopath, a natural-born killer. That's why they put him away for so long. Apparently that crazy little boy grew up to become a crazy adult." He borrowed Max's fabricated logic to perpetuate the lie rather than face the potential consequences of the truth. "It only makes sense, honey. It has to be him. Who else could it be? The treehouse, the noose, the meadow. It's like he's recreating his little brother's murder for some sick reason, who knows why?"

Margaret had no reason to suspect that her husband was holding back anything of importance that might further explain Christopher Koenigs's motivation for murdering Jimmy Kelly. Tim, of course, knew there was more to the story, but he reassured himself that withholding information was a lesser offense than telling an outright lie. Besides, he had made a pact with Dickey, Max, and Jackson never to speak of that long ago night; frightened little children sworn to an oath of silence regarding their role in Michael Koenigs's demise. Jackson had broken that oath, but for some intangible reason, more than likely self-preservation, Tim still felt duty-bound to honor it.

The blood drained from Margaret's face, siphoned away by a heart that pumped wildly with the bone-chilling realization that a maniacal killer was in their midst.

"What about Tony and Billy? Do you think they're in danger?" she cried in panic, raw fear oozing from her voice and etched across her contorted face.

"If that crazy son of a bitch is back in Broadaxe, we're all in danger," Tim warned, needlessly fueling the formidable fires that threatened to consume her.

*   *   *

It had been a long, unproductive day, and Sauter offered a word of thanks as he enjoyed the pink hues of the sunset that signaled its end. He had nearly nodded off several times on the previous night's drive from Broadaxe back to Turtle Creek, but when he finally arrived home and collapsed on his couch, the sleep that his body craved became predictably, and annoyingly, elusive. Each time he closed his eyes, Dorothy Kelly's haggard hallucination appeared, her disembodied face floating in the void, desiccated and scowling scornfully.

"The blood of my boy is on your hands, mister, and mark my words, the blood of more children will be spilt here in Broadaxe before all is said and done, blood that will further stain the hands of the sinners . . ."

The acerbic words scraped incessantly across the inside of his skull, sharpened fingernails screeching with unnerving import along the blackboard of his brain. The grating voice echoed outside of his memory, as if spoken aloud, and washed over Sauter in sensuous waves with such immediacy that he swore he felt the warmth of the apparition's breath and tasted its fetid odor.

"You could've saved my boy, mister, but you're just as guilty of killin' Jimmy as the rest of 'em. You were onto 'em. You were onto 'em all along, but you lost your nerve and let

'em run you out of town, and now my boy's dead."

Ceding the night to insomnia, Sauter subjected himself to a stream of insipid infomercials, wishing he had a handful of the magic pills that had brought blissful sleep to his Broadaxe jail cell. Eventually, as he always did when he lay awake, staring at the ceiling with mounting frustration, Sauter surrendered and retreated to his office. He arrived just after four in the morning, oddly comforted by the hushed hallways and unkempt cubicles, familiarities which made the Ojibway County Sheriff's Department seem, sadly, like a home away from home. He avoided interaction with any of the unfortunates who were stuck working the graveyard shift, slipping into his sanctuary unseen and locking the door. Undetected in a building filled with detectives, he sat undisturbed, ignoring the intermittent phone call and watching the time tick away on a lost Friday.

It all seemed so distant – the dead child, the beating, the time behind bars . . . the talk with the enchanting Amelia Devine. He winced when he thought of her, hanging on the phone, hanging still, denied the courtesy of a return call and an apology for the rude way he abruptly ended their introductory conversation. Sauter knew she must also be concerned, wondering if he was still in jail and a suspect in a young boy's murder, or if the real killer had been caught – or if there was any connection to Christopher Koenigs. *Christopher Koenigs.* It was imperative that he make the call, make amends with Devine and find out if Koenigs had been located, or if he was still on the loose. There was so much to do, yet he remained inert, lost in a sleep-deprived, cataleptic haze.

A barely perceptible pounding crept into Sauter's fragmented consciousness, originating in some far away place, then slowly pitched upward in intensity until it roused him from his pathetic paralysis. The opaque window of his office door rattled with each recurrent rap of knuckles on wood, bringing him back from the brink, back into an office he found surprisingly dark, save for the dim light of the desk lamp that had given him away.

"Hey, are you in there Sauter?" the slender silhouette on the other side of the glass called out impatiently. Sauter recognized Colins's manufactured Midwest accent immediately, but he stubbornly refused to respond, gripped unwillingly by a stifling torpor that originated from some unseen, outside source. "C'mon, I know you're in there," Colins whispered, an unbidden conspirator in Sauter's idiosyncratic game of hide and seek. "I saw your Bronco parked out in the lot and I see your light on in there right now. Open up, will you, people have been trying to get a hold of you all day. Didn't you hear your phone? It's been ringing off the hook!" The shadow outside the door shifted as Colins pressed his ear against the glass, listening for any signs of life within. "There's been a doctor calling from out in New York, a shrink I think she said, name of Amelia Devine. She's been pretty persistent, said she needed to talk to you, that it was urgent."

The ensuing silence caused Colins to suspect that he had been speaking to an empty room, or, less flatteringly, was being summarily ignored. He was about to walk away when the click of the lock revealed, disappointingly, that it was the latter. By the time he opened the door Sauter had already slouched back into his seat, sequestered by the inescapable ennui that sapped his strength and forbade him from functioning when he could ill afford to sit idle. Colins slipped stealthily into the darkened office and tripped the harsh, unforgiving overhead lights, unprepared for the decrepit creature that emerged from the shadows.

"What the heck happened to you?" he implored with an empathetic grimace, as if his own tissue ached vicariously upon the sight of Sauter's multi-colored disfigurement.

"I had a little accident. My face bumped into somebody's boot," Sauter said dryly, adding incredulously, "As if word of what happened hasn't made the rounds by now." Nodding at the clock on the wall above his desk, "Is that right?" he asked Colins, who double-checked his wristwatch.

"I've got 10:35 p.m., so yeah, it's pretty close." The dawning realization that the day had been stolen from him angered Sauter. He felt distressed, violated, as if an invasive spirit had wormed beneath his skin and deliberately shut him down, holding him in abeyance until his services were once again required. Lucid, listening to the hypnotic, haunting voice that had reclaimed his thoughts, he assumed that time had arrived.

"Go to the treehouse . . . save yourself . . . save the innocent child . . ." The raspy words rumbled around his brain, intermingling with the recurrent recollection of Dorothy Kelly's rantings, *". . . And I will dash them one against another, even the fathers and sons together, saith the Lord: I will not pity, nor spare, nor have mercy, but destroy them . . .",* until his mind reeled in abject confusion.

"Hello, are you still with me?" Colins waved his hands, trying to summon Sauter back from wherever it was he had drifted off to. "I'm sorry, but I've seen people laid out in a casket who looked better than you do right now."

"Thanks, Colins, thanks for the reassuring words, but those folks in the casket probably felt a helluva lot better than I do right now, too." He smiled thinly, trying to recapture some sense of normalcy. "What are you doing here so late, anyway?"

"Actually, I'm here early. My shift doesn't start for another half-hour," he explained with earned weariness, "I'm pulling a double, really, worked most of the day already. How long have you been here?"

"All day," Sauter admitted.

"Then why didn't you take your calls? Like I said, that doctor from out East was pretty insistent, I bet she left you a dozen messages, at least," Colins claimed, pointing to the blinking red light on Sauter's telephone as proof.

Sauter felt no compulsion to explain, didn't think Colins would understand how he had been helplessly held prisoner inside his own unresponsive body when he couldn't comprehend it himself. Determined to compensate for the forced forfeiture of the past 24 hours, he anticipated yet another long, sleepless night.

"Anything else of interest happen around here in the past couple of days that I should be aware of?" he inquired. "What have you heard about what happened over in Broadaxe? Tell me anything you know, Colins. I need all the information I can get my hands on before I talk to Dr. Devine."

"I really don't think I'm going to be able to tell you anything you don't already know, Sauter. Obviously, I'm aware of the fact that a little boy was murdered over in Broadaxe, but that only happened two nights ago, Wednesday night, and as far as I know there haven't been any new developments since then," Colins conceded, disappointed that he couldn't be more help. He averted his eyes, uncomfortable with what he had to say next. "There's a rumor around here that you're involved in that boy's death somehow, that you were actually being held as a suspect over in Broadaxe. Is that true?"

"It's all a matter of perspective. Let's just say I was in the wrong place at the wrong time," Sauter equivocated, certain that Colins knew more details than he was letting on. "I remember you boasting about being a professionally-trained journalist, slash police officer hybrid, that you had a nose for the facts. Now, you mean to tell me that you don't know *anything* else. I must say, I am disappointed, son."

Colins took the good-natured gibe in stride. He habitually removed his wire-rimmed glasses and assiduously cleaned the small oval lenses, his hazel eyes twinkling with a mischievous confidence. Of course he knew more.

"I never said I didn't know anything else, all I said was I couldn't tell *you* anything that *you* didn't already know," he elucidated. "I know the murder victim was the son of Jackson Kelly, a name I heard for the first time when we stopped at Tingle's Tuesday afternoon, after we went and checked out that treehouse that, um, freaked you out. Kelly was one of the four men we witnessed visiting the same treehouse the following morning, Wednesday, when we were on the stake-out." He hesitated, certain that he was about to offend, "He was one of the four children you harassed, stalked actually, after Michael Koenigs was hung; one of the four who you blamed for that boy's death. You do blame them, don't you Sauter." It wasn't a question.

"Not directly, no; that's not true," Sauter played a game of semantics. "I always thought they knew more than they were telling us, that's all; something that would have helped explain such a senseless loss."

"And that's what you were obsessed with? That's why you were so relentless in your harassment of those kids?" Colins had done his homework, and in turn was unconvinced. "Some of the things I read in the case files, some of the things you put those poor kids through, frankly, Sauter, it creeped me out. You snatched each of those boys, one by one, and dragged them kicking and screaming back out to that treehouse, trying to frighten them into some sort of confession. You made them look at crime scene photos of Michael Koenigs hanging beneath the treehouse, you intimidated and bullied those boys mercilessly. When it became physical, when you roughed up Richard Mann in front of his teachers and classmates, that's when you finally went too far. I don't know, maybe you really don't blame Jackson Kelly and his friends for Michael Koenigs's death, but it would sure make your behavior back then more understandable if you did. If it wasn't for the fact that Christopher Koenigs is unaccounted for . . ."

"Then what, Colins, then you'd jump to the conclusion that I had something to do with Jimmy Kelly's murder?" Sauter snapped. He'd had his fill of the rookie officer's insolence. "There are some things you can't learn about a case, some nuances that you can't possibly understand by reading through some outdated files more than two decades after the fact. If you want to stand there and pass judgment on me, be my guest. You won't be the first and I can guarantee you won't be the last – just make sure you know what the hell you're talking about. Unless there's something else you need to tell me, get the hell out! I've got a phone call to make."

Not allowed to finish his thought, and therefore misunderstood, Colins tried to make amends. "What I was trying to say, Sauter, before you interrupted, was that if Christopher Koenigs hadn't escaped I wouldn't know who to suspect in Jimmy Kelly's murder. Certainly not yourself. It has to be Koenigs, don't you think?"

"That's what I intend to find out," Sauter didn't acknowledge the veiled apology. He removed the receiver from the phone's cradle and put it to his ear, expecting Colins to take the hint and vacate the premises. He started to retreat but stopped just short of the door, hoping to wheedle his way back into Sauter's good graces.

"You know, I did a little research on muskies, too. Thought I better since I made the mistake of calling them huskies the other day." He began to feel better when Sauter shared a smile at the recollection. "Muskies are a fish, huskies are a dog. I won't make that mistake again. Muskies, or muskellunge, are a very large, edible pike of North America," he quoted the dictionary definition, noting Sauter's bored, unimpressed expression. *"Esox masquinongay,"* he added furtively, recalling Sauter's penchant for identifying trees in a like manner, "the king of freshwater fish, the fish of one-thousand casts, the state fish of Wisconsin. The world record, which some folks still dispute, weighed in just shy of seventy pounds and was caught in Wisconsin, west of here, in the Chippewa Flowage."

Sauter dropped the receiver from his ear and let it rest on his shoulder. He saw the pleased look cross Colins's face and, for some reason, couldn't resist wiping it off.

"Catching a fish is like catching a criminal, Colins. Good luck netting either one with your nose stuck in a book or buried in case files," he parceled out the unsolicited advice, reinforcing his earlier admonition. "You learn from experience, son, spending time in a boat casting plugs, or out in the field sifting through evidence, getting your hands dirty. Book smarts will only take you so far, remember that, and without the experience to back it up, most often you'll come out looking and sounding like a damn fool."

"I'm willing to learn," Colins confirmed. "Maybe you can teach me, you know, the nuances, some of the secrets experience has taught you about solving a crime, or catching a fish."

"Let's talk about this some other time." Sauter dismissed Colins for the final time, putting the phone back to his ear and punching the flashing red button to replay his accumulated messages.

Hello Henry, this is Amelia, Dr. Amelia Devine, calling from out in New York. Please call me back as soon as you get this message, I don't care what time it is, we need to talk. I'm worried Henry, about you, about Christopher Koenigs, I'm worried about a lot of things.

Colins wasn't exaggerating. There were at least a dozen similar messages from Devine. Sauter dutifully listened to each one with a growing sense of remorse for not having had the decency to call back sooner. He gathered that Christopher

Koenigs's whereabouts were still unknown, but for some reason he still resisted the transparent possibility that he had returned to Broadaxe, a deranged killer after all.

"Go to the treehouse . . . save yourself . . . save the innocent child . . ."

Relegated to the recesses of his brain through sheer willpower, the onerous chant nevertheless beckoned Sauter back to Broadaxe with a diabolic magnetism. The grating voice, the asthmatic whistle, so comfortingly familiar, yet brutally antagonistic at the same time. He suppressed the overwhelming urge to bend to its bidding in blind obedience, to rush to the meadow and stand among the irresistible purple cones of the undulant lupines. There was nothing there, no reason to return, he assured himself, unable to ascertain the mysterious origins of his ardent desire to do just that.

It was after midnight out East, but Devine had left her home number with an explicit plea to call no matter the time. Sauter imagined Devine in bed and curled up on her pillow, anxiously awaiting his call, once again titillated with the anticipation of hearing her sonorous voice. She answered on the first ring.

"Hello, Henry, is that you?" she asked expectantly.

"Yes, it's me Amelia, please accept my regrets for taking so long to get back to you," Sauter apologized, still confused by his distorted perception of time.

"It's only been a little more than a day, Henry," she reminded him. "I'm the one who should be apologizing for leaving all those messages. I must have come across like some hysterical fool."

"No, no, don't be foolish." He cringed at the poor choice of words. "I mean you're not foolish, you didn't sound like a fool at all. You sounded concerned and you had every right to be. You want to talk about hysterical fools, you should have seen me running down the hallway of that jail after you told me about Christopher Koenigs. Quite the scene, let me tell you."

"Speaking of jail Henry, are you . . .?" she asked unthinkingly, momentarily forgetting the time of night herself.

"They let me go yesterday afternoon, but I've been

pretty busy trying to catch up on things since then," he lied, rather than admit he'd spent the past twenty-four hours in a vegetative state.

"Believe me Henry, I can empathize. Things have been pretty crazy around here all week, as you can imagine."

"So, Koenigs still hasn't turned up, I take it?"

"No, unfortunately, there's been no sign of him yet, but he is the focus of a pretty intensive manhunt out here, so it should only be a matter of time until he turns up. His face has been plastered all over the television and the newspapers."

"Do you really believe that he's still out in your neck of the woods, Amelia? Word of his escape has already made its way to Wisconsin and let me tell you, folks around these parts are convinced that Christopher Koenigs is back in Broadaxe, that he came back and killed Jimmy Kelly."

"What do you think, Henry?" Devine asked reluctantly, fearing that she already knew the answer, "Do you think Christopher Koenigs killed that little boy? Do you think he returned to Broadaxe?"

The line fell silent as Sauter considered his response. He had staked his reputation on Christopher Koenigs's innocence long ago and had suffered the consequences ever since. Devine had done the same, fighting for and eventually winning his release, so Sauter understood the ridicule and remonstration she would be subjected to if Koenigs was, in fact, Jimmy Kelly's killer.

"Look on the bright side, at least he's taken the heat off of me." Sauter tried to inject a bit of humor, but Devine wasn't laughing. "Listen, Amelia, I'm not willing to go that far yet. I'm not ready to just pin this murder on Christopher Koenigs in the absence of any solid evidence. Is it a possibility? You bet, but there are other possibilities, as well. It's already crossed my mind that someone may have been trying to set me up to take the fall for Jimmy Kelly's murder. Maybe somebody's trying to set up Koenigs, somebody who has a vested interest in making sure he remains locked up."

Devine immediately thought of Perkins, but just as quickly dismissed the ridiculous notion. Sauter, predictably, was thinking of none other than Richard Mann, the ringleader of the childhood cadre that had helped put Christopher Koenigs away in the first place.

"Henry, I have to be honest with you, I do have my doubts," Devine unburdened herself. "Ever since you told me about that young boy's murder, I've been trying to convince myself that Christopher Koenigs had nothing to do with it, that the man I helped set free was incapable of such brutality. I can't believe I could have been so wrong, that I could have been duped so completely." Her voice broke. "It could be him though, you know. Then what?"

The exact same thoughts had run through Sauter's mind so often it was as if Devine was reciting his own words. He longed to reach out and touch her, felt strangled by the insurmountable distance that separated them, and in the end harbored an unequivocal disgust for the atrocity that bound them tenuously together. Redemption or ruin awaited, each dependent upon locating Christopher Koenigs.

"I agree, it *could* be him, yes, but I meant it when I told you I'm still not convinced that it *is* him." Sauter wasn't just trying to assuage Devine's anxiety, he was telling her the truth.

Sauter the detective took a pragmatic approach to any puzzle, judiciously exhausting all available options before settling upon a solution. In the search for Jimmy Kelly's killer, he hadn't even scratched the surface of that tedious process. Sauter the man listened to his instincts, trusted in an innate clairvoyance that had been both a blessing and a curse. It told him Christopher Koenigs was not the killer, yet he could not shake the festering feeling that the present was somehow connected to the past. Unavoidably, the detective and the man were locked in an internal struggle for Sauter's allegiance.

"Let me handle things out here on this end, Amelia, I'm sure you've got enough to worry about," he commiserated.

"To put it mildly," she replied drolly. "I'm already taking a lot of flak for what's happened with Christopher Koenigs. I can't help feeling he let me down, you know? Really just ripped my insides out after all I'd done for him, the faith I placed in him. The truly scary thing is, I'm the only one around here who knows that a little boy was murdered out in Wisconsin two days ago, hung from a treehouse in Broadaxe, just like

Michael Koenigs twenty-two years ago." She sighed heavily into Sauter's ears. "I haven't had the nerve to tell any of my colleagues yet, especially Sarah Perkins. Do you think I should tell them? About Jimmy Kelly's murder? I don't even want to think of the repercussions if . . . when they find out."

"I'd hold off on that if I were you," Sauter advised. "Why subject yourself to something so unpleasant if there's no need to, if Christopher Koenigs isn't the killer? Who knows? Maybe we'll catch the murderer out here and you'll catch Koenigs out there, and your fellow doctors will be none the wiser. What d'ya say?"

"I suppose you're right, Henry, but promise me you'll keep in touch. You don't know how comforting it is to hear your voice, to have someone to confide in." She stroked his ego and he melted into his chair. "I'm feeling much better about things already, having talked with you, and I'm sure you're right, everything will work out. You know, when it is all over with Henry, it would be wonderful if we could finally meet, in person."

The thought alone set Sauter's blood to boiling. Each of Devine's letters added impetus to his fantasies of a first meeting, evolving from a platonic handshake to a full-blown lover's tryst. Now, daunted by the intriguing possibility of an actual face-to-face encounter, he was suddenly ashamed of his presumptive daydreams.

"I'd be lying to you, Amelia, if I were to tell you that I hadn't . . ." Sauter was on the cusp of baring his soul, by his guarded standards, with the admission that he had long hoped to look into her eyes someday. The loud banging on the door broke his concentration and his resolve, an aggravating interruption that added heat of a different kind to his heightened temperature. "Excuse me for one moment, Amelia, there's someone knocking on my door," he said calmly, his tone and demeanor changing as soon as he covered the receiver with his hand.

"What is it?" he snarled, greeting Colins with a distasteful sneer intended to convey his displeasure with the mal-timed intrusion, "This better be good!"

"Sorry Sauter, but I thought you'd want to know as

soon as possible," Colins apologized breathlessly, his slender frame quivering with uncontained excitement beneath his crisp khaki uniform. Despite the purported urgency, he hesitated for a split second, long enough for Sauter to impatiently jump down his throat.

"Well, spit it out, son, can't you see I'm on the phone," he barked menacingly.

Flustered, Colins's face reddened a shade darker than his strawberry blond hair, "Ah . . . ah . . . um, another boy is d-d-d-dead," he stuttered before regaining his composure. "Believe it or not, word just came in that another boy was murdered over in Broadaxe, found hung out at that treehouse, the same as Jimmy Kelly."

Sauter nearly dropped the phone, just as he had the day before in the hallway of the jail when Devine informed him about Christopher Koenigs's escape. He stared at Colins for a moment in wide-eyed disbelief, then shooed him away with a dismissive wave of the hand as he tentatively raised the receiver to deliver the devastating news.

"I guess it's time to tell your colleagues what's happening here in Wisconsin after all," he said somberly. "We've got another dead child on our hands."

Sauter sat in his dimly-lit office for an indefinite amount of time, waiting for a response that never came. He reluctantly returned the phone to its cradle when he finally realized it was his turn to be left hanging on the line.

NICHOLAS

The headlights cast an eerie glow across the back yard, smoky, luminescent pillars reaching into the milky mist swirling above the restive waters of the Rice River. Nicholas was having a difficult time deciding what to do. His dad had been acting funny all night, funny in a scary kind of way, but he had just fallen asleep and Nicholas remembered Mrs. Schumacher saying that he needed his rest. He didn't think he should wake him. That might make him mad.

But someone needed to turn the headlights off. Nicholas knew that if they were left on, the battery would go dead. That would certainly make his father mad. Under strict orders not to leave the house by himself until they found out what happened to his friend Jimmy, Nicholas nevertheless determined that was his best course of action, to turn the lights off on his own. If his father found out the consequences would be the same; he would be mad, so what difference did it make. Anyway, why did his father have to find out?

Nicholas tip-toed to his father's bedroom door one last time to make sure he was asleep. He hoped he had awakened, it would make things so much easier; but he was still happy to find him sprawled on his back, snoring loudly. Maybe when he did wake up he'd be better, more like he usually was, not so scary anymore. Nicholas knew he had made the right decision. It was nearly impossible to stir his father from a deep sleep, so he could turn off the lights and be back in the house without a worry.

Nicholas hurried to the sliding glass door that opened onto the flagstone patio he had helped his father lay last summer. He quietly opened the door just wide enough to turn sideways and squeeze through. The smooth silver stones cooled the bottoms of his bare feet, which were subsequently dampened as he trotted furtively across the dewy grass. The beams of light flickered with his shadow as he cut through the pillars, causing the hazy vapors to swirl turbulently in his wake.

A fetid odor billowed from the minivan when Nicholas opened the driver's side door. It smelled as if an animal had crawled under one of the seats and died, he thought, so he held his breath and made a hasty inspection. He crawled through the minivan, checking beneath each seat, but found nothing. The rancid smell seemed to be fading anyway, so he jumped back out, killing the headlights and vaulting himself into a sudden and complete blackness. An unearthly wheezing emanated through the ebony wall that temporarily blinded him, and he wheeled in a panicked circle as he searched helplessly for its source.

The searing surge of pain buckled his knees and brought a flood of tears to his bulging, unblinking eyes. He heard the soft popping of the tender skin on the side of his neck and felt the warm rivulets of blood running down his chest and back, released by the crushing, bony fingers impaling his throat. It was a queer, unfamiliar sensation, the weightless buoyancy that mercifully diverted his mind from the unbridled agony otherwise engulfing his body.

Nicholas had been so big for so long, and had been deprived of a mother at such a young age, that he had no memories of being held, of ever being picked up off the ground. When he wrestled no one could budge him, as if he were glued to the mat, anchored by the unrelenting pull of gravity upon his unwieldy mass. What in the world could possibly have a hold of him now? he wondered hopelessly, whisked away from his home like a feather in the wind.

The chilled, roiling waters of the river licked at his heels as he bounced along the rocky bank. Tiny points of light flickered before him, sometimes the stars whirling overhead and sometimes the visible flashes that accompanied the punishing jolts of pain. A low, guttural moan alternated with the shrill scream of the congested whistle, and the ice-cold knives plunged deeper into his neck. Footfalls splashed lightly on the water ahead of him and he skittered across the river, the waves wetting his clothes, which were torn violently away as his back scraped the jagged rocks on the opposite bank.

Nicholas caromed off the gnarled trunks of trees and was slashed by the grasping thorns tangled in the underbrush as he careened helplessly through the forest in the clutches of his unseen assailant. Soon, the soft petals of flowers brushed against his blistered and bleeding skin, bathing him in a placid pond of infinite purple. He levitated for a fleeting moment at the base of the oak, staring upward at the yawning portal into the blackened bowels of the treehouse. The rancid smell of death rolled over him once again as he was swallowed up by the shadows. The noose dropped from the darkness and draped itself around his punctured neck, tightening relentlessly until blood spurted from the jagged line of unplugged holes poked into his throat. No longer weightless, crumbling beneath the resurgent pull of gravity, he fell fast toward the groping field of flowers, imagining how mad his father would be . . .

CHAPTER TWELVE

"Amelia? . . . Amelia?"

Nothing.

Sauter repeated the name several times, remaining on the line until the connection clicked off and the dial tone screamed in his ear. He rested his finger on redial, then reconsidered. She obviously needed some time to collect her thoughts, to come to terms with the dreadful truth, that she may have been responsible for releasing a killer back into society. Sauter felt helpless, lost, wanted desperately to call her, but he reluctantly hung up the phone. It rang immediately.

"We certainly have a strange way of ending our conversations," he answered, assuming it was Devine.

"Excuse me?"

Sauter didn't recognize the voice.

"Isn't this . . . I'm sorry, I was expecting someone else." He regretted taking the call, but it was too late. "This is Detective Henry Sauter."

"I realize that detective, I called you. This is Officer Corcoran with the Broadaxe P.D. Do you have a few minutes?"

"For you Officer Corcoran, of course, how can I be of help?" Sauter asked nonchalantly, curious to see how Corcoran would broach the subject of the most recent hanging.

"I was hoping you could tell me where you spent the evening detective, say from about 9 p.m. on."

Still under suspicion, Sauter mused. "I've been right here in my office, officer, all day and all night, as a matter of fact. Why do you ask?"

"Is there someone who can confirm that?" Corcoran pursued her line of questioning, unimpressed by Sauter's supposed ignorance.

"Yes, certainly there is," he declared without elaboration.

"And who would that be, detective?" Corcoran asked testily, quickly tiring of the irksome detective's mind games.

"Officer Seth Colins," he stretched the truth, since Colins could only attest to his whereabouts for the past hour or so. "Again, if you'd be so kind officer, I'd like to know what this is all about." Sauter injected impatience into his voice.

"There's been another murder here in Broadaxe," she caved, no longer caring whether or not he already knew. "Another young boy, name of Nicholas Ferguson. He was abducted from his home sometime after 9 p.m. and his body was found shortly after eleven."

"Who found him?"

"Chief Kunick would like to speak with you, detective." Corcoran was done doling out information.

"Put him on."

"No, detective, he wants you here, in Broadaxe, as soon as you can get here."

"Where is here, officer? Should I come to the station?" Sauter really wasn't sure.

"No, here as in the crime scene, detective. You'll have no trouble finding it, it's a place you're quite familiar with – so we'll see you in an hour, is that about right?"

"Forty-five minutes," Sauter promised, regretful that he hadn't obeyed the voices in his head after all. If he had, Nicholas Ferguson might still be alive. On the other hand, he may have ended up back in jail, two murder counts hanging over his head. There were no voices now, but he was equally unnerved by the abrupt cessation.

Sauter stopped in the men's room and splashed cold water on his face, which did little to alleviate his disheveled, somewhat monstrous, appearance. The mirror reflected a face unrecognizable even to himself, the disjointed nose and bruised flesh proving too painful to look upon. He wore a gray tweed jacket that was crumpled and creased, the collar sticking up on one side and laying flat on the other, and faded black jeans that were similarly wrinkled. Sauter had not slept for nearly thirty-six hours, but it looked as if he had just rolled out of bed.

"Fuck it," the stranger in the mirror concluded, and Sauter agreed. There was no time to clean up the mess.

The night was as black as Sauter presumed it would be, shadowless and opaque, the moon tucked away below the horizon and the stars blotted out by a dome of indiscernible clouds. Michael Koenigs died on such a night, as did Jimmy Kelly, and now, Nicholas Ferguson. The darkness never departs, Sauter need not remind himself, for it had been his constant companion for far too long. It had descended the moment he laid his hands upon Michael Koenigs's dangling corpse. It crawled beneath Sauter's skin, became entrenched, the enemy within, thwarting all his efforts to shed some light on the mystifying murder. Two more dead children. It was taunting him now, rubbing his face in it.

"There will never be another night like this!" he cried out in desperation, his head tilted back and his arms spread out, beseeching the heavens for a reprieve from the madness.

"I hate to burst your bubble, but it's supposed to be like this for the next week," Colins forecast from the bumper of the Bronco, completely missing the deeper meaning in Sauter's plea. Assuming he was alone in the parking lot, Sauter was not pleased with the startling surprise.

"Jesus Christ, Colins, what the hell are you trying to do? Give me a heart attack?" he lashed out at the featureless figure emerging from the gloom. "What are you doing, sitting out here in the dark?"

"I want to go with you," Colins explained without hesitation.

"Go with me? You don't even know where I'm going." Sauter believed it, severely underestimating the young officer's instincts.

Colins took offense, "Please, how stupid do you think I am?" he huffed indignantly, resuming before Sauter offered his opinion. "You're going to Broadaxe, to the treehouse, where those two little boys," he corrected himself, remembering Michael Koenigs, "three little boys, I guess, were murdered. I'd like to go along."

"Not a chance, the last thing I need right now is a rookie cop getting in my way. This is serious stuff, son, this isn't a game. The police over in Broadaxe have two unsolved murders on their hands and . . ."

"And how am I supposed to get the experience that you just told me I needed? This is a great opportunity for me Sauter, I could learn a lot from you," Colins resorted to flattery. "Besides, you'll never even know I'm there. I promise I won't get in your way. And if you don't mind my saying, I'm not nearly as invested in this whole deal as you are, so it might be helpful to have the perspective of somebody who's, you know, more detached."

Sauter envied the young cop's enthusiasm for the job, something he'd been sorely lacking himself for the past few years. He didn't derive the same satisfaction from solving a crime and putting the perpetrator behind bars, not with Michael Koenigs's murder still unresolved, at least in his mind. The recent hangings certainly rejuvenated his interest, which had finally begun to wane due to ceaseless disappointment and disillusionment. Colins also happened to be his alibi for the evening, so it might not hurt to have him along.

"Get in," Sauter acquiesced, smiling to himself as Colins hurriedly climbed into the Bronco before he had a chance to reconsider. "Better buckle up. We need to make up for lost time, thanks to our little chat. See what I mean? We haven't even left yet and you're already a pain in my ass," he added in jest, his good humor deflated by Colins's dour expression. "Nobody gets me anymore," he lamented.

Colins would never have guessed that the rusty old Bronco was still capable of attaining such a dizzying speed. He queasily recalled his first white-knuckle ride with Sauter two days prior, a ride in the park compared to this reckless race down the curvy, tree-lined highway. Green eyes blinked back from the roadside brush occasionally, whitetail deer that threatened to leap in front of the speeding vehicle at any moment.

"What happens if one of those deer decides to cross the road at the wrong time?" he asked haltingly.

"Then we have venison for dinner," Sauter deadpanned, "if there's anything left of the poor bugger."

"It's not the deer I'm worried about," Colins confided, nervously checking to make sure his seat belt was still fastened. Sauter surprised him with a hearty belly laugh, which leapt like a contagion to Colins, momentarily taking his mind off imminent death. "I had something I wanted to ask you, Sauter, about the oak tree, the one you showed me the other day with the treehouse in it, where we're headed now – you said that it was a bur oak, *Quercus macrocarpa*," he flaunted his newly-acquired knowledge, much to Sauter's amusement. "Are you certain that's actually what it is, a bur oak?"

"No doubt in my mind." Sauter was intrigued. "What makes you think otherwise?"

"Well, I don't know, that tree is just so humongous, upwards of one-hundred foot tall I'd guess, and the diameter of its trunk must be a good six-foot," Colins estimated, pleased with himself when Sauter nodded in agreement, "Bur oaks just aren't supposed to grow that big this far north, from what I read. The bigger bur oaks are typically found in southwestern Wisconsin, where they appear more commonly in what's called the 'oak opening', where the soil drains better. This tree would even be huge down there, so what gives? Is it a fluke or an abnormality? Or what?"

The kid was beginning to grow on Sauter. He had seen the bur oak just once, and only for a short time, yet he was observant and astute enough to nail down its dimensions with the naked eye alone. He was obviously curious and a quick study, more than willing to take the time to inform himself about subjects that were unfamiliar, such as trees and fish. With a little experience, he'd probably make a damn good cop. Sauter pulled off the highway and climbed the two-track dirt road, parking the Bronco behind Corcoran's unoccupied police cruiser, glad that he had brought the kid along.

"There's nothing normal about that tree, son, not one damn thing," Sauter warned. "There's nothing normal about the whole shootin' match – the meadow, the oak, or the treehouse – things are about as far from normal around here as it can get. You make damn sure you keep that in mind when we're back there."

A yellow, plastic band of police tape enclosed the meadow, strung from tree to tree in one continuous strip that fluttered ever so slightly despite the uncanny stillness of the surrounding forest. A stanchion of bright lights illuminated the entire crime scene, powered by the small gas generator that coughed and sputtered at its base. The field of purple lupines provided a beautiful backdrop to the ghastly vision at the center of the maleficent meadow, where Nicholas Ferguson's bluish body still hung beneath the treehouse. Max Ferguson stood next to his departed son, arms crossed and eyes defiant, threatening any man who dared to approach.

"Goddammit Bobby, why in the hell is that boy still hanging from that fucking treehouse?" Sauter directed the profanity-laced tirade at the back of Kunick's encephalitic head. Kunick didn't flinch. He was on the outside of the police tape looking in, his own arms crossed just like Ferguson's and locked in a stare-down with the grief-stricken father.

"We've been waiting on you Sauter, that's why," Kunick explained disdainfully.

"What! What for? I've seen this shit twice before Bobby, same as you, so you should understand why I'm a little more than pissed off at being subjected to it again! Goddammit, where's your decency?"

"You're pissin' on the wrong leg, Sauter. You need to have a talk with your buddy there." Kunick, still facing away from Sauter, dipped his head toward Ferguson. "He said his boy stays right where he is until he had a chance to talk to you. We tried to talk him out of it for chrissakes – what the hell do you take us for, anyway? But he was pretty darn adamant. He found his kid hanging there himself, called his buddies, and they called us. We haven't been able to get close. Don't worry Sauter, it doesn't look like he has a baseball bat."

"Ferguson demands to see me, and you just stand back and let him hijack your crime scene? You gotta be shittin' me! And I thought I'd seen it all." Sauter brushed past Kunick and ducked beneath the fluttering yellow tape, determined to take the child down from the noose himself.

"Now that you've had your say, gone and gotten all high and mighty on me, maybe you can calm down and put yourself in my shoes." Kunick didn't think he deserved to be painted as the bad guy. "This man's been through a lot the last couple of days, Sauter. If anybody can empathize with that, it should be you. His best friend's son was murdered just two days ago, he puts a beating on the wrong man because of it and ends up in jail, now his own boy is dead. What would you have done, Sauter? Stormed the meadow? Overpower Max Ferguson? Look at the size of him! Imagine what that tussle would have done to the crime scene. I did what I thought was best.

Don't you think I wish I could have spared *any* of us from having to go through this again? Believe me when I tell you it tears me to have to admit it, but I need your help, Sauter. I need your help catching whoever it is that's killing our children."

With the meadow lit up like a Broadway stage, a dead child and his distraught father sharing the spotlight, Sauter hadn't noticed the cast of characters assembled in the shadows. Kunick wore the wilted retrograde of sleepless nights, his bloodshot and bleary eyes baring the toll of his miserable burden. Corcoran stood behind him and off to the side, fairly brimming with hostility at being relegated to the roll of ineffectual bystander. True to his word, Colins kept his distance, hanging well back in the trees in an exaggerated effort to stay out of Sauter's way. A handful of uniformed county cops and state troopers were stationed at intervals along the outside of the police tape, some with firearms in hand, which Sauter found unnecessarily threatening considering the circumstances. Lastly, he looked upon the actors who – like himself, Kunick and Max Ferguson – had recurring roles in this deadly drama; Richard Mann, Jackson Kelly, and Tim Schumacher. They huddled together near the rumbling generator, wary of straying too far from the light or from each other, a triumvirate of trembling consternation.

Sauter plucked one of the lupines, the "wolf flower" he preferred to call it, and twirled the vibrant purple spike between his fingers. The subtle hues of the individual petals sparkled in the artificial light, more radiant and beautiful than any flower he had ever seen. Yet the very presence of the lupines was disquieting, as if the timing of the prolific late-season bloom was not merely coincidental, but choreographed. Sauter handed the flower to Kunick and the two old, estranged friends shared a tired smile.

"What'd we ever do to deserve this, huh Bobby?" Sauter watched the lupine fall as Kunick let it slip from his hand, then turned and tentatively made his way toward the middle of the meadow. He was concerned about the reception awaiting him beneath the treehouse, but his worries waned as Max's angry defiance surrendered to heartbreak and contrition.

"Don't you think we ought to let your boy down from

there?" he suggested sincerely, stopping well short of Max's considerable reach. "The child shouldn't be left hanging there like that, it's time to bring him down." Max cut a much more imposing figure than Sauter remembered, and he blanched at the thought of the behemoth working him over with a bat. Sauter's hand instinctively went to his cracked rib cage.

"I owe you an apology for that," Max conceded, acknowledging Sauter's silent recollection of the beating he received beneath the treehouse two nights prior. "I know we've had our differences in the past, Sauter, but I had no right to do what I did. But seeing poor little Jimmy hanging there like that, just like my boy Nicholas here," he motioned to his strangled son's twisted neck, "something just came over me, I lost control. It seems crazy now, but at the time, I thought you killed Jimmy. I don't think that anymore, I *know* you didn't kill Jackson's boy."

It was the second time Sauter had been exonerated of any involvement in Jimmy Kelly's death since he arrived at the meadow, a pleasant surprise considering Corcoran's accusatory phone call summoning him to the scene. Kunick said Max had beaten the wrong man, now Max had agreed. Still, he couldn't comprehend why Nicholas was left hanging from the noose, his blank, bulging eyes following Sauter with a derisive death-stare.

"How about it, Max? Your boy . . .?" Sauter tried again, but Max still had a message to deliver.

"I wanted you to come here so you could see what's happened to my boy, Sauter, and to tell you that we're both to blame for his death. Jimmy's too," Max confided, confusing Sauter with his apparent flip-flop.

"You just told me that you didn't think I killed Jimmy, now you're telling me I'm to blame not only for his death, but for your son's, as well? Why don't you explain your meaning while I take that rope off his neck." Sauter decided not to wait for permission any longer, sickened that he was about to lower a third dead child to the same small patch of the forest floor.

Max caught Sauter's wrist as he reached up for the noose, yanking his arm down and pulling it towards him. Sauter felt the cool, clammy flesh of the corpse press against his skin as he and Max squeezed the dead child in an awkward hug. The life had been drained from Max as well, the spark had been extinguished, all that remained was an impassioned plea for understanding and forgiveness.

"I hadn't slept for three days, Sauter. I had voices in my head, I was hearing things . . . I thought I was losing my mind! I didn't think I could sleep if I tried, I didn't want to sleep. I was afraid, afraid for my boy," Max wailed, his grip tightening around Sauter's wrist. "But somehow I *did* fall asleep and now look what's happened to my Nicholas. I should have been watching out for him, I shouldn't have been asleep, and now he's gone!" He dropped Sauter's arm and wrapped himself around his son, burying his face into the dead boy's chest and sobbing convulsively.

Sauter stepped back from the heart-wrenching scene, allowing Max a moment to pour out his grief. The child's slowly stiffening body buckled over, bent in half by the father's constricting bear hug. The desperate weeping abated into intermittent gasps as Max fell limp and gradually collapsed to the ground, sliding slowly down the length of the dead body. When he finally let go, Nicholas swayed back and forth at the end of his tether, and the treehouse groaned overhead with menacing satisfaction. Sauter steadied the corpse and lifted it just enough to slacken the rope, straining against the dead weight of the man-sized boy. He worked the noose free from the broken neck and knelt down, gently laying the departed son next to the incapacitated father.

The lupines stiffened with a whispered rustle of purple petals, rising in a collective breath before slumping over in dull, lusterless sorrow. A choking stench descended from the treehouse and filtered through the drooping crop of flowers, inundating the meadow with the reeking aura of death and decay. The repulsive smell rolled like a phantom fog across the forest floor in a tidal retreat, mercifully dissipating into the cool night air as quickly as it had come. The diffused light encased the meadow in an insular bubble, an incandescent island adrift in the darkness.

Sauter stood and whirled in a confused circle, harried by the suspicion that he had been lured into a trap. He probed the inkiness beyond the rim of light, searching desperately for someone, some *thing,* uncertain what it was he expected to discover. There *was* a watcher in the woods, always at his back, slithering away as he turned, an all-encompassing eye ogling its handiwork with perverse delight. There was nothing normal about this haunted hole in the forest, he reminded himself, *nothing.*

"Is somebody gonna bring a blanket for my boy? He's cold and needs to be covered up." Max made the indirect request from his supine position, void of emotion, no longer wanting to obstruct the gruesome proceedings, "You and Bobby have work to do and I've been holding you up, but you needed to see my boy, Sauter. You needed to see what he did to my Nicholas."

"Who are you talking about? Who do you think killed your son, and Jimmy Kelly?" Sauter posed the leading question, offering Max a hand and yanking the despondent hulk to his feet. "And just a moment ago, when you said you and I both share in the blame, what did you mean by that, Max?" Sauter was sure he knew the answer to the first question, but was more circumspect regarding the second.

"You know who I'm talking about, Sauter, you damn well know who I think the killer is," Max couldn't bring himself to say the name, not in the shadows of the treehouse. "I'm willing to bet you know who it is, too. If that's the case, well, you've had the answer to your second question all along."

"It's Christopher Koenigs, that's who you believe killed your boy, I realize that," unhindered by superstition, Sauter boldly uttered the taboo name. "But where do we enter the picture, Max? How are we to blame?"

"Jackson Kelly's boy? My boy? You think it's just a coincidence that our sons were the ones hanging under this goddam treehouse? I guess I gave you more credit than you deserved, Sauter. I thought you had this whole mess figured out a long time ago," Max confessed, brushing by Sauter and prematurely curtailing the question and answer session before his curiosity was satisfied.

Kunick and Corcoran, wending their way through the field of faded   flowers, met up with Max as he exited in the direction of his three cohorts hunkered down by the generator. Kunick placed a hand on Max's shoulder, offering condolences for his loss and assurances that the killer would be captured. Corcoran stood deferentially to the side, a gray wool blanket draped over her arm. She nodded constantly during the brief exchange, then fell in step behind her boss as he continued on toward the treehouse. Colins loitered on the fringe of the light, ducking under the yellow police tape with unconcealed excitement when Sauter beckoned him to the base of the big bur oak.

"What was that all about?" Kunick inquired, referring to Max's insistence upon seeing Sauter before his son could be taken down from the makeshift gallows. Corcoran placed her palm on the dead child's forehead, then brushed the lids shut on his unseeing eyes and carefully covered the exposed corpse with the blanket.

"Just my luck I guess," Sauter replied, still trying to make sense of the morbid situation himself. "Max wanted me to see his son while he was still hanging from that treehouse. I think he wanted to impress upon me how important it was for us to catch whoever's responsible, as quickly as possible." There was no need to elaborate. "Somebody should really keep tabs on that guy. In his condition there's no telling what he might do, especially when the reality of what's happened here tonight finally sets in."

"I wouldn't mind being privy to that conversation," Kunick said, pointing to the four friends engaged in an animated discussion beneath the brilliant lights, their voices drowned out by the hum of the generator, "Look at 'em, they're at each other's throats for chrissakes! You'd think they'd be consoling each other, wouldn't you? Hold on to your hat, Sauter, but by god, I believe I'm finally coming around to your way of thinking, that those fellas have been holding onto a secret for all these years. I'll tell you what, it must be a doozy. I'm betting it would go a long way toward explaining why Christopher Koenigs is back here in Broadaxe, killing their kids."

Sauter dared not deny himself some semblance of satisfaction from the dilatory vindication of his oft-ridiculed suspicions, but the damage had long been done. Three children were dead and another life had been ruined. A tarnished reputation seemed a small price in comparison.

"Maybe somebody should just go over there and ask them," Colins suggested, emboldened by Sauter's invitation into the inner circle, "I can't imagine that they'd withhold any information that might help catch the killer when their own kids are being targeted."

"It's a done deal now, son, and they know it," Sauter surmised, memories of the heavy-handed attempts of a young cop trying to extract the information flashing before his eyes. "Anything they had to say should have been said many years ago, back when Michael Koenigs was hanging from this treehouse. There's no putting the genie back in the bottle now, as they say. They may know *why* Christopher Koenigs is back in Broadaxe – if, in fact, he is – but they don't know where to find him. That's our job, Max Ferguson just reminded me of that; so the next step is figuring out how we're going to go about doing it." He respectfully deferred to Kunick, "Bobby, what's the plan?"

"Wait a minute," Corcoran took her turn, addressing Sauter, "If I'm not mistaken you just implied that the killer might not be Christopher Koenigs. Am I correct?" Sauter nodded his agreement. Corcoran countered, "I think it's safe to say that as of right now we're operating under the assumption that Christopher Koenigs *is* the killer."

"Well, one shouldn't assume . . ."

"Oh please, Sauter, don't tell me you're going to pull out that old 'ass out of u and me' line," Corcoran protested.

"Actually, no. Unfortunately, I'm not that clever. That's a good one, though. I'll have to remember that one," Sauter said sarcastically, then finished his thought with reproachment. "I was going to say that there's no place for assumptions in a properly conducted police investigation. Suspicions? Instincts? Sure, that's all-together different, but you better have the facts to back it up. Once you start assuming things the facts have a funny way of fitting right in, tailored to reinforce those as-sumptions through your own biases. It's tough to arrive at the truth when you're too busy chasing yourself in circles. It's fine to have your suspicions about Christopher Koenigs, to listen to your instincts, but it's a bad idea to blindly assume that he's our killer."

"No problem, Sauter, I'll play your little game. I have my suspicions about Christopher Koenigs, strong suspicions, and my instincts tell me that he's the hangman. Do I know that for a fact? No, I don't, but I still say our top priority should be finding out where he's been for the past week," Corcoran reasoned.

"There you go, now you're catching on. I agree with you one-hundred percent," Sauter inflated his accord, hiding the disparity of his own instincts. "That brings me back to my original question – where do we start, Bobby?"

Kunick leaned against the gnarly gray bark of the bur oak, hands in the pockets of his rumpled pants and legs crossed at the ankles. He sniffed the air with a wrinkled nose, tasting the faint traces of the rotten smell still wafting over the meadow. Suffused with stolid determination, he didn't hesitate to propose his first order of business.

"As soon as we complete the crime scene investigation, the first thing we're going to do is tear that goddam treehouse down," Kunick commanded, tilting his head back to examine the underside of the scurrilous structure. "The killer is extremely cautious. There wasn't a clue left behind after Jimmy Kelly's murder, but maybe he, or she, made a mistake this time around." He dropped his gaze to the blanket covering Nicholas Ferguson's corpse.

"Are you sure that's a good idea, Bobby? Tearing down the treehouse, I mean," Sauter countered.

"I'll be damned if I'm going to allow one more child to hang from it, so it's coming down," Kunick bellowed. "Maybe that would be just the thing to make our murderer mad, mad enough to make a mistake. Maybe we could force his hand."

"Or force the murderer away," Sauter argued. "Think about it for a minute, Bobby, this treehouse is the only connection we have to the killer. Tear it down, and we've got nothing. I don't think we should be so hasty. I don't think that's the right way to go."

"I'm listening," Kunick vacillated, willing to hear Sauter's alternative.

"Leave it up and let the killer come to us," he suggested, "The murderer obviously went to a great deal of trouble to recreate the scene where Michael Koenigs died. Look at that treehouse for chrissakes, Bobby. It's identical to the one I tore down myself twenty-two years ago. The murderer isn't going to abandon it now, not when it serves as the centerpiece of the sick little game that's being played."

"So you're proposing a stake-out, correct?" Kunick stroked his chin, impressed by the inescapable logic of the idea.

"Exactly. I doubt the killer is going to come back during daylight hours, but just to be safe we should have at least one person out here tomorrow to keep an eye on things. Corcoran, maybe. Nothing's going to get past her," Sauter offered the compliment as appeasement for his unwelcome involvement. "Colins and I will come back before dark . . . is that okay with you Colins?"

"I'm in," Colins eagerly offered his services.

"Great! If you're out here tomorrow night too, Bobby, the four of us should be able to cover the meadow and the surrounding forest without bringing unwanted attention to ourselves. I'm convinced the killer comes back here every night. I don't think he has the willpower to stay away. When he shows up, we'll be waiting for him," Sauter predicted grimly.

"I'll spend the day out here tomorrow if that's what Chief Kunick wants me to do," Corcoran qualified her willingness to cooperate, displeased and dismayed with Sauter's apparent shift from suspect to savior.

"That's precisely what I want, Corky." Kunick pushed off the tree and placed a placating arm around her square shoulders. "Do me a favor too, will ya? Leave the hostility at home. Sauter's not as big a nut-job as some folks led you to believe – myself included, I suppose," he confessed meekly, "Besides, if we're dealing with Christopher Koenigs – and *my* instincts tell me that we are – there's nobody else around these parts who can provide the same insight. Hell, he's lived and breathed Christopher Koenigs for half his life. If anybody can track that crazy son-of-a-bitch down, it's our man Sauter here. Isn't that right, Henry?"

"I'll see what I can do," Sauter equivocated, once again the lone holdout in the rush to judgment against a possibly innocent man.

"What about your contact out in New York? The one that's associated with the mental hospital Koenigs walked away from? Have you spoken recently? What's happening out there? Anything we should be aware of?" Kunick fired off the questions in rapid succession.

Sauter imagined Devine lying awake in the darkness and under considerable duress, staring despondently at her bedroom ceiling, dreading the impending confrontation with her adversary, Dr. Sarah Perkins. Maybe she had felt a responsibility to inform Perkins of the hangings in Broadaxe immediately, thereby explaining why she had abruptly ended their phone conversation earlier that evening. If that were so, Devine was almost certainly being subjected to an insufferable harangue replete with accusations and I-told-you-so's from the woman who had affixed Koenigs with the 'genetic sociopath' label. Was there any way, he wondered, to keep such incendiary news from ever reaching Perkins at all?

Unbeknownst to Sauter, it was already too late. Ironically, the same subject was being discussed just outside of the yellow police tape, where Richard Mann preached a sermon of reassurance to his three dispirited disciples. The noise of the generator insured that no one outside of his immediate circle could eavesdrop upon his oration.

"I'm telling you, I've taken care of everything, just like I always have," he boasted unconvincingly. "I called Dr. Perkins tonight, right after I found out about Nicholas. I told her about the hangings, the treehouse, everything! She was appalled, of course, and very apologetic for her colleagues' severe misjudgment. She said she's going to come out to Wisconsin as soon as she can."

"A hell of a lot of good that will do!" Max scoffed.

"Hold on, hold on, that's the same thing you said when I wrote to Dr. Perkins back when Koenigs was about to be released here in Wisconsin," Richard protested, referring to the anonymous letter he had written to Perkins many years ago suggesting Koenigs was an ideal candidate for her studies. "That worked out fairly well for us, if you recall."

"Goddam it Richard, don't you understand?" Max

railed. "There's not a fucking thing you or Perkins, or anybody else for that matter, could do that would make a damn bit of difference to Jackson or me! Both our boys are dead you stupid asshole, and there's no bringing them back. Christ, Jimmy hasn't even been buried yet and my Nicholas is still laid out underneath that treehouse."

"Jimmy's funeral's tomorrow. He done gets buried tomorrow," Jackson poignantly reminded his friends. "Yous fellas is all gonna be there, eh?"

Max sneered contemptibly, "Nothing matters anymore, can't you see that? Christopher Koenigs, the treehouse, our little pact, none of it matters."

"What about *our* boys, Max?" Tim implored, his voice trembling with fright. "Our boys are still alive and are still in danger. They still matter. I know you don't want to see anything happen to Richard's boy, Terry, or to Tony or Billy. My heart goes out to you Max, you too Jackson, you both know that. I'd do anything to bring Jimmy and Nicholas back, I'd take their place if I could, but that's impossible. My point is we can't abandon each other now. Now is when we really need to pull together."

"Fine, whatever, you don't have to worry about me, I'll keep my mouth shut. I've got nothing to gain, certainly nothing to lose anymore. I'm done, I've had it. Keep your secret, let Perkins come to Wisconsin, I just don't give a shit," Max groaned mournfully, a lost soul, utterly defeated. He stepped out of the arc of light and was swallowed up by the night.

Sauter watched him go, surprised to see Max leave while his son's dead body remained, gradually growing stiff beneath the gray blanket. Distracted, Sauter tried in vain to remember what Kunick had just asked him, but his blank, unfocused expression unmasked his inattention before he could recall the conversation.

"Try and stick with us a little bit longer here, Sauter," Kunick pled impatiently. "I know you're tired, we're all tired, but none of us is going to get much sleep until we track down Christopher Koenigs. So what about it, huh, your contact out East?"

His mind refreshed, Sauter answered, "Jimmy Kelly's

hanging hasn't hit the radar out there yet, as least as of earlier this evening, but I'm guessing that's going to change now that a second child died under the same circumstances. Koenigs is the focus of a pretty massive manhunt in New York state as we speak, I've been told. His picture is all over the news, so if by chance he's still out there, somebody should spot him eventually. If he's here in Broadaxe, which seems to be the consensus, the onus is on us, at least for now. I imagine we're going to have plenty of company soon enough, whether we like it or not."

"We've got some work to do, so let's start by wrapping things up right here so we can get this child up off the cold ground. Corky, I need you to . . ." Kunick started to issue his instructions when the generator spit and gurgled as it choked on the last of the gas. The lights dimmed, then faded to black as the machine slowly droned to a stop.

The totality of the ensuing darkness was intensified by the abrupt dissolution of the artificial light. Sauter held his hand less than a foot in front of his face but was unable to discern any movement from his wriggling fingers. The blackness besmirched the meadow with ominous portent and a collective chill scurried down the spines of its sightless hostages. The silence itself was equally oppressive in the sudden absence of the generator's persistent hum, but it was maliciously shattered by a clear, omnipresent whistle that echoed through the forest. Sauter immediately recognized the shrill, piercing tune. The lyrics, in turn, crept unbidden into his head, haunting words that hurtled through the unsuspecting minds of everyone in the meadow.

Christopher Koenigs sittin' in a tree
K-I-L-L-I-N-G . . .

CHAPTER THIRTEEN

The parquetry shimmered with the reflective afterglow of the mop, capturing the energy of the thin fluorescent tubes lining the ceiling and saturating the dismal corridor with a gilded aura. Devine stood at the top of the stairwell, slightly winded from the early morning climb up four flights of concrete steps. She held the wooden handrail and leaned out into the hallway, chagrined to see the janitor lazily wetting the floor midway between herself and her destination. It was a woman, grossly overweight and clad in stiff-from-the-package olive green coveralls tucked into brown, knee-high rubber boots. The obese charwoman waddled down the center of the corridor, methodically swinging the soaked, stringy head of her mop back and forth between the walls.

Not surprisingly, the newly washed floor presented a slippery challenge to the slick leather soles of Devine's powder blue high heels. She tucked her briefcase under one arm and used her free hand to steady herself as she shuffled along the wall. Her shoes matched her twilled cotton outfit, a conservative business suit consisting of a form-fitting, knee-length skirt and tailored jacket with dark blue piping accenting the cuffs and collar. Tiny, colorful Kachina dolls decorated the barrette that secured her black hair in a bun at the back of her head, presenting a professional, put-together image that seemed unnatural for quarter of six on a Saturday morning.

The hangings in Broadaxe had stolen a sound night's sleep from one more victim, yet Devine felt remarkably refreshed and prepared to face the unpleasantness of her planned meeting with Dr. Sarah Perkins. The call came moments after she had cut short her conversation with Detective Sauter, an unintentional gaffe prompted by the shocking news of the second murder. Devine was contemplating the best approach for sharing the news with her contentious colleague, but when she answered the phone, expecting a return call from Sauter, Perkins tersely relieved her of that responsibility.

"Christopher Koenigs is back in business. Meet me at my office at 7 a.m. sharp."

That was the extent of it, no hello, no goodbye, just a vague declaration and presumptuous command delivered in the haughty, self-righteous tone that Perkins could have patented. "What a bitch!" Devine had mumbled to herself as she slammed down the receiver, irked by the mean-spirited lack of consideration. It was an intentional affront, Devine presumed, designed to leave her anxiously dangling in tormented suspense about the nature of Christopher Koenigs's "business." Her truncated conversations with Sauter had spared her the suspense, yet she still tossed and turned until the wee hours of the morning. Rather than count sheep, she wiled away the time by repeating a dubious mantra intended to bolster her wavering conviction – "It can't be Christopher Koenigs," she tried to re-assure herself, "it just can't be."

The cleaning woman plopped the dirty mop into the sieve of a wheeled, rusty metal bucket and pushed against the rubber-handled lever, leisurely squeezing out the soiled water. She arched her strained back, trying to work out the kinks in her overburdened muscles as the trickling liquid gradually quieted to the occasional drop. Her corpulent face was bright red and glistening from the subdued effort – a heart attack waiting to happen, Devine thought – framed by the tufts of graying brown hair peeking out from the damp folds of a paisley-patterned bandana. A severely upturned snout, high chubby cheeks, close-set eyes and flabby, chinless neck all contributed to her distinctly porcine appearance.

Devine was several steps away when the woman noticed her, appearing none too pleased that she had trod upon her as yet unfinished chore. She narrowed her gaze and sneered, forcing Devine to turn and take notice of the dimpled tracks she had left in the slowly drying surface. Water splashed out onto the floor as the offended cleaning woman forcefully plunged her mop up and down in the bucket to illustrate her irritation.

"I'm sorry, I don't typically come into the office this early on a Saturday morning," Devine felt the need to explain herself. "Actually, I don't normally come into the office at all on Saturdays, but there was a last minute meeting called that's scheduled to start in a little more than an hour from now so I came in early to prepare."

The sneer faded to a glazed disinterest, which quickly bled into annoyed impatience.

"Well, if you'll just excuse me then," Devine answered the rudeness with courtesy, refusing to be drawn into a senseless confrontation. The meeting with Perkins promised to deliver enough combative discourse for one day.

Still hugging the wall, she tried to hurry by before the cleaning woman resumed her work, but her early morning adversary wasn't willing to cooperate. The mop spewed an arcing gray stream in its hasty withdrawal from the bucket, nearly soiling Devine's powder blue shoes. The cleaning woman wielded the mop like a water-soaked weapon, sweeping it to and fro across the width of the corridor with calculated vigor. Devine stutter-stepped on the slippery floor, waiting for the opportune moment to pass, hesitating like a sidewalk stroller trying to avoid the overreaching spray of an oscillating lawn sprinkler. She slipped through the oddly amusing obstacle course unscathed, unable to suppress a smile as she strode away with sure-footed confidence down the dry, unwashed half of the hallway.

Devine fumbled with her keys as she hurried to open her office door, prodded by the perceived urgency of the ringing within. She jiggled the lock and the door popped open, but instead of rushing to the phone she paused at the threshold and snuck a peek down the corridor. The cleaning woman, head bowed and elephantine hips swaying, had fallen back into her indolent rhythm, swinging the mop and shuffling her rubber-booted feet with sluggish insouciance. Ducking into her office, Devine decided to let the answering machine screen the incoming call.

Hello Amelia, this is Detective Sauter, um, Henry, I tried to phone you at home but . . .

The answering machine screeched in protest as Devine lifted the receiver and intercepted the recording. She kicked off her shoes and pitched the jangling key chain onto the corner of her well-ordered desk and dropped the leather briefcase into a chair. The keys slid off the desk and fell noisily to the floor, joined shortly by the briefcase as it caromed off the tight coils of the cushion.

"Good morning Henry, this is Amelia. I'm glad I caught you, I stepped into my office just this second," Devine trilled in a tone too chipper for such an early hour. "You must have had a long night last night. How are you holding up?"

"I'm hanging in there . . . Good morning, by the way," Sauter's response lacked any such exuberance. "I'm calling for the same reason, as fate would have it. I'm guessing you didn't get much shuteye yourself."

"No, I sure didn't."

"So what happened? Did you contact Perkins right away last night and inform her about the hangings, or is that what brings you into the office at this hour on the weekend?"

"Well, that *is* why I'm here in the office, to meet with Perkins regarding Christopher Koenigs, but she's the one who contacted me," Devine clarified. "She called me as soon as we hung up . . . I'm sorry, as soon as I hung up. I do apologize for that Henry, I don't know what came over me."

"What do you say we just call it even and try to end this conversation with a civil 'so long' for a change," Sauter suggested with a soft chuckle.

"That shouldn't be a problem, should it? I'm hoping both of us have depleted our supply of bombshells," Devine concurred playfully.

"So how did Perkins react when you dropped your bombshell on her," Sauter asked. "I imagine she really went off when you told her about the hangings."

"Oh, as I was about to say, she contacted me because she already knew about it, Henry."

"She already knew about *both* the hangings? How do you suppose that bit of news reached her so quickly? Apparently you're not the only one with a connection out here in Wisconsin," Sauter surmised.

"Actually, Henry, Perkins didn't come right out and admit that she knew two children had been hung in Broadaxe," Devine elucidated. "She only said that Christopher Koenigs is back in business. Those were her exact words, back in business, and she told me to meet her here at Municipal Mental Health this morning. That's it, that's all she said, but what else could she possibly mean? Somebody from Broadaxe must have contacted her last night after the second child was found, there's no other explanation. She knows, Henry, otherwise she never would have called me in the middle of the night."

"When are you supposed to meet with her?"

Devine checked the clock, "In about forty-five minutes, in her office at seven."

"Do me a favor, would you please? See if you can find out who her contact is out here. I'm curious to see who was so anxious to share the news with her," Sauter requested, wondering whether her source was a member of the Broadaxe Police Department or a citizen of the community at large.

"I'll see what I can do, Henry. Is there anything else right now? I can get in touch with you again later, but there are some things I need to look over before I meet with Perkins."

"I guess I was holding out hope that you'd have some news for me about Koenigs. Everybody out here is convinced that he's the killer, Amelia, everybody but me. My gut keeps telling me that he's not our man, that things aren't as cut and dried as they appear," Sauter confessed. "Christ, here I am again, the lone ranger, same as I was back when Michael Koenigs was killed. I keep telling myself that everybody else is turning a blind eye to the truth, but I don't know, maybe it's me after all."

There was a moment's pause before Devine spoke, "I'm sorry Henry, I'm still here. I was just checking the messages on my computer. You're not going to believe this, but there have been a number of unconfirmed sightings of Koenigs at several locations in northern and eastern New York state. All of the alleged sightings were last weekend, but this is the first time I've seen or heard anything about it. The sightings place him as far north as the Canadian border. If it's him, and if he was headed for Wisconsin like everybody seems to believe, he certainly took a circuitous route to get there. I'll see if I can learn more later on today, Henry, but I really do have to get going now."

"It's better than nothing, Amelia, which is what we've been working with up to this point. I hope some of those sightings can be confirmed and we can get some idea which direction Koenigs actually headed when he walked away," Sauter assessed the news optimistically, hastening to add, "Listen, I know you're in a hurry, but there's one more thing you need to know, about the hangings," he paused a beat, "The two boys who were killed, Jimmy Kelly and Nicholas Ferguson, there's a connection there to Christopher Koenigs. The fathers, Jackson Kelly and Max Ferguson, well, they were two of the four local children who were present the night Michael Koenigs died. Their sworn statements reinforced the popular theory that Christopher Koenigs was a mentally disturbed individual who killed his younger brother, with premeditation. It's hard to argue with the notion that the past provides Koenigs with ample motive to commit the current murders. I just thought you should know that before you met with Perkins, that's all."

"Oh my god, Henry, my head is swimming," Devine sighed, "I really don't know what to think anymore. I fully intend to defend the decision to release Christopher Koenigs to the halfway house. I really have no choice at this point; but Henry, oh my god . . ."

"Try not to fret, Amelia, we're keeping the treehouse – the scene of the murders – under twenty-four hour surveillance," Sauter offered reassuringly. "I don't expect anything will happen during the day, but I have a hunch the killer will be back tonight, then we'll have the answers to all our questions. Trust me, Amelia, we're going to catch the person responsible for these murders. If it turns out to be Christopher Koenigs, we'll deal with the consequences then, okay? Goodbye Amelia, and good luck."

"Goodbye Henry, it was so nice speaking with you," Devine signed off with ingrained kindness, thankful that she still had a good half-hour to collect herself before butting heads with Perkins. She retrieved her keys and briefcase from the floor and carried them with her to the window. Wedging the briefcase between her nyloned-knees, she twisted open the vertical, white linen slats of the window blinds, pausing to survey the empty courtyard below her fifth floor window.

Enclosed on all four sides by the staid brick façade of the aging institution, the grassy basin of the rectangular courtyard was interlaced with the narrow cement walks radiating from the small water fountain at its center. Two wooden benches overlooked the fountain, an unadorned concrete bowl ejecting a single stream of water that spurted no more than two feet in the air before tumbling back downward in a spray of individual droplets. The benches, and the courtyard, per usual, were unoccupied. Devine never went there herself, blaming flawed architectural design for the courtyard's gloomy, uninviting ambience. It was, in her mind, a reflection of the facility as a whole. With five more stories above her, the building's high walls shielded the courtyard from the warming benefit of direct sunlight on cool days and, conversely, trapped the oppressive heat of muggy summer afternoons.

The briefcase slipped from between her legs and thudded to the floor for a second time, nudging her away from the window and back to her desk. She sat down with the briefcase on her lap and flicked open the brass latches with her thumbs, opening it just wide enough to dip in a hand and fish out a Polaroid photograph of Christopher Koenigs. It had been taken just over a week ago, the day he was released from cell C-28, Block 3 of the Municipal Mental Health Center, the day he disappeared. The photograph was only distributed to the media after the holiday weekend when Koenigs turned up missing, Devine recalled, explaining why the alleged, week-old sightings were just now filtering in. She studied the image, gazing beyond the photograph itself, questioning whether the subject possessed a soul that the camera could steal. She had snapped the picture herself.

Koenigs stood in the doorway of his cell, clutching a canvas satchel too large for his spartan supply of undergarments and toiletries. He cradled the remainder of his meager personal belongings in a cardboard shoebox tucked in the crook of his arm. It was a head-to-toe shot, posed to capture the transformation a mere change of clothes could make in a man. He wore white tennis shoes, tan trousers, and a tan windbreaker over a white tee shirt. Far from dapper in the department of corrections issued duds, but a drastic change in appearance from the crumpled, oversized orange jump suit that had been his only apparel for the past twelve years.

In truth, the new outfit affected no meaningful change.

Koenigs certainly no longer cut such a droopy, stoop-shouldered figure, but his somber, careworn expression belied the defeated heart that beat within. Resigned to the cruel reality fate had handed him, he stared back at the camera with vacant eyes, a thirty-year-old man who had eroded at an accelerated pace. His thin, graying hair nearly matched the colorless pallor of his sagging skin. He was nondescript, invisible, the next door neighbor or the factory worker waiting at the bus stop at the end of another agonizing shift. Devine imagined him slowing walking away from the halfway house and dissolving into the surrounding scenery.

The photograph surrendered no secrets, reaffirming Devine's conviction that there were no secrets to conceal. Christopher Koenigs was harmless. He was not a 'genetic sociopath' at the mercy of a mind programmed for murder and mayhem. He was, in fact, a victim of a system that had unjustly robbed him of the prime of his life. He did not return to Broadaxe to murder innocent children. That is what she intended to tell Dr. Sarah Perkins, fully aware of the scorn and ridicule she would open herself up to by expressing that belief. She had no other choice. If her judgment and intuition were so blatantly fallible, or, worse yet, if she had simply been duped by a deranged but clever criminal mind, she was obviously ill-suited to continue with her current profession. The thought didn't frighten her, for her career no longer seemed to matter when a life, or lives, were on the line.

Invigorated by the carefree confidence that commitment to one's principled beliefs engenders, Devine chucked the photograph back into her briefcase and headed for the showdown with Perkins empty-handed. It was 7 a.m. The hallway was empty, sparing her another dance with the contentious cleaning woman's mop. She serpentined between the damp patches that still glistened against the dull backdrop of the faster drying sections of the parquetry. Perkins occupied the corner office at the far end of the corridor, a short stroll away, but Devine was in no hurry to get there. She derived a certain amount of guilty pleasure picturing Perkins glaring impatiently at the clock, chafing for the opportunity to gloat over her prescience regarding Christopher Koenigs's apparent recidivism.

The door was propped open at the bottom with a hard-rubber wedge, but Devine still knocked and waited deferentially for her summons into Perkins's inner sanctum. The shade was drawn down on a slightly open window, its weighted bottom rising and falling with the gentle puffs of cool air filtering into the room. Perkins was seated behind her desk, long legs stretched out and clasped hands resting in her lap. Her attire was atypically casual, selected since it was a Saturday, Devine presumed, self-consciously second guessing her own choice of a more formal business outfit. Perkins appeared enviously comfortable in flat-bottomed sandals, pressed black jeans and a peasant-collared white shirt unbuttoned to reveal just a touch of cleavage.

"Come in, Dr. Devine, come in," she waved a beckoning hand with a gregarious smile that Devine found unsettling, "I appreciate your willingness to meet me here this morning on such short notice – a Saturday morning no less! Please, pour yourself a cup of coffee and make yourself comfortable. It's a delicious dark roast blend of beans from Peru, ground fresh this morning. It's one of my favorites, so please, help yourself. Take a seat."

Anticipating more hostility and less gentility, Devine had defensively puffed herself up with piss and vinegar, her father's favorite colloquialism for her inherent feistiness. The rich aroma proved intoxicating. She was a sucker for a good cup of coffee, but she didn't see why she couldn't sip a fine dark roast and remain indignant at the same time. Wisps of steam corkscrewed out of the piping hot brew and vanished as she filled a white ceramic cup so small that it could have been a piece of a young girl's tea set. Perkins's red lipstick smudged the rim of the regular-sized mug sitting on her desk and Devine noted the disparity, amused that the favored Peruvian blend was rationed out to guests in comically small doses. She downed her first cup in two hearty swigs and poured another, curious if there was a cut-off point.

"Make sure you leave enough for the others, Amelia," Perkins scolded, stingily supplying the answer to Devine's unspoken question.

"Drs. Karet and Welsch, I presume?" Devine inquired,

referring to the remaining members of the medical examiners board who had voted, along with Devine, to grant Koenigs's release.

"Yes, yes, of course," Perkins confirmed, wondering if Devine had just made a reasonable assumption or somehow already knew the subject of the meeting, "They won't be here until seven-thirty, however. I thought it would be nice to have a little time to chat first, just you and I, catch up on things. It certainly is a beautiful morning, wouldn't you say? By the way, I meant to tell you how great you look! I love that outfit, it's perfect on you," she gushed.

The coffee's delicious, dark chocolate essence was suddenly overpowered by the bitter taste biting at Devine's tongue. Perkins's cloying behavior struck her as obscenely superfluous. She was sickened by the smug satisfaction Perkins exuded as she broke from character and attempted to engage in mistimed small talk. It was unimaginable that an individual, even one as Messianic as Perkins, could derive such selfish pleasure at the expense of another's suffering. There would be no *chat*, no *catching up*.

"My God! You're actually enjoying all of this, aren't you?" Devine exploded. "Two boys have been murdered, Sarah! Two families have lost a child! Is that an equitable trade off in your estimation? The lives of two children in exchange for your own sad self-aggrandizement? Two children are dead, Sarah, doesn't that mean anything to you?"

Perkins flew out of her chair and slammed her clenched fists down on her desk. "Don't you dare come into my office and start preaching to me, Dr. Devine, not when I'm the only one in this room who has a clear conscience as far as those two unfortunate boys are concerned. Those children would still be alive if you had listened to me, if you hadn't been in such a rush to set a depraved killer free!"

"You know this for a fact? You *know* that Christopher Koenigs killed those kids? Somehow, sitting behind your desk here in New York, you've managed to solve two murders that occurred out in Wisconsin – two murders that are still under investigation, I might add." Devine had calmly lowered her voice, hoping to avoid a shouting match. Perkins's tone, in contrast, pitched aggressively upward.

"Please! Are you kidding me?" she screeched. "I don't know who you're getting your information from, I don't know how you found out about the killings and I don't really care, but you're obviously sorely lacking in specifics. All of the evidence indicates that it's him."

Devine remained impassive, "What evidence would that be? Specifics tend to do more harm than good if they're false or misleading, Sarah. There is no evidence, other than circumstantial, but don't let that bother you. Most of the folks out in Broadaxe have jumped to the same conclusion."

"Who have you spoken to in Broadaxe?" Perkins demanded, miffed that she had lost the upper hand provided by a monopoly on inside information.

"I thought you didn't care," Devine reminded Perkins of her feigned indifference. "Does it really matter? Maybe you'd be willing to tell me who your contact is, maybe it's the same person." She made a clumsy attempt to extract the name per Sauter's request.

"I'm sworn to confidentiality," Perkins scoffed at the idea with a half-truth, "but I can guarantee you that we're not getting our information from the same source."

She and Richard Mann had never actually agreed to a confidential arrangement, it was always just assumed. The anonymous letter initially tipping Perkins off to the Koenigs case remained just that, anonymous. Based on Richard Mann's subsequent and persistent interest in all things Christopher Koenigs, which she obtusely never questioned, Perkins had come to believe that he had in all likelihood penned the introductory missive. There was an odd symbiosis to their relationship, each happy to use and be used to achieve a common goal – keeping Christopher Koenigs incarcerated.

"We both have reasons for protecting our sources, Amelia, but the who, after all, isn't nearly as important as the what, at least not in this case," Perkins suggested, no longer shouting. "Perhaps you'd be willing to share *what* you know?"

Devine sensed the set up and could see that Perkins was poised to pounce regardless of her response. If she balked and pretended not to know about the incriminating similarities between the recent hangings and Michael Koenigs's death, Perkins would accuse her of acting out of ignorance. Confessing what she knew would give Perkins ample ammunition to make a mockery out of her insistence on affording Christopher Koenigs the presumption of innocence until he was factually linked to the murders. She decided to have her say, hoping to surprise Perkins with her candor.

"A young boy named Jimmy Kelly was murdered Wednesday night, and another child, Nicholas Ferguson, was murdered just last night. The murders occurred in Broadaxe at the same location where Michael Koenigs was killed," she regurgitated Sauter's narrative. "The killer went to a great deal of trouble to recreate the scene where Koenigs died more than twenty years ago, hanging the boys from a replica of the treehouse out of which Christopher Koenigs purportedly pushed his younger brother to his death," she paused, ruminating. "Oh, and one other thing, the fathers of the boys just killed were two of the children present the night Michael Koenigs died."

Perkins stiffened and averted her quizzical blue eyes. The early morning meeting was not progressing as she had planned. She anticipated delivering the surprises, not receiving them. The biggest surprise was Devine's comparatively intimate knowledge about the hangings in Wisconsin. Until Devine had provided more details, Perkins had only known that two children had been killed in the past week, hung from a treehouse in Christopher Koenigs's hometown, and one of the boys was to be buried that afternoon. That was the extent of the information delivered to her by an anxious Richard Mann, but it was enough to convince her that Koenigs had returned to Broadaxe upon his escape. She didn't believe in coincidences, not on that scale.

A strong gust of wind flapped the shade and a handful of papers fluttered to the floor from a nearby shelf. Perkins knelt and collected the scattered documents. She tapped the papers on the floor until the corners were aligned, then returned them to their place. The window creaked when she pushed it shut, cutting the cramped quarters off from the invigorating flow of fresh air. She opened the shade without bothering to look out upon the dismal courtyard, then changed her mind and pulled it back down, shutting out the feeble light. Slowly, she turned and faced Devine, perplexed by her colleague's incomprehensible commitment to a lost cause.

"So Amelia, you're telling me . . ." she stopped and touched a finger to her lips, rethinking her approach. "Based on everything you just told me, I can't help but conclude that Christopher Koenigs is the most obvious suspect. The victims' fathers provide an unquestionable connection between the past and the present. Amelia, how can you continue to deny what's happening here? I'm at a loss trying to understand your way of thinking, I really am, but apparently I'm not the only one whose motives are being influenced by some degree of self-interest."

Devine surrendered the point. "I suppose that's true, I'm probably just as guilty of that as anyone else, but I don't believe it's kept me from assessing the situation with an open mind."

"Are you calling me close-minded?" Perkins blurted, needlessly defensive in Devine's estimation.

"I'm not calling you anything, Sarah. I was talking about myself," Devine attempted to play nice, then decided not to pull any punches. "But, now that you mention it, I do believe that you have blinders on where Christopher Koenigs is concerned. It's a human being we're talking about here, Sarah, not some laboratory mouse that can be kept running around in the maze until he drops over dead."

"No, of course not, much better to give the meek little mouse his freedom," Perkins sneered. "The only problem I have with that untenable comparison is that, unlike yourself, I never believed Christopher Koenigs to be a mouse. I judged Christopher Koenigs for what he was, is, and always will be, a monster and a murderer."

Dr. Barry Karet cleared his throat to announce his presence, "So that's what this emergency meeting is all about, another kick at the cat." He entered the room and breathlessly took a seat, trailing the stale perfume of cigarette smoke clinging to his clothes. "So I take it our friend Koenigs has been located and we need to figure out what to do with the happy wayfarer. Is that it?"

"Christopher Koenigs has been found? Oh, thank god," Dr. Ruth Welsch made her entrance, arriving on the heels of Karet, both conscientiously prompt for their 7:30 a.m. summons.

Karet had carried Perkins's casual Saturday morning style one step further, donning a gray, hooded sweatshirt, stained brown chinos and soiled running shoes for the occasion. His thick black hair was matted by the pillow on one side and stood up in an uncombed mess on the other, while his bloodshot eyes and cherubic cheeks shone with the afterglow of the previous evening's cocktails. Welsch, always prim and proper, had her dyed black hair impeccably styled and wore a conservative gray skirt and jacket that complemented the lighter highlights near her temples. Her broad, misplaced smile of relief made Devine uneasy, fearful of the toll that the unsavory reality would wreak on Welsch's fragile constitution. Perkins, predictably, entertained no such qualms.

"Actually, Koenigs hasn't exactly been located as of yet, but we, excuse me, *I* believe I know where he's been for the past few days – and you're not going to like it," Perkins grinned insensitively, once again irritating Devine with her callous derivation of perverse delight.

"What do you mean?" Welsch directed the question at Perkins, her relief instantly trammeled by disquieting confusion.

"It would be best if Dr. Devine explained the present situation," Perkins suggested shrewdly, implying that her antithetical colleague had been less than forthcoming about current affairs. "She seems to know quite a bit more than she's been willing to share, so I respectfully defer to her expertise on the matter. If you'd be so kind, Dr. Devine, please tell our associates what you know in regard to all that has happened this past week."

Devine willingly obliged, hoping to instill a predisposition of doubt pertaining to Christopher Koenigs's whereabouts, "I take it none of you had time to check your messages this morning, otherwise there would be no need for me to tell you that there were several unconfirmed sightings of Christopher

Koenigs last weekend." She saw the impact of her unexpected tack reflected in Perkins's unknowing eyes, "The sightings were reported in northern New York state, all the way up to the border, so it appears as if Koenigs may have made a run for Canada."

"Wait just one minute!" Perkins again pounded her desk, beside herself. "Have your senses completely abandoned you, Dr. Devine? Canada?"

"Have you checked your messages?" Devine asked serenely, nodding her head at Perkins's darkened computer screen.

"No, I haven't checked my messages! This is ridiculous! I do not care if Koenigs was supposedly sighted heading toward Canada and I do not care if he was seen boarding a boat bound for Cuba! He is in Wisconsin, Dr. Devine, Broadaxe, Wisconsin!"

Perkins was livid, red-faced and ranting, frustrated by her inability to manipulate the proceedings as she had intended. In contrast, Devine was restrained, rational. Karet and Welsch sat stone-faced, trying to decipher if, in fact, anything was actually known about Koenigs's current location. They watched Perkins cautiously, disquieted by her cryptic late night phone call and present rage.

"Well, that's my point I guess," Devine reasoned. "He wasn't spotted on his way to Cuba and he wasn't spotted on his way to Wisconsin. All of the sightings had him headed north, or east."

"*Unconfirmed* sightings," Perkins clarified pointedly. "Don't say I didn't warn you, Dr. Devine. You are committing professional suicide with your misguided attempt to concoct an alibi for a convicted killer who is back in business."

"Whoa, back up the bus a second here," Karet interrupted in his smoker's rasp. "If you'd please be kind enough to clue Dr. Welsch and myself in on just what the hell is going on here, we'd very much appreciate it! Your message last night was very dramatic indeed, Dr. Perkins – Christopher Koenigs is back in business – now you've just said it again, but I still don't know what the hell it means! I guess I assumed he was captured too, back in the business of getting his head examined, you know."

Perkins gladly dispelled the misconception, "Two children have been killed in Broadaxe, Wisconsin, Christopher Koenigs's boyhood home. Both boys were hanged, just like Michael Koenigs, hanged from the very same tree! The murders were committed within the last three days. The victims' fathers were there all those years ago when Michael was pushed to his death by his older brother. They witnessed the entire thing. Do you understand now what I meant when I said Christopher Koenigs was back in business?"

"Sure, now I understand, but is there any evidence, anything at all linking Koenigs to what's going on in Wisconsin right now?" Karet winked at Devine as he assumed her accustomed role as devil's advocate.

"Did you listen to anything I just said? What is it going to take to convince you people? More dead children?" Perkins shook her head in rebuke.

"It would take evidence to convince me," Welsch chimed in assuredly. "I'd need to see solid evidence to convince me either way, guilty or innocent. You didn't answer Dr. Karet's question. Maybe you could, Amelia. Is there any evidence that Christopher Koenigs is involved in these deaths?"

Perkins laughed derisively and continued to wag her head, "The evidence seems pretty overwhelming to me, let me tell you, but if you're talking about fingerprints and DNA . . ."

"There isn't any," Devine broke in. "All of the evidence is circumstantial, Dr. Welsch. The killer has been very cautious. There hasn't been any evidence collected at the crime scene implicating Christopher Koenigs, or anyone else, for that matter. There has been no evidence of any kind left behind."

"The crime scene itself is ample evidence," Perkins countered, working to conceal her seething temper. "Somehow, Dr. Devine conveniently omitted a description of the murder scene. These two boys were hanged from a treehouse, but not just any treehouse. It's an exact replica of the original treehouse that was there when Michael Koenigs was killed."

"The original treehouse was torn down many years ago, that's a known fact," Devine added, hoping Karet or Welsch would pick up on her lead. "I've also learned from a reliable source that the new treehouse was built fairly recently."

Karet made the connection and considered the logistics, "So, let me get this straight, Dr. Perkins. If you're saying Koenigs set this all up – which it sounds like you are – that would mean he would have had to travel from New York to Wisconsin, obtain the necessary materials and tools, construct a treehouse from childhood memories, track down his intended victims, abduct them, and, finally, kill them both. All in one week's time, never heard nor seen. It seems highly improbable, if not outright impossible."

"Maybe if he had an accomplice, you know, somebody back in Wisconsin who set everything up for him and assisted in the murders," Devine only offered the possible explanation so she could point out its absurdity. "Highly unlikely though. We all know that. Koenigs had no family, no friends, he never communicated with anybody, inside or outside of these walls."

"How soon we forget! He kept in touch with his dead baby brother, the brother he killed with his own hands," Perkins recalled facetiously. "Need I remind you, this is a mentally unstable individual we're talking about here, a certified genetic sociopath. He was committed to the extensive examination beyond mandatory release program for a reason, and, if I dare say, I cautioned each of you about the potential ramifications of releasing him prematurely."

"Christopher Koenigs was eight years old when his little brother died and he spent the next twenty-two years locked away in mental institutions," Devine protested, her traditional lament. "I'd hardly classify his release as premature."

There was a break in the conversation and a contemplative hush descended on the dreary corner office. It had turned uncomfortably stuffy in the absence of the refreshing breeze that had rattled the shade. Perkins cracked the window and opened the shade halfway, allowing the diffused light of the courtyard to filter into the room. She weighted the stack of papers with a gray metal stapler, holding the documents in place as the influx of air rustled the loose edges. Devine filled herself another thimble-full of coffee despite Perkins's earlier admonition. She didn't feel guilty. Nearly half a pot remained, a good ten to fifteen of the tiny tea cups. Devine amused herself with the estimation.

Perkins was apparently through playing hostess, anyway, not bothering to offer Karet or Welsch a taste of her precious Peruvian blend in the first place. Karet looked like he could have used it. It would have given him another cigarette substitute to stick in his mouth besides the tooth-pocked number two pencil he gnawed on habitually. Welsch, on the other hand, conducted herself with confidence and composure, infusing Devine with as much relief as the gentle wind rolling across the room. The news of the recent hangings coupled with Koenigs's escape could have proved devastating to Welsch, most certainly would have in the past, but Devine could see by the set of her jaw and the determination in her eyes that she wasn't going to allow unchecked emotion to cloud her judgment.

"Premature," Perkins reignited the debate, leaving the lone word hanging by itself as she crossed her arms and sat sideways on the edge of her desk. Karet and Welsch looked up at her from their low profile chairs, like pupils awaiting a well-worn lesson from the teacher. Devine declined Perkins's invitation to sit. She knew what was coming. They all did. It was only a matter of time.

"Premature," Perkins repeated the word with a crooked grin. "Let's pick a pithy saying shall we? It's the same old song and dance. It's déjà vu all over again. Been there, done that. Old so soon, smart so late. I could go on, but I'm sure you all get the idea. Karl Meriter and Nadine Kasten. Need I say more?" she asked rhetorically. "When I adamantly opposed their release what was my argument? Do any of you recall? I said their release would be *premature*! I wasn't wrong then, and I'm not wrong now."

Karet removed his pencil from his mouth, "I understand your point, Dr. Perkins. You've certainly made it often enough. But does anything that happened back then really have any bearing on what's occurring now?"

"I have one more saying for you, Dr. Karet. If you fail to learn from past mistakes, you're destined to repeat them. It was a mistake to release Meriter and Kasten, and it was a mistake to release Koenigs. The similarities are staggering. Karl

Meriter was nine years old when he locked his friends in an ice shanty and lit them on fire. Nadine Kasten was an eleven year old babysitter when she dissected an infant. Christopher Koenigs was eight when he hung his little brother from a treehouse. This is where the stories diverge, however. Meriter and Kasten were released at the age of eighteen. Again, *I* said it was premature, but the argument that they were just little kids when they committed their crimes and had served their time eventually won out. That's the same argument I listened to when Koenigs was up for release on his eighteenth birthday and it's the same argument I'm hearing now. It doesn't wash, not with me, not knowing what I know, what we all know."

Perkins took it upon herself to remind them, "Upon his release, Karl Meriter barricaded his halfway house and incinerated its occupants, while Nadine Kasten abducted an infant from a shopping mall and impaled the baby on a barbecue spit. Koenigs didn't have that opportunity as an eighteen year old, thanks to the terrible lesson we learned from the Meriter and Kasten fiasco, but it seems we've only delayed the inevitable by delaying his release." She had turned predictably patronizing. "Koenigs disappears and kids start turning up dead back in his hometown. Sure, that's right, the past has nothing to do with the present."

Perkins tucked a wayward strand of long blond hair behind an ear and assessed the impact of her impassioned oration. Welsch rose from her chair and walked over to the window, her calm exterior masking the inner turmoil unleashed by abhorrent memories, memories of a decision that nearly stole her sanity, her career, and her life. As she gazed blankly out the window, she assured herself there would be no breakdown, no pills and alcohol, not this time around. She stubbornly refused to believe she could have made the same unforgiveable mistake twice in one lifetime.

"Even though you take every opportunity to remind us of the past, Dr. Perkins, you can rest assured that I live every day of my life with regret," she spoke with her back turned to the room. "I argued persuasively for the release of Meriter and Kasten, but what's done is done. I agreed to Koenigs's release as well, but this is far from over. I'll stand by what I said earlier. I need evidence, not mere supposition, to convince me of that man's guilt or innocence."

Devine lent her support. "Exactly, that's the logical approach." She addressed Perkins, "Do you really believe we can go about this any other way, Sarah? *We* turned Koenigs loose, *we* determined that he was not a threat to society, *we* bear responsibility for the ramifications of that decision. I for one will not admit that I was wrong, not yet, not until Christopher Koenigs is located and the murders in Wisconsin are resolved."

"*We* are obviously at an impasse," said Karet. "Some of us think Koenigs killed those kids in Wisconsin, some of us don't," he alternated glances between his colleagues, "but guilty or innocent, Canada or Cuba, like Dr. Welsch just said, it's all supposition until Koenigs is found. With that in mind, maybe you could explain to me why we all needed to come into the office so damn early on a Saturday morning." He was agitated, desperate for a smoke. "You could have just told us what was happening over the phone, or waited until Monday morning, for that matter. What the hell are we going to do? Sit here on our thumbs? Hold a vigil until Koenigs shows up?"

"No, I'm not going to sit idly by while others have to deal with the mess that's been made," Perkins said. "I'm going out to Wisconsin, to Broadaxe, and I'm going to do whatever I can to help locate Christopher Koenigs before he takes another child's life. I was hoping that some, if not all of you, would join me. It's the least we could do."

"I'm not going to Wisconsin. I'm not going on some wild goose chase," Karet protested. "I'm buried in work here as it is. I don't have time for that nonsense. I'm a doctor, not a detective, for chrissakes! Count me out."

Welsch remained by the window, but she turned and faced the room. "I'm afraid that I have to agree with Dr. Karet. I have nothing to contribute to a murder investigation, I'd just be in the way. Those folks know how to do their jobs, I'm sure. They don't need me sticking my nose in where it doesn't belong."

"Dr. Devine?" Perkins tried her last resort.

"Sure, I'm in," she didn't hesitate. It had been years since she had been back to her home state, back to Wisconsin, and she thought it would be nice to return, even under such unfortunate circumstances. "When were you planning on leaving?"

"As soon as possible," Perkins said. "The funeral for one of the children who was killed takes place this afternoon and it would have been nice to make an appearance, to get a feel for what's happening there in Broadaxe. That would be pushing it, though. We'd never make it. Besides, I still have some things to take care of around here and I have to pack. I'm sure you have some loose ends to tie up as well. Let me see what kind of arrangements I can make."

Devine didn't know if this was such a good idea. Like her colleagues Karet and Welsch, she didn't know what she could possibly contribute, but those were secondary concerns. She was secretly thrilled by the prospect of finally meeting Detective Henry Sauter, and she felt silly for fretting about what she was going to wear.

CHAPTER FOURTEEN

The small log chapel was filled beyond capacity. Grim-faced parishioners were crowded into the rows of solid oak pews so tightly that their black-clad torsos overlapped. The aisles were impassable, clogged by reverently hunched bodies that spilled out of the open doors, down the steps, and into the parking lot. Shards of prismatic, pastel light snuck through the arching stained glass windows, probing the emptiness beneath the hand-hewn rafters of the high cathedral ceiling. Large wax pillars lined the altar, tipped by dancing flames that left a smoky residue lingering above a mesa of white, long-stemmed lilies.

The casket was simple, unadorned, an apt reflection of the shattered family that was laying its only child to rest. It was a small pine box, easily mistaken for a tool chest or storage bin, but the precious little boy asleep within transformed it into a sacred vault. Jimmy Kelly lay in peaceful repose, his fiery red hair dancing on the coffin's stark white pillow like the candle flames above him. He was dressed in a new blue blazer, white shirt, and matching blue tie. An arrangement of tea roses and pine boughs decorated the lid of the closed lower half of the coffin, along with a framed photograph of the young boy striking a menacing pose in his wrestling uniform.

The wooden pews creaked, hymnals rustled, feet shuffled and throats were cleared, but the chapel was otherwise silent. Absent were the uncontrolled sobs, the primordial wailings and the persistent sniffling that provided the normal soundtrack to a young child's funeral. There was sorrow, but there were no tears. It was a congregation too shocked to properly mourn, a community still reeling from the unconscionable news that another of its children had been slain; that Nicholas Ferguson had also been taken from them; that they were destined to repeat this awful ritual yet again.

Margaret closed her eyes to ward off the claustrophobic malaise that had plagued her throughout the funeral service. She was pinched into one of the pews, back turned to a bearded woodsman who reeked of the chainsaw oil and sawdust imbedded in his flannel shirt and blue jeans. Her left arm rested on the back of the pew behind her boys' bowed heads, and it had fallen asleep. Tim's right arm stretched over the top and he gripped her bicep, the moisture from his palm dampening the sleeve of her charcoal dress. Tony and Billy were sandwiched between them, sitting partly on the hard wooden bench and partly on their parents' more comfortable laps. The illogical panic subsided and she blinked open her eyes, trying to ignore the impenetrable morass of humanity pressing in on her from all sides.

God has a plan for all of us . . .

The minister had spoken the words with reverential sincerity, yet to Margaret the belief was imbued with a triteness she found disturbing and inappropriate. She questioned how one was expected to worship a god who was the architect of Jimmy Kelly's short and unfortunate life, an ignored child of alcoholic parents destined to die at such a young age and in such a heinous manner. It only made sense to Margaret that a deity capable of crafting such a plan had to be more demented than the killer fated to carry it out. This god obviously charted a similar course for Nicholas Ferguson, and it frightened Margaret to think that more children, perhaps her own, could be sacrificed to the grand scheme.

It was the only thing she absorbed from the mercifully short service – *God has a plan for all of us . . .* She wondered what the plan was for herself, for her family, and if there was any chance of opting out. Billy looked up at her with eyes pleading to be released from the torturous confinement and she nodded her head sympathetically, letting him know that she shared his pain. The funeral service was over, but no one dared leave until every last drop of lament was wrung from the sullen ritual.

The minister circled the casket, trailing puffs of musky smoke that belched from the ornate brass incense holder he swung from a heavy chain. Two somber morticians materialized from the jungle of lilies, tottering black jackets adrift in an ocean of white. The men were ancient, frail and ashen with neatly combed, snow-capped domes. They positioned themselves at each end of the casket and methodically worked their way to the center. One removed the flower arrangement and photograph, while the other doted on the small corpse with long, slender fingers. Together, they ceremoniously lowered the casket lid and locked little Jimmy Kelly away forever, the irony of the youthful loss etched upon their grim, humorless faces.

The minister proceeded down the center aisle, parting the sea of sympathizers before him with each forward swing of the smoldering incense. The aged attendants turned the casket until it faced down the aisle, then stepped aside so the pall bearers could place their hands on the coffin and escort it from the chapel. It was a motley crew of high school wrestlers, shaggy-haired teenagers shuffling along listlessly in oversized suits bearing bored expressions revealing a callous indifference to their forced participation.

Jackson and Dorothy Kelly fell in step behind the pine box carrying their sole progeny's physical remains, side by side but not together, a microcosm of their tumultuous married life. Margaret watched them pass from the corner of her eye, careful not to stare, her claustrophobia erased by morbid curiosity.

Jackson stumbled along in the vacuum of inconsolable grief, oblivious to the well-wishers offering words of comfort as he mechanically dropped one foot in front of the other. The starched collar of his white dress shirt choked his thick throat and rubbed a raw, red rash into the overlapping skin. His gray tweed jacket was much too tight in the shoulders, stretching the coat open and exposing a taut, pregnant beer belly that forced him to buckle his short black trousers well below the waist. He was bleary-eyed, not from drink, but from an ancillary sadness stoked by the demoralizing realization that his son had rarely, if ever, seen him sober. While she gave him credit for trying to kick away the crutch, Margaret imagined Jackson would eventually hobble back to Tingle's for the shot of courage required to face his solitary existence in the absence of his son.

It was well beyond his wife's limited capacity to lend any kind of support. Dorothy had plunged even deeper into the bottle since Jimmy's death and she had no intention of swimming for the surface. She weaved down the aisle behind her husband in a drunken stupor, responding to the proffered condolences with a dopey, gap-toothed grin. A pale, pointed tongue darted in and out of a mouth garishly decorated with ruby red lipstick, hiding her thin, colorless lips beneath the uneven smudges of a trembling hand. Clumps of ratty beige hair worked free from the loose knot tied atop her head, exposing bald patches cleft by dark veins that cut into the alabaster skin of her scalp like jagged cracks. Aside from the skeletal outline of her collarbone and pointed shoulders, her sparse frame was otherwise lost beneath a loose black frock buttoned from neck to knee with triangular brass studs.

The shiny silver cap of a metal flask poked from the purple velvet lining of the imitation leather handbag Dorothy clutched securely, protectively, to her side. Margaret noticed the flask and quickly averted her glaze, focusing instead on the fringed, ankle-high moccasins strapped to Dorothy's sliding feet. White beads sewn into the dusty red leather held Margaret's attention for too long, she realized belatedly. The moccasins shuffled to a stop and when she hesitantly looked up Dorothy teetered at the end of the pew, glaring back with penetrating gray orbs and mouth ajar. She lingered for what seemed like an agonizing eternity, then slowly ambled away, never diverting her eyes, turning her head to stare at Margaret as she departed.

"Boy, if looks could kill, Megs, it would be your funeral that we'd all be attending next. What'd you ever do to her?"

Margaret didn't realize that Richard was seated in the pew directly behind her, so she was startled when he leaned forward and whispered unexpectedly in her ear. It didn't take much, shaken as she was by the brief stare down with the grieving mother. She should have ignored the comment, just let it drop, but for some reason, she couldn't. Richard was still leaning forward when she turned to respond, close enough so his cheap cologne overpowered both the heady perfume of the incense and the odiferous woodsman seated next to her.

"The woman is obviously bereaved, Richard, any idiot can see that! Do you have any concept of common decency," she chided, also in a whisper. "And another thing, have you forgotten that we'll be burying another child soon?" Her voice cracked with the reference to Nicholas Ferguson, his surreal death slow to transform from abstraction to reality. She wondered where Max was at the moment, if he was somewhere in the crowded church, how he was coping.

"Of course I have not forgotten about Nicholas! I was there last night. I saw Max's son hanging from that tree. I'm well aware that we're going to have to bury that boy, Megs, believe me, you don't have to remind me. How can you imply such a thing? I was only being facetious, trying to make a joke, lighten things up . . . oh, whatever!"

"This is a *funeral*, Richard, so spare me, would you? Just keep your moronic sense of humor to yourself! There is a time and a place, you know, and this is neither." Margaret turned away, refusing to acknowledge the persistent taps on her shoulder.

Richard whispered one last thing into the back of her head before settling back into his pew, "Please Megs, I've asked you many times before, it's Dickey, please call me Dickey."

That struck Margaret as absurdly funny and she bit back a sudden urge to giggle, to turn back and ask "Excuse me, did you say Cheeseball?" but the inappropriate spasm of mirth evaporated when she caught a glimpse of her husband from the corner of her eye. She thought Tim might at least share a knowing smile at Richard's expense, but his distrait manner betrayed a preoccupied mind sequestered inside invisible walls. Tim had heard none of the exchange between herself and Richard. He was somewhere else, had gradually withdrawn from her since Jimmy Kelly's death. He withdrew further under the added burden of Nicholas Ferguson's murder, barely speaking since he returned home from the crime scene early that morning. She wondered when, and if, she'd ever get him back.

One by one the pews began to empty. Margaret kept a watchful eye on her husband as he rose and robotically took his place in the stop-and-go procession down the center aisle. She corralled her children and followed closely behind, afraid to let Tony and Billy out of arms reach, even within the benign sanctuary of the chapel. For all she knew, the killer could be nearby, milling about among the mourners, a predator slyly scanning the crowd for potential prey. Neighbor regarded neighbor with mutual distrust and neither took offense, each cognizant of the other's primary responsibility to protect their own flesh and blood. She wondered if Christopher Koenigs was in fact the culprit, and, if so, presently watching over the proceedings. Perhaps he had brazenly melted into the large crowd or was hidden among the sheltering shadows of the surrounding forest. Tony and Billy wriggled in protest as she wrapped them beneath protective wings.

The reflection of the chapel's carillon crept along the polished flanks of the hearse as it crunched slowly down the gravel shoulder of the road. Margaret hugged her boys to her hips as the ornate funeral wagon passed, capturing a trio of bewildered faces that stared back from glossy windows decorated with white lace curtains. The infinite expanse of pale blue sky allayed her constricting phobia and she was ambushed by the abrupt liberation of repressed sadness. Story hour at the library would never be the same without the adorable little redhead's contagious enthusiasm. A twinge of claustrophobia returned when she considered the young child locked inside that pine box. Life itself had been irrevocably altered. Jimmy Kelly and Nicholas Ferguson were dead. *Dead! Murdered!* It seemed fantastical, an unimaginable nightmare, yet there was no escaping the disturbing reality. She squeezed Tony and Billy even tighter as tears rolled freely down her cheeks.

Billy tugged at her dress. "Are you alright Mommy? Don't cry," he pleaded, distressed to see his mother upset.

"It's okay Billy. I'm just sad, but it's okay to be sad right now. It's okay to cry." Margaret wiped the tears away and did her best to put on a brave face. She scanned the dispersing crowd for any sign of Max, even though she didn't expect to see him; not so soon after his own son's murder, not with his own boy's funeral to plan. She swallowed hard at the thought.

The motorcade crawled forward, a long line of vehicles bumper to bumper with headlights glowing dimly in the mid-afternoon sun. Tim had insisted upon retrieving the truck with motives based more on a desire for a snippet of solitude than masculine gallantry. Margaret saw him idling in the queue, both hands gripping the steering wheel and his disconnection still discernible through the guise of sunglasses. She decided to meet him halfway, dutifully herding her boys before her as she headed for the truck. Tim leaned over from the driver's seat and opened the passenger side door, settling back behind the wheel as his family joined him without a word.

The short, silent drive to the cemetery was prolonged by the interminable snail's pace of the funeral procession. Margaret alternated glances between her boys, her husband, and the wall of pine trees bordering the highway. Tony and Billy were behaving in accordance with the solemnity of the occasion, heads hung low and hands to themselves, raucous little devils miraculously transformed into becalmed young angels. Tim remained distant, inaccessible, slain himself in mind and spirit. It was a beautiful autumn afternoon, the type of day Margaret hated to spend inside a foul smelling gymnasium, which is where she would have been at the moment had the murders not forced the cancellation of the weekly Saturday wrestling tournament. What she wouldn't give to be there now, cheering on her boys as they tumbled about the mats, listening to her husband shout words of encouragement.

Sweep, Billy, sweep!

Margaret closed her eyes and pictured herself sitting on the hard wooden bleachers, could almost smell the mingled odor of fried food and sweat, sweet rather than repugnant in her exalted imagination. She saw her little Billy locked in combat against a much larger, more menacing foe, a bully who fell helplessly to the mat when his undersized opponent heeded his father's advice and adroitly swept the legs from beneath his faceless adversary. Father and son embraced joyfully on the mat, joined by Tony, Jimmy, and Nicholas, and even Richard's scrawny little stickpin, Terry. It was a blissful, fleeting escape to a time that had, until recently, encompassed her family's idyllic existence. Margaret opened her eyes, painfully aware that those halcyon days were gone forever.

A rustic wooden arch spanned the entrance to the cemetery, a small non-denominational burial plot carved from a stand of septuagenarian white pine. Whittled branches nailed to the arch spelled out *Cemetery of the Pines*, the final resting place for turn-of-the-century lumberjacks, pioneering homesteaders, and their varied descendants. And, shortly, Jimmy

Kelly. Then, soon after, Nicholas Ferguson. Margaret shuddered as the despairing caravan rolled to a halt among the cold gray tombstones.

"Tim, are you going to make it honey? You don't look so good . . ." She unbuckled her seatbelt and leaned across the front seat, placing an open palm on her husband's ashen forehead. " . . . We don't have to do this, you know, we can just go home right now if that's what you need. We've paid our respects. What do you think?" Tim's unresponsive indifference to her concern, her touch, suddenly seemed selfish and petty under the trying circumstances. "You're hardly the only one - this is extremely difficult for all of us," she snapped, glancing at her attentive boys in the backseat with an immediate twinge of regret. She forced an awkward smile and softened her impatient tone. "You can't just shut us out, Tim, not now," she pleaded, "The boys and I, we need you, and, well, it's pretty obvious, isn't it honey? You need us, too."

Nothing. Only the lost, vacant stare, the unnerving trance of emotional paralysis manifested as one man's means of coping with an incomprehensible turn of fate.

"Hello . . . Tim . . . Are you in there? Hello!" Margaret sighed, not expecting a reply to what for the moment would be her final, half-hearted attempt to break through the fog. "Jesus, what am I . . ." she murmured in surrender before dropping the thought, her attention diverted by the staggered clumps of mourners drearily weaving their way through the maze of engraved tablets jutting from the manicured ground. Tears filled her eyes, yet stubbornly refused to fall to her cheeks. Sunshine cut through the pines and the sky above shone clear and blue. Still, Margaret gazed out through a rain-streaked window, unblinking. Through the trees, at the top of a shady knoll, a small pine box hovered above a perfectly symmetrical, rectangular hole cleft from the soft, sandy soil.

" . . . and as young Jimmy Kelly, the son of Jackson – our friend Jackie, of course – the son of Jackson and Dorothy Kelly, as Jimmy was, as are we all, of the earth, so shall he now be returned to the earth . . ."

That's it! Margaret thought, *That's god's plan for us all, a guaranteed reservation with a hole in the ground!* She stood at the fringes of the final ritual, hunched backs obscuring her view of the graveside service. Tim stayed in the truck, frustratingly impenetrable, too far away to trust with the boys, who once again wriggled beneath her suffocating grip. The simple casket and the bereaved parents were shielded from her sight, unlike the minister, who stood with arms raised at the end of a small seam between the reverently bent bodies. The sleeves of his starched vestment stretched from his side like the wings of a resplendent white butterfly, which Margaret found oddly comforting. Drained of tears, she watched him intently, a crisp, clear image earnestly sharing a sermon she no longer heard.

The seam of vision widened as restless feet shifted and resettled, suddenly offering Margaret a glimpse of the young boy's casket. Stepping behind the catafalque, the minister slowly folded his wings, synchronizing his solemn movements with the inevitable lowering of the pine box, little redheaded Jimmy's preordained return to the beckoning soil. The grave greedily swallowed the tiny coffin just as the preacher's outspread arms dropped back to his sides, unveiling a desolate visage beyond, a tortured face peering out from the trees. Margaret's reflexive gasp at the sight of Max, desultory and determined to hide his bulk behind the bole of a white pine, added an incongruent note to the chorus of sobs and moans ascending in pitch with the casket's descent. Her heart leapt out to him and her body followed. She lurched forward.

His own son, his only son, Nicholas, dead no more than a day – *two dead boys*, Margaret had to remind herself. *Christ, is this really happening?* And she marveled at the courage and compassion it must have taken to bring Max to the cemetery that day. Symbolic handfuls of sun-hardened soil fell upon the flat wooden lid of Jimmy Kelly's coffin with empty thuds as the bereaved hesitantly began to disperse. Margaret craned her neck from side to side, maneuvering to keep an eye on Max as the last of the straggling minglers passed before her. She needed to talk with her old friend, desperately wanted to offer her condolences for his unimaginable loss.

"Okay, Tony, Billy, here's what I want you guys to do," Margaret squatted to speak to her boys, breathless and throaty with urgency, "I'm going to walk you back toward the truck and when you can see it, and see your father, I want you to run as fast as you can to get there. I want you to get inside the truck and wait for me with your father until I get there. Okay?"

"Where are you going, Mommy, why can't we go with you?" Billy's lip quivered, frightened into asking the question by his mother's obvious anxiety. Tony stood behind his little brother, eagerly nodding in agreement.

"I just saw Max and I have to speak with him, no big deal, huh buddy?" She tried to comfort her son, rubbing his shoulders as she spoke. "I need to tell him how sorry we all are about Nicholas, right? I need to see if there's anything we can do for him, how we can help him out . . . and I need to talk to him alone. So, I want you to do as I ask and . . ."

"Oh Jimmy! I'm so sorry Jimmy! It's all my doin', it's all my doin' you'se bein' dead! How could I let you'se get kilt like this, kilt for somethin' I done!" Jackson knelt beside the rectangular hole in the ground and cryptically pled forgiveness from his departed son.

"C'mon Jackson, keep it together now buddy, keep it together," Richard bent down over his faithful sidekick, imparting directives more than sympathy, "Quit talking nonsense! It does no good making a martyr of yourself. This is not your fault, do you understand? You know that, don't you?" He paused before demanding a response. "Answer me, you know who's to blame! You know who put your boy in the ground, and soon enough Max's boy, as well! Answer me!"

Jackson fell limp, the sadness, pain, and remorse visibly draining from his overwrought soul and seeping into the hallowed ground beneath him. His head dipped, an imperceptible nod of debatable intent, yet adequate to satisfy Richard's heartless manipulation of his friend's emotional catharsis. Jackson wept softly as Richard prodded him to his feet, teetering at the lip of the grave and nearly joining his dead son at the bottom of the hole.

The commotion had drawn Max closer to the grave, closer to Jackson. He extended an arm, trying to offer the comfort of his touch. Margaret, still squatting with her arms around her sons, looked into his pained blue eyes and soundlessly mouthed his name. Max turned away and dropped his head, seemingly ashamed to accept her empathy. He retreated into the forest with agitated haste.

"Now, boys, now! Get to the truck, do you hear me? No more questions!" Margaret pushed her children from behind, roughly herding them on a zig-zag dash through the head-stones. Tim, still gazing blankly through the windshield, never turned, never noticed as she gave the boys one last shove and raced away in search of Max. "Get in the truck! Now!" She called back over her shoulder, voice restrained out of superstitious respect for the dead underfoot. In the mad rush to find Max before he left the cemetery, Margaret was unaware of her children's hesitancy to obey her command. With great unease, they clutched hands and woefully watched their mother go.

Max had nearly reached his minivan when Margaret spotted him. He noticed her approaching and quickened his pace. Wounded by her old friend's obvious intention to avoid her, Margaret nearly stopped dead in her tracks before resuming the pursuit in an all out sprint.

"Max, please, what are you doing?" She called out breathlessly, again with deferential restraint. "Don't do this! Don't run away!" Her voice quavered as she ran. Without looking back, Max hurried into the minivan and started the engine. Margaret slowed to a walk, then broke off the chase completely. She inhaled deeply, hands on hips, expecting Max to seize the opportunity and drive away. "Please, I really want to talk to you, Max." She spoke loudly enough for her request to be heard above the sputtering motor. In desperation, she threw back her head and bellowed with complete abandon and utter disregard for the deceased, "Somebody please talk to me!" Fighting back tears, resisting weak knees and the sense of impending collapse, Margaret was slow to react when the cemetery fell soothingly quiet.

Desperately wishing to escape, Max instead had cut the minivan's motor. Fate had cast his lot where Margaret was concerned long ago, a victim of unrequited love who found solace with precious little satisfaction through their enduring friendship. Even now, wracked with grief and devoid of hope, he looked upon the forlorn figure hunched in his rearview mirror, and, as always, surrendered. He saw the pain and uncertainty carved into her face as she tentatively made her way along the side of the minivan, transforming from the image in the mirror to flesh and blood as she stepped to the open window. She placed a gentle hand upon his shoulder and began to weep.

"I'm so, so sorry Max . . . I just wish there was something, anything that I . . . Nicholas was such a great kid, you know, and he was really lucky to have a dad who loved him as much as you did . . ." Margaret tilted her head and tried to gain his attention, to look Max in the eye, but he refused to turn to her. Her heart jumped when she noticed the rifle resting against his knee, the blue steel barrel and burled stock toylike in his ponderous grip.

"If you had been my wife there would have been no secrets between us, Margaret, I can assure you of that," Max mumbled, monotone, head still turned and voice barely audible.

Margaret withdrew her hand, certain what she had heard and stunned into silence by the odd topic's awkward introduction. She, too, remembered Max's flattering adolescent attempts to woo her, amorously encouraged by her amicable invitation to fish and swim at Pine Point Cabins, her parent's old resort out on Cattail Lake. From the very beginning she never insinuated a desire for anything more than friendship. The one-sided infatuation was understood but never mentioned. Until now! Now, of all times! They were teenagers, juniors in high school, for chrissakes! That's when Max brought Tim into her life and resolved the matter. She fell in love with Tim and dashed Max's misguided dream of making her his own, and life went on.

Margaret . . . it suddenly dawned on her . . . *He called me Margaret!* It had been the reggae-accented *Redlocks* ever since the long ago day in the school library when he introduced himself. *Girl, I love your redlocks, mon.* It would be too easy to say it seemed like yesterday. It seemed remote, a time out of reach, a scene from another lifetime. *Margaret* . . . A queer reminder that nothing would ever be the same, that reality had been indelibly altered.

"Your wife Max, really?" she asked in dismay. "After all these years, now, with our children being murdered, that's what you want to talk about? I don't know what to say . . ."

"Then don't say a damn thing, try to listen for a change," he growled, snapping his head around to face Margaret for the first time. "If you would have been listening, you would have heard what I was trying to tell you. I was talking about secrets, that between a husband and wife, there should be no secrets. That's all, no secrets, do you understand now?"

"You're scaring me Max, what secrets? Are you talking about me and Tim? That is what you're talking about, isn't it? What makes you think we have any secrets?"

"All I can tell you is that I'm truly sorry, Margaret. Somebody should have told you the truth, you deserved that much, at least," Max softened, "Somebody should tell you the truth now."

"Why not you, Max? Why don't you tell me the truth?"

"I'm not that somebody," he answered matter of factly. "Your husband, he's the one you need to talk to, he's the one you need to hear it from, not me. He's had you all these years, the best years, and as soon as things turn dark, well, I'll be damned if I'm going to do his dirty work for him."

"I know the truth, I know all about Christopher Koenigs. Tim explained everything to me," Margaret stated with conviction.

"Quit fooling yourself! You may think you know everything, but believe me, you don't have any idea."

"How can you be so sure? How can you . . ."

"Because if you knew everything you wouldn't be talking to me right now, that's why I'm so sure!"

"But I am talking to you right now, Max, so why don't you tell me? If I don't know everything I should, why don't you explain it to me?" She felt alone, an outcast making a plea for inclusion. "You're the closest friend I've ever had, Max, and best friends don't keep secrets from one another either, do they?"

"Sometimes friends *keep* secrets because friends *have* secrets," Max tried to explain his predicament, "If that makes any sense."

"So you won't tell me, is that your point?"

"I *can't* tell you, that's what I'm trying to make you

understand!" Max slumped forward and drummed his forehead against the steering wheel, letting the rifle slip from his grasp. It caromed off the dashboard and clattered to the floor. He leaned across the seat and retrieved the firearm, wedging it back against his knee and nervously clicking the safety on and off.

"What's with the gun Max?" Margaret asked, guessing it was loaded, worried that he might turn it upon himself.

"This was my son's weapon. It belonged to Nick." Max changed the direction of the leading question, turning the rifle to reveal the boy's initials, patiently carved by hand into the underside of the wooden stock. "He would've been old enough next fall to hunt. He was going to use this rifle to get his first deer. He wanted to put a notch in the wood for each deer he shot, right next to where he whittled his initials there."

Max pressed a thick finger into the lettering and tenderly traced the precise cut of his son's monogram. He worked his way back to the safety and resumed the methodic, metallic click. Margaret placed her hand back on his shoulder and he turned once again to face her. There was nothing in his eyes, no pain, no grief, nothing, reinforcing Margaret's fear.

"What are you doing with the gun, Max?" She pursued an explanation, considering the possibility that vigilante justice, not suicide, could be on his mind. "I want to know what you plan on doing with it." Either alternative frightened her.

Oblong shadows fell from the dark side of the tiered headstones, otherwise alight from the descending sun's horizontal beams. Blinded by the shifting light, Margaret hid behind Max to shield her eyes, his unruly black beard aglow at the edges. She jumped when he turned the key and aggressively revved the motor, and panic rolled through her when he shifted into gear. By ignoring her question, Max had provided Margaret with the answer she feared most. The rifle would be his escape from a life suddenly devoid of meaning. She couldn't let that happen. She needed to buy time.

"Max, I want your word that you'll meet me later tonight. This is no time for you to be alone," Margaret played to his weakness, his devotion, his inability to deny her wishes. If he made a promise to her, he would keep it. "Please Max! Let's say an hour from now. I'll run Tim and the boys home, then I'll come over to your place and we can . . ."

"No," he interrupted, stunning Margaret with an abrupt denial that momentarily convinced her that she had lost him. "Not my place, I don't want to go there," he continued, reviving her fading hope. "I'll be at Cattail Lake, the fishing pier at the boat landing, one hour."

Alone in the cemetery, watching Max depart into the dwindling daylight, Margaret thought she would crumble beneath the crushing weight of the heavy burden that had befallen her. In the next hour she would find no words of consolation for the inconsolable, nor hope for the hopeless, yet she was left with no alternative but to try. She shuddered at the thought of the hidden piece of the past, a secret shared by those she held most dear, a secret kept from her. Her husband obviously hadn't trusted her enough to tell her, preferred to live a lie rather than test the strength of their bond. It made him seem weak, pathetic, and it saddened her to think it.

Weak and pathetic. Margaret knew she would be no better if she didn't fight against the insidious darkness, if she allowed the specter of the past and the fear of the future to render her helpless. Instead, she gave herself over to the anger that slowly consumed her. She was finished feeling sorry for everybody, sorry for herself. She was pissed at Max for making *her* fight for *his* life, at Tim for his spineless deceit, at Richard because she knew he was involved and always hated the asshole anyway, at herself for missing the clues that were surely there, for tripping along in ignorant bliss. Margaret tasted the hatred for Christopher Koenigs and savored the sensation, used it to focus her strength and build her resolve.

"Nobody's going to harm my boys," she vowed to the departed souls that passed beneath her feet as she ran through the cemetery. No amount of anger could quell the terror evoked by the daunting reality that her children were in danger. Margaret cringed at the mental picture that flashed through her mind, the disturbing image of her boys hanging at the end of a rope, two more innocent victims of a distant tragedy. Tim would tell her everything if she had to slap it out of him, an image that held much greater appeal.

Margaret staggered to a disbelieving stop as she neared the truck, now the lone vehicle parked in the deserted cemetery. There was only Tim, slack-jawed and slump-shouldered in the front seat, a mere shell of the man she proudly called her husband. *Tony and Billy! Oh my god! Where are they!* A jolt of raw fear burned over her flesh and sizzled inside her. Margaret whirled in a frantic circle, feverishly scanning the bleak terrain in a desperate search for her children. She heard them first, muted snippets of laughter mingled with tiny voices. Billy's voice, then Tony's, rising from a hollow in an overgrown, neglected corner of the cemetery. Giddy with relief, Margaret rushed to the crest of the slope.

"Tony! Billy!" She called to them before she saw that they were not alone. It took her a moment to place the other child, but then she remembered seeing the boy once before. It was in her own front yard, the day after Jimmy died. She recognized the tufts of dark brown hair and noticed he wore the same clothes; a faded red tee-shirt, cut off bluejeans and black high-top tennis shoes. The little stranger commanded her boys complete attention, just as he had in her front yard the first time she laid eyes on him. If they heard her call now, they gave no indication. The child's back was to her once again, his face indiscernible and his small frame partially hidden by an ancient, vine-covered tombstone. Nicholas had told her the boy had *funny eyes*, she recalled.

A narrow dirt path cut through the encroaching, tangled undergrowth. Margaret hurriedly followed the pointy-toed impressions of her boys' small dress shoes down into the dreary depths of the ravine. She strained to keep the children in sight, but the three boys disappeared behind the tombstone when the trail bottomed out. Hazelbrush and blackthorn bushes clawed at the delicate gray cloth of her dress and overhanging branches tangled in her red tresses as she struggled to reach the headstone. For some odd reason, she wasn't surprised to find that the mysterious child with funny eyes wasn't there to greet her when she arrived.

"I thought I told you two to wait in the truck! You scared the dickens out of me!" Margaret admonished, maternal instincts momentarily overriding her piqued curiosity about the anonymous child's identity. "Now no more games, you hear me?" she forewarned, stridently reminding her boys about their unwillingness to cooperate the last time she asked them about their new friend. "I want you to tell me that boy's name and I want you to tell me which way he ran off! Now!" Tony sheepishly shrugged his shoulders, just as he had before, then pointed his finger in one direction while Billy extended his arm in the other. "Do you hear me?" she fumed. "Who is that child? What did he want? And where did he go?"

A jeering cackle resounded through the hollow, mocking laughter that seemed to rise from the depths of a sunken grave nearly lost beneath a shroud of twisted roots and branches.

"Dare say I know who that boy is, truth be told."

Dorothy Kelly squatted on her haunches at the head of the neglected grave, the square white marker serving as a makeshift backrest for her cadaverous frame. Drunkenly amused with herself she cackled again, a scratchy bark she soothed with a sip from her silver flask. Margaret stumbled forward, pushed from behind by her boys' frightened dash for the shelter of her body. Tony peered around one hip and Billy the other, wide eyes transfixed on the ghostly figure hunched atop the tomb.

"Sure'nuff I know that child, guessin' I know what he wants, too, but can't rightly say I know where he gone to, though I could likely guess that, I s'pose," she slurred, snorting derisively. "I ain't gonna tell, though, no siree, I ain't! You best keep those young'ns close, just like that, less'n you done want 'em to end up dead like my Jimmy! That I can tell!"

The boys tightened their grip and Margaret winced as sharp little fingernails dug into the tender flesh of her lower back. Dorothy took another long pull off the flask and lit a cigarette. She tilted her head and smoke streamed from her flared nostrils. Glaring contemptibly through a smoggy halo, Dorothy rose suddenly and lurched toward Margaret, waving the cigarette dismissively.

"Go away! What're you still doin' here anyhow? Why you even here in the first place?" she howled through decaying, yellow teeth, "Git outta here, git! I don't want you 'round here no more!"

Margaret backed away tentatively, her boys in tow, uncertain what to expect from the crazed woman waving withered fists in her face. Dorothy's sanity had long been in question, in Margaret's estimation, but the poor woman could hardly be held accountable for her present behavior having just buried her son.

"I came to extend my deepest sympathy, Dorothy, to tell you how badly we all feel about what happened to Jimmy." Margaret spoke with quiet respect as she departed, hoping to escape from the hollow without further confrontation. She looked beyond Dorothy to the plain white headstone marking the long forgotten grave and her knees buckled in horror and disbelief. It was inscribed simply, a name and dates, yet it stole the breath from her lungs.

Michael Koenigs
1979 – 1985

Margaret wheeled and shoved her children down the bramble-lined path. Small and nimble, the boys ducked below the grasping branches and scrambled up the steep hillside.

"I ain't needin' your sympathy! Don't you talk to me 'bout my boy, you hear me?" Dorothy screeched at Margaret's back as she pursued her boys down the trail. "You ain'tnever figured it out, have you? You one dim bulb, you know it? You ain't got no idea'r what's really happenin' here, no idea'r why Jimmy done got buried . . ." the raspy voice trailed off and fell silent.

With her heart pounding out a heavy cadence that echoed in her head and her flesh afire with thorn-scarred welts, Margaret struggled to join Tony and Billy at the top of the slope. She buried their tear-streaked faces into her heaving breast and looked back down upon the eerie scene at the bottom of the hollow. Dorothy Kelly had hunkered back down on Michael Koenigs's grave, partaking in delusional conversation and gesturing emphatically, the silver flask glinting in the remnant rays of a waning sun.

CHAPTER FIFTEEN

Tim resisted Margaret's efforts to replace him behind the wheel. She hadn't asked him to move over to the passenger seat; she had simply opened the truck door and pushed. He didn't resist voluntary, it was more akin to the dead weight of a big black lab sprawled out at the foot of the bed.

"Goddamit Tim, slide over!" she grunted, and pushed harder. "Enough with this bullshit, I don't have time for it! I'm running you and the boys home and then I'm going to meet Max, so move your ass over!"

"Mommy, you're scaring us," Tony tugged at her sleeve, frightened by her hard-edged, cursing commands. Billy clung to his older brother and both looked up to their mother for reassurance through moist eyes.

"Good, you should be scared!" she snapped instead, glaring at the boys harshly, causing them to recoil from the stranger inside their mother's skin. "You two did not listen to me when I told you I wanted you in the truck, did you?" Neither responded, wrongly assuming the question to be rhetorical, as often was the case with their mother's rebukes. "Answer me! Did you?" The chastised children wagged their lowered heads back and forth. "There will be no more of that, do you understand me? From now on, when I tell you to do something, you do it! No questions, no backtalk, you just do it!"

"But Mommy . . ." Billy started to sputter through his sobs. Margaret immediately cut him off.

"There are no buts! Didn't you hear a word I just said?" She took Billy by the shoulders and tried to shake the seriousness of the situation into him. "Two of your friends are *dead*! Someone *killed* Jimmy and Nicholas! You heard what Jimmy's mom said, that the same thing could happen to you! Well, I don't intend on letting anyone hurt you, but you have to listen to me, you have to do as I say!"

Tony and Billy were bawling now, terrified into uncontrollable tears by the thought of their friend Jimmy locked inside a box and buried beneath the ground, terrified that they could be next. It heartened Margaret to see the fear overtake her boys, just as anger had overtaken her. She planned to use those raw emotions to her advantage. She planned to keep her children alive.

"I'm sorry, Margaret, I'm so, so sorry," Tim emerged from his trance and whimpered the apology, finally ceding the driver's seat to his wife at the same time. Without prompting, her two mewling children jumped into the truck and followed their father as he retreated wearily across the bench seat. Margaret stepped hard on the gas and the rear tires of the vehicle bit into the cemetery road's loose gravel.

"Save the apologies, Tim, it's a little late for that. I want answers, I want the truth," she demanded sternly, alternating glances between the road and her husband. He placed an index finger on the bridge of his nose and slowly slid his sunglasses to the top of his head. The black frames disappeared beneath the thick curls of his soft white hair and tears trickled from the crow's feet at the corner of his eyes.

"What *really* happened that night in the treehouse, Tim, the night that Michael Koenigs died?" Margaret persisted, now callously indifferent to her husband's own suffering. "Max said you've been keeping something from me, that all of you guys, Richard and Jackson, have been hiding something all these years. What happened, Tim? Why did Christopher Koenigs come back? Why did he kill Jimmy and Nicholas? Why does he want to kill our boys?"

The front tires of the truck chirped loudly against the pavement and the back tires kicked up a cloud of gravel dust as Margaret cranked the wheel and departed the cemetery. She turned her head and met Tim's disbelieving eyes. Mouth agape, he nodded at Tony and Billy on the seat between them, still teary-eyed but listening attentively to every word. Margaret knew what her husband was thinking.

"Don't worry about the boys, they can hear whatever it is you have to say. They need to hear it. We can't be kept safe if we're kept in the dark, so spare me the look already and tell me your secret. Max wouldn't tell me, he said he couldn't tell me. He said you had to do that, Tim, that you should have told me a long time ago, so spit it out."

Tim pressed his face into his bicep and rubbed his eyes

dry with the sleeve of his suit coat. He leaned back into the headrest and inhaled deeply. His pursed lips fought against the gradual release of the pent up air, puttering softly as tears once again welled at the corner of his eyes and trickled down his reddened cheeks. He rolled down his window and cocked his head, breathing in the sweet scent of pine on the cool evening air.

"Max was right, you know, I should have told you. I wanted to tell you so many times, tried to tell you, but for some reason I never could. I was always too scared, I guess, scared that you might not understand and I'd lose you," he prefaced his confession, hoping to salvage some sympathy. "Each time I tried to tell you what happened and couldn't, the longer it went on, that made it even harder to tell. So much time went by that it just got to the point where I could never tell you. It got so I knew you'd never be able to understand, where you'd never be able to forgive me for shutting you out. I know you don't want to hear it, Margaret, but I am sorry. I never meant to hurt you or the boys, I never meant for . . ."

"For chrissakes quit stalling!" Margaret fumed in exasperation. "I have to meet Max out at Cattail Lake in less than twenty minutes and I can't be late. I'm afraid he might hurt himself, that he might even kill himself, and I need to know what really happened with Christopher Koenigs before I go out there. Maybe if I can tell Max that I know . . ."

"We killed Michael Koenigs," Tim blurted cathartically. "I mean, Richard was the one who put the rope around his neck, he was the one who pushed him out of the treehouse, but it was all our faults, all of us, myself, Max, and Jackson, all of us. We could have stopped it, we could have done something, but we just played along."

"My god Tim, how could you? How could you 'just play along' with something like that?" Margaret gasped.

"We were only trying to scare those boys, just a bunch of kids fooling around in that treehouse, but then things got out of hand," Tim continued to purge, "I don't know how or why it happened, but at some point things turned from fun and games to mean-spirited. We teased those Koenigs boys, tormented them really, pretending we were going to hang them both. It was mean, like I said, but we were just joking. Then Richard put the rope around Michael's neck and . . ." Tim paused and swallowed hard, his Adam's apple jumping in his throat, " . . . and Richard threatened Christopher, he told him that the only way he could save himself was to push his brother out. If he didn't, Richard said that they both were going to die."

"So, what, Richard coerced Christopher Koenigs into killing his little brother, is that what happened?" Margaret asked incredulously.

"No, Christopher wouldn't do it. He started crying and went a little nuts. He punched Richard in the face, knocked him down and bloodied his nose. Christopher tried to take the rope off Michael's neck, but then Richard went crazy. He was embarrassed because Christopher was just a little kid and he had put him on his ass in front of all of us. Richard jumped up and started wrestling with Christopher, trying to keep the rope around Michael's neck while Christopher tried to get it off. Richard couldn't shake the little kid. Christopher was strong, scared shitless, so Richard yelled at us, told me and Max and Jackson to get off our asses and grab Christopher. We listened to him, just like we always listened to him, and we pulled Christopher away. Then . . ." Tim lowered his head and stopped, choking back tears.

"Then what, Tim, what happened when you pulled Christopher away?" Margaret asked with breathless anticipation. Tim turned to her with faraway eyes.

"Then Richard smiled, that dopey smile he still gets whenever he has a bad idea, and he just shoved Michael out the treehouse door. One second the little boy was standing there with a rope around his neck, crying, and the next second he was gone. Just . . . gone. The rest of us couldn't believe what we had seen, we didn't want to believe it. We just let Christopher go and he ran right over to the treehouse door. I was hoping the rope broke or something, that the kid wasn't hurt, but I'll never forget seeing Christopher Koenigs's face after he looked out that door. I had never seen anybody in shock before, like he was after seeing his brother at the other end of that rope. He just dropped down and curled up in a fetal position."

Margaret turned into her driveway as Tim finished telling his grotesque secret, struggling to comprehend all of the ramifications of what she had just heard. Richard Mann was a murderer. Her husband, along with Max Ferguson and Jackson Kelly, were accomplices in that act. Christopher Koenigs not only witnessed his brother's death, he was wrongly accused and convicted for it, and had languished behind bars for the ensuing twenty-odd years because of it. Now he was back, seeking revenge against those who had so maliciously wronged him.

"How could you let this happen, Tim? How could you allow your own children to be placed in such danger?" Margaret asked compulsively, not really thinking the question through.

"It happened a long time ago, a few years before I even met you, Margaret. I was just a little kid myself. Hell, I was only 13 years old!" Tim groped vainly for an explanation. "We were all scared as hell, and we were stupid, stupid to listen to Richard. After Christopher curled up in a little ball we all jumped out of that treehouse and got the hell out of that meadow. We just ran past Michael hanging there. He was already turning blue. Richard concocted the whole goddam idea, of course, to tell the police the whole story about Christopher going crazy, threatening us and all, hanging his brother. Richard had the bloody nose and bruised face to back his story up. He knew we were scared. I guess it was easy for him to convince us to go along with it, telling us we'd be the ones going to prison if we didn't. Everything just happened so fast and got out of control so quickly, and most everybody swallowed it hook, line and sinker. Everybody but the one cop, Sauter. He was the first one to show up at the treehouse and he never believed any of it from the very start. You know, I never thought . . ."

"Shit!" Margaret's heart raced when she looked at the dashboard clock and realized she had to meet Max in five minutes. It was a good ten minute drive out to Cattail Lake and she feared that he wouldn't wait long if she failed to show on time. She hated to leave her boys alone with Tim. She no longer trusted the man, yet she knew there was no other alternative.

"Remember what we just got done talking about boys, that you're to do exactly as I say." She stepped out of the truck and her children followed obediently. "I want you to go up to your room, close the door, and wait for me there until I get back. Don't open that bedroom door for anyone, not even your father, you got me?" Having just heard the terrible tale of the treehouse themselves, the boys both glanced back at Tim with mistrust in their eyes as well. They nodded their heads eagerly at their mother and tore off toward the house, bursting through the front door and racing up the steps to their room.

"Get out, Tim, now! And if you let anything happen to a hair on either of those boys' heads before I get back, I swear I'll . . ."

"Margaret, you know I . . ."

"Shut up! Just shut the fuck up and get out! Now!"

Crestfallen, Tim grudgingly obliged. He set one foot on the ground and hesitated, but Margaret wasn't going to wait any longer. She dropped the truck into gear and hit the gas. Tim bounced off the seat and landed on his knees, dragging from the door momentarily before letting go. Margaret leaned over and pulled the door shut. She drove away without a backward glance.

The tall pines framing the calm blue waters of Cattail Lake hid the setting sun. A red streak singed the jagged silhouette of the tree crowns along the horizon, fading upward into a broader band of orange that finally bled golden into the approaching darkness. Speeding westward to the lake, Margaret had squinted into the departing light and had watched with ominous portent as the red stain spread across the sky. *Sailor's delight my ass*, she had thought to herself, finding the colorful sunset more sinister than serene.

Max was there on the fishing pier, as promised, dutifully waiting for her. Hemmed by a water garden of slender green reeds and lily pads, the slatted wood walkway bridged the shallows to a railed platform suspended over a bed of deeper, green weeds. Resting on his elbows, Max bent over the weather-warped rail and gazed into the water, the rifle at his side. The dock creaked and bounced from Margaret's weight, creating tiny wavelets that rolled across the surface with each step. The ripples dispersed through the reeds and the stalks swayed gently, waving a silent greeting as she passed. Max didn't greet her. He didn't flinch a muscle as she approached. Margaret joined him at the railing and mimicked his pose, bending over her elbows and scanning the weeds in silence.

Small fish floated through the undulating vegetation, jittery prey species that occasionally scattered into hiding. Soon enough the unseen threat would pass and the fish would reappear, a pack of little wolves on the prowl for their own meal. Margaret studied the foraging schools, multi-colored sunfish and vertically-striped yellow perch. Food chain bottom dwellers. She saw her face faintly reflected in the mirror of the water's surface and, for the first time in her life, she felt like she was a little fish. A predator was lurking, but Margaret refused to swim for the safety of the weeds. She and her boys would not be easy prey.

Several moments passed in silence. The foreboding hues drained from the lip of the evening sky and the first pale stars twinkled dimly overhead. Margaret was content to wait Max out, to see what he had to say, if there was anything of consequence he could say, without any prompting of her own. She suddenly wondered why she had even come, if she wasn't just wasting her time. Panic-induced adrenalin spiked when she thought of her boys. She felt stupid for choosing to meet Max when she should be at home with her children, comforting and protecting the only two people who mattered to her anymore. Max, her old friend Max; it dawned on her that he didn't matter. Tony and Billy were in danger and he was partly to blame. He could do whatever he wanted with the rifle. She realized she didn't care.

"Some of my best memories are of time spent out at this lake," Max straightened and shifted his gaze from the water to the far shore, "but that's all I've got now, memories, nothing else. The future holds nothing for me, now that Nicholas is gone, especially how and why my boy died. Standing right here, hell, we're not that far from that goddam treehouse. Anywhere I go around here I'm not far enough away from that meadow – my own house, the woods where I hunt, down at the high school gymnasium – that evil place is always right there. I only agreed to meet you because . . . shit, I don't know why the hell I said I'd be here. I've got no reason to go on, Margaret. A father shouldn't have to bury his son, ever, especially not as payment for his own sins."

"My boys aren't going to die because of you, Max, or in spite of you. I'm going to make sure of that. As for yourself, Tim, the whole fucking lot of you, come what may, I can't afford to give a shit right now," Margaret admitted, comfortable with the newfound notion that she no longer cared.

"So, your husband waited until it was too late before he finally . . ."

"You're goddam right he told me what happened to Michael Koenigs! How could you, Max? That bullshit about *friends keep secrets because friends have secrets*, that's all that is, Max, bullshit! We were never friends, never truly friends. Christopher Koenigs is here, killing our children, Max, and you know the real reason why, but you, my *friend*, you keep your secret, you all do – you and your *true* friends Tim, Richard, Jackson," the mere names tasted foul in her mouth, "acting like you're still those fucked up, sadistic teenagers in that treehouse!"

Max picked up the rifle and backed away from Margaret, her harsh words body blows buffeting him into the opposite railing. The platform rocked and groaned as he retreated, slapping the water and sending the jittery fish into the shelter of the weeds. Margaret knew the words had to hurt, but they were the only words she had.

"We were just kids, scared, stupid kids," Max timidly repeated Tim's simplistic explanation, "but don't get me wrong, I'm not saying that's some kind of excuse. There was no excuse for what we did, Margaret, none at all. You don't think I know that? Not a day went by when I didn't regret what happened in that treehouse. A part of me died that night with Michael Koenigs, and a little piece of me has died every day since. I've decided I'm done dying a slow death, it's time for me to just be . . . dead. I don't know what else there is for me to say. Goodbye Margaret. I'm not going to waste my breath asking your forgiveness, not when I can't forgive myself."

Margaret had no qualms letting Max go, a little fish desperately trying to hide from the predators within, a stranger who had masqueraded as her friend. Part of her had died as well, died just that day when she learned her life had been fated by the whim of an unimaginable, long ago lie. The anger pulsed through her veins and contracted her muscles, a consuming fire she fed upon to forge ahead. She was pushed to the precipice through events out of her own control, a precipice leading from one life to another. Through clenched teeth she vowed to bury the old and embrace the new.

Alone on the pier, Margaret struggled to rein in her reeling mind, to quell the cacophony of thoughts fogging her brain. She needed to clear her head, to *think*. She needed help. The cop, *Sauter,* that's who she needed. She would tell him what she knew, what really happened to Michael Koenigs that night in the treehouse. She would confirm his suspicions and he would track down Christopher Koenigs before he could hang another child, she was certain of it. That would have to wait until morning. Tonight there were two frightened, confused boys who desperately needed their mother. *Tony and Billy!* Spurred by a stab of panic, she hurried from the creaking, rocking dock.

Margaret slowed when she neared her truck and noticed the minivan still parked where she had found it upon her arrival at the lake. Presuming that Max had gone, in fact hoping that he had, she was momentarily taken aback. The dome light was glowing dimly inside and reflected faintly off the empty seats. Margaret peeked inside, helpless against the gnawing unease swelling within her. Max was gone, and he'd taken the rifle with him. The sickness jumped suddenly to her throat, the acidic burn nipped at the base of her tongue. It surprised her, the creeping sense of surrender, the intrusion of hopelessness. She beat back the impinging weakness mercilessly, hardening her heart against emotions that no longer served any useful purpose.

The surrounding woods were quiet. Black clouds appeared overhead. Margaret scanned the lengthening shadows of the trees with a hard, cold stare. She barely jumped at the sharp crack of the shot when it creased the silence. Exploding from the hidden hollows of the forest, the report echoed through the pines and rippled across the lake, a rolling peal of thunder that faded unceremoniously into the far shore. The night again fell

Treehouse

silent. Nicholas's rifle had earned its first notch.

*   *   *

Sauter cocked his ear toward the muted rumble. He looked up at the dark clouds hanging above the treetops, a black shroud slowly unfurling across the sky and threatening to presumptively extinguish the diminishing daylight.

"Sounds like we might be in for some rain."

Colins offered the observation as absent-minded small talk, diligently cleaning his wire-rimmed spectacles as he assessed the weather.

"That wasn't thunder," Sauter dismissed the mistaken forecast impatiently. Colins felt the burn of embarrassment upon the fair flesh of his cheeks. "Don't tell me you can't tell the difference between a rifle shot and thunder. That was a rifle shot, *officer*, and it wasn't all that far from here. Sounded like it came from over by Cattail Lake, wouldn't you say Bobby?" Sauter turned to Chief Kunick, who knelt beside him on one knee. "Awful late in the day to be hunting. Tough to see your target and get a good killing shot in this light."

Kunick twisted the top off a metal thermos perched atop his bent knee. He emptied the dregs of the lukewarm coffee into the dented, stained lid and took a measured sip. Grimacing at the bite of the bitter brew, he poured the remainder on the ground and rose to his feet.

"We'll let the game wardens worry about that," he grunted as he stood. "Wouldn't be the first time they pinched some poor bastard for shooting after hours, and up here, you know it won't be the last. I'd be willing to bet you've squeezed off a shot or two in the dark yourself, Sauter. That experience may come in handy tonight."

"That's something I never did, Bobby, never hunted after hours or out of season. Poaching was never my idea of sport." Sauter spoke the truth, unaware that the distant rifle shot signaled another addition to the growing list of victims connected to the treehouse cradled in the branches above him.

"Sure, fine, whatever you say," Kunick cynically doubted Sauter's idealism, "My point is, let's be prepared for anything here tonight, okay? Christopher Koenigs may . . ." he paused and rephrased the proposition in deference to Sauter's doubts, "The *murderer* may or may not show his or her face, but our friend Sauter here seems to think the perpetrator can't stay away from here, that he's drawn to this meadow and to this treehouse. Let's hope he's right and we catch the son-of-a-bitch tonight, put a bullet in him if we have to and put an end to this goddam nightmare."

"Nothing to report from today chief, no suspicious activity, but I didn't really expect the murderer to show up in broad daylight." Corcoran dutifully provided the uneventful details of her daylong stakeout of the meadow, casting a scornful glance at Sauter. The stakeout was his idea, after all, and she felt it was a waste of precious time, her time. Clad in camouflaged fatigues, her features indistinct beneath green and gray face-paint, Corcoran positioned her stout frame defiantly with arms crossed and legs spread in an open stance.

"It was a long shot, I'll grant you that, Corcoran, but somebody needed to maintain surveillance here at the crime scene." Sauter sensed her resentment and tried to massage her wounded pride. "Chances are when the killer returns it'll be at night, but I for one was glad it was you out here today. I understand you don't always see things my way, but I know you're the kind of cop who can put personal feelings aside and do your job. I was confident that you would handle any potential situation appropriately."

The conciliatory rapprochement had little impact based upon Corcoran's unflinching outward demeanor. A tight-lipped scowl constricted her face and she maintained her rigid pose, determined not to let a few condescending words soften her indignation. There was a moment of awkward silence before she finally granted Sauter a terse nod of recognition.

"Well, I'm going up," Colins chimed in, pointing a slender index finger at the treehouse above. "It's going to be dark soon and I don't suspect that the killer is going to just walk right up to us while we're standing here chatting beneath this bur oak. It's time we all got in position for the night shift."

"Is that an order, sir?" Sauter asked facetiously, sharing a knowing wink with Kunick. A broad grin spread over the rookie officer's youthful face and Colins tried unsuccessfully to suppress a short burst of nervous, high-pitched laughter. Sauter and Kunick shared in the contagious, ill-timed mirth and chuckled softly. Corcoran sniffed contemptuously as she turned on her heels and retreated to her predetermined position among the pine trees.

"Okay, I guess that's our cue," Kunick concluded, shaking his wide head as he watched her depart. "I'll be tucked in behind the generator manning the lights, according to plan, but I'm not kicking them in until I get a signal that somebody's entered the meadow or if I see someone enter myself. You want light, two clicks on the radio and you've got light. Like I said earlier, let's hope tonight's the night and we arrest this guy or put him down. We all straight? We all good to go?"

Colins saluted and shimmied up the thick, knotted rope dangling from the darkened door of the treehouse. Though he was slight of frame, the warped wood still screeched beneath the burden of his swaying weight. Kunick headed for the patch of thick balsam concealing the generator, while Sauter stayed beneath the tree until Colins reached the top of the rope.

"God . . . almighty, it . . . reeks in here," Colins whispered through a   sputtering cough.

"Hang in there kid, the night is young," Sauter whispered back, giving a thumbs up to the eagerly nodding head of strawberry blond hair peering down from the treehouse door.

Darkness fell heavy upon the meadow. Sauter watched as the last handful of stars peeking through the trees along the horizon blinked out and disappeared behind the low ceiling of clouds. He waited patiently while his eyes adjusted to the blackness. At first he could barely see a hand held at arm's length from his face, but over time his diminished field of vision expanded until the vague outline of the giant bur oak materialized from the shadows. Sauter crouched down adjacent to the trail leading into the meadow. Kunick was positioned on his right flank, with Corcoran to his left and Colins directly in front of him inside the treehouse.

It was a black night befitting this haunted hole in the woods, Sauter surmised, drawing the inescapable comparison to the awful darkness that had pervaded this same meadow so many years ago. It was a malevolent, sinister gloom cast upon the forest on that faraway, unforgettable night, the night that he had released Michael Koenigs's limp, blue body from the death grip of the noose. Now, alone with his thoughts, he wrestled with the questions that always plagued him when he was forced to confront the forces of darkness and light, good versus evil.

There were always shadows lingering in the forest. Darkness never fully disappeared. It was tucked away beneath the thick, matted fronds of waist-high ferns. It lurked inside the rotting hulls of enormous white pine deadfalls or lazed beneath the outstretched arms of a mature oak. Darkness retreats into the low-lying cedar swamps, wrapping itself around the twisted trunks and clinging to the wet, spongy bog, holding the light at bay on the highground. Darkness descends on the forest with little sign of struggle. Do shadows fall upon the soul as easily? Are there a fortunate few who radiate light, souls unburdened by a hidden, darker side waiting to shatter the calm surface? There are certainly souls who face a daily struggle against the shadows lurking within. It was just as certain that there were blackened souls, souls that traded in despair and evil as though forever trapped in a midnight woods . . .

Sauter surrendered, let himself be taken back as he often did when the philosophical storm raged through his brain. He could hear Christopher Koenigs cry out for his baby brother, the chilling sobs and low, guttural moans rolling relentlessly out of the darkness. He felt the damp bark of the massive oak, hand pressed against the trunk to steady his wavering knees. Vividly, he saw the small boy hanging beneath the treehouse, the coarse, blood-soaked rope tearing into the flesh of Michael Koenigs's tiny neck. Sauter heard the bone-chilling shriek of madness, felt his body recoil in rigid terror, and saw Christopher Koenigs racing through the forest with his baby brother's dead body dangling like a rag doll from his arms. Michael's swollen little hand waved at Sauter, beckoning for eternity to be saved.

This black night would pass from the forest. Morning would come, and with it, the light. The darkness that descended upon this meadow the night that Michael Koenigs died, however, the same sinister darkness that had returned to claim two more innocent lives, that was a darkness that blackened souls forever. Sauter had lived a lifetime in that lengthening, despairing shadow, and had long ago surrendered any delusion of escape.

It was stunningly quiet, a quiet so complete that the cool night air hummed with the deafening absence of noise. Sauter tried to shrug off the unnerving suspicion that something suddenly wasn't right. He felt unseen eyes boring into him, a nagging sense that the watchers were being watched. With a finger poised on his radio transmitter, he peered into the forest and listened intently, straining to discern any movement among the faded trees. There was nothing out there, nothing he could see or hear, only a nagging feeling that would be hard to explain if he sent Kunick the signal to light up an empty meadow. He slid his finger off the button and trained his ear on the silent forest.

The treehouse moaned in the bur oak's branches, a low, drawn-out lament amplified by the still night air. Sauter recognized the familiar chorus of the wailing wood. It sang out the night he had held Michael Koenigs's lifeless body in his arms. It had reverberated through his nightmares ever since. Laid out before him in the gloom, the treehouse and the meadow might have been plucked from those haunted dreams. *I tore you down myself* . . . a rookie cop ripping the warped gray boards from the covetous grasp of the oak's gnarled limbs, filling the forest with his own mournful cry. Sauter cringed at the faraway vision, startling in its clarity, regretting how soon one is dispossessed of youth and passion. Maybe Bobby was right, maybe he should have listened to his old friend the chief and torn the goddam thing down again.

This was his deal, though, the stakeout. He had sold the idea to spare the deranged replica from demolition. That's what stuck in Sauter's craw, the fact that someone went to a hell of a lot of trouble to recreate the scene of Michael Koenigs's demise. A sick bastard like that can't stay away from his twisted creation for long, not even for a night, Sauter was certain of it. Catch the killer of those two little boys, *then* rip the treehouse down. Sauter considered the beautiful bur oak, *Quercus macrocarpa*, and knew he could never take a chainsaw to the magnificent tree, menacing though it may be. He wondered who would wander into the meadow on this night, hellbent to catch the killer who thrust his nightmares into the waking world.

Two little boys, Jimmy Kelly and Nicholas Ferguson, innocents who ended up connected to the treehouse by a noose because of their fathers' connection to the past. Slovenly Jackson Kelly and physically precocious Max Ferguson. Sauter could hear their jittery, youthful voices explaining the death of Michael Koenigs with suspiciously identical detail. That was twenty-two years ago, nearly to the day, not far from where he currently sat alongside the trail. Richard Mann and Tim Schumacher provided nearly verbatim accounts as well, rounding out the adolescent cadre that conspired to pin the blame on Christopher Koenigs. Sauter was immediately convinced back then and he still believed it to this day.

The children of two of those conspirators had already met the same fate as Michael Koenigs. Sauter suspected that the children of Richard Mann and Tim Schumacher were next on the killer's list. He had checked into it after the first two deaths and learned that Mann had one kid, Terry, a scrawny runt just like the old man, and Schumacher had two boys, Tony and Billy. He considered putting the three young boys under surveillance rather than the treehouse, but if the killer was a copycat plucking random victims, this was the final destination. The more he thought about it, the more Sauter questioned his decision.

It has to be Christopher Koenigs!

Sauter could draw no other conclusion despite the visceral burn deep inside. He typically trusted his gut feelings, inborn instincts that had always served him well. In an autumn woods with bow and arrow, he would feel the burn, *feel* the whitetail buck hidden from his view. As a cop, the burn sorted lies from the truth and separated the guilty from the innocent. Still, he needed to *see* the buck to be certain it was there, much the same as he needed facts to prove that his intuition was correct. The burn told him Christopher Koenigs wasn't the killer, yet logic and circumstance told him otherwise.

Jimmy Kelly and Nicholas Ferguson died at the hands of Christopher Koenigs. Sauter repeated it to himself, let the idea sink in. It felt more comfortable than he would have thought possible, reaching the conclusion that Koenigs, the man he had defended so passionately for so many years, was in all likelihood a murderer. In a strange way, he took it as a measure of vindication. There were six boys in the treehouse that night twenty-two years ago. By Sauter's reckoning, one died and four lied. Back then, filled with the idealistic enthusiasm of a novice cop, he vigorously pursued that theory. In the ensuing years, the pursuit had morphed into an obsession. He had stepped on too many toes, and his solitary quest was met with ridicule and contempt. Yet now, the sixth child in the treehouse, the boy who was ambushed by that orchestrated lie and locked away, was back in Broadaxe.

A scared little kid wrapped up in a policeman's parka, that was the enduring image of Christopher Koenigs that Sauter had carried with him for more than two decades. He could still bring the child's heartrending sobs into his ears, grief-stricken cries for a dead little brother laid out on the ground beneath the treehouse. Sauter wished he could forget the piteous sound. He couldn't, nor could he erase the horrific vision of Michael Koenigs's dead body cradled in his older brother's arms, an ashen-faced corpse bouncing maniacally in the mad dash from the meadow. That had clouded Sauter's thinking, the picture of that frightened child, the memory of a child blamed for his baby brother's death and subsequently branded a sociopath. That was the Christopher Koenigs Sauter knew, the innocent young boy. He didn't know the man, the man who had returned to the meadow in search of revenge, but he expected to meet him soon.

Sauter narrowed his gaze and peered into the shadows of the forest, trying in vain to pick out Corcoran hunkered down in her camouflage to his left or Kunick to his right at his post by the generator. His gaze finally settled back upon the treehouse, no longer lamenting, permitting silence to retake the night. Colins remained concealed within its fetid interior, inhaling the stench, the same awful odor that cloaked the meadow three nights prior when Sauter had taken the rope from Jimmy Kelly's twisted neck. The smell was as much a mystery as the treehouse itself, not to mention the resilient lupines spreading from the base of the oak. Sauter did his best to ignore the slow burn rekindling in the pit of his stomach, but he *felt* someone out there, like a buck at his back during bow season.

Two hours into the stakeout and it could have been twelve. The still air had turned damp and cold. Sauter's tired muscles and joints stiffened, his broken ribs and bruised face screamed with the damage done by Max Ferguson's baseball bat. When was that? He wondered. The sobering events of the last few days dissolved into a jumble inside his overtaxed brain. He tried to piece things together in his mind, working backward chronologically.

It's Saturday, the eighth of September. The Ferguson kid was hung yesterday, Friday the seventh. The killer took Thursday off, the day I spent in jail. The first hanging, Jimmy Kelly, that was Wednesday, the fifth. Okay, that was the day after I got back from my muskie fishing trip . . .

The end of the Labor Day weekend, Tuesday, September 4. Sauter stopped cold when he backtracked to that fateful day, the day he had learned that Christopher Koenigs had finally been paroled. It made him think of his conversations with the intriguing Dr. Amelia Devine. Panic-fueled blood ran fast and cold through his veins. His heart thumped in this chest. The mere thought of telling Devine about his change of heart made him queasy. The assurances he offered when they spoke on the phone just last night and again this morning would seem like empty promises, as if he never truly believed in Koenigs's innocence. Devine was the only person who had as much invested in Koenigs and it was comforting to share that burden.

Sauter understood the grave implications for himself and Devine if Koenigs was indeed the killer he waited for in the woods. There would be no vindication; he was only kidding himself. It didn't matter if Koenigs had returned to Broadaxe to avenge a past injustice, to seek revenge against those who had played a role in his brother's death. Devine had led the charge to win his release. She would be vilified for setting a murderer free. That self-promoting shrink, Perkins, would be merciless. Sauter envisioned the probable outcome and slumped in bitter resignation. It would be too easy for Perkins. Jimmy Kelly and Nicholas Ferguson were dead because her anointed "genetic sociopath" couldn't control the same inbred homicidal urges that caused him to hang his brother Michael. Perkins would reclaim her little guinea pig and retreat to New York, Devine would be discredited, and Sauter would be right back where he started.

It was a debilitating realization. He would never know what had happened in the treehouse the night Michael Koenigs died. Two more children were dead and he still had no answers, had nowhere to turn to find them. Maybe he had been a fool, maybe Koenigs did kill his little brother, maybe he was a blackened soul. Why couldn't he accept that? Sauter probed his psyche. What made him so sure he was right about Koenigs, that he didn't kill his brother, that everyone else was wrong? A *feeling*? he thought self-mockingly, a burning inside that's more likely indigestion than intuition?

It was there now, stronger than ever, goading Sauter. Someone was dangerously near, stalking the perimeter of the meadow, Sauter was convinced now. He had just got done questioning his instincts, had mocked the inner burn, but in the end, he couldn't ignore it. Sauter tucked the radio inside his coat to muffle the sound and clicked the transmitter twice, squinting in anticipation of the blinding transition from total darkness to bright light. Nothing. Agitated, Sauter quickly signaled Kunick a second time. The meadow remained dark.

"Bobby, what in the hell are you doing? Hit the lights!" Sauter hissed into the radio in a loud whisper, reluctantly breaking the silence. "Hit the lights! There's somebody out there!"

A shadowy blur dashed through the trees to his left and Sauter leveled his service revolver instinctively. He withdrew the weapon when he recognized that it was Corcoran racing toward the oak, her own gun drawn and her panicked voice cutting into the night.

"The lights! Turn on the lights chief, there's someone in the treehouse with Colins!" she screamed out as she broke free of the trees and entered the field of flowing purple lupines.

Sauter kept his eyes on the treehouse as he bolted for the base of the oak tree. A bright orange flash suddenly illuminated the shadowy interior and the piercing bark of a pistol ricocheted loudly through the pines. The muted rustle and thump of a scuffle bumped across the wooden floor and Colins suddenly materialized in the darkened portal. He teetered momentarily at the precipice of the treehouse door, then jerked forward convulsively. The wooden planks sang their familiar dirge as Colins reached the end of the rope and his pendulous body swung back and forth at the end of the noose. Corcoran reached Colins first and immediately hoisted his thin frame above her head to slacken the rope, never diverting her eyes from the treehouse overhead.

"C'mon Sauter, let's go, get the rope off his neck!" Corcoran grunted as she tried unsuccessfully to hold Colins up with one arm and loosen the noose herself with her free hand. "What in the hell is going on with Chief Kunick? Where in the hell are those lights?" Sauter could detect the frightened suspicion underlying Corcoran's questions as he rushed to her side and loosened the rope from Colins's bent, broken neck.

"Jesus . . ." Corcoran gasped, dropping her tough cop persona momentarily, ". . . that looks bad." She recovered quickly, "Cover me Sauter, I'm going up. We've got this son-of-a-bitch treed!"

"Careful Corcoran, he might have a gun!" Sauter warned, but she was already snaking her way up the knotted rope leading to the treehouse door.

"Don't think so, Sauter, he could've shot us easily just now if he wanted to," she grunted again as she pulled herself into the treehouse without hesitation.

Sauter braced for the fight, betting on the feisty female cop to come out on top. He could hear Corcoran walking on the wooden planks as she circled the floor slowly and returned to the door. She peered down at Sauter, eyes wide with disbelief.

"There's nobody home, Sauter, the treehouse is empty!"

"Bullshit Corcoran, how can that be? Look again!" Sauter immediately realized the absurdity of the request. Corcoran looked at him quizzically. "I know, I know, it's a treehouse." He waved a hand above his head as he spoke, "It's only so big, there's no place to hide, but what the hell . . . "

Colins sputtered and coughed, stubbornly clinging to

life on the cold bed of decaying oak leaves. Startled, Sauter spun around and dropped to one knee. He felt guilty for letting the kid lay there alone while he and Corcoran puzzled over the empty treehouse. A rivulet of blood ran from the corner of Colins's thin white lips and his cheeks were painted with the pallor of death. Sauter brushed a shock of strawberry blond hair back on Colins's forehead and removed the tilted wire-rimmed glasses from the young officer's slender nose. He wiped the smudged lenses clean as he'd watched Colins do so many times himself, then placed the glasses back on his freckled face.

"Who did this to you son? Who pushed you out of that treehouse?" Sauter pressed the dying man for information. "There's nobody up there, Colins. Corcoran says the treehouse is empty. There had to be somebody up there with you, right? Who was it? Can you talk?"

"I saw somebody go up the trunk of the tree, thin, small guy, quick as a cat." It was Corcoran giving her account from her perch in the treehouse door. "That's when I signaled the chief. That's when I headed for the treehouse. I'm coming down. I've got to go check on the chief. Something's obviously happened to him. There's no way he . . ."

The generator finally coughed to life in the underbrush and bright light flooded the meadow. Kunick stumbled through the lupines, the purple petals once again lusterless and pale. His prodigious head was stained red from the blood that continued to flow from a deep gash on the side of his scalp. He fell to his knees opposite Sauter and pressed an open palm over the cut.

"What the hell happened?" Kunick slurred, blinking eyes knocked out of focus by a concussive blow.

Sauter waved Kunick's question off and turned his attention back to Colins, who was bravely struggling to speak. His weak voice gurgled through the warm liquid pooling in his throat, forcing Sauter to lean close to discern the cryptic words. The acquired Midwestern accent had vanished, replaced by the soft southern lilt of his Georgian upbringing.

"Michael . . . Koenigs . . . died just . . . like this Sauter, ain't that right?" Colins asked in a sputtering drawl, "He died right here . . . just like I'm gonna. This here is . . . his mead-

ow . . . his treehouse . . . these lupines . . . belong to him."
Colins blinked slowly and the life faded from his colorless pupils. He hissed his final words clearly with the exhalation of his last breath. "He don't want you to forget that."

CHAPTER SIXTEEN

A soft, Sunday rain misted the windshield of the police cruiser. Steering subconsciously, Corcoran allowed the moisture to accumulate until the concrete melted into a wriggling gray ribbon. She virtually ignored the highway and kept an anxious eye on Kunick slumped beside her in the passenger seat, his head wrapped in a blood-soaked bandage. Forced to watch helplessly from the back seat as Corcoran careened blindly down the narrow, rain-slicked road, Sauter was thankful he didn't shit himself. He would have, however, rather than say a word.

What could he say? *Keep your eye on the road, Corcoran, what are you trying to do? Kill somebody?* She could shove those words back down his throat. Kunick was passed out with a cracked cranium and Colins was tucked inside a black body bag down at the county morgue. Sauter dolefully shouldered the blame for both. There was no need to give Corcoran the opportunity to remind him just how horribly wrong things had gone in the meadow, how *his* idea to stake out the treehouse resulted in the death of one police officer and left another gravely injured.

It was dark. The digital clock glowed 4:40 a.m. in the dashboard. The rain fell hard and straight now. The liquid fog forced Corcoran to finally hit the wipers. She reluctantly eased up on the accelerator, scowling at the weather all the while. Sauter gazed into the deluge and grimaced himself. He thought of Colins, red-faced after being admonished for mistaking a rifle shot for thunder last night in the meadow. Sauter wondered why he couldn't just let it slide, why he had to be an asshole and make the kid feel stupid. *Sounds like we might be in for some rain,* that's all the kid said, something like that anyway, his made for TV voice not yet stolen by the noose. Sauter cracked his window and put his hand out into the cold, wet spray, hoping to wash away the hard lump pressing into his gullet.

"How're you doing chief? You feeling okay?" Corcoran turned her scowl on Sauter as she posed the questions to

Kunick, who was apparently awakened by the open window.

"Never mind that! Where in the hell are we going?" Kunick snapped to attention quickly. He glanced over his shoulder and nodded at Sauter – an I'm okay, you can count on me nod.

"We're taking you to the hospital," Corcoran answered authoritatively. "That's a nasty cut and lump. A doctor should take a look at that."

"To the hospital! Is that right? Eh Sauter? *We're* taking me to the hospital?" Kunick gingerly fingered his throbbing skull and checked the tips for blood.

"Not *we*, Bobby, I'm only along for the ride. As far as I'm concerned, *you* can go wherever you'd like," Sauter decided the hell with it and threw his two cents worth in from the backseat.

"Your goddam right I'll go where I want!" Kunick's temper flared. "And I'll tell you where I don't want to go, I don't want to go to any goddam hospital!" He sat back and took a breath. "*We're* going to the station, Corky. Now! Don't you worry about me, I'll be just fine."

"Hey, the station was good enough for me." Sauter pointed to his own bruised face. He didn't want to waste time with doctors and nurses. "Hell, I was damn near beaten to death and I didn't need a hospital, did I Bobby? I healed up just fine down at the station, in one of your cells. That reminds me, in light of what happened tonight, I take it I'm officially off the suspect list."

"Don't test my patience Sauter." Kunick was looking over his shoulder again, a raised eyebrow pushing the sagging bandage upward. "No matter how you want to cut it, old friend, fact is you show up back here in Broadaxe and people wind up dead. *People*, mind you, two little boys and a cop, no less! Folks around here did an admirable job of putting that whole Christopher Koenigs mess behind them, but trust me, Sauter, they all remember. They remember Koenigs, they remember you." He turned away.

"What's that supposed to mean, Bobby?" Sauter resented the implication.

"You know damn well what it means! Most everybody

but you believes Christopher Koenigs killed his little brother. It's guilt by association, Sauter. People never wanted to see Koenigs anywhere near these woods again, and the same could be said of you. Nothing personal. It's not like I'm telling you anything you didn't . . . oh shit, of all the people . . . talk about timing."

"Do you want me to keep going, chief?" Corcoran crept along the side of the road in front of the police station, poised to pass right by if given the command.

"Hell no I don't want to keep going! What in the name of . . . you're starting to worry *me* Corky. Pull over, I've got a police department to run." Kunick opened his door with the tires still rolling. "Sauter, you make sure and keep your cool, is that understood? Let me handle him. I'll meet you inside – Corky, you too. We need to talk. You two are going to tell me what happened last night."

"Hey Bobby, just so we're straight," Sauter grabbed Kunick by the sleeve, "I'm looking at one of the locals who never wanted to see me again."

"Nice work, detective." Kunick stood, rotated his head to shake the cobwebs, then leaned back inside the door. The rainfall abated, but enough still fell to mottle the back of his tan jacket with damp splotches. "Richard Mann is a man cut from a unique mold, particularly for these parts, I'll grant you that, but we all know the history between you two. So I'm telling you, Sauter, just pass on by. I'll get enough heat for having you around here as it is, without you shooting your mouth off."

Richard was sheltered from the rain in the small alcove at the front door of the one story police station. It looked to Sauter as though he hadn't been waiting long. His clipped blond hair was matted to his head and wet patches dulled the glossy finish of his pale blue track suit. White from the box tennis shoes reflected in the puddle at his feet alongside the down-turned face of his stickpin son, Terry. The frail child clutched at his father's retracted hand and wept copious tears.

"Take a look at what you've done to my boy." Blocking the entrance, Richard barked at Sauter as he followed behind Kunick's and Corcoran's strategically-positioned wedge. "Ever since Jimmy Kelly's funeral yesterday afternoon, this is all the child does, cry like a baby." He looked down at his son and whispered harshly, "Stop it now, Terry, you're embarrassing me!" then turned his attention back to Sauter, "How many more of this town's children have to die because of you, Sauter, because of you and Christopher Koenigs? How many . . ."

"Whoa, whoa, whoa!" Kunick set his feet and pushed back hard when he felt Sauter lunge forward from behind. Corcoran grabbed his forearm and he shook her off, fists clenched. Kunick held his ground and Sauter silently relented.

"I'll tell you this once, Dickey, and I want you to listen to what I have to say," Kunick wagged a finger and chided Richard, "Sauter had no part in those hangings. He had nothing to do with those murders, not with Jimmy Kelly, not with Nicholas Ferguson," he paused, "not with Michael Koenigs, for that matter. Is that clear enough for you?"

Richard listened to the police chief respectfully, attentively, then went right back at Sauter. He was agitated, eyes frantic and rheumy from lack of sleep.

"Don't try and tell me that you weren't happy when Christopher Koenigs was released, detective. That's what you've wanted all along isn't it? To set a murderer free? Well, you got your wish, you've seen what's happened, you saw those two boys hanging from that tree! Are you happy now? You were on Koenigs's side when he killed his brother. Are you still on his side?"

Sauter retreated two paces and folded his arms across his chest. He eyed Richard's son with pity as the boy begged his father's attention, only to be rebuffed and rebuked for "acting like a baby." There was still something about Richard Mann that set Sauter off, an inherent distrust that unfailingly ignited the slow burn inside. Frustratingly, as always, there was nothing he could do about it.

"Where are the three stooges, Richard," Sauter asked, unaware that one of the three, Max Ferguson, had had his face planted at the business end of the rifle shot he heard the night before. He noticed Richard's odd, distracted demeanor and couldn't resist tweaking him for old time's sake. "Nobody's got your back anymore, I see. How does it feel to be abandoned when the past comes back and bites you in the ass? Think you can keep this up on your own? Or would you rather just come clean about what happened the night Michael Koenigs died?"

Kunick had heard enough, however.

"That's it!" he bellowed. "Sauter, didn't I just tell you to keep your mouth shut?"

"That's right, keep your mouth shut, Sauter," Richard interjected.

"Shut your goddam mouth yourself, Dickey! And move the hell away from that doorway so we can get inside." Kunick put his hands out, palms up. "It's raining out, if you haven't noticed. Unless you have something constructive to add, anything that can be of any help, get out of the way and let us go about our business."

Richard slowly sidestepped out of the alcove and ceded the front entrance. Little Terry skittered behind, still crying, still irritating his unsettled father. Corcoran unlocked the glass door and ushered a resistant Sauter inside. Through the rain-streaked pane, he watched Richard catch Kunick by the arm and hold him back. He wished he could hear what was being said.

" . . . Dickey, the best thing you can do right now is go home and take care of your family, try and get some rest," Kunick tried to console Richard, hoping to get rid of him at the same time. "We'll track down Christopher Koenigs, you have my word, but you have to trust me, you have to give me some room to do my job. Coming down here, ranting and raving, trying to pick a fight, that's not doing anybody any good."

"But you don't understand, chief, I swear I'm about to snap," Richard mewled, his voice tinged with panic. "I think I'm going crazy, losing my mind."

"Calm down, what are you talking about?" Kunick wasn't keen on playing shrink.

"I'm talking about voices, Bobby, voices in my head. The last two days, it just won't quit. It started the night Nicholas . . ." Richard choked up, ". . . I can't shut them off!"

"Relax, Dickey, like I said . . ." Kunick felt sorry for the poor guy, didn't really know what to say.

"Relax! Were you listening to a word I just said? I'm

hearing voices in my head, plain as day, same as you talking to me right now." Richard's distrusting eyes darted back and forth; he lowered his voice secretively, "Jackson and Max, it was the same with them, they heard the voices, they thought they were losing it." He corralled Terry by his scrawny shoulders and thrust his son before Kunick. "Jackson and Max heard voices and their sons ended up dead! My boy can't hang from that treehouse, that can't happen to me! I could never forgive myself!"

Richard ended the self-pitying rant in a high-pitched wail. Terry sobbed heavily, gasping "I don't want to die" in sporadic bursts. The divot in Kunick's skull throbbed to life. Richard Mann had worn out his welcome.

"It's time to take your boy and head home now, Dickey, can't you see you're scaring him?" Kunick suppressed his bubbling impatience, measuring his words. "Try not to get yourself so worked up. At times like this you need to get control of yourself, for your boy, you need to be strong for Terry. I won't sleep until we put an end to this, I promise you that." Kunick looked Richard in the eye. "Now you run on home. You take care of your family."

"What about him?" Richard pointed to Sauter, hovering like a watery mirage behind the glass door, straining to pick out words and trying to read lips. "He has no business being here in Broadaxe, you know that as well as I do, chief. We took care of that problem a long time ago. Sauter shouldn't be here! Christopher Koenigs shouldn't be here! This wasn't supposed to happen. As police chief, Bobby, it's your . . ."

"Go home, Richard," Kunick cut and ran.

There was no way in hell he was going to stand in the rain with a blistering headache and take advice on how to do his job. Besides, he wasn't like all the rest, he had never sought solace in delusion. He knew it would all come back some day, the malignant cancer that had been manipulated into a long, tenuous remission. Kunick regretted missing his chance to excise the exacerbating tumors long ago, before they had a chance to fester and grow into a fatal disease.

"I want Sauter off this case, Chief Kunick! I want him out of town!" Richard fired one last salvo at Kunick's moist, retreating back. Sauter heard the déjà vu demands as the door swung open. He greeted Kunick with a wry smile as the harried chief slipped into the sanctuary of the station.

"The more things change, the more they stay the same. Isn't that what they say, Bobby?" Sauter didn't care if it sounded hackneyed. It was true. "So what did my old friend Richard Mann have to say? Anything interesting?"

Kunick averted his eyes and brushed by Sauter. He shook off the damp chill as he trundled down the hallway to his office. "Corky," he bellowed, motioning with a wave for Sauter to follow. Kunick flipped on the overhead lights in his office, recoiled from the humming, halogen glare, then quickly turned them back off. He cannon-balled into his desk chair and rolled slowly backward across the hard plastic floor mat, stopping just short of the chipped drywall where the ride often ended. Sauter went straight for the corner couch, not bothering to remove the accumulated clutter before he stretched out on his back, hands interlocked behind his head.

"You want to know what that sorry son of a bitch said?" Kunick surprised Sauter. He assumed his curiosity had been summarily ignored. "His boy is standing right there in front of him, scared shitless and crying as it is, and he talks about the kid getting killed, you know, hung, like his friends. The kid was right there! But get this, this is the part that's vintage Dickey, he says this can't happen to *me*, worried more about himself than his own child. I could have slapped that stupid, selfish asshole senseless right then and there."

"Why didn't you! I had front row seats for the show and believe me, I definitely would have enjoyed it, probably would've called for an encore," Sauter satisfied himself with the mental picture.

"Oh yeah, then I could have phoned his attorneys myself, and packed my bags. Stop me if this sounds familiar. You've been down that road before, Sauter. I'm sure you could've walked me through it." Kunick laughed, a forced, uncomfortable titter. He shuffled his feet and wheeled back to his desk, settling in on his elbows. "Richard Mann . . . a certified piece of work. He's persistent, I'll say that for him, just like his old man. I was under a lot of pressure after the Koenigs deal,

Sauter, I . . ."

"Let's not go back there then, Bobby. That was a long time ago," Sauter stared blankly at the ceiling, mellowed by his cushioned repose. "Everybody did what they thought they had to do, myself included. If Richard Mann wants to follow in his father's footsteps and run me out of Broadaxe, I won't fight it, not this time. No worries, Bobby. As soon as we catch the killer, I'm gone."

"Well hell, I'm not worried Sauter. What's that supposed to mean anyway?" Kunick wasn't going to let it drop, insistent about revisiting unpleasant memories. "You certainly didn't leave me many options. Talk about persistent! No offense, but you may be more like Richard Mann than you'd care to admit. I warned you plenty of times, Sauter. I told you what would happen if you didn't let it drop, but you didn't listen. You and your cockeyed ideas about Christopher Koenigs!"

"Cockeyed ideas!" Sauter swung his feet to the floor and sat up in the center of the sofa, sweeping a folded newspaper and a yellow note pad from the cushion with his legs. "I'm telling you, Bobby, there's a reason Christopher Koenigs returned to Broadaxe, there's a . . ."

"Listen to yourself!" Kunick pounded his fist on the desk. "Christopher Koenigs is a murderer, Sauter, a murderer! He killed his brother Michael, he killed Jimmy Kelly, he killed Nicholas Ferguson, and he killed Officer Seth Colins! And you're going to provide a plausible rationale? Are you kidding me? Are you that pig-headed? That you'd keep defending a killer rather than admit you were wrong?"

Sauter wasn't prepared to make that admission, not yet. He stood and paced the confined floor space in front of the couch.

"You're way off base, Bobby. I think you've always misread my intentions. I'm not defending what Christopher Koenigs has done, I'm simply trying to explain it. As cops, isn't that what we're supposed to do?" He stopped beside the desk and looked down at Kunick. "It always seemed funny to me though, after Michael Koenigs was killed. Folks around here didn't bother to ask why, they were too concerned with a quick resolution."

"I *know* you're not suggesting any impropriety on my part." Kunick reacted defensively, too defensively, in Sauter's estimation. "The investigation of Michael Koenigs's death was open and transparent. Nothing was swept under the rug. There was no cover up. There were four eyewitnesses who provided not only the why, but the what, where, when and how of Michael Koenigs's death."

The words "cover up" struck Sauter like a cold slap in the face. He considered incompetence to be Kunick's greatest sin in his handling of the Koenigs case, the error of an inexperienced police chief allowing public opinion to steer the course of the investigation. Sauter disdained conspiracy theorists; but, for the first time, he regarded his old friend with an unsettling suspicion.

"And it's just coincidence that the children of two of those eyewitnesses are dead?" Sauter stepped back from the desk, turning his back to Kunick when he spoke. "There's a *reason* Christopher Koenigs targeted Jackson Kelly's and Max Ferguson's sons. Richard Mann looked mighty scared to me, Bobby, and I imagine he should be. You saw his little boy. He's even figured out that he could be next."

Kunick pushed himself upright behind the desk and limped to the door of his office. He scratched the back of his large, round head, looking down the empty hallway one direction, then the other. "Goddam it, where's Corky gone to?" he grumbled beneath his breath. He stepped back into the office and closed the door. "Yeah Sauter, sure, Richard Mann is frightened. I guarantee you every parent with a small child in this town is frightened. But you're right, I'm not going to argue about this one with you. If I were Richard Mann, or Tim Schumacher, for that matter, I would certainly have more reason to be concerned. Dickey said as much himself."

"What did he say?" Sauter turned and faced Kunick.

"Actually, the poor bastard is starting to crack under the strain. He told me he's hearing voices, said that Jackson Kelly and Max Ferguson heard voices right before their boys were killed. That's why he thinks his son Terry is next, said that if anything happened to the boy he could never forgive himself."

"Voices?" Sauter asked weakly, his own trailing off. He

remembered the voices in his own head – *go to the meadow, save the child* – the voices he ignored. "What did he mean, voices? Did he tell you what the voices said?"

"Voices, that's all he said. Voices in his head. He didn't get specific, just that it was driving him crazy. He looked crazed, that's the best way to explain it. I stood right in front of him, my bleeding head wrapped in bandages, and he never asked what happened, didn't even seem to notice it." Kunick stepped closer to Sauter and eyed him skeptically. "You alright? Is there something I'm missing here?"

"No, Bobby, no, nothing," Sauter screwed his puzzled face straight. "It's just odd, the thing about the voices, that's all." He veered off quickly, "Last night in the woods, what happened? Do you remember anything at all? Did you see anything before you got clunked on the head?"

"No, not one goddam thing! Didn't I make that clear earlier?" It irked Kunick to recall his embarrassing contribution to the botched stakeout. "That's what we're supposed to be trying to figure out right now." His patience depleted, he opened the door and yelled Corky's name directly into her surprised face. She sidestepped Kunick and entered the office, flipping on the overhead lights with her elbow. She clutched a tray that carried a towel, a bowl of water, a small bottle of antiseptic cream and a clean roll of gauze.

"Come and sit down, chief," she gave a gentle command and set the tray on the desk. "We need to clean and re-dress that wound."

"Doesn't anybody listen to me?" Kunick pointed to the nameplate above the breast pocket of his shirt. "Chief Robert Kunick. That's me, I give the orders around here, and I said there's no time for that," he protested.

"Just sit down, Bobby, let Corcoran fix you up," Sauter interceded. "We can talk about last night while she changes that bloody dressing. It's nasty, so just let her do her thing. How about it? It's kind of ironic, hey Bobby, people always making fun of that beg melon of yours, and here it probably saved your life."

Kunick surrendered and stomped back to his chair. "Fine, make it quick, Corky, you hear me?" He rubbed the prodigious dome and frowned. "People make fun of my head? Really?" Sauter and Corcoran exchanged glances, eyebrows raised.

"If nobody has any objections, I'll start it out and run through last night from my point of view," Sauter suggested, nodding deferentially at Corcoran, who nodded her assent back. "Okay, well, I wish I had something more tangible to contribute. At some point I had a feeling that somebody else had entered the meadow, but I didn't see or hear anyone, so I held off on the radio. You know how quiet it was out there. How could anybody possibly move through those woods without being heard?"

"I've been wrestling with that one myself," Kunick acknowledged with a wince. Corcoran removed the soiled headband and daubed the deep, sensitive gash running slightly above and parallel to his left temple. "I didn't hear anything, I didn't see anything, hell, I didn't even feel anything, at least not until I came to, but by then it was too late."

"This could sting a bit chief," Corcoran issued the warning at the same moment she applied the antiseptic cream to the wound with a wet cloth.

"Son of a . . ." Kunick bit his lower lip and slightly arched his back, "How anybody was able to get the drop on me last night," he dealt with the pain and continued his thought, "I never even had an inkling that somebody was closing in, but you did, is that right, Sauter? Why was that again? Why did you think we had company?" The cleansed cut shone like a bright red feather, a jagged cleft in a mesa of swollen flesh.

"Dammit, Bobby, that has to smart!" Sauter leaned in for a closer inspection of Corcoran's handiwork. "Nicely done, officer, but you wouldn't happen to know how to put a suture or two in, would you?" He noticed Kunick's sour expression and slowly backed away.

"Okay, right, back to last night. It was just a feeling, that's all, a feeling that someone else was out there with us, someone who didn't belong. I ignored it at first, but I couldn't shake it. It got to the point where I couldn't ignore it, so I actually signaled for the lights, Bobby, but you must have already been, um, incapacitated. I signaled a second time, still nothing. It was fairly obvious something was up by then, so I said the hell with the silent signal and tried talking to you directly. That's when Corcoran caught the corner of my eye. She was running toward the treehouse, shouting for the lights. You must've tried unsuccessfully to signal." He waited for her nod. "There was gunfire in the treehouse, a single shot, actually, and you could hear the sounds of a scuffle. I saw Colins in the treehouse door with a rope around his neck and . . ." Sauter paused to collect himself ". . . and then he fell out, more like he was pushed from behind, really, but I'll be damned if I saw who was in there with him. We tended to Colins initially, but Corcoran climbed into the treehouse within seconds. There was nobody up there, Bobby, that quickly, gone, as if nobody had ever been in the treehouse with Colins at all."

"I told you last night, Sauter, I *saw* somebody climb the trunk of the tree and enter the treehouse, just before the shot was fired," Corcoran bristled. She coated a clean bandage with the antiseptic cream and pressed it into the tender wound more forcefully than Kunick would have preferred.

"I wasn't speaking literally, Corcoran. I wasn't suggesting that Colins was actually alone in the treehouse." Sauter was surprised by the need to clarify. "All I'm saying is that someone snuck in right under our noses and snuck right back out, and it simply doesn't seem possible."

"Of course someone was in the treehouse with Colins!" Kunick exploded from his seat, slapping away Corcoran's doting hands as she finished securing the new bandage with sticky white tape. "Do you think Colins shot off his pistol, did a little jig up there in the treehouse, put a noose around his neck and jumped? Do you think I stumbled and hit my head on a rock? Can either of you two tell me *anything* that might help make some sense of this god-awful mess?"

"Well," Corcoran hesitated, then plunged ahead, "it was your firearm that was discharged in the treehouse, chief. Whoever knocked you unconscious apparently acquired your weapon."

"Did I miss something?" Kunick's dander was up. "Colins wasn't shot dead, was he? No, he was hanged! Someone put the rope around his neck and pushed him to his death, and you're the only one here who saw that someone, Corcoran."

"I didn't get a very good look at the individual, chief. It was difficult to see that far in the dark and it all happened so fast." She lowered her head, ashamed by the admission.

"C'mon, Corcoran, anything at all," Kunick pressed. "Did the person you saw climbing the tree match the description of Christopher Koenigs?"

"Hold on, Bobby, she just got done saying that . . ." Sauter tried to intervene, but Kunick snapped his fingers and repeated the question.

"Did the individual you witnessed match the description of Christopher Koenigs?"

Sauter noted the barely perceptible nod that accompanied Kunick's leading question. A contagious nod. Corcoran gradually began to bob her head, aping the chief. The up and down movement seemed to jar something loose. Sauter saw the flicker of implicit recognition cross Corcoran's countenance. She stiffened – shoulders back, stance wide, hands clasped behind her back – and in a clipped cadence rattled off a report Sauter found remarkable in its newfound detail.

"The perpetrator, a man, small stature, appeared to be approximately five-foot-five to five-foot-seven inches in height, slight of build, 125- to 135-pound range. Thinning hair, light brown to gray in color . . ."

"Are you kidding me?" Sauter, looking directly at Kunick, broke in, "One minute ago it was too dark, things were happening too fast," he turned his attention to Corcoran, "you admitted you didn't get a good look at the . . ." he actually flicked quotation marks in the air, his tone mocking, "perpetrator."

"I didn't get a good look at his *face*." Corcoran, defiant, glared at Sauter. "It was dark and the perpetrator was already climbing the tree, the trunk of the tree. Very quick, very agile." She paused, narrowing her eyes in reflection. "His back was turned to me the entire time. When I climbed the tree in pursuit . . ."

"Fine, Corcoran, fine," Kunick resumed control. "Sauter went over this already. Koenigs made his escape while the two of you tried to save Colins's life."

"Well, that's not exactly how I'd describe what occurred," Sauter attempted to clarify, "Corcoran was up that tree in a hurry herself – half a minute, a minute, at most – from the time Colins was pushed out the door until she was in the treehouse herself."

"And we've heard this all already," Kunick lamented with an overdramatic flare. "The treehouse was empty! That's the way you put it, Sauter. It's all the same to me, merely semantics. Christopher Koenigs sucked in the lure but we failed to set the hook. You're the muskie fisherman, Sauter, maybe you'd prefer that analogy. I'll stick to plain old Americanese. We had him, we had our killer, but we let him escape."

Sauter placed his hands atop his head, fingers interlaced. With his elbows extended and flapping like wings, he ambled over to the couch and sunk back into the cushions. His hands fell into his lap, palms upturned, unable to hide his incredulity.

"The lights hadn't come on yet, Sauter. It was still pitch black when we were working on Colins, when I searched the treehouse," Corcoran tried to answer his unspoken questions. "It doesn't seem possible, but Koenigs must have shimmied down the backside of the tree and slipped away in the darkness. He snuck into the meadow. We thought that was impossible, so I don't see why he couldn't have slipped back out. It's tough to admit. Believe me, I can empathize with that, especially with, well, with what happened to Colins and all, but I don't see how we can deny it."

A respectful hush descended upon the room with the mention of their fallen fellow officer. Corcoran turned away and busily tidied up the medicine tray, the muscles of her jaws working to grind away the welling emotion. Sauter and Kunick masked their own guilt and remorse with stolid contemplation, both tortured by a barrage of second guesses. The extended silence chafed Sauter. There was no time to reflect, to stagnate with regret. He tried to rally the flagging troops, but he lit Kunick's fuse, instead.

"That's the conclusion then, it was Christopher Koenigs in the meadow last night," he offered in agreement.

"Goddammit, Sauter!" Kunick blustered in red-faced

fury, misinterpreting Sauter's intent, "You heard Corky's description, a pretty damn good match with Koenigs as far as I'm concerned. What the hell is truly the matter with you, Sauter? Are you one of those kooks who sees a conspiracy wherever he looks?"

The misguided harangue struck Sauter as overly defensive, adding to his unease about Kunick's queer behavior since his private meeting in the rain with Richard Mann. The unprovoked references to a cover up and a conspiracy left Sauter cold. He was about to share his revelation in the woods, when he had gazed upon the meadow and the treehouse, and reluctantly convinced himself that Christopher Koenigs killed Jimmy Kelly and Nicholas Ferguson. Sauter wanted to assure Kunick that they were on the same side because he didn't want to end up back outside. The phone rang before he had the chance.

"Chief, didn't you notice? You haven't even checked your messages yet," Corcoran pointed out the flashing red light as she reached for the phone. Kunick beat her to the receiver.

"Broadaxe P.D., Chief Kunick here." He skipped a beat and his eyes danced furtively. "Oh, um, could you hold on one second." Irritated, he waved Sauter and Corcoran out of his office, gesturing for privacy. Corcoran came around the desk, tray in hand, and herded a recalcitrant Sauter into the hallway. Muffled yet distinct, he heard Kunick reengage the caller as Corcoran struggled to simultaneously pull the door shut and balance the tray.

"Dickey, what the hell are you doing calling me here already? Didn't I just get done telling you I'd take care of this? Just like I did before . . ." Corcoran won her battle with the door and cut Sauter off from the curious conversation. She used the tray to repulse his undisguised attempt to continue eavesdropping and cocked her head to gain his attention.

"Don't beat yourself up too badly, detective. It was a good plan, poor execution," she surprised Sauter with the sincere declaration of support. "I didn't agree with it at first, the stakeout, I'll admit it, but the killer showed. You were right, he couldn't stay away. We just underestimated who we're up against. We won't make that mistake again, will we?"

"You know Corcoran, I figured if Christopher Koenigs was back, he couldn't hide out for long and not be seen, not in Broadaxe. After what I saw last night – what I *didn't* see, I guess, I'm not so sure." Sauter shook his head, still baffled by the display of uncanny stealth. "Downright unbelievable though, wouldn't you say? The way he got in and out of there on us?"

"Unbelievable? Yes. Impossible? No."

"Colins, right before he died, when he referred to Michael Koenigs, what'd you make of that?"

"Shock." Corcoran didn't hesitate. "It wasn't even his normal voice. He was talking in that odd accent."

"He was from Georgia, lost the accent because he wanted to be a television news anchor, went to school for it," Sauter regurgitated the little he actually knew about Colins. "His old man was a cop, larger than life type, steered his son into the police academy when his television dream tanked. Colins came up to Wisconsin because he didn't think he could live up to his old man's expectations, didn't want to spend his life in his shadow. I need to send his old man a letter, maybe with a commendation, let him know his kid died in the line of duty, that he didn't die in vain."

Corcoran sensed doubt in Sauter's voice. "Colins *didn't* die in vain, detective, we have to make certain of that. The description I gave of the perpetrator, I know you thought it fit what the chief was asking for a little too conveniently, that I was only telling him what he wanted to hear, but I swear on my badge I was describing exactly what I saw out there last night. It *could* have been Christopher Koenigs. Is that really a surprise? Maybe he gave Colins the message about his brother Michael before he pushed him out of the treehouse, who knows? I consider myself a damn good cop, detective. I don't misconstrue the facts for anybody. Is that clear?"

Kunick's voice rose and fell behind the closed door, unintelligible, but obviously irritated. Sauter realized nothing had changed. He was still stuck on the outside looking in, whether he liked it or not, evidenced by his old friend's unsettling duplicity concerning Richard Mann. Kunick would no doubt bend to the pressure once again. Sauter understood he was running on borrowed time in Broadaxe. Corcoran might never be his ally, but he couldn't afford to make her an enemy.

"I wasn't insinuating anything of the kind," he cajoled, lying himself. Her initial, murky recollection of the man climbing the oak in the dark cleared too quickly when Kunick pressed her, but Sauter had to admit that he didn't truly doubt Corcoran's integrity as a police officer. "If that's the way I came across, please accept my sincere apology. I've always played the devil's advocate on this one, but now I agree that Christopher Koenigs is responsible for the most *recent* killings." He purposely stressed the word. "When Bobby just jumped down my throat in there, I suppose he thought I was being facetious when I said that, but I meant it. I intended to ask for suggestions on what to do next."

"Catch Koenigs, quickly, before he kills again," obdurate toward the apology, Corcoran supplied a simplistic solution.

Sauter smiled thinly, "I can't argue with that, so the next question is how? I was hoping we could talk about that with Bobby when he's finished with his phone call. Sounded like it was Richard Mann. Is there some connection that I'm missing? Are the chief and Dickey, as he calls him, do those two stay in fairly close contact?"

"Follow me, I put a pot of coffee on when we came in, we can discuss that over a cup -- how to go about catching Koenigs, that is – the chief's business is just that, the chief's." Corcoran started down the corridor toward the back of the station. "I know I could use a little caffeine. I'm running on fumes."

Sauter lingered by Kunick's office door, still hoping to hear a snippet of the conversation within. Corcoran stopped and impatiently tapped her foot on the glossy linoleum. She had requested his company for a cup of coffee, and she wasn't going to be denied. Sauter wanted to oblige, knew it was in his best interest to stay in her good graces, yet he couldn't help himself. He turned away and brazenly opened the door.

The call had ended and Kunick was seated behind the desk, scowling at the phone. Ignoring Corcoran's protestations, Sauter strode into the office and settled back into the sofa. Corcoran quickly materialized in the doorway, tray still in hand, looking quite distraught.

"I'm sorry chief, I tried to . . ."

"Close the door behind you, Corky. I need a minute with our friend Sauter here." Kunick flicked her from the room with his fingers. He didn't look up. Corcoran obediently followed orders, displeased at being summarily dismissed.

Sauter suspected she loitered in the hallway, just as he had, listening in. He spoke loudly, hoping she heard what he had to say.

"If you think I'm going to make it easy on you and just leave Broadaxe, Bobby, sorry, not this time." Sauter leaned forward and leapt onto the offensive. "You and that little piss ant, Richard Mann, so you two are pretty tight, you and *Dickey* . . ." he allowed the contempt to linger, ". . . Something's not right with that guy; you'll never convince me otherwise. Now I'm wondering, Bobby, maybe something's not right with you."

A bright red dot turned Kunick's white bandage into a miniature Japanese flag. He swiveled in his chair and leaned back, throwing his legs atop the desk. Metal screeched as he reached down and opened the bottom drawer. The bottle of whiskey was half-empty, the brand backshelf, and Kunick licked his lips in anticipation as he slowly unscrewed the cap.

"Look at yourself, Sauter. You're a goddam mess. Your face is as bruised as the bottom banana." He grinned and swallowed hard, wincing at the alcohol's bite and wiping his mouth on his sleeve. The cap stayed off, but he didn't offer the bottle to Sauter. "I warned you right after you got your ass beat, after Jackson Kelly's boy turned up dead, I told you right then and there to get the hell out of Broadaxe."

"For chrissakes, Bobby, one minute you were holding me as a suspect in the kid's murder, the next you're begging me to help you catch the real killer." Sauter melted into the sofa as if he intended to stay awhile. "I could help, or I could be a scapegoat, pretty sweet deal either way from your angle. You wanted me out of Broadaxe like you wanted that lump on your head."

"Lucky me, I've got you, and the lump. Hell, I've got

the lump *because* of you." Kunick dropped his feet to the floor and propped his elbows on his knees. The smile was gone. "You're fast becoming a liability, Sauter, and you know from experience that I'm a man with little or no tolerance. Sure, mister smarty pants detective, you've got it all figured out, Richard Mann does want me to run your sorry ass out of Broadaxe, but know this my friend, nobody tells Chief Bobby Kunick how to run his town, nobody." He mellowed. "Besides, it appears you're a mighty popular guy."

Kunick stabbed the phone with his stubby index finger and the answering machine beeped to life:

"Yes, hello, this is Margaret Schumacher calling, I'm trying to get in touch with Detective Henry Sauter. I contacted his office over at the Ojibway County Sheriff's and was told to call here, that the detective was in Broadaxe working on the recent hangings. I have some important information, but I'll only talk to Detective Sauter. As I said, it's very important, so if you could please relay this message and have him return my call at . . ."

Kunick killed the recording, "There were several more calls from Mrs. Schumacher. I wrote down her number." He waved a small notepad at Sauter and punched the red button a second time:

"My name is Dr. Sarah Perkins. I'm a psychiatrist with the Municipal Mental Health Center, a state-operated facility in New York that until recently had Christopher Koenigs enrolled as one of its patients. I understand that your department is currently investigating the murder of two children in your town and that Christopher Koenigs is being sought as the prime suspect. Myself and a colleague will be flying out to Wisconsin to offer any assistance . . ."

Kunick snuffed the tape prematurely once again. He tipped a short sip of whiskey and watched intently for any reaction. Sauter sensed the chief's mischievous anticipation and did his best to subdue the mixed rush of excitement and dread pulsing through his veins. Dr. Amelia Devine, *the colleague*, would be arriving, in the flesh, in the very near future. Kunick waved the whiskey under his nose and thought about another drink. He capped the bottle, settling for a sniff of the fumes, and withheld comment on the message from Dr. Sarah Perkins. That would normally set the insular chief off, the imminent arrival of *outside* interference, so Sauter prodded to elicit the source of Kunick's powerful preoccupation.

"And this makes me such a popular guy because . . .?" he asked nonchalantly, familiar with the chief's penchant for suspense.

"I thought you'd never ask."

Smirking, Kunick hit the button and played the final message. Sauter recognized the voice immediately:

"Hello, I'm hoping that this message can be forwarded to Detective Henry Sauter. This is Dr. Amelia Devine. I apologize for the short notice, it's early Sunday morning, September ninth, and I'm just about to board a flight here in New York and expect to arrive in Wisconsin at approximately 7:30 a.m. It's imperative that Detective Sauter meet me at that time, let me see, at the Ojibway County Airport at that time. Again, I'm sorry for any inconvenience, but if every effort could be made to get this message to Henry – I'm sorry, Detective Sauter – it would be greatly appreciated. Thank you for your assistance with this matter."

Kunick clicked off the answering machine with a flourish and rose from his chair. He raised his eyebrows and cooed playfully, "Henry?", looking and acting much too smug for Sauter's liking. "Shall we go and meet Amelia? – I'm sorry, Dr. Devine – She would greatly appreciate it." Smug, and mocking. Kunick stepped to the sofa and stood above Sauter, uncomfortably close, his enormous, bandaged head blotting out the overhead light. "It seems as though somebody has, oh, how should I put it? A *special friend* out East, a special friend who happens to be the director of the nuthouse where Christopher Koenigs was locked up. Amelia Devine, the shrink responsible for Koenigs's release, and you two on a first name basis. A sweet deal, indeed!"

Kunick hovered interminably, towering over Sauter until his annoying persistence turned threatening. The muscles tensed in Sauter's lower back. The tension rolled over his shoulders and down his arms, bottoming out in balled fists. Kunick ripped a sheet of paper from his little notebook and dropped Margaret Schumacher's telephone number into Sauter's lap.

"My head hurts, so you're driving." Kunick extended a hand to Sauter, who reluctantly allowed himself to be yanked to his feet. "Our unexpected and uninvited visitors arrive in less than an hour." Kunick turned and exited the office, finally venting his displeasure with the changing situation. "Goddammit, what do these two women think they're going to do here in Broadaxe besides get in the way?" Still grumbling, he disappeared down the hallway.

Sauter took a deep breath and relaxed, allowing the defensive anger to drain from his rigid frame. Kunick had baited him and he'd nearly bit, and it pissed him off. To make matters worse, he felt foolish for being so flustered by the prospect of a face-to-face meeting with Amelia Devine. He self-consciously brushed off his crumpled tweed suit coat and wrinkled black jeans, suddenly distressed that he hadn't changed clothing in more than three days.

"Goddammit, Sauter, you coming or what?" Kunick bellered from the front of the station. "The message said it was imperative that you were there to greet the plane when it arrived, not me, but I'm the one standing here twiddling my thumbs."

"Hold your horses, Bobby, I'm coming, I'm coming," Sauter hollered back, pausing a moment as he looked from the phone number in his hand to the phone on the desk.

The paper snapped with each flick of his finger. The call from Tim Schumacher's wife intrigued him. She barely registered in his memory, yet he seemed to recall a quiet redhead, the daughter of the folks who used to run the resort out on Cattail Lake. Could she possibly know anything of value? he wondered, or was she in a panic like Richard Mann, frightened for herself and for her family.

"Sauter!" Kunick again, very agitated.

Whatever the reason for Margaret Schumacher's call, she would have to wait, unlike Amelia Devine. Hesitating, he tucked the paper into his coat pocket and made a mental note to return the call later that morning, when he had more time.

Kunick scowled at Sauter when he finally emerged

from the office, then flagrantly ignored him during the ride to the airport. It was more precisely an airfield, a single strip scarred black from years of touchdowns and takeoffs. The spartan facilities consisted of a white mobile home that served as the terminal, per se, along with a handful of low-slung hangars and a smattering of maintenance sheds and small outbuildings.

Bright orange windsocks fluttered in the breeze, flanking a pair of planes parked one beside the other at the end of the runway. The rain had stopped and the clouds splintered, allowing patches of filtered sunshine to mottle the ground. Two men were busy inspecting the larger of the two aircraft, a sleek Gulfstream jet that made the adjacent single wing turbo prop appear ancient. Sauter parked next to the mobile home and surveyed the scene for any sign of the female doctors, anxious to put a face to Dr. Devine's voice, in particular. There were only the two men. Sauter pegged one as a pilot, the other a mechanic. Sated with Kunick's ill-tempered company, he killed the ignition and strolled out onto the tarmac. Ambivalent about all things aviation, Sauter was nevertheless drawn to the aircraft with a kid's curiosity.

"Hello, excuse me. Henry, is that you?"

Sauter walked another two or three steps before he pivoted toward the familiar voice calling out behind him. Amelia Devine smiled cautiously and waved from the wrought iron steps of the makeshift terminal. She wore faded jeans with flared bottoms, brown, square-toed boots and a brown corduroy blazer over a white blouse. Her shoulder-length black hair was gathered in a loose ponytail and her complexion shown with a natural, unadorned radiance. Sauter felt the warmth of her beautiful brown eyes burrowing into his chest and his jaw slackened in response. Devine stopped waving, cocked her head. Mortified, Sauter caught himself in the stupefied stare.

"Yes, it's me Amelia, Henry," he spoke casually, hid the embarrassment, "I'm sure you understand, it's been a hell of a long week." She smiled reassuringly.

"Henry? Amelia?"

Somehow, Sauter hadn't noticed the long, alluring legs propping up Dr. Sarah Perkins in the open door frame of the mobile home. She hit him hard with her blue eyes, as well, but it was a cold burn, an icy stare. What Sauter knew of Perkins he didn't like, her manipulation of Christopher Koenigs, her reputation as a self-promoter, a ruthless bitch. Still, he had to admit, all that ugliness was packaged quite appeasingly. Tall, blond, and statuesque, she was Ginger to Devine's Mary Ann. Sauter smiled back at Amelia. He had always preferred Mary Ann.

"Well, Dr. Devine, it didn't take long to learn who you've been getting your information from here in Wisconsin," Perkins sniffed, handling the grated iron steps gracefully in her high heels. The peach-colored shoes matched the pastel, knee-length skirt clinging to her shapely hips. A matching coat was draped over her bent arm and the unbuttoned top of her silky pearl blouse exposed an enticing hint of alabaster cleavage.

"I only learned of that interesting little connection myself just moments ago." Kunick joined the reception, gallantly extending a hand to aid Perkins's descent. "Dr. Perkins, I presume. It's a pleasure and an honor to finally meet you in person. Chief Robert Kunick." They shook hands; he continued to fawn, "Most folks call me Bobby. I certainly do appreciate you taking valuable time from your busy schedule to come all the way out here to our little town of Broadaxe. I give you my word as a sworn officer of the law, we'll find Christopher Koenigs for you."

"And is this what you have to show for it so far?" Perkins snorted contemptuously, nodding to Kunick's bandaged head and Sauter's battered face. The quartet had formed a small circle at the foot of the steps.

"Detective Henry Sauter," Sauter extended his hand to Perkins, pointedly ignoring the cheap shot. Appraising his disheveled appearance with obvious distaste, she recoiled quickly from the awkward handshake.

"I hate to interrupt the heartfelt introductions." Devine did so, nonetheless, with a surprising announcement. "I received some information just before we left New York. It's the reason why it was so important that you meet me here at the airport, Henry. I believe that I've located Christopher Koenigs."

There was a moment of stunned silence. Finally, not

trusting his own ears, Sauter had to repeat what he had just heard. "Christopher Koenigs? You've found Christopher Koenigs?" he stammered. "What? I mean, how did you find him? Where is he?"

Devine surveyed the three stunned faces gaping at her in disbelief, certain that the veracity of what she was about to aver would be immediately in doubt.

"Canada," she stated confidently, "Ontario, Canada."

CHAPTER SEVENTEEN

The ink had faded to a pale blue, blending the tattoo into the burnt red skin of the weathered knuckles drumming the map. Sauter was able to make out four letters, all lowercase, starting at the index finger and running to the pinky. *b u n a*

"Due north of here, the neighborhood of Lake St. Joseph, that's where I'm at." The owner of the tattooed digits tapped the yellowed page of the atlas, pointing vaguely to the vast, roadless expanse of northwestern Ontario. "Name's Zebulon Munga, owner and operator of Munga's Outpost, huntin' and fishin' lodge, pretty remote, fly-in. That's my plane." He nodded at the aged turbo prop. "Only got room for three more. Sorry, Dr. Amelia, can't take all four of you."

Devine raised her hand before the quizzical quiet of Sauter, Kunick, and Perkins devolved into a barrage of questions. The owner of the outpost had taken her mention of Canada as his cue to enter their circle of conversation. He politely doffed his tattered gray tam to Perkins and nearly shook the arms off Sauter and Kunick, his lower lip distended in a tobacco chewer's grin. Oil spotted the leather and sawdust gathered in the creases of his boots. The sun had faded the olive hue of his worn dungarees and collared shirt, with darker green clinging to the stitched seams and pockets.

"So you're a pilot," Sauter couldn't help himself. "I had pegged you as a mechanic on a first impression."

"A man can be more than one thing." Munga turned and squeezed a brown stream through the gap in his front teeth. "That said, maybe you'll keep that in mind and forgive my impatience when I say there aren't enough hours in a day." He bowed his head deferentially to Devine. "So, if you don't mind, Dr. Amelia?"

"Yes, of course, I'm sorry Mr. Munga. I understand you've sacrificed valuable time to volunteer your services," blushing, she apologized hastily. "Mr. Munga is the individual who contacted me regarding the whereabouts of Christopher Koenigs. Please, Mr. Munga, it would probably be simpler if you explained."

"Feel free to call me Zeb, Dr. Amelia." He clawed the gray cap from his head and uncorked a disheveled crown of dirty gray hair. "Short and to the point, the feller you call Christopher Koenigs has been in my employ up at the outpost going on a full week now."

"Christopher Koenigs? Working at a hunting lodge? In Ontario, Canada?" Perkins awakened from her brooding silence and bit the words off with dubious contempt. "Preposterous! If time is indeed such a valuable commodity, as you claim Mr. Munga, I find it very interesting that you have no qualms wasting not only yours, but *ours* as well."

Munga screwed the lid back over his unruly mane and manufactured a faint, forced smile, "A huntin' *and* fishin' lodge, which I can safely assume you won't be visiting any time soon, Doctor . . . Perkins, is it?" He met her hard, uncompromising glare. "Very well, that makes room for the rest of you folks, those who do plan on making the trip, that is. Makes no difference to me who wants to tag along, Dr. Amelia. It's time to saddle up. I offered to fly down here as a courtesy, only trying to be of help. I didn't come all this way to be insulted." He spit tobacco into the shallow puddle of drying rain at his feet and suddenly retreated to his plane without another word.

Perkins defensively responded to Devine's admonishing stare. "Don't give me that look, Amelia! If I offended Mr. Munga, so be it. I meant every word I said! Do you realize how foolish this makes you look? Your willingness to lend credibility to far-fetched claims from the likes of . . . him?" She nodded derisively at Zebulon Munga, who was busy saying his good-byes to the crisply-uniformed pilot of the chartered jet that had carried her and Devine from New York to Wisconsin.

"Sarah, his story is plausible." Devine stubbornly attempted an explanation while purposely withholding information. "Living in the middle of nowhere, he gets his news from the Internet. That's where he came across a picture of Christopher Koenigs and immediately recognized the face. Munga worked an outdoors show in northern Maine last weekend and Koenigs showed up at his booth, asking for a job. He swears the man in the photo and the man he hired are one and the same. He did some research on Koenigs, read some articles he found on-line. That's where he got my name. Why would he contact me? Why would he go to all this trouble if he wasn't convinced that it was Christopher Koenigs?"

The turbo prop's blades rotated into a silver blur as the plane's engines sputtered to life. The tail of the aircraft rolled across the runway in a one-hundred and eighty degree arc until it faced directly down the center of the aging concrete strip. Eyes masked behind dark teardrop lenses set in gold frames, Zeb Munga routinely flipped a handful of switches and scribbled a short notation across a sheath of wrinkled paper crimped in a clipboard. He looked through the small, smudged side window of the cockpit and throttled the engines into a high-pitched whine, signaling his imminent departure.

"What are you waiting for, Dr. Devine, your flight of fancy awaits," Perkins condescended. "Christopher Koenigs is here in Broadaxe, Amelia, we both know that, that's why we came here. Run away to Canada on a wild goose chase, keep deluding yourself. I'll stay here and see if I can't help bring some resolution to the mess you've made."

Devine slowly backed away. "Henry?" She sought out Sauter with pleading eyes, unprepared for the obvious implications of his grim-faced silence. She suddenly felt stupid for assuming unquestioning acquiescence on his part, for expecting anyone to accept the veracity of Zeb Munga's unlikely tale as readily as she had.

"Amelia, I . . . don't know what to say," Sauter stammered, painfully aware that he was about to abandon the only ally he had left. "It's just that I can't . . . ."

"You can and will!" Kunick interceded, his voice booming authoritatively. Looking quite pleased with himself, he inched closer to Perkins and tucked his thumbs behind the thick brown leather of his belt. His wrinkled khaki trousers were bunched at the top of his ankle-high slip-on boots and perspiration stained the underarms of his short-sleeved shirt. The blood on his bandaged head had dried and darkened to deep crimson.

"Can and will what?" Sauter inquired testily, well aware of what Kunick was suggesting.

"You can accompany Dr. Devine to Canada and you

will!" Kunick barked the command, pompously raising a finger to punctuate his point.

"Is that some kind of order, Bobby,? Or a threat? For one thing, I don't need to . . ."

"You need to goddam do as I say, detective, and I say you're going to Canada with Dr. Devine to follow up on this important lead!" Kunick smirked and preened unapologetically in an obvious attempt to impress Perkins with his inflated self-importance. "It's not just *some* kind of order, it's a direct order! Lest you forget, detective, this is my jurisdiction and this is my investigation. You've been a participant out of my good graces. You want to continue working this case, you get on that plane and let me know what you find when you get to Canada. Or don't go, it's your choice, but either way I want you the hell out of Broadaxe for the time being. Is that clear?"

"Crystal clear, Bobby, you'd better believe it," Sauter seethed. "Be sure to give my best to your pal Dickey when you call him to give him the good news."

Kunick bit his bottom lip and lowered his gaze. "You'd better run along now Sauter." He looked to Devine as she backpedaled slowly toward the plane. "Don't bother considering your options. You've only got one."

It galled Sauter, Kunick's heavy-handed bravado, yet there was no time to argue, nothing to argue about. Like it or not, he was being banished from Broadaxe once again. There was only one option, Kunick was right on that count; albeit a suddenly attractive option that carried with it a modicum of guilt, a nagging discomfort generated by the feelings of excitement and anticipation evoked by Amelia Devine. Two children were dead! He chastised himself; Colins was dead! The killer was here in Broadaxe, not in Canada, but there was no denying the impulse to simply fly away with the unwitting centerpiece of his middle-aged daydreams.

"I'm turning around and coming right back after I find out what this is all about," he warned Kunick. "Good luck back here in Broadaxe while I'm gone, Bobby. I'm afraid you're going to need it."

"Don't you worry about me . . . excuse me, about *us*," Kunick nodded deferentially to Perkins, who looked down her nose disdainfully, jaw set and face grim. "We'll be just fine. Nobody knows more about the way Christopher Koenigs's mind works than Dr. Perkins. Isn't that right, Sarah? You don't mind if I call you Sarah?"

Perkins ignored Kunick's cloying attempt to inject familiarity into their relationship. "Dr. Devine's knowledge of Koenigs is as intimate as my own, maybe more so. Isn't that right Amelia?" She raised her voice to be heard over the plane's engines. "It would be hard to face him again, Christopher Koenigs, under these conditions, wouldn't it? Go to Canada, avoid the unavoidable for now if that's what you need to do. Just remember that you can't hide from your mistakes forever. There will be repercussions!"

Devine absorbed Perkins's goading with quiet confidence. The threatening, accusatory words collided with her calm exterior and fell harmlessly away, vaporized by her sudden indifference. When she turned to Sauter, her eyes were cold and dispassionate, focused with the certainty of conviction. He interpreted the message she was sending, that she somehow *knew* Christopher Koenigs would be waiting at the other end of the flight, that she was prepared to go it alone.

Sauter shrugged his shoulders and manufactured an apologetic smile. "Looks like I'll be making the trip to Canada after all," he offered timidly. Devine nodded her less than enthusiastic assent and quickly climbed into the open hatch in the plane's dimpled metal fuselage. Sauter jogged across the damp pavement of the runway and jumped in the door just before Munga impatiently pulled it shut. Devine was already buckled into the blue vinyl shotgun seat on the right hand side of the cockpit. Head cocked, she gathered a handful of thick black hair into a ponytail and gazed out the windshield.

Sauter settled into the seat directly behind Devine and fumbled in the hip pocket of his crumpled tweed suit coat. He fished out Margaret Schumacher's phone number and once again flicked it with the nail of his index finger, reminding himself to make the call immediately upon his return. He wondered what she knew, wondered if he wasn't about to fly away from the answers to questions that had plagued him ever since that long ago night when he lowered Michael Koenigs from the noose.

"This feller that I'm taking you folks to see, this feller I've got working for me up at the outpost," Munga placed a reassuring hand on Sauter's shoulder, sensing his doubt, "it's him, it's Christopher Koenigs, you can bet your bottom dollar on that."

In one motion, Munga slid into the pilot's seat and eased the throttle forward. The plane lurched ahead and gradually gained speed, rising unsteadily from the runway and banking sharply to the left as it cleared the tiered green crowns of the pine forest dropping away below. Sauter peered back down at the airport, searching for Kunick and Perkins, questioning whether they could catch the killer before someone else turned up dead. He shoved Margaret Schumacher's phone number back into his coat pocket and leaned forward into the cockpit until his head was perched between Devine and Munga.

"So what's our ETA anyway? How long of a flight are we looking at here?" Sauter inquired, not just making small talk, but already trying to lay out a timetable for his return to Broadaxe.

"Three and a half, four hours, give or take." Munga flipped a pair of silver toggles above his head as he offered the estimation. He continued to fly the plane west, Sauter noticed, despite his earlier claim that the Canadian outpost was situated due north. Sauter recognized the wide, white crested waters of the Flambeau River and recalled many successful fishing trips at its deep, wide junction with the Turtle River farther back to the east. He knew the outlay of clear blue lakes passing below intimately by land and water, but from the air he found it surprisingly difficult to correctly identify a given body of water with any certainty.

"So tell me, Zeb . . . you don't mind if I call you Zeb, do you?" Sauter continued after Munga nodded his approval. "Forgive me if I seem overly skeptical," he spoke indirectly now to Devine, as well, "but I've recently arrived at the conclusion that Christopher Koenigs returned to Broadaxe after he disappeared out east, that he's the only one with any plausible motive for the killings that have taken place. The motive and the method, the victims, the timing, everything fits. Now you come along and tell me that's not possible, that Christopher Koenigs works for you, that you're his boss. You've obviously convinced Dr. Devine that it's Koenigs, maybe you can convince me, too."

Munga leaned back and stretched out his legs as far as he could in the cramped cockpit, nonchalantly guiding the vibrating controls with a single finger. He retrieved a dented green thermos from beneath his seat, wedged it between his legs and unscrewed the silver cap. He filled the lid with tepid coffee and offered the thermos to Devine.

"It's running on the cool side now, but the caffeine's still up to strength, I'm sure. You folks are welcome to your share, but I'm afraid you'll have to sip right from the jug." He raised the silver cap in an informal toast and slurped the cold coffee through pursed lips. Devine and Sauter both declined his generosity.

"I started flying planes as a kid, in the air force. Flew a bunch of combat missions at different locations around the globe when there wasn't supposed to actually be any combat occurring, if you know what I mean. Top secret sort of stuff," Munga confided, apparently taking the long route in response to Sauter's request.

"Is that where you picked up the tattoo? The letters on your knuckles? In the service?" Sauter asked with genuine curiosity. "Are those initials? A nickname? Stand for anything in particular?"

Munga splayed his fingers and displayed the tattoo, chuckling, "In the service, yep, a nickname, given to me after a certain something happened to me at a certain someplace during a particular leave, the details of which I'd rather not discuss in mixed company," he grinned at Devine to hide his embarrassment, "b u n a," he recited the individual letters, "pronounced like hot dog bun, only with an a, buna. Many a man only knows me by that name, buna, or buna munga. My given name, Zebulon, well, that come down through the generations as a result of my great granddaddy's association with Lt. Zebulon Montgomery Pike's 1806 expedition down the Arkansas River drainage. Tried to summit the mountain that now bears his name, Pikes Peak in Colorado, but were undone by a snowstorm and inadequate preparation. Made the trek to the peak myself, by foot mind you, even though there's been a drivable road to the top since the turn of the century."

The plane finally banked to the north and Sauter watched the lake dotted forests of north-central Wisconsin give way to the agricultural fields perched above Lake Superior's Chequamegon Bay. Sunshine reflected in tiny pin pricks of silver off the blue expanse as Munga steered the plane out over the deep waters of the largest of the Great Lakes. Sauter listened respectfully to the tales – top secret missions, Pikes Peak – and began to worry that he may have been hijacked to Canada by a crackpot with an overactive imagination.

"That's all very interesting, buna," an army man himself, Sauter felt obligated to use Munga's military nickname, "but if you could get back to Koenigs, how you met him, why you're so certain he's the man working for you. Dr. Devine mentioned you first crossed paths with the man you think is Koenigs at a sport show last weekend, somewhere out east?"

"Maine, Presque Isle Maine, that's where we met," Munga turned and looked at Sauter over his right shoulder, "and for the last time, believe you me, it is Koenigs! I'd wager my plane on it, and I make my living with this plane." He wandered off subject once again. "Bought this aircraft with two other fellers who ran outposts up near my place, split the purchase price, maintenance costs, the whole shebang, made it affordable. Since then, both those fellers ran afoul of the law and I ended up with the plane. Now it's mine outright. Use it to fly my clients in and out of the lodge, to go to sport shows. Without it, my business dries up and goes away. When I realized it was Koenigs I had hired, a man on the run from the law, I called Dr. Amelia here right off the bat. I wanted it on the record that I cooperated, that I didn't try and hide nothin'. Like I just said, I can't afford to lose my pilot's license and that's the first thing taken when trouble comes calling."

"How, if you don't mind my asking again," Sauter tried to conceal his mounting impatience, "how did you come to the conclusion that it was Koenigs?"

Munga narrowed his eyes and scanned the changing horizon as he eclipsed the North Shore of Lake Superior and left Chequamegon Bay behind. He fingered each of the three switches aligned horizontally above the steering column and didn't flip any on the first pass. Returning quickly to the center switch of the trio, he reluctantly triggered the toggle button without any noticeable effect.

"Well, I like to work a booth at the smaller shows, shows like the one in Presque Isle. Folks who book a trip tend to be the type of folks I'd be glad to have back year in and year out." He spoke slowly, stubbornly intent upon taking the long route to the short answer Sauter was seeking. "People who appreciate the splendid isolation, respect the fish and game they come up here after, people who are thankful for the experience, that's what I'm talking about. Don't go to the big shows anymore – Chicago, Atlanta, and the like – got burned one too many times. Excuse my salty tongue, Dr. Amelia, but the odds go up greatly that a booking from one of those shows turns out to be too big of a pain in the ass for the pay. The type of person I like to call an asshole. No patience, no respect, no appreciation, just a big wad of green in their wallet. Well, I say, keep it!"

Turning first to Devine beside him then to Sauter behind, Munga bobbed his head righteously for emphasis. Unexpectedly, the plane hit an air pocket and plunged several feet. Sauter steadied himself by grabbing the two head rests above the front seats, clumsily entangling his fingers in Devine's black tresses in the process. Munga started to snicker when he noticed the predicament, stopping abruptly when it became apparent he was alone in his mirth. Devine reached around and matted her hair against her scalp as Sauter worked his way free of the snare.

"Go on Zeb," she urged softly, her voice barely audible above the purring engine, "you were about to tell us about your first meeting with Christopher Koenigs." She quickly redid her ponytail to straighten Sauter's mess.

"Yep, I was working my way around to that," he exhaled, sour-faced, "but I've got one more thing to say about the difference between the folks from the small town shows and the big town shows, to finish making my point." He looked over his right shoulder. "You a fisherman, Sauter?"

"Sure, muskie mostly, you bet." Sauter played along; he could always talk fishing.

"Perfect! This just happens to be a story about a muskie, as a matter of fact!" Munga was grinning again, scanning the skies. "Not just any muskie, mind you, but a bona fide record breaker, pictures to prove it. Never weighed it though, never measured it, just snapped a photo and let 'er go! She was a six-footer, easily, pushing 80-plus pounds. The Presque Isle types, those folks get it, they understand why I put that fish back in the lake. The clients from the big city shows, they think I'm the dumbest son of a bitch that ever pitched a lure for not killing it. I culled those types out of my client list a long time ago."

The left wing dipped and the plane nosed slightly to the northwest. Sauter looked out the window at the scraggy pines clinging to the thin soil atop the gray rock outcroppings of the Canadian landscape. He pictured the plane carrying him further and further away from Broadaxe and couldn't fight the ominous sense of utter futility. *This guy is a world class bullshitter!* He thought despondently, furtively eyeing the tale spinning pilot. *Top secret combat missions! Great granddaddy the intrepid explorer! Namesake of Lt. Zebulon Pike! Climbed the peak himself!* Sauter found the cumulative body of stories suspicious, but the claim of a world record muskie brought Munga's credibility seriously into question. *Bullshit!*

"Bullshit!" he blurted impulsively, warmed by his flaring temper. "Christopher Koenigs is waiting for us up here in Canada my ass! Give me some proof that you're not yanking my chain or turn this goddam plane around! Now!"

"Henry! Don't make a fool of yourself, of both of us!" Devine spun in her seat and scolded Sauter, cheeks already flushed with embarrassment. "Do you really think I'd be making this trip without good reason? . . . that I would have asked you to come if . . ." she shook her head in frustration and turned away.

Sauter placed his hand on Devine's shoulder and squeezed gently. "I still don't believe Christopher Koenigs killed his brother Michael, Amelia, you understand that, don't you?" He attempted to explain his blatant skepticism. "As for the recent hangings in Broadaxe? Well, truthfully, it only makes sense; it has to be Koenigs. The two dead boys, their fathers were in the treehouse with Christopher when Michael was hung. I didn't want to admit it either, Amelia, but Christopher Koenigs is back in Broadaxe, seeking revenge for his brother's death."

"Now, that's a load of bullshit!" Munga hooted and slapped his knee. "This is the ace detective you were telling me about, Amelia? The cop you were so anxious to bring along?" Devine's pink cheeks flamed to a darker red. Sauter bit back a self-conscious smile. "Well, detective, I hate to be the one to shoot your well-reasoned theory down, but someone other than Christopher Koenigs is killing the little boys of Broadaxe. Let me finish my story, then decide if you still think I'm full of crap."

A small red light began to flash on the instrument panel, then fell dark once again when Munga rapped the corresponding gauge with a tattooed knuckle.

"Nothing to worry about, minor electrical problem," he reassured, then continued, "As I was about to say, it was the final day of a three-day show up in Maine, good show, booked a number of clients, talked with a lot of old friends. I just started breaking down my booth when he showed up. Stood there at first, thumbing through my brochures, thought he was just a window shopper out to kill a Sunday afternoon. Looked like the typical sad-sack husband dreaming about a trip the wife would never let him take. The guy never moved on though, just kept hanging around. Then out of the blue, bang, he works up the nerve and asks me if I'll give him a job."

"So you hired him, a complete stranger, right on the spot," Sauter interjected dubiously.

"You just can't let a man finish, can you?" Munga looked at Devine and rolled his eyes at Sauter's expense. "As fate would have it, I was in the market for a warm body. My best worker up and quit at the end of the summer season. Saved up enough of his earnings and headed back south of the border, went back to school, hopes to be an engineer someday. Kid could fix anything, build anything. Anyway, this guy standing at my booth says he'll work for room and board on a trial basis, that we could talk about compensation after he completed a probationary period the length of my choosing. How could I go wrong?"

"Any number of ways, as I see it," Sauter opined.

"I asked him what his story was and he answered all my questions. I'll admit it, the guy was a little sketchy about his background, but that didn't surprise me much. A guy shows up at my booth asking for a job in the middle of nowhere, it's no secret that he's probably dodging something. In his case it was a mid-life crisis; that's the way he explained it, anyway."

"A mid-life crisis?" Sauter scratched his head when he asked the question.

"That's right, a mid-life crisis, said his wife left him so he up and quit his job, said he desperately needed a change."

"A change from what? What was his job? Did he say?" Sauter prodded, hastily adding, "What about a name, did he give you a name? Did he . . ."

"Hold on, don't get ahead of yourself," Munga raised his hand, "this is the clincher right here. He said he worked his entire adult life as a psychiatrist for the state of New York, said he was suffering from a serious case of burn out." Sauter's lips parted momentarily as he processed what he just heard. "The feller reached out and shook my hand, looked me straight in the eye, told me his name was Amelia Perkins." As Munga finished Sauter's jaw dropped completely open and his hand fell heavily from Devine's shoulder. She turned as it slid away.

"It's him, Henry, so you'd better brace yourself." Her voice was deep, oddly detached. "It's been a long time since you've seen him."

"Wait a minute, wait a minute," Sauter wedged further ahead until he dropped to a knee on the cockpit floor between Devine and Munga. "Amelia? A stranger, a strange *man*, solicits a job and drops the name Amelia on you? You said yourself you figured he was dodging something and then he gives you a woman's name? And you hire the guy?" He laughed, sounding derisive when that wasn't his intention.

Munga had been dropping altitude almost imperceptibly until the plane leveled off just above the stunted pine forest. The proximity of the trees enhanced the perception of speed and transformed the flight into an unwelcome thrill ride. Devine squeezed the blue vinyl armrests between white knuckles and her posture stiffened. Sauter clenched initially, then focused on Munga, combat pilot on a secret mission, and the tension drained. Munga ignored the uncomfortably close scenery himself and returned Sauter's stare.

"First off, weren't you paying attention when I introduced myself?" His grin was spreading, exposing more of the saturated brown cud clinging to his bottom lip, "Zebulon Munga! Detective, from a young age on I never put much stock in a person's name. You've heard of a boy named Sue? How do you do!" The aircraft remained level as it raced above the treetops, even though Munga's chuckling had put his body to shaking. He continued to steer blindly, much to Sauter's growing discomfort.

"Thing is, you're wrong again, detective, the feller didn't give me a woman's name at all. Introduced himself as Emile at first, no last name, just Emile. Wasn't 'til I started thinking about hiring him, that he told me his last name was Perkins. Emile, not Amelia. Emile Perkins."

Still clinging to her seat in paralyzed terror, Devine began giggling through clenched teeth, an eerie giggle that slowly ascended into maniacal laughter. The plane breached an opening in the forest and nosed downward precipitously, provoking an amusement park scream that mercifully ended Devine's unnerving revelry. Munga pulled back on the controls and the aircraft returned to horizontal above the calm blue waters of a sprawling freshwater jewel.

Sauter was surprised by the number of modest log cabins dotting the shoreline of Munga's Outpost, a rustic sportsman's retreat hewn from the Canadian wilderness. He sat perched upon the back of a golf cart, facing to the rear, wishing the bumpy ride from the airstrip to the main lodge over. There was still a chance that it wasn't Koenigs, he told himself, that the name was a freakish coincidence, that the stranger from the sports show truly was a retired psychiatrist from New York. Better that Koenigs was really back in Broadaxe, a killer with a name, a face and a reason to be there. If not, Sauter despaired, he was trapped miles away from a ruthless murderer operating in complete anonymity, and he was helpless to do anything about it.

The thin tires of the golf cart skidded to a stop on a bed of decaying pine needles. Munga jumped off the machine while it was still rolling and ran around to assist Devine to her feet, an act Sauter jealously construed as savage chivalry.

"You two make yourself at home here in the lodge while I track down Emile," Munga paused, "you know who I mean. Door's open, go on in," he insisted as he jumped back in the cart. "I've got a pretty good idea where I'll find him."

The lodge was musty and gloomy inside. The four walls, stout vertical logs stained nearly black, swallowed up the paltry light peeking through windows rendered opaque by accumulated years of grime. The cleanest window filled an entire wall and offered a beautiful view of the lake, flat and rinsed colorless by the midday sun. The décor was predictable – animal and fish mounts, a bar with a handful of stools and a brass foot rail, a billiards table with well-worn felt, a juke box stocked with forty-fives, and a wall of framed, black and white photos. Sauter scanned the pictures.

"Holy shit!" he gasped, propping himself on the end of the pool table.

"What is it?" Devine stepped in front of him and peered at the wall. Arms crossed, she wheeled to face Sauter and smiled knowingly. "Yes, Henry, no bullshit, Christopher Koenigs is here, not in Broadaxe."

Sauter moved closer to the photographs. The first was very old, a group of parka clad men surrounded by expedition gear with a snow-capped peak as the backdrop. Two of the faces were circled and labeled with red ink, great granddaddy Munga off to one side and Lt. Zebulon Pike, front and center. Directly below, Zebulon Munga smiled broadly standing atop the peak after succeeding where his great grandfather and the original Zebulon Pike had failed. There were several gold-framed photos of Munga standing astride the wing of an air force jet, the surrounding landscape dark and exotic. The pictures were blurred, the plane's numbers and identifying marks illegible.

"Holy shit!" he repeated, unhooking the final photo

from its nail to get a closer look. "This fish is . . . it's huge!" Munga knelt in the stern of a snow-dusted boat sporting his customary grin, only much larger. The sky was low and gray behind him, a dismal hue that reflected off the choppy surface of the water. The striped midsection of the muskie rested on his bent knee, while he held the broad tail with one hand and the massive head with the other. It was, without question, the largest muskie Sauter had ever seen. "I'll be a son of a bitch," he murmured, "I'm looking at a world record fish!"

"Damn right you are!" Munga kicked open a rickety screen door and entered from the lake side of the lodge. "You were saying bullshit to my fish story as much as my claim that Koenigs is my newest employee. I figured as much." He snatched the photo from Sauter and hung it back on the nail, eyebrows raised. "Why, I suppose you didn't believe a word I said."

Sauter nodded at the photo montage. "Seeing is most definitely believing for me, I'll admit that." He stole another wistful peek at the enormous fish. "What about your right-hand man, Emile? Did you find him?"

"I hired him last Sunday, week ago today as a matter of fact, and this afternoon is the first time that little bugger has taken off. I had to make him do it, told him he didn't have a choice. Hardest working feller I've come across. It's a shame. When he should be relaxing, the poor man has to deal with you, instead." Munga clarified himself sheepishly, "I wasn't speaking of yourself, Dr. Amelia. I hope I didn't offend."

"Did you locate him?" Devine suspected Koenigs wouldn't be overjoyed to see her, either. She didn't care if she was encroaching on his day off. "Enough beating around the bush! Can we see him, please?"

"Follow me." Munga shuffled sullenly back out the screen door, Devine and Sauter on his heels. "Maybe it was a mistake bringing you folks here," he mumbled. "This man don't strike me as the murdering kind, and I've had the misfortune of meeting a few of those in my day. That tragedy with his little brother, the hanging, I read all about it, fished up some old articles off the 'Net, the Internet. A lifetime ago, that's what I say. If this feller's a so-called 'genetic sociopath', I'm

Ethel Merman!"

The terrain sloped gently from the lodge to the lakeshore, a mix of sand and scrubby vegetation atop shallow bedrock. From above, Sauter could see the rock descend into the water from the shore of the lake, wide gray steps leading into a bottomless well. He pictured a fish the size of Munga's lurking in the shadowy depths, hunting for a meal, and wondered if he'd be welcomed back as a client or culled like the big city folks. Munga stopped half-way down the slope and pointed to his left.

"There he is," he said, almost regretfully, and trudged back up the hill.

There were four long, wooden docks reaching into the lake. A lone figure sat in a folding chair at the end of the furthest, his back to the shore and an open sketch book in his lap. Koenigs didn't look up to see whose hollow footsteps were thudding down the pier as Devine and Sauter approached, yet he greeted their arrival with prescience.

"Hello, Doctor Devine." Head down, he dipped a thin brush in purple paint and dabbed it on the crisp white paper of the book. "Hello, Detective Sauter."

"Did your boss tell you we were coming?" Sauter inquired, curious if Munga tipped Koenigs off, gave him a chance to flee. He wondered why he didn't take it. It was Christopher Koenigs, in the flesh. He couldn't help but stare.

"No, not Mr. Munga, he didn't mention it," he answered quietly.

A small island lay just off shore, a square boulder poking from one end like a snout and a tree leaning nearly horizontal over the water at the other, bringing to mind a tail. A loon bobbed between the island and the dock, its red eye alert and probing. The diving bird's black and white feathers glistened with droplets of lake water. Sauter leaned over Koenigs's shoulder to assess how closely the painting resembled the idyllic scene. Unprepared for the subjectivity of the artist, he rocked back and nearly stepped off the pier.

Lupines. A field of purple, cone-shaped lupines.

The loon called, startling Sauter with its haunting tremolo. He searched for the bird. It dove, leaving rings in its wake on the lake's glassy surface. Shaken by the painting, the beautifully rendered lupines, flowers that could have been plucked from the meadow beneath the treehouse, Sauter stared blankly at the water, waiting for the loon to reemerge. He never saw the bird again. *The treehouse, the dead children, Seth Colins.* A sickness surged through Sauter, a queasiness that weakened his legs and caused the dock to rock like a small boat in the waves. Christopher Koenigs was here, within reach, no longer the wailing child who had just lost his little brother, no longer the child who had wailed within his mind ever since. Sauter suddenly felt the eyes upon him. Koenigs was standing now, shoulder to shoulder with Devine, who had taken possession of the sketch book.

"It's only a painting detective. I'm sorry that it upset you so," Koenigs apologized in a calm, soothing voice.

Speechless, Sauter looked closely at Christopher Koenigs for any trace of the boy that may have been left behind in the man, but found none. The gray hair at his temples would soon be gone if the thinning strands atop his head were any indication. He was small, not so much in size, Sauter decided, but in stature, as if he'd earned his stoop-shouldered demeanor through constant beat downs. His skin didn't look right, pallid and too loose on his bones. Pale, lifeless pupils attached themselves to Sauter in a vacant stare.

"Yes, Christopher, and a very nice painting at that," Devine interceded, flashing Sauter a look that said *What the hell's the matter with you?* "Do you mind if we sit down? We traveled a long way to see you, Christopher, and we'd like to have a talk." As she spoke, she sat down on a bench attached to the dock and propped the painting up against the rusted white hand rails of the swim ladder hanging from the end. "Christopher had a painting just like this hanging on the wall of his cell back in New York, isn't that right? You did many paintings just like this, didn't you Christopher."

The metal legs of the folding chair scraped across the wood dock as Koenigs backed away and dragged it with him. Sauter stepped around him and took a seat next to Devine on the bench, deliberately averting his eyes from the unsettling picture. Koenigs swung the chair behind his legs and slowly lowered himself onto the interwoven nylon straps, watchful and wary.

"Excuse me if I misunderstood, but I assumed you wanted to talk with *me*, not with each other," Koenigs quietly interrupted Sauter's whisper into Devine's ear, "or am I allowed to keep secrets, too?"

Sauter forced himself to look at the field of lifelike lupines bursting from the page. "No secrets. I was just telling the doctor that there was something she needed to know about this painting, about the flowers in the painting, to be more precise." He faced Koenigs. "I've seen these flowers several times before, a meadow of purple lupines exactly like the ones you painted here. The painting reminds me of things I'd rather forget, but we know that's not possible, don't we Christopher?"

"It's easy to forget something you never had a recollection of in the first place, detective," Koenigs gazed at the painting himself now, "that is, unless something, or *someone*, constantly recreates the memory for you."

"Did you remember me?" Sauter asked, lucid again, "from the meadow that night many years ago, the night your brother was killed? I was the cop who put my parka over your shoulders, the one who took Michael down from the treehouse. I wouldn't have recognized you, Christopher, not from my memories of that night. How did you recognize me?"

Koenigs crossed his legs and placed both hands, one over the other, atop the upper knee. The stiff material of his new mechanic's coveralls, dark green and creased at the folds, swallowed whole his sparse frame. It reminded Devine of the inmate's uniform, the oversized orange jumpsuit she was accustomed to seeing him in. The white tennis shoes were the same that he wore when she saw him last, the day he stepped from cell C-28, Block 3 on the seventh floor of New York state's Municipal Mental Health Center for the final time. It was surreal, sitting here with him now, at the end of a dock on a lake in northern Ontario.

He spoke softly, "I recall a young police officer brought to his knees by what he encountered that night, overwrought by the senselessness of Michael's death, by my hysterical reaction, no doubt. What I'm about to tell you will explain everything, detective, if you'll just be patient, if you're willing to listen, to *really* listen. You've heard this before, Dr. Devine; this is old news to you, most of it, anyway. It sealed my fate as a certified lunatic, but that's of no concern to me now. I'm never going back there, never," his eyes locked on Devine, "I pose a threat to no one, I'm not a murderer. I didn't kill my brother and I certainly didn't kill those two boys in Broadaxe, nor the police officer last night. Your trip here confirms that."

"Officer Seth Colins. He was hung last night, from the treehouse," Sauter answered Devine's questioning look. He didn't intend the oversight; but the stakeout, the previous night, seemed so distant and removed, a scene from an alternate reality. Like Devine, there was no way Koenigs could know about Colins's death, yet he did, somehow, causing Sauter great discomfort.

"You look alarmed, detective. Get used to it," Koenigs warned before he continued. "These are my memories of that night. It's blank as far as what happened in the treehouse, permanently erased by the shock of it, I suppose. I vaguely remember the coat being wrapped around me, the dawning realization that I was bawling like a baby. You covered Michael with a blue blanket after you took the rope off his neck and laid him on the ground. There were just the three of us beneath the treehouse at that moment. As I said, you were on the ground as well, your head was down. It was nightmarish, unimaginable, and it was more than you could bear."

Koenigs paused and watched Sauter until he meekly nodded his assent to the less than flattering account. The crumpled coveralls bunched at his knees and ankles when he rose and stepped to the end of the dock, hands behind his turned back. Devine placed her hand on Sauter's forearm. They looked into each other's eyes for the first time and found comfort in the reflection of their own apprehension. When Koenigs continued, speaking toward the lake, she reflexively squeezed, then quickly withdrew her hand.

"It was then, as you clawed at the soil, that I saw Michael staring at me. He was an awful shade of blue, his neck was torn from the noose, but his eyes were wide open, seemingly alive, calling me to come get him. I was silenced by Michael's imploring eyes, and was drawn toward them at the same time. When I picked his body up it was limp and cold at first. Then there was something, something *alive* in my little brother's corpse. Those were screams of sheer terror you heard, detective, screams I couldn't control as I carried Michael from the meadow, into the darkness of the forest."

The sun was descending in the late afternoon sky, chilling the autumn air and casting a golden pathway across the surface of the water. Sauter stared into the reflection until the image remained when he closed his eyes. The child's terrified screams filled his head, and he pictured Michael's wilted body bouncing wildly in his brother's arms, almost . . . animated. He opened his eyes and once again found Koenigs watching him.

"When you return to Broadaxe, detective, do me a favor. Ask Chief Kunick where my brother is buried, ask him to show you Michael's remains." Koenigs returned to his seat and crossed his legs.

Sauter picked up the painting and shook his head. Insert the bur oak and the treehouse into the scene and it would be indistinguishable from the meadow back in Broadaxe. He wondered what the hell was going on, if he correctly understood what Koenigs was trying to tell him.

"What are you trying to say, Christopher?" Sauter prodded with growing impatience. "You were going to explain everything, isn't that right? Well, I've been listening, just like you asked, and I'm still listening, so cut to the chase."

"There is no body, detective. Michael was never seen again after I took him from the meadow, not by anyone other than myself, not until recently."

"Oh, I see . . ." Sauter raised his eyebrows and nodded at Devine, concluding that Koenigs was indeed insane, after all.

"No, you don't see, detective, and you weren't truly listening." Koenigs remained unruffled, his tone calm and confident. "Dr. Devine didn't listen; neither did Dr. Perkins. None of the doctors listened. They all looked at me like I was crazy, the same way you're looking at me now. The brother I knew died that night, detective, but the soul-deprived shell of Michael Koenigs survived."

"Okay, Christopher, I believe you. I don't think you're

crazy." Sauter claimed unconvincingly. He allowed himself to hope that Koenigs might actually have credible answers to his questions, answers that would help catch a killer. Instead, he was confronted with a man still haunted by his brother's ghost.

"I appreciate the condescension, detective, but humor me, if you will. Michael was disappointed in you. You didn't want to play with him. You ignored him, and two children died as a result."

"What are you talking about?" Sauter protested.

"Don't pretend you didn't hear him when he spoke to you. Michael told me about the game he tried to play with you, the game you refused to play. He told you to *go to the meadow, to save the child,* but you didn't listen, did you? That doesn't surprise me. How could you know?"

The damp chill crawled across Sauter's prickling skin as he replayed the relentless voice that had crept inside his skull, the voice urging exactly what Koenigs claimed. *Go to the meadow. Save the child.* It was true, he hadn't listened.

"You see, Michael is an imp, detective," Koenigs elucidated, "a demon trapped inside a little boy's body."

"Have you seen him?" Sauter asked, helplessly swept away by the fascinating claim.

"Yes, Christopher has seen his brother Michael many times since his death," Devine interceded with a clinical explanation, "but we explained to him repeatedly that it was only a figment of his imagination. Granted, a frighteningly realistic, distorted figment of his imagination, a schism in his mind created by the trauma induced when he witnessed his brother's death. That's the blank spot in his memory of that night. That's one way it manifests itself. Another is hallucinations, or delusions."

"What does he look like now, your brother?" Sauter persisted, much to Devine's chagrin.

"Michael would have revealed himself to you eventually if you had listened, if you had played his game. When you didn't he grew bored and moved on, as any child would." Koenigs took advantage of the cathartic opportunity to share his curse. "It's the corpse of a dead child, to put it succinctly, a vision I struggle to put out of my mind. Occasionally, when he visits, I do see the Michael I remember. There is a rasping from the torn neck, where the noose ripped the flesh, and when it catches, as it sometimes does, when the rasping stops, the dead skin flashes pink, the black eyes twinkle blue, and thick brown hair sprouts anew. Inevitably, the rasping returns and Michael withers."

Devine stood, a hand on one hip and the other extended, palm up. "Christopher, this is not real! Michael is dead! It's all in your head. We established that long ago, when you first came to the institute. You know you have to accept that if you expect to have any chance at functioning like a normal human being."

Koenigs rose and faced Devine, tenderly enclosing her hand between both of his. He smiled, faintly, betraying the first sign that he hadn't been completely stripped of emotion by his bleak existence.

"There's nothing normal about me and there never will be." The smile evaporated. "Michael Koenigs will always be my brother. That's my reality. I know I didn't kill him. He filled in that blank spot in my memory long ago. He told me what happened that night in the treehouse. The figment of my imagination? Well, it killed those two boys in Broadaxe, and that poor police officer, although that wasn't part of the game. It's a game called revenge, and Michael's not finished playing."

CHAPTER EIGHTEEN

Dyed pink, the sun floated in a sea of red mist, still a good fist's width above the pine tops reaching skyward from the far shoreline.

"Wild fire west of here, over 'round the provincial parks near the Manitoba border." Munga clutched a metal stringer of bronze-sided walleye, some still alive and jingling the chain link tether in writhing protest. "Good for the forest and good for us. We've been enjoying some mighty pretty sunsets 'round these parts as of late." A fillet knife was tucked in his armpit, its slender silver blade, razor sharp, carelessly unsheathed. In the same arm, he cradled the busted flywheel from an outboard motor, coating the crook of his elbow with black grease.

"Well, I fetched you all the way up here with the best intentions, Dr. Amelia; but you should know, I've been doin' some thinking," Munga kicked his toe into the pine duff, spit tobacco. "If Emile don't want to go back with you, count me out. You'll have to make other travel arrangements."

"Christopher, Christopher Koenigs," Devine corrected Munga, but her eyes were on Sauter, beseeching his advice. She was high and dry on the shoreline end of the dock, restlessly tapping her foot on the weathered wood. Below her, sinking into the lip of moist sand rimming the lake, Sauter tucked his hands into his coat pockets and exhaled slowly, shrugging his shoulders in response. Small waves rolled into the shore, saturating the sand and sucking Sauter's brown leather shoes beneath the mire.

"Not only is the man certifiable, he's corny to boot,' he scoffed. *"It's a game called revenge, and Michael's not finished playing!* His brother, the killer! Are you kidding me?" Sauter pointed to Koenigs, crouched in the folding chair at the far end of the dock, obsessively painting purple lupines. His hunched silhouette turned black in the blushing face of the setting sun. "The man was judged sane and released. Wow!"

Clad in knee-high, rubber muck boots, Munga splashed ankle deep in the shallow water on the other side of the dock from Sauter, with Devine perched above and between them. The fish clipped to the stringer struggled with less frequency, dying weight that bulged the muscles in Munga's forearm.

"Hold on one second here," confused, his face contorted, "I thought his brother Michael was dead."

"He is!" Devine and Sauter barked, both equally emphatic in the simultaneous response.

"Then what the hell . . ." Munga mumbled, turning to Devine for an explanation, "Dr. Amelia?"

"The mind responds to a traumatic episode in different ways, dependent upon any number of different factors," she tried to keep it simple, to the point. "In Christopher's case, as a mechanism to cope with witnessing his brother's death, his child's mind created a realistic delusion that persists to this day. He still sees his little brother, even converses with him, even though Michael has been dead for twenty-two years."

"Maybe its necromancy," Munga suggested earnestly.

"Excuse me?" Out of the blue, the notion blindsided Devine.

"Divination through communication with the dead, necromancy," he elaborated, straight-faced. "Maybe he's not delusional, maybe he's a necromancer. Who's to say for sure? Can you say with certainty that he isn't being contacted by his brother, from beyond the grave? Some folks believe in that sort of thing, you know."

"Those folks didn't hold Michael Koenigs's dead body in their arms," Sauter stepped up and joined Devine on the dock, struggling to free his feet from the suction of the wet sand. "Dead and gone, that's the way I see it. No coming back, no catching up on old times with the kin folk. It's fantasy for people who have a problem coping with their own mortality. Although this has been exceedingly interesting, it's also been a waste of time. I'm no closer to catching the killer now, further away, if anything. I don't care what you decide to do with Koenigs, Amelia. Bring him along if you want, but I need to get back to Broadaxe."

Munga grinned and hoisted the stringer of walleye at arm's length. "You'd like it if I could just jump back on that plane at your beck and call, I'd imagine, but as you can see

I've got some chores that I need to tend to first off." He nodded at the greasy motor part. "Got some paperwork, correspondence I need to address after I fillet up these walleye and fix this flywheel. Business don't run itself, after all."

"You don't understand, Munga, there's a murderer . . ." Sauter didn't get a chance to finish.

"I'm not the one lacking understanding here," Munga spoke slowly, for emphasis. "We'll leave when I'm good and ready, when I get things put in order, no sooner. And another thing, you obviously weren't listening to me a moment ago. I'm not taking him anywhere," he glanced at Koenigs, "not on my plane. Either way, nutcase or necromancer, that little feller is harmless. And did I mention, he's the hardest working bugger I've ever had in my employ at the Outpost, bar none."

"Amelia?" Sauter turned to Devine for back-up, but she didn't seem as anxious to depart.

"Hold on one second," she put Sauter off and strolled out to the end of the dock. Koenigs didn't look up until she sat down on the bench across from him. The two talked briefly before the fiery backdrop of the red-rimmed horizon. Devine leaned forward and placed a hand on his knee. Koenigs shook his head, then nodded. A moment passed before he carefully closed the sketch book and reluctantly ceded it to Devine.

"I've got everything I need," she proclaimed upon her return, sketch book in hand. On Sauter's behalf, she tried to coax Munga into adjusting his timetable. "I understand that you're a busy man, Zeb, that you have some work to do, but the sooner the better, alright?"

"Morning, first light, that's the best I can do for you," he insisted, eyes set and lips pursed, the usual grin constricted into a grim slit.

"Morning!" Sauter howled, but Munga slammed the door on any further discussion.

"Take it or leave it." He spit the words out with his tobacco plug, dripping a sluice of brown juice down his chin. He wiped his face with the back of the hand holding the stringer of fish. With a mischievous twinkle in his eye, he swept the hand horizontally across his mouth, leaving the natural, stain-toothed smile in its wake.

"Got a cozy little cabin for you right down the shore, two bedrooms, mind you," he pointed to a tiny log structure with a screen porch, allowed the implication to linger a moment. "You're welcome to it. I'll come fetch you sun up. I'll get you back down south, don't you worry. In the meantime, you're welcome to enjoy all the amenities here at the Outpost." With that, he sloshed from the shallows and headed up the sloping shoreline, swinging the slowly dying walleyes at his side as he walked away.

Sauter trailed Munga for two or three steps and stopped. Defeated, he watched him go, then stared blankly at the vacant trail after he was gone. Devine cleared her throat, stirring Sauter from the doldrums of self-pity. She was walking down the shoreline when he turned, toward the little log cabin, the sketch book pressed against her swaying hips. Sauter waited for the glance over the shoulder, the check to see if he followed, only to find himself helplessly seduced as she sashayed through the lengthening shadows. Devine didn't look back, not for him, not for Christopher Koenigs. She had found what she was searching for here in Canada, Sauter supposed, vindication of her belief in Koenigs's innocence. He should have embraced it himself, had earned the right, yet there was no sense of satisfaction, no relief, not while children were still being murdered.

"Farewell, detective. I wish you a safe return to Broadaxe in the morning, too late once again I fear; but, sadly, your last chance to play my little brother's game."

Sauter pivoted, startled to find Koenigs standing behind him on the trail, a fish gasping for air, mercifully released from the stringer. He stared long and hard at Koenigs, hoping that the broken man before him could somehow erase the haunting memories of the terrified child and his mournful cry. Koenigs represented one piece of the puzzle, a broken, discarded piece that no longer fit neatly into the bigger picture.

"Michael is dead, Christopher." Sauter backed away, his heart pounding with deafening import in the stillness of the evening. He dropped his head and spun on the trail, hastening to the cabin, to Amelia Devine.

"I'll be sure to remind him of that the next time I see him," Koenigs spoke into Sauter's back, a sober whisper that chased him down the shoreline. He hesitated, listened for foot-falls behind him on the trail, the blood red lake to his left and the darkening forest to his right. The whisper faded into the gloaming quiet. Ahead, lights flickered yellow, illuminating the windows of the cabin. Sauter watched Devine's shadow mov-ing within the log walls, floating from one glowing pane to the next. He felt Koenigs pressing in from behind on the narrow path and he pivoted quickly to confront the ghost from his past one last time.

"What'd you mean by that? Too late once again?" Sauter posed the question into the empty evening air, an impul-sive curiosity that would remain unanswered.

Koenigs was gone, inhaled by the forest faster than his whispered words. Not far from shore, the loon cried, shattering the oppressive stillness that had descended, a familiar, mourn-ful wail that further chilled the icy liquid pulsing through Sauter's veins. It mimicked the sobbing child, the boy crouched beneath the treehouse, left to grieve for the slain brother who would live forever inside his tortured mind.

Sauter backpeddled down the trail cautiously, una-mused by the sudden onset of irrational disquietude. The sun fell below the treetops, leaving behind the graying remnants of an inconclusive day. The crying stopped – the loon on the lake, the child in Sauter's memory. He cocked his ear to the forest. Silence. His eyes twitched between the tree trunks and scanned outward toward the lake, eventually settling upon the unoccu-pied dock where Koenigs had sat sketching purple lupines only moments before. Sauter pictured Colins struggling at the end of the rope, hanging beneath the treehouse, dying above a mead-ow of purple lupines . . .

"Amelia!"

Sauter heard the panic in his voice as he hurtled himself down the shoreline path. He didn't react when he heard the cabin door slam shut, the screeching metal coil, the slap of the wooden frame, not at first. It wasn't until he noticed that the lights were off, that Devine's silhouette no longer danced in the windows, that's what finally set him to running. When he saw someone walking toward the lake, body bent and laboring be-neath the cumbersome weight slung over a shoulder, he called out in alarm.

"Amelia!"

Wrinkled with bewilderment, Devine's wide-eyed face peeked over the top of a flimsy mattress she wrestled awkwardly toward the dock adjoining the little log cabin. Grunting, she paused a full beat, then stubbornly continued on, unwilling to squander her momentum.

"Henry, trust me, I'm not trying to be funny here, but you look as if you've just seen a ghost," Devine panted, muscling the mattress down the length of the pier. She flopped it heavily across the cold, hard frame of a metal bench that faced the lake and pumped her clenched fists in mock triumph. "I hated to waste a gorgeous night like this, *our* only night, stuck inside that musty cabin," she pinched her nose and smiled, "You're welcome to join me if you'd like, Henry . . . well, I'd like you to join me, actually." She lowered herself onto the cushioned bench. "The last folks who stayed here were kind enough to leave some beer in the fridge. If you come out, would you please grab me one, Henry? A beer sounds pretty good to me right now."

Bent over, hands on his knees and his heart still racing, Sauter tried to rouse himself from what he decided must certainly be a dream. He would awaken in his own bed, in Wisconsin, never having been to Canada, never having met Christopher Koenigs, or Amelia Devine. He watched her, seated at the end of the dock, leaning back against her arms, gazing upward at the evening's first stars. Still stooped and clutching his crumpled black jeans, Sauter swiveled his head toward the cabin. A fishing pole leaned invitingly against the porch, a muskie bait dangling from an eyelet by the barb of a sturdy treble hook. Suddenly, Sauter found himself yearning for a long, sound sleep.

The green glass clinked together as Devine selected one of the four beer bottles wedged by their slender necks between the fingers of Sauter's left hand. He set the fishing pole on the dock and the lure unhooked, falling just short of the water and bouncing the tip of the rod.

"Got an opener?" Devine asked dubiously, handing her capped beer back to Sauter. She picked up the pole and held it

Treehouse

at arm's length, peering down the five-foot length of the long, fiberglass shaft with one eye shut.

"Have you ever used one of those?" Sauter snapped the cap off one bottle, set it at his feet, then opened a second. "An open face reel like the one in your hand? Those can be kind of tricky if you've never cast with one before."

Devine tucked the pocked, corked butt of the rod under her arm and pushed a button on the reel with her thumb. The lure, a black wooden plug with a metal lip that made it dive and wiggle like a fish, plunged into the water. She cranked the handle and reeled in the slack line, adjusting the reel's drag at the same time. When she depressed the button again, the lure descended very slowly. Devine smiled, thumbed the spooled line, and effortlessly flicked a cast that sent the lure arcing gracefully over the water.

"That answers that question." Sauter stepped to Devine's side with a beer in each hand. She watched her line intently as she retrieved the lure.

"You can take the girl out of Wisconsin, but you can't take Wisconsin out of the girl. Fished a lot when I was a kid, right up until the time I moved, actually, both north and south in the state." The lure materialized from the deeper water, swimming frenetically into sight atop the gray boulders tumbling from the shallows. "Even made a trip to Canada once, believe it or not. Fished for both muskie and walleye."

Before she lifted the lure from the water, Devine automatically dipped the tip of the pole beneath the surface and swam the bait around several times in long, sweeping circles.

"I'm impressed, a figure eight." Sauter commended the effort sincerely, eyeing the lure intently himself, "Too bad there wasn't a fish following." He extended one of the open beers. "Here you go."

"Hold on to that for just one second." Devine temporarily declined the beer she had requested and fired off another cast, then another, and another, diligently swimming the bait beneath her each time, anticipating a muskie below. Sauter sipped his beer and watched the lure's repeated approach, not expecting to be a spectator but content nonetheless. He saw the fish before she did.

"There's one!" He pointed with unconcealed excitement, rendering the shaken beer bottles rabid with regurgitated white foam.

It was a thick fish, a typical Canadian muskie, much heavier than a fish of similar length back in Wisconsin. It was below the lure and to the left, toward deeper water, a good two feet away but closing fast. Its wide, red tail fanned the water, sending a whirlpool to the surface. The lure and the muskie arrived simultaneously at the end of the dock, directly below Devine. The fish writhed, prepared to strike, flaring bright red gills and exposing jaws lined with razor sharp teeth. Devine quit reeling, didn't keep the lure swimming as she had on every other cast. Instead, she allowed it to float harmlessly to the surface.

"What are you doing?" Sauter shrieked, unable to contain his disbelief, "That fish was going to hit."

The wooden plug danced on the water. Denied a meal yet still tempted, the muskie lingered just below the lure, its dorsal fin sporadically breaking the surface. Dark bars offset the lighter, luminescent green scales covering the muskie's flanks. Opaque eyes bulged from atop its alligator head, assessing the lure's odd behavior, elusive quarry that no longer scurried from its gaping jaw. The hungry fish grudgingly lost interest and it sank, almost imperceptibly, laying for a moment just above the rocky bottom. With one strong kick of its tail and a neon green flash, the muskie disappeared into deeper water.

Devine gazed into the lake, her lips parted into a wide, satisfied smile, a contagious smile that remained long after the fish had departed. It spread to Sauter, who found himself grinning despite what he had just witnessed, erasing the petty regret that the rod wasn't in his hands with an aggressive fish on the prowl. Devine reeled in the lure and set the pole on the dock. She finally claimed her beer, tapping the neck of her bottle against Sauter's and downing a good quarter of its contents in one gulp. He sipped, too distracted to drink, too tempted by the fish out to fill its belly. With a catchable muskie calling to him, the urge to pick up the fishing pole nearly overwhelmed Sauter.

"Come and sit with me, Henry. We haven't even had a chance to talk." Devine adjusted the flimsy mattress and sat down on the metal bench, patting the spot next to her with an open palm. He followed blindly, a fish chasing bait, and was seated beside Devine without realizing he had even moved.

"Why did you stop reeling, Amelia?" He focused on the water, visualized the fish about to strike the black wooden plug. "Why didn't you figure eight? You could've buried some hooks into that fish, no doubt about it! That would've been a helluva fight!"

Devine tipped back her bottle and swallowed generously. Sauter compared his beer, nearly full, to her's, already one good slug away from empty.

"I suppose it seems a little selfish on my part, putting that poor fish through so much pain for my own gratification, for a few seconds of fleeting excitement," she explained, still smiling broadly. "We would have just let it go anyway, right? Besides, I derive more than enough satisfaction from the privilege of just being able to see such a beautiful creature in its natural environment." She drained her beer and immediately handed Sauter a second bottle to open.

"You weren't kidding with that whole can't take Wisconsin out of the girl spiel, were you?" He raised the empty bottle with feigned disapproval, then obliged her request for another.

"Well, here's to a beautiful creature," Sauter started the toast in reference to the spared muskie, but spoke directly into Devine's gentle brown eyes as he finished. She blushed, turned away, and placed the bottle to her lips without drinking. Flustered, Sauter let the cold amber liquid flow freely down his throat.

Reflected stars twinkled on the glassy surface of the lake. The calm waters were halved down the middle by the luminescent swath of the Milky Way, the melded light of the distant celestial bodies intensified by the arrival of total darkness. Devine tucked one leg under the other and crossed her arms, constricting her body to fend off the chilled night air. Reluctantly, Sauter removed his crumpled tweed sport coat and draped it over her shoulders, wary that the stressful week's worth of wear might offend her feminine senses.

Devine freed her thick black ponytail from beneath the collar and pinched the coat tightly around her neck, "I never intended to take Koenigs back with me, Henry. I have no desire to get my hooks into him again. I'm not entirely sure why, the motivation behind it, but I came to Canada just hoping to see Christopher one last time." Her eyes reflected the sadness in her voice. "I needed to see if he was going to survive, I guess, to assure myself that he wasn't going to go belly up after being released. That makes perfect sense, doesn't it?"

Sauter finished his beer and rolled the bottle back and forth between his palms, dispersing the filmy suds clinging to the inside of the green glass.

"Truthfully, nothing makes perfect sense to me at this point, nothing makes any sense at all," he admitted, his voice tinged with a hint of exasperation. The spent bottle tipped over and rolled in a semicircle when he tried to set it on the dock. Bending forward on the bench, he plucked the last beer up and rocked back into the improvised cushion.

"You were surprised to actually find Koenigs here in Canada, weren't you Henry?" Devine plucked the thoughts from Sauter's racing mind. "You believed he returned to Wisconsin and murdered those two children. That *does* make sense, Henry. I was coming to that conclusion myself. We talked about that over the phone."

Sauter held the unopened beer in both hands, one fist atop the other, "Two children and a cop," he said softly. "An officer was killed last night, hung from that treehouse just like those boys, even though I was right there."

"Henry . . . oh my god . . . I didn't . . ." Devine stammered, releasing the lapels of the sport coat and allowing it to fall open in the crisp air, "Everything has just been happening so fast, we've hardly had a chance to talk." She craned her neck until Sauter finally looked her way. "Are you doing okay, Henry? Was it someone you knew well? A friend?"

"A friend, sure, I suppose you could say that," Sauter conceded, pained by the dawning realization that the rookie cop with the strawberry blond hair qualified for that designation by default. "His name was Seth Colins, only just met him

– let's see, when was it – end of the summer I guess. Kid grew up down south, wanted to be a newscaster but ended up a cop just like his old man. He was as green as that muskie, but I could see the makings of a good cop." Sauter paused, popped open the beer and took a drink, swallowing hard. "We were staking out the treehouse, where the two boys were found hanged, same as Michael Koenigs way back when, and I did come to the conclusion that Christopher Koenigs had to be the primary suspect. Everything fit, but I still had to convince myself because my gut was telling me otherwise. I wasn't surprised that Koenigs was here, I was just hoping like hell that he wasn't because I've got nothing else."

"No other suspects?" Devine didn't conceal her surprise. "Nobody? What about the others? The ones who were there the night that Michael Koenigs died? You told me you always thought they were hiding something, that they've got something to do with this? They're the ones who gave you that black eye, aren't they?"

Sauter's fingers instinctively went to his cheek and re-acquainted themselves with the forgotten, puffy flesh. The swelling had subsided and the blue-black bruise was beginning to yellow at the edges. His ribs were still tender and painful, but only when he thought about it, apparently, since it had quit bothering him until just now. He stood up and walked to the edge of the dock, arching his back with raised arms to stretch his weary muscles and aching bones, groaning involuntarily.

"Max Ferguson did most of the damage, with a baseball bat, but his boy Nicholas was the second victim," he spoke toward the lake, as much to himself now as to Devine. "Ferguson was in the treehouse when Michael Koenigs was hanged. So was Jackson Kelly, and his boy Jimmy was the first victim. I figured Christopher stewed over Michael's death for the past twenty-plus years and started taking out his revenge at the first opportunity. I was wrong about that, obviously, so what am I missing?"

"Not a necromantic, I take it," Devine offered playfully, an impulsive attempt to lure Sauter back to the bench. "Not even going to consider the ghost of Michael Koenigs theory?"

"Richard Mann, he was mighty anxious to ship my ass

out of Broadaxe," staring out over the lake, Sauter continued with his train of thought as if Devine had never spoken. "Why? He lied the night Michael Koenigs died and convinced his friends to do the same. I've always believed that, but what really happened in that treehouse?" Sauter revisited the agonizing questions and eagerly considered a new twist to the familiar tale. "A lie that he would kill for, a lie he couldn't afford to have exposed? Kill his friends' sons? Friends who were in the treehouse that night, let's not forget, friends who could expose the lie . . . then why not just kill *them*?" he wondered, unaware that Max Ferguson's corpse lay rotting in the woods near Cattail Lake, his son's rifle still clutched in his hands. "Why kill the children and leave Max and Jackson alive? Why now, after all these years? One other person was in the treehouse that night, Tim Schumacher, and he has two boys who . . ."

Sauter stopped mid-thought, spun on his heels, and hurried toward Devine with arms outstretched. She felt a warm rush through her body as he reached out for her, pleasant warmth rudely replaced by a cold shiver when he unexpectedly snatched his suit coat from her shoulders.

"Hey!"

Devine uttered the mild protest with furrowed brow. Despite the chill, she downed another swig of her icy beer, set the bottle back down and pulled her knees to her chest. She watched with waxing curiosity as Sauter rifled through the coat pockets once and came up empty handed. Agitated, he searched again with the same results.

"Lose something?"

"A phone number." He checked the pockets one last time. "Son of a bitch!"

"Somebody important, apparently," Devine saw her breath form wisps of smoke, trembled, and squeezed herself into a tighter ball.

"Oh shit, sorry." Sauter wrapped the coat back around Devine and rubbed her upper arms rapidly, heat through friction. "It *could* be important. It was Schumacher's wife, the phone number I mean. It was Margaret Schumacher's. She wasn't in the treehouse, but she married somebody who was there. The last couple of days she's been trying to get a hold of me, insisted on talking with me and nobody else, I guess. Christ, I should have called her back, but like you said, Amelia, everything is happening so goddam fast I never had the chance, never made the time. I wish I would have, wish I could now, but no, I had to lose the damn number!"

Devine fumbled inside the ponderous coat and finally freed a hand. Two quick raps on the cushion and the hand disappeared.

"Sit back down, Henry. I checked my cell phone earlier. Munga's Outpost is out of my coverage area." She smiled, a comforting, reassuring smile, pulling Sauter down onto the bench like an obedient puppy. "Besides, there would be nothing you could do tonight, not here in Canada, no matter what she had to say. In the morning, when we get back to Wisconsin, you'll sort this all out."

Sauter sat close enough to share the warmth of his body, yet he had drawn no nearer, distanced from Devine by deep, deliberate thought. She didn't try to reel him in, allowed him to sink away, content to be alone, at his side.

The night proved deceptively quiet, an underlying silence that surrendered to the minutiae of negligible noises amplified inside nature's amphitheater. Devine leaned back, listened. The murmured call of an owl, far off in the forest, preparing for the nighttime hunt. The grating rasp of sharp claws digging into tree bark. She envisioned a raccoon or porcupine, climbing to safety. The soothing rhythm of the water, lapping against the dock, almost keeping time with the tenor songs of frogs and the throaty bass of toads rising from the shoreline behind her. The mesmerizing chorus carried Devine away.

"It'll be too late."

The baritone of Sauter's voice reached her, yet she had floated off far enough to squelch the import from the words.

"Excuse me?" She drifted back, looked at Sauter quizzically. "Did you say something, Henry?"

"Too late," he repeated stolidly, "Morning will be too late."

"What do you mean? Too late for what?"

Christopher Koenigs's cryptic warning had been bouncing around inside Sauter's head, but he was reticent about sharing that with Devine after he had just finished mocking the maligned man's unfortunate dearth of sanity. Still, no matter the origin, the familiar burn seared his gut; his instinctive, inbred warning signal.

"I've got a bad feeling, Amelia," Sauter confessed, now fully engaged, no longer sequestered in the recesses of his own mind. "I'm afraid another child's life is in danger. I'm afraid another child is going to die tonight, die beneath that goddam treehouse! The killer is back in Broadaxe and I'm up here in the middle of nowhere!" he lamented. "Nice work, detective."

"Don't even say that Henry!" Devine scolded. "Why beat yourself up over something that hasn't even happened yet? Might not even happen at all? Put your focus where it belongs," she counseled, hoping that she could help Sauter sort things out and ease his distress. "So, this Richard Mann. Do you consider him a suspect, or not? Do you think he's somehow involved in all this now that Christopher Koenigs has been eliminated from the equation?"

"I'm having trouble making the leap from manipulative liar to murderer . . ." Sauter paused, reflected. "Hell, I just dealt with that pain in the ass, when was it . . ." he checked his watch, 11:15 p.m. ". . . Huh! It was only just this morning, at the police station in Broadaxe. He was ranting, a mix of fear and anger, and that's a scary combination. His kid was with him, a scrawny little fella, bawling, scared shitless, with good reason. Two of his classmates, his buddies, gone forever, and he's pleading with his father for a little comfort, a little security. What does Richard Mann offer his distraught son instead? Quit crying! Quit acting like a baby! Quit embarrassing me! Then he makes the public pronouncement that the child's been wetting himself, literally pushed the poor kid away, like he was a nuisance!"

Devine shook her head. "Not on the short list for father of the year, by the sound of it."

"The asshole was more worried about himself. He came right out and admitted as much for chrissake!" Sauter seethed, embittered by the recollection of the frightened, emotionally abandoned child.

"Okay," Devine recapped, allowing Sauter to simmer.

"Afraid and angry, heartless and cold-blooded, obviously self-absorbed, but is he a killer?" She persisted, "That's what you need to figure out, detective."

Sauter held up his beer, gauged the contents, then finished the remaining half-bottle in a series of short, sequential gulps. "We go way back, me and Richard Mann, back to the very beginning of this whole deal, back to the night Michael Koenigs died, a night that changed the direction of so many lives." Absently, he put the empty bottle to his lips, realized the beer was gone, and placed it at his feet. "The story that he and his pals concocted, *their* explanation about what occurred in the treehouse, I didn't buy it from the get go and I pushed the issue, pushed it pretty hard, too hard for some folks' comfort, Richard Mann's father being one of them. Seeing how I was the cause of that discomfort, I was exiled, banished from Broadaxe. Certain folks had something to hide, that's the message I got."

"Still haven't figured that one out yet though, have you?" Devine ventured, cautious not to offend or chafe a raw nerve.

Sauter bowed his head, shook it somberly from side to side.

"Just to be clear, I'm only playing the devil's advocate here, trying to consider all the angles, okay," she continued to tiptoe, "but have you considered the possibility that maybe those folks don't have anything to hide after all? Maybe you are just chasing Michael Koenigs's ghost, metaphorically speaking, of course."

"Christopher Koenigs murdered his younger brother in an episode of uncontrolled rage," Sauter scoffed, "a crazed, inhuman killer after all, is that what you're saying, doctor? I was led to believe you were never an adherent to that theory. And let's get one thing straight, Michael Koenigs's ghost has been chasing me!"

Devine rolled her eyes, "Henry, please!"

"That's the logic I'm following here," he insisted. "If certain folks have nothing to hide, that could only mean one thing, those folks are telling the truth. That truth is based on the tenet that Christopher Koenigs is an incorrigible killer necessitating special dispensation. That's how he ended up in your lap, doctor, thanks to certain folks in Broadaxe and your pal Sarah Perkins."

Sauter's sudden condescension irked Devine, especially his patronizing tone when he called her *doctor*. She bit back her Irish temper, the temper that had too often brought out her father's belt in his steadfast attempt to tame the rebellious girl, to break her as if she was just another animal on the farm. Oddly, she flashed back to her pet pig, Frenchy, and his unfortunate demise, a memory strong enough to trigger the stench of the pork chops steaming on the kitchen table. The memory bled to Christopher Koenigs, as it always did, the broken soul in the oversized orange jump suit, meek and mute at the precipice of the slaughterhouse.

"The proposition that nobody is hiding anything could certainly mean more than one thing, detective. I would think you would understand that better than anyone else." She draped a calm exterior over the slow boil just beneath the surface. "Richard Mann and the Koenigs boys, the other three children who were there that night; that's just it, Henry. We can't forget these are, *were*, children. They witnessed a traumatic event, the horrible death of a child, a playmate, and those young minds could easily have processed a version of the incident entirely different from reality. Right or wrong, that would be their truth, Henry, an unconscious truth formed without malicious intent. Christopher Koenigs believes his brother is still alive. That's his truth, that's his reality. The mind truly does work in mysterious ways."

"And the moral of the story still doesn't change, Christopher Koenigs gets royally screwed, although from a different position." Sauter understood where Devine was coming from and appreciated the fresh perspective. He felt shitty about copping an attitude. In the end, however, he was unconvinced. "I'll tell you *my* truth, *my* reality. Somebody's hiding something!" He smiled at Devine, pleased to receive the same in return.

"Go on . . ." she prodded, insisting on a fuller explanation behind the instinct-driven theory.

"I was pissing and moaning about it just a minute ago, the fact that I'm stuck here in Canada while there's a murderer stalking the children of Broadaxe," he obliged, "And why am I here in Canada? Funny you should ask! Because Richard Mann wanted me gone, just like dear old dad, desperately wanted me gone. I'll say it again, something to hide, that's the message I get."

"If you ask me, Chief . . . Cooney? . . ." Devine fumbled for the correct pronunciation.

"Kunick," Sauter provided it, "Bobby Kunick."

"I was only going to say, from what I saw the chief was awfully eager to see you go himself," she resumed the thought. "He was prepared to carry you out onto Zeb Munga's airplane himself, if need be. From my perspective, he was the one doing the banishing."

"At Richard Mann's bidding." Sauter unwittingly alluded to a conspiracy.

"Whatever," she persisted, walking through the door he had opened. "The chief was elated to be rid of you whether it was his idea or not. Maybe he and Mann are in cahoots. Tell me, was Cooney," she butchered the name again "a member of the police force when Michael Koenigs died?"

Sauter bit his bottom lip. Devine had probed until she uncovered the raw nerve she had tried to avoid, the unthinkable notion that had festered in the fringes of his consciousness since Kunick had first ushered him from Broadaxe under the guise of genuine concern. Sauter had assumed there were ulterior motives involved, there always were, but he considered the enormous pressure heaped upon Kunick in the wake of Michael Koenigs's death and cut the chief some slack for the decision. Most importantly, he couldn't have afforded to jeopardize his relationship with Kunick, his last remaining link to Broadaxe, to the unresolved murder of an innocent child.

Sprays of white mist swirled above the surface of the lake, the day's stored heat escaping from the water and colliding with the cool night air. The smoky vapors blurred Sauter's vision and he blinked hard to clear his sight, to break through the melancholy fog. He leaned forward and adopted Devine's orphaned beer from below the bench.

"Sometimes, if the stars happen to line up just right," he shifted his gaze from the hazy surface of the lake to the twinkling canopy overhead, "a person is fortunate enough to have the opportunity to lead his life. Most often though, sad but true, it's the other way around. Life does the leading. That's the way the coin flipped for me the second I entered that meadow and took the rope from Michael Koenigs's neck." He took a drink, swallowed hard, then tipped the bottle once more. "Bobby Kunick was on the force alright, he was already the chief of police when the Koenigs case hit. He sent me packing back then, too."

Devine confiscated her pilfered beer, quivered as she drank, and quickly ceded the bottle back to Sauter.

"What does that tell you?" She could see that he was following, lured by her logic, and she slammed the hooks home. "Does the chief have something to hide as well, or are you getting a different message."

Sauter offered Devine the last of the beer; she declined, so he finished it off. He exhaled, heavily.

"I'm the patsy in that picture, the dopey detective played and put out to pasture. Not an attractive option. Are you one-hundred percent certain the man we just met with was actually Christopher Koenigs and not Emile Perkins?" He shredded Devine with a sad-eyed, tired smile. "The scenario you're suggesting is a tad bit more delicate and quite disturbing, to say the least. Collusion on the part of the chief of police to cover up or at least obstruct both past and present murder investigations? Jeez!" He wiped his forehead with the back of his hand for dramatic effect. "Christopher Koenigs fit the part much more neatly, offered a much cleaner resolution. If I wouldn't have just talked with him myself . . ." he trailed off.

"Perhaps that's what the real killer, or *killers*, intended all along," Devine flipped the final card from the conspiracy theory deck. She rocked back and forth to free her feet from beneath her buttocks and wiggled her legs to shake out the tingling sleep.

"One problem," Sauter cautioned. "It's tough to frame someone for a crime that's committed when said someone isn't even in the same country."

"No one knew Koenigs was here in Canada!" Devine dismissed the argument with a laugh. "Admit it, Henry, you doubted it right up until the minute you laid eyes on him! I was skeptical myself when Zeb Munga first contacted me, of course I was, but he convinced me that the man he had hired was Christopher Koenigs. It's even harder to outrun the long arm of the law in the computer age, maybe even impossible. Munga saw the *have-you-seen-this-man* photo of Koenigs posted online, the photo distributed by the police after he walked away from the halfway house."

"So you were certain it was Koenigs before you even arrived in Wisconsin?" Sauter sprang from the bench and gaped down at Devine, incredulous. "You *knew* he was in Canada, that he had no connection to the killings in Broadaxe, yet you didn't bother sharing that with me?"

The tweed suit coat slipped from her shoulders and fell onto the bench as Devine bounced to her feet and squared up to Sauter. "What difference would that have made? It was Canada or anyplace else other than Broadaxe, remember? Those were the two options Chief Cooney offered you."

"Kunick," Sauter interrupted to make the correction one more time. Devine thanked him with an icy glare.

"This is the option you chose," she made a sweeping gesture with one outstretched arm, "although I certainly don't know why!" Miffed, she didn't back down. "I am not obliged to share anything with you, is that understood?" *Irish temper.* It reflected in Sauter's eyes. He stepped back. Smoldering, she tamped the flaring embers and reined herself in. "Having said that, I'll have you know that I planned to tell you, Henry. I *wanted* to tell you! Again, don't ask me why. There was no time, we were never alone. Sarah Perkins thought it was ludicrous, you heard her! She was *so* certain that Christopher Koenigs had returned to Broadaxe. Well, that was just fine with me. I by no means wanted her on that plane, no matter what we found in Canada. If it wasn't him, if it turned out to be a wild goose chase as she predicted, if she were here and he was killing children in Broadaxe, I'd have never heard the end of it. If she found him here, as we did, she would have insisted on returning him to New York, insisted upon his placement back in the institution. You saw him, you talked with him. He's harmless. He's suffered enough in one lifetime."

"Does she trust you?" Sauter ventured, wary of fanning the flames. Devine scrunched her eyebrows. "Will she take your word for it, that's what I'm asking. Like I said, if I *hadn't* seen him and talked with him, I'm not so sure *I* would have believed you." A bit late, he added, "Considering the circumstances and all."

"Thanks! Thanks a lot!" Devine softened her harsh tone and defensive posture. Decompressing, the chilled night air crept back upon her. She retrieved Sauter's coat from the bench and covered back up.

"No offense, Henry, really, I understand," she paused a beat, "considering the circumstances and all. By the way, very insightful, detective. Dr. Perkins would *not* have taken my word. Christopher Koenigs in Canada? Not so big a deal. Christopher Koenigs a recidivist killer returned to the scene of his infamous childhood crime? Sarah Perkins would bathe in that limelight! I can only imagine the look on her face when I show her the sketchbook." She wagged a finger at Sauter. "That reminds me, you didn't bother hiding your opinion of Koenigs's art work. I thought you were going to throw his paintings into the lake. What got into you?"

A meadow of purple lupines flashed before Sauter. His heart thumped in his chest. Page after page of purple lupines painted on crisp white paper, the defiled meadow reborn through Christopher Koenigs's hand.

"Why the sketchbook?" he lapsed into his best nonchalance and bypassed Devine's inquiry. "What's the significance?"

"It's not the book, obviously, it's the paintings in the book," she elucidated. "Christopher Koenigs the artist can best be described as prolific. Inventive? Creative? Not so much. The same painting, the *exact* same painting, over and over and over, a field of purple flowers. He hung one on his wall at the institution."

"Lupines," Sauter clarified, "the flowers are lupines, lupines in a meadow, not a field."

"A field of flowers, lupines in a meadow, sounds like a matter of semantics," Devine countered. "Art *is* subjective, after all."

"Not this art. This art is specific, its objectivity the result of its origins," Sauter critiqued. "It's not just a field of flowers or lupines in a meadow, Amelia. It's a painting of the meadow where his brother Michael died, of the lupines that covered the forest floor that night."

"Henry, I didn't . . . I just thought . . ." Devine stuttered.

"Not what I expected to see when I peeked over his shoulder, kind of caught me off guard." Sauter finally got around to explaining his visceral reaction to the painting. "All that's missing is a big bur oak with a treehouse in its branches. Michael Koenigs, Jimmy Kelly, Nicholas Ferguson, Seth Colins, all dead in that meadow. Each time, purple lupines, an early summer flower blooming like gangbusters in autumn. That's got me scratching my head." He bent forward, hands on knees, and slowly lowered himself onto the flimsy mattress. "It's the kind of art I don't need to be subjected to, that's all."

Sauter kept his head down and wallowed in the weary beer buzz. Morning couldn't come soon enough. The fateful first meeting with Amelia Devine had fallen short of his middle-aged fantasies. Christopher Koenigs had drawn them together, only to somehow, in some way, push them apart. He considered a gallant retreat to the cabin, could almost hear a bed calling out, an overdue respite for his battered body and spirit. The effluvium of the past few days pressed down, souring Sauter to the brink of self-loathing and solitary introspection. Then, almost magically, Devine breathed new life into the deflated mood of the northern Ontario night.

The neglected reel of the fishing rod screamed, a nail-on-the-blackboard screech that resounded like sweet music in Sauter's ears. Metal hooks jangled, tracing the arc of the lure until it slapped down upon the surface of the water. He raised his head and watched Devine furiously crank the reel handle. Drowning in his sport coat, she retrieved the lure rapidly and mechanically fired off another cast. Sauter noticed she didn't figure eight the lure at the dock and decided he couldn't blame her in the blinding darkness.

"I can't remember if I read this somewhere, saw it on a fishing show, or what, but I recall hearing that this is a productive way to muskie fish at night. That the fast-moving lure trig-gers strikes," Devine looked back over her shoulder at Sauter as she continued to reel and cast, reel and cast. "You ever heard that?"

"My philosophy's always been that you can't catch a fish if you're not fishing," Sauter replied. "Other than that, I really don't give it much thought."

Devine quit after a dozen casts and carried the fishing pole back to the bench. She tempted Sauter with the rod, hold-ing it out to him with the black wooden plug dangling free.

"That's alright," he surprised himself with the demur-ral. "The fish you spared earlier might come back and I'd prob-ably just end up catching it."

Rolling her eyes, Devine carefully hooked the lure to the pole and laid it down on the dock amid the empty beer bot-tles. She plunged her hands into the flapped pockets of the coat and plopped down next to Sauter, brushing against him as she settled in. He inhaled her earthy essence, reveled in her near-ness, and no longer felt depleted. From the corner of his eye, he saw the white puffs of her warm breath form and fade when she spoke.

"It's funny, you know, what you said earlier, about sometimes leading your life, sometimes life leading you. When I was younger I always thought I was doing the leading, but as time went by I came to realize that probably wasn't the case, much like you." She turned and faced Sauter. "I believe life led me to Christopher Koenigs. I believe our paths crossed for a reason. On the farm back in Wisconsin, when I was a little kid, there was this pig . . ." she hesitated, realized she was commit-ted, and forged ahead. "Well, I made the mistake of treating this pig like a pet, named it and everything. At times I thought that pig was the only friend I had in the world. Long story short, my father butchered the pig, served it for dinner, and life went on, but I was no longer doing the leading. It's called fate, Henry, and you can't fight it."

Unsure why, Sauter felt compelled to share his own sad pet story. "I had a dog when I was a boy, a stray pup I found wandering around in the woods, half-starved. I figured that was fate, so I named the pup accordingly, Kismet, means fate, or destiny. Only I spelled it with a 'z' instead of an 's' so I could call her Kizzie. *My* long story short, I nursed that pup back to health and grew too attached in the process. Only had her a short time before she was run over by a truck right before my eyes. Life does the leading, you've got that right. It should go without saying, I try not to tempt fate, Amelia."

Devine slipped her hand out of the coat pocket and squeezed Sauter's fingers inside her soft, warm flesh.

"Don't give up on fate just yet, Henry," she purred, "after all, it brought us together, didn't it? It's late, it'll be daylight soon. Why don't we head into the cabin where it's warm? Why don't we make the most of the night? Who knows what fate has in store for us tomorrow?"

A hot surge of excitement pulsed through Sauter's veins. He cupped Devine's head in his hands and gently kissed her forehead. They rose from the bench together and embraced, lingering a moment longer on the dock, savoring the anticipation.

"Detective!"

It sounded distant. Sauter tried to ignore it, to wish it away. He felt Devine flinch and pulled her closer.

"Detective!"

Munga stomped down the dock waving the tattered gray tam in one hand and toting a square black satchel in the other. The long-imagined moment vaporized. Fate. Under his breath, Sauter cursed it.

"You got a phone call, detective, that big-headed police chief back in Wisconsin, says it's urgent," Munga extracted an elongated telephone receiver from the satchel and handed it to Sauter. He noticed the empties and the fishing rod. "Sorry to interrupt," he grinned, his voice dripping with insincerity.

"What's up Bobby?" Sauter snarled, still chafing at the importune timing of the call. As he listened, nodding his head intently, the color drained from his cheeks. He returned the receiver to Munga without another word.

"We have to leave immediately, Zeb, we can't wait until morning," Sauter issued the command in a stern voice, "Christopher Koenigs was right. I'm already too late. Richard Mann's boy, Terry, he's dead!"

The clothes in the back corner of his closet were beginning to reek, the mounting heap of urine-soaked underwear and pants Terry kept hidden from his disapproving father. The windows could only remain open for so long before his bedroom filled with the cool autumn air and made him shiver. Once shut, the stink crept bank into the room, stinging his nostrils and eyes with an ammonia burn. It made him weep, the confusion over what he should do, and he felt like he was going to wet himself again.

But he would not! Terry promised himself that he would do as he was told and quit crying, quit acting like a baby, quit wetting himself . . . quit embarrassing his father. Yet the tears still glistened on his cheeks and the pile of soiled clothing continued to grow and fester in his closet. It was so frightening to think of his friends – Jimmy Kelly buried beneath so much dirt and Nicholas Ferguson trapped inside a box down at the funeral home, waiting for his turn to be put in a hole alongside the other dead bodies in the cemetery.

Terry ran to the bathroom and relieved himself just in the nick of time, sparing him the confrontation with his father that he desperately wished to avoid. He wore his last clean pair of underwear and his last clean pair of pants. He felt terribly alone, abandoned by his parents when he needed them most. His mother was too frightened herself to be of any help, to secretly wash his dirty clothes, to hug and kiss him and tell him everything is going to be all right. She was frightened by the unknown killer just like everyone else, but she was frightened by his father, as well, and he wondered why.

It was all his fault, Terry concluded, it had to be. Things would be better for everyone if he weren't around. His father wouldn't be embarrassed any longer. Maybe then he wouldn't be so mean to his mother. Maybe the two of them would be happier together if he wasn't there to cause so many problems. No one likes a crybaby, especially one who goes to the bathroom in his pants. Terry wanted to make his father proud, to prove he was a man and not a baby. It would be best to run away.

The sun had just set and the sky was growing darker. He had to hurry. Some of the underwear was still damp when he stuffed it into his backpack on top of the dirty pants. The smell was awful, but he couldn't possibly leave the clothes behind in the closet for his father to find. He emptied his piggy-bank onto his bed, careful to keep the silver coins from jingling too loudly as they tumbled out. There was also a roll of crisp green bills, the allowance he had been saving to buy a skateboard. Terry scooped the money up and stuffed it in his front pockets. He slipped his arms into the padded straps of the backpack and looked around his bedroom one last time.

The coast was clear when he cracked the door and peered down the hallway. He listened for a moment. The house was quiet. It was a straight shot to the back door, making it easy to sneak outside. Hunched over to make himself less conspicuous, Terry waddled across the open yard. At the edge of the tree line he straightened, broke into a sprint, and ran headlong into the forest. When he finally stopped, the darkness beneath the towering pines squeezed what little air was left from his heaving chest.

Terry sniffed the air, surprised that he could still smell his clothes through the backpack. Then he realized the odor was different, stronger yet, and putrid like the rotting flesh of a dead animal in the roadside ditch. Terry heard the strange, garbled wheezing closing in on him from the shadows, echoing off the trees in every direction. Determined to be brave, to make his father proud, he pinched his eyes shut and pledged not to cry.

Terry screamed instead, screamed at the searing pain that radiated out into his body from the tips of the hot, sharp knives digging into the back of his neck. There was no sound, the scream was silent, muted by the unbearable agony. The backpack separated from his body violently, the bones and sinews of his shoulders snapped and torn by the pull of the padded straps. Liquid trickled down the length of his spine, warm like the liquid that ran down his legs when he wet himself. The burning talons dug deeper into his neck and lifted him off the ground.

Intermingled with a soft, sinister laugh, the gasping,

gurgling wheeze intensified as Terry's last clean pair of jeans scraped and skidded over rocks and roots. The intense pain ebbed into a dull ache and his consciousness dimmed. Rough, scaly skin scratched across his cheeks and slapped him back awake. Purple flowers surrounded him now and stroked his abraded skin with grasping, clutching petals. Terry glimpsed the foreboding, gaping maw of the treehouse. He kicked and wriggled in vain, powerless to fight against the fiend who had snuffed the life from Jimmy and Nicholas, terrified that he was next. Skittered up the trunk of the oak and deposited into the noxious belly of the treehouse, his body fell limp. Terry surrendered to the noose bravely, his eyes free of tears and his pants unsoiled. As he tumbled to his death he wished his father were there, there to see that he had quit crying, quit acting like a baby, quit wetting himself . . . there to see that he would never be an embarrassment again.

CHAPTER NINETEEN

"Is that oversized skull of yours crammed full of rocks Bobby? What the hell is the matter with you?" Sauter leaned on his knuckles and stared across the desk at Kunick, stunned by the chief's stubborn stupidity.

Kunick refused to look Sauter in the eye, "Watch yourself, detective," he mumbled the ineffectual warning.

The flight back to Broadaxe had been bumpy, the mood inside the plane owly and antagonistic. Munga took umbrage at Sauter's unequivocal demand for immediate departure and only acquiesced after extorting – Sauter's spoken interpretation – extra cash to cover the inconvenience. Frustrated by the untimely interruption to their impending tryst, Devine shared the foul disposition that pervaded the cockpit. Nerves frayed and patience disintegrated.

"If you're accusing Detective Sauter of lying, chief, that means you're calling me a liar as well, and I take offense to that!" Devine stood at Sauter's side and glared at Kunick. "It was Christopher Koenigs. We *saw* him. We *talked* to him! If you refuse to believe that, if you still think he's here in Broadaxe, that he's the killer, well, you're sadly mistaken . . . and you're a stupid, stupid man!"

"Nobody comes into my office and talks to me like that!" Kunick fired back, pouncing to his feet. The blood-stained bandage was gone and the red lump rose garishly from the side of his head. Bloodshot, tired eyes contrasted the sudden spike in his temper.

"Where is Christopher Koenigs now, Dr. Devine?" Legs crossed and hands folded in her lap, Dr. Sarah Perkins sat off to the side and posed the calculated question with smug turpitude. "Why didn't you bring him back with you doctor? Detective?" She looked from Devine to Sauter as she spoke. "The man is a fugitive from the law. He escaped from a secure halfway house operated by the State of New York. It was your duty to return him to custody. I agree with Chief Kunick. I don't believe Christopher Koenigs is in Canada. I don't believe either of you, whether it offends you or not!"

Sauter threw his hands in the air and let gravity pull them back to the top of his head. He clutched fistfuls of his disheveled, gray-black hair in each hand. "This has got to be the most goddam, unbelievable . . ." he gasped in exasperation.

Kunick shuffled sideways from behind the desk and ambled slowly down the worn linoleum path leading to the hallway. He pushed the door shut and drew the blinds. Spreading apart two of the metal, horizontal slats with his fingers, he peered absently into the narrow shaft of light penetrating the dingy office.

"I should have left well enough alone," back turned to the room, Kunick spoke softly. "I should have left your sorry ass in Canada, Sauter, but I was fool enough to believe that you might actually help me solve these murders, might help me catch Christopher Koenigs. It's time to give it up, Sauter, this misguided crusade of yours, this unconscionable defense of a depraved killer." He slipped his fingers from the blinds and turned to Devine. "That goes for you too, doctor."

"Hold it right there, Bobby, there's something that you should know . . ." Sauter protested, hoping Devine would take his cue and produce the sketchbook. Kunick didn't give her the chance.

"You hold on, detective!" The chief's broad face flushed red and his voice suddenly boomed loudly in the enclosed space. "Christopher Koenigs *is* here in Broadaxe! Christopher Koenigs *is* the killer! Dr. Perkins explained everything, how Koenigs is the prototypical . . ." he scratched his temple ". . . what was that term again, doctor?"

"Genetic sociopath," Perkins chimed in confidently.

"That's it, genetic sociopath," helplessly beguiled by the long-legged, blond haired doctor in his office, Kunick spewed out her psychological doctrine like a trained parrot. "A natural born killer, not by choice, just hard-wired that way, couldn't change if he wanted. It all makes sense. It's the *only* thing that makes sense – the victims, the crime scene," he deferred to Perkins, "I'm sure the good doctor could explain it all much better than I. Dr. Perkins?"

Sauter caught Devine's eye and for a fleeting moment they shared their amazement at being summarily dismissed and labeled outright fabricators. The sketchbook was tucked in a canvas shoulder bag Devine had slung behind her back. She slid the bag to her hip and wagged it unobtrusively at Sauter, tacitly asking if it was time to display the painted pages of purple lupines. Sickened by their intractable ignorance, Sauter was content to watch Kunick and Perkins dig themselves a deeper, self-righteous hole. He waved Devine off and she shifted the bag off her hip.

Never tired of her own voice and always willing to expound upon her career-launching theory, Perkins cleared her throat and uncrossed her legs. She stood, brushing off the green, crushed-suede suit clinging to her ample curves. Long lashes blinked over impassive blue orbs, and thick, lustrous locks of gold tumbled to her broad, pointed shoulders. Sauter could hardly fault Kunick for his blind infatuation with the comely doctor.

"The innate or genetic sociopath is a term I coined to describe the inherent psychological affliction which predisposes certain individuals to violent, sadistic personalities from birth." Perkins spoke in the measured cadence she had mastered long ago while working the lecture circuit. "As such, these individuals are destined to commit amoral, antisocial acts at a very early age. These crimes tend to be specific, dependent upon the individual. Arson for instance, or cannibalism," she paused for effect, "or hanging children from a treehouse. Given the opportunity, these individuals will continue to display this aberrant behavior and will revisit, or recreate, the original deviant acts. I can cite examples." She turned to Devine, who knew what was coming. "As a nine-year old, Karl Meriter locked some of his playmates in an ice shanty and burned them alive. At the age of eighteen, upon his mandatory release from psychiatric supervision under the guidelines at the time, Meriter locked seven people in a pantry at his halfway house and burned them alive. At the age of eleven, Nadine Kasten dissected an infant she babysat for and ate the internal organs with a bowl of ice cream. Upon her mandatory release at the age of eighteen, Kasten kidnapped an infant from a shopping center and barbecued it on an open spit for dinner. Christopher Koenigs was eight when he put the noose around his brother

Michael's neck and pushed him from the treehouse. Thanks to my groundbreaking work with genetic sociopaths, he wasn't released at the age of eighteen, but as you can see, that only delayed the inevitable. At the first opportunity he returned to Broadaxe and started pushing children out of that treehouse, the only thing he knows how to do."

Sauter greeted the conclusion of Perkins's speech with sarcastic applause. "I must admit, doctor, I admire your conviction and may have swallowed your logic hook, line, and sinker like the chief here, but there's one small problem," he raised his voice and slammed his fist down on the desk, "Christopher Koenigs did *not* return to Broadaxe! Christopher Koenigs is *not* pushing children out of that treehouse! He's in Canada and we *can* prove it!"

Devine stepped forward and pulled the strap of the canvas shoulder bag over her head. She set the bag at her feet, removed the sketchbook, and handed the bound package of crisp, white paper over to Perkins. Hesitant at first and eyeing Devine suspiciously, Perkins finally turned back the thin, cardboard cover and stoically scanned page after page of purple lupines.

"What is this, Amelia? Some kind of joke?" Perkins sniffed dubiously. She closed the sketchbook and passed it into Kunick's eagerly awaiting hands.

"It's no joke, Sarah. Christopher Koenigs gave me that sketchbook in Canada . . . where we found him, where he's been for the last week," Devine tried to explain, well aware that Perkins remained skeptical.

"What? I don't get it," Kunick interrupted as he rifled through the sketchbook with his stubby fingers. "A bunch of paintings of flowers? That proves Christopher Koenigs is in Canada? Unless I'm missing something here, I don't see how this changes one goddam thing!" Again, he deferred to Perkins. "Doctor? Isn't that right? This doesn't prove anything?"

Deaf to his imploring tone, Perkins didn't answer Kunick. She was focused on Devine, searching her colleague's face for any sign of deception. Jaw set with unwavering certainty, Devine didn't blink. Perkins's lips parted slightly, but she had trouble finding her voice. Faint red blotches stained the porcelain skin stretched over her high cheekbones and the air of superiority sucked audibly from her constricted lungs. Speechless, for once, she slumped back into her chair in shocked resignation.

"Would somebody fill me in?" Kunick whined the plea as he assessed Perkins's reaction with apprehension.

"Take a good look at those paintings, Bobby. Try and pay attention," Sauter suggested, "then tell me what you see."

Kunick thumbed through the sketchbook a second time, more deliberately, turning each page with grave recognition. He didn't close the book until he had studied each of the identical paintings with equal intensity.

"The meadow," he mumbled despondently. "It's the meadow." Confusion still corkscrewed his expression and his impatience bubbled over. "I'm a little thick in the head so somebody give me some goddam answers now!" he growled. "Quit beating around the goddam bush!"

From a distance, her voice barely audible, Perkins acceded to the undeniable truth, "Those paintings were created by one hand and one hand alone. Hundreds, perhaps thousands, wouldn't you say, Amelia?" she looked up at Devine with contrition. "That's how many times Christopher Koenigs painted that exact same scene in his cell at the institution. The paintings in the sketchbook are identical, all but the final painting, which I'm sure you all noticed was left unfinished, quite recently, it would seem." Perkins raised her right hand and extended the index finger, exposing the underside of its slender tip, smudged purple with the damp residue of recent brush strokes.

Devine tried to wrest the sketchbook from Kunick, who initially resisted before he grudgingly released his grip. She tucked it back into the canvas bag and looped the strap over her shoulder.

"I didn't bring him back because he's suffered enough, Sarah. If you want to bring Christopher Koenigs back to New York, that's your prerogative, I guess. You go to Canada and track him down," Devine offered the suggestion with a major caveat, "but he's not a so-called genetic sociopath, whatever that is. He's an unfortunate soul who lost much more than his brother that night in the meadow. My advice, for what it's worth, is let him go. Let *it* go, Sarah."

Perkins nodded her head and straightened her posture, shrouding her shaken composure beneath a hastily-erected facade of forced indifference. She stood, head bowed, and walked slowly to the office door.

"I'm sorry I couldn't be of more help, Chief Kunick. I sincerely believed that Christopher Koenigs . . ." her voice trailed off as she grabbed the doorknob. "I'm afraid I'll only be in the way now. I'm going to return to New York, immediately. I think that's best. Good luck with the investigation. I'm sure you'll catch the killer shortly. Dr. Devine?"

"Yes?" Devine missed Perkins's implication.

"Will you be accompanying me? Back to New York?"

Devine's eyes shifted to Sauter reflexively. "No, I think I'll stay behind," she decided on impulse, recalling their recent flirtation with intimacy. "I haven't been back home to Wisconsin in a number of years," she added, somewhat self-consciously.

Perkins appeared surprised, oddly disappointed. "Very well," she exhaled the words. "I realize you're very busy, but if I could just trouble you for a ride to the airport, Chief Kunick? Then I'll be out of your hair."

Still reeling from the sudden, unanticipated turn of events, Kunick rubbed the expansive top of his bald head, "Well, I don't really see that as a problem. You won't be in my way," he offered a half-hearted attempt to change her mind, saddened by the imminent departure of such an attractive ally, "but if you insist."

"Yes, I insist," Perkins dashed the chief's unrequited expectations, exiting the office and retreating down the hallway. Sauter grabbed the collar of Kunick's khaki shirt when the smitten chief started to follow the departing doctor.

"You're the chief of police for chrissakes, Bobby, not a chauffeur," he admonished. "We're not done here, not by a longshot. The good doctor can call a cab, hell, she can walk for all I care, but you're not leaving this office, not until we hash some things out."

Kunick angrily slapped Sauter's hand from the back of his neck, "A cab," he grumbled, "you know damn well . . ." he frowned deeply, Sauter smiled faintly. "Corky!" Kunick leaned his head out the door and hollered for his trusted junior officer. He swiveled his head in each direction and noticed Perkins standing outside the front door, patiently awaiting her escape from the backwoods town of Broadaxe. "Taxi cabs, up here in the woods," more grumbling, then another distressed shout, "Corky!"

Corcoran rounded a corner at the far end of the building and trotted stiffly down the hallway, arms bent at the elbows. Laden with keys, radio, firearm, and various other law enforcement implements, her black utility belt bounced heavily on her wide hips. Sauter marveled at her fresh face and crisp, clean uniform, mistakenly assuming that the breakneck pace of the last week had left everyone worn and haggard.

"Chief?" She greeted Kunick with a terse salute, nodded at Sauter, and ignored Devine.

"Do me a favor, Corky. Run Dr. Perkins out to the airport." He tipped his head toward the front door, "Make sure she hooks up with her pilot. Don't just leave her stranded out there. Get her whatever she needs, then get back here to the station, pronto."

"Right chief, I'm on it." Another quick salute and she broke back into her trot. Halfway down the hall, she spun around and continued to jog away backwards. "I almost forgot, detective," she called out to Sauter, "that woman who's been trying to get a hold of you, Margaret Schumacher, she's here in the station with her two boys, back in the lunchroom, said she wasn't leaving until she had a chance to talk with you, only you." She backed out the door and whisked Perkins away.

Sauter bristled, "Just when were you planning on telling me Margaret Schumacher was here, Bobby? Are you worried about whatever it is she has to say?" He raised his eyebrows. "It's looking more and more like you've got something to hide, old friend."

"Hide? Hide what? I honestly didn't know she was here. Corky never mentioned it to me," Kunick unconvincingly pled ignorance. "Need I remind you, another child died last night, Sauter, so excuse me if I haven't kept track of your appointments," he looked past Sauter to Devine, "social, or otherwise. Go have your chat with the selective Mrs. Schumacher, see if I care. Contrary to your belief, I've got nothing to hide. By the way, you can go straight to hell."

Sauter smirked at Kunick's put-upon posturing, "Nothing to hide, but you were in one hell of a hurry to get me out of Broadaxe. You were more than happy to do Richard Mann's bidding. You were dead set on pinning the hangings on Christopher Koenigs, probably thought it would be easy, just like the last time. Christopher Koenigs didn't murder his brother Michael and he didn't murder Jimmy Kelly, Nicholas Ferguson, Seth Colins, or Terry Mann. But you persisted, even *after* Dr. Devine and I told you that Koenigs was in Canada and couldn't possibly have committed the crimes."

"*I* called *you* and told you Terry Mann was dead," Kunick shrieked defensively. "I gave you the green light to come back to Broadaxe, to rejoin the investigation! You tell me, does that sound like the actions of somebody with something to hide?"

"You only brought me back here because you were so certain that Christopher Koenigs was the killer," Sauter countered. "You changed your tune in a hurry after I told you Koenigs was in Canada. Something about wishing you'd left my sorry ass up there? Does that ring a bell?" He shifted gears. "Maybe you could explain what happened last night, how another child was allowed to die out in that meadow. I thought you were going to tear that goddam treehouse down!"

Kunick locked on Sauter with penetrating, hollow eyes. "I did rip it down, me and Corky, yesterday morning, right after you left for Canada. We burned the scrap wood right there in the meadow beneath the bur oak. The flames charred the tree's bark, turned those purple flowers into ashes."

"Maybe I misunderstood," Sauter rubbed his temples to assuage an encroaching headache, "but I would've sworn you told me the Mann kid died just like all the others, that he was hung from the treehouse."

"That's right," Kunick confirmed the contradiction, failing to elaborate.

"Goddamit Bobby!" Sauter barked in frustration.

"Don't ask me for an explanation, because I ain't got one," Kunick lowered his voice and looked about for unseen eavesdroppers with madness in his eyes. "We found Terry Mann hanging from that treehouse, just like the others, as if Corky and I never did tear it down. We did, I can assure you of that, we did, but it was right back in the oak's branches, and you know what else?" Kunick dropped to a whisper and he glanced furtively down the hallway. "That bur oak, the flowers, all back to normal, no charred bark, no ashes. The goddam meadow looks the same, Sauter, the *same*."

Sauter tried to digest what he was hearing and noticed Devine standing silently in the background, wide-eyed with wonder at the improbable tale.

"Who found the Mann kid? You? Corky?" He prodded Kunick for more information. "When did you learn that he was missing? That he was dead?"

"Dickey called me, Dickey Mann," Kunick made the admission sheepishly. "He's the one who found his son hanging from the treehouse. He was waiting for us in the meadow with his dead boy."

Sauter grimaced and shook his head in feigned surprise. "Richard Mann!" The name passed slowly through his lips, as if it were almost painful to speak it. Kunick noticed Sauter was talking to Devine now, a shared secret, and he didn't appreciate being left out of the loop. It took a bit, but the switch finally flipped.

"You two can't be serious? Dickey?" Incredulous, Kunick's eyes darted back and forth between Sauter and Devine. "We're talking about his own flesh and blood! Dickey Mann? C'mon, not just his own boy, but two of his best buddies? Their sons? Jiminy jumpers, Sauter, I know you've had a hard-on over this guy for a long time, but I didn't realize your brains rushed out of your head with the blood!"

Sauter peered down the hallway, now more anxious than ever to hear from Margaret Schumacher. There was a deliciously tempting unknown that tied all of the murders together, an intangible rolling around on his taste buds, but he was having trouble identifying the flavor. It had staled many times in the intervening years since Michael Koenigs's death. Now it was back, biting and bitter.

"Well, it's not Christopher Koenigs, Bobby. We've established that, so maybe you'd be willing to share any new theories you have about who the killer may be." Sauter started to back down the corridor, his curiosity pulling him toward the lunchroom. "I'm throwing Richard Mann out there as a prime suspect. Maybe Dr. Perkins is right after all, maybe there was a genetic sociopath in the treehouse the night Michael Koenigs died. The way she explained it, that type of individual would have no qualms about killing his own kind."

Kunick shooed Sauter away with both hands, "I don't even have Dickey on the radar. You wouldn't either if you'd have seen him last night with his dead boy in his arms. He's a broken man, a shattered soul, took the child's death mighty, mighty hard, kept blaming himself. Does that sound like a cold-blooded killer? A madman? Dickey Mann is *not* a suspect, not in my book, so you may want to come up with another name to throw out for my consideration."

"Michael Koenigs."

Standing on her left foot just outside Kunick's office door, her back against the wall, arms crossed and her right leg bent at the knee, Devine clearly stunned Kunick with her unexpected contribution to the conversation.

"Michael Koenigs," she repeated calmly, irked by the chief's condescending demeanor and off-hand dismissal of Sauter's suggestion. "There's another name for you." Devine saw apprehension creep across Kunick's face. "Christopher Koenigs claims his deceased little brother is the hangman, so there's another name you can mull over. Michael Koenigs."

Kunick sneered at Devine with sudden contempt, "I'm not sure what kind of game you're playing, doctor, but I have no time and precious little patience for such foolishness. I think you should have gone back to New York with Dr. Perkins, had the good sense to get out of the way and let me do my job, like she did." His cheeks blanched ashen and the color bled from his pursed lips. "Michael Koenigs! For chrissakes, what kind of cockamamie . . ."

Intrigued by Kunick's discomfiture, Sauter teetered in a tug of war between Margaret Schumacher and the chief. There was something he needed to ask Kunick, it was there, just on the tip of his tongue . . . The question popped into his head, an echoed recollection of Christopher Koenigs's soft voice requesting an intriguing favor. He sidled back to Kunick.

"Where is Michael Koenigs buried, Bobby? I'd like to exhume the body, take a look at his remains. Can you set that up for me?"

Dumbfounded, Kunick shuffled backwards and glanced into his office. He wavered, lowered his head, and made a quick stutter-step toward the door. Devine slid along the wall, and filled the portal, blocking his quizzical attempt to escape. Kunick raised his large right paw, an open palm poised to slap the cowering, diminutive Devine across the face. Hissing through clenched teeth, he slowly lowered the threatening hand to the back of his neck and began to massage the tension building at the base of his skull.

"That poor family disintegrated because of what happened, surely you remember that, Henry," Kunick kept his eyes averted, staring straight down at his feet. "Hell, the Koenigs family ceased to exist, what with one son dead and the other the killer. The folks lit out from Broadaxe right quick. Not long after, hell, couldn't have been more than a year gone by, the old man offed himself. Mother followed shortly, died of a broken heart I imagine."

Sauter tired of Kunick's stalling. "The grave, Bobby, where is it?" He kept an even tone. "I'll get the court order myself – what time is it?" He glanced at his watch, surprised that the day was slipping away. "Midday Monday, Bobby. I'll have the court order from the county this afternoon. I still have some friends *there*. Just tell me where Michael Koenigs is buried and I'll take care of the rest."

"Take care of the rest? The rest of what?" Kunick swiveled his bowed head, suspicion seeping through the narrow slits of his eyelids. "Tell me, where'd this crazy notion spring from? Just what do you expect to find out there in the cemetery?"

"It's beginning to look more and more like nothing, does that sound about right, *chief*," Sauter twisted Kunick's title off his tongue disrespectfully.

"Yep, that sounds about right. Nothing," Kunick tugged at his belt, too eager to agree. Relief rubbed away his furrowed brow. "It was a long time ago now, but if memory serves me right Michael Koenigs was buried in an unmarked grave out in Cemetery of the Pines. I honestly don't know where that grave site is. I don't believe anybody does." He ogled Sauter with cheeks spread wide in a checkmate grin.

"I do, I can take you to Michael Koenigs's grave."

Margaret Schumacher extended the offer in a frail, tired monotone. The grin jumped from Kunick's lips and landed on Sauter's face.

"I stumbled across it the other day, literally. It was Saturday, following Jimmy Kelly's funeral. The grave is not unmarked, there is a headstone." She had snuck into the hallway from the lunchroom unnoticed and had quietly moved within a few feet of Sauter's turned back. Her red curls jutted in a messy jumble from her head and jagged red streaks marred the whites of her haggard green eyes. Cowering behind her and clinging to the loose belt of a long black coat that reached to her ankles, two young boys peered out around her hips, wide-eyed with instilled fear. "If I take you there, to the grave, Tony and Billy are coming with," she tousled the unkempt hair on the top of her sons' heads. "They're not leaving my side."

Margaret tipped her head back and pointed at Sauter with the fine line of her jaw. "You're Sauter, the detective. I recognize you. I've been trying to get a hold of you. My husband, Tim Schumacher, he was one of the boys in the treehouse the night Michael Koenigs was hung. I'm his . . ." she cleared her throat, "I'm Margaret Schumacher. There's something I need to tell you, there's something you need to know, detective."

Sauter held up an apologetic finger and put Margaret on hold. He turned his head to Kunick.

"Bobby, that court order, can you help me out with that so I can speak with Mrs. Schumacher here?"

Kunick spread his stance and crossed his arms, obstinate. His face went blank and he didn't budge.

"Mrs. Schumacher, bring your boys and follow me into the chief's office." Sauter stared Kunick down to let him know he wasn't asking for permission. "I need to make a quick phone call, and then we can finally talk." Kunick didn't look pleased as the door closed in his face.

Sauter immediately placed the call for the court order to exhume Michael Koenigs from his long lost grave. He perched on the edge of Kunick's desk with the phone cradled in the crook of his neck. Margaret sat upright on the couch with her youngest, Billy, tucked beneath one arm and his older brother, Tony, hugged tight in the other. Faces scrubbed clean, the dispirited little boys locked on Sauter with leery mistrust. Tony's red mop burst from his head like a rocket blast, cheeks shiny from dried tears and bottom lip folded out in a sad pout. Billy's short-cropped brown hair complemented his compact, athletic build. His stare sizzled with defiance above a sternly set jaw and clenched fists, the protector rather than the protected. Unlike his brother, submissive in his mother's embrace, Billy squirmed against the pampering constraint.

Margaret answered Sauter's mimed offer of food and drink with a curt shake of her own red locks. He hooked up with his contact at the Ojibway County Courthouse and called in some chips, exacting a promise that the court order would arrive in Broadaxe later that afternoon. When he hung up the phone, he noticed Margaret sizing up the unwelcome guest standing with her back to the shuttered office door.

"What's she doing here?" Margaret's eyes didn't leave Devine when she asked Sauter the question. "I thought I made it clear to the police officer, Officer Corcoran, what I have to say I say to you alone."

Sauter attempted a comforting smile. "I'd prefer that she be allowed to stay, Mrs. Schumacher . . ."

"Margaret, I'd prefer to be called Margaret."

"Very well, Margaret," Sauter continued, "this is Dr. Amelia Devine. She's a psychiatrist from the institution out East where Christopher Koenigs was confined. She came all the way out to Wisconsin to try and help solve . . ." he glanced at her boys.

"Don't worry about them," Margaret caught Sauter's drift. "The time's long past for mollycoddling. Ignorance will get you killed." She assessed Devine with blossoming enmity. "Did you get Christopher Koenigs released? Were you involved in that somehow?" Devine nodded. Margaret clicked her tongue and shifted her attention to Sauter. "She can stay.

She *should* hear what I'm about to tell you, then maybe she'll understand why Christopher Koenigs came back to Broadaxe to kill our sons."

"I'm sorry, but there's something you should . . ." Devine flexed defensively.

"Hold on, let's hear Margaret out. She's been very patient," Sauter cut Devine off with remonstrating eye contact. "You're certain that Christopher Koenigs is the killer." Margaret nodded her assent, "Tell me why."

Margaret surrendered the protective grip on her boys with obvious trepidation. Tony continued to burrow into her side, a little bird scratching for the protective cover of its mother's wing. Billy slid down the sofa cushion and settled just beyond arm's reach, scowling. Margaret responded with a disappointed frown.

"I'm sorry about my boy acting up like he is, but Billy's been going a little stir crazy as of late," Margaret apologized needlessly. "That's about as far away as I've let him get since the murders started. He's only 10 years old. He should be out running around in the woods, fishing, playing, just being a kid. I'm trying to put a healthy scare in him, make him realize how serious this is, but he might be too young to truly understand the gravity of the situation."

Billy jumped to his feet and struck a wrestler's pose. "I'm not too young! And I'm not afraid of Christopher Koenigs!" he boasted, chest puffed.

"Billy Schumacher! Don't even say that!" Margaret gasped, unveiling her own susceptibility to the ingrained superstition. She grabbed Billy's elbow and yanked him back to her side, prodding him for an apology until he mumbled "I'm sorry" unconvincingly.

"Let me start over, or let me just start." She tightened the vise on her headstrong child. "I guess I didn't get the chance before I was interrupted." Billy got the message and went limp. Margaret jumped straight to the point.

"Richard Mann killed Michael Koenigs, detective. Richard put the noose around that boy's neck and pushed him out of the treehouse."

Watching Sauter intently, Margaret paused until the

dazed expression faded from his face.

"That's right. It wasn't Christopher Koenigs after all. He didn't kill his little brother. It was Richard Mann!" She snapped at Sauter, "You suspected as much, didn't you detective, but you didn't do your job. You couldn't solve the case! Now children are dying again and it's your fault as much as anybody's." She graciously included Devine. "Same goes for you, doctor."

Arms crossed, Sauter rocked himself off the edge of the desk and turned his back to Margaret. He walked slowly to the far wall, glancing at Devine out of the corner of his eye. She gaped back with a holy shit expression which he found oddly amusing. Although Margaret's blunt revelation initially zapped Sauter like a stun gun, he cautiously stepped back from blind acceptance of her claim.

"Margaret, that's one hell of an accusation you're leveling there . . ."

"It's not an accusation, it's the truth!" Margaret blistered, "Max Ferguson was my best friend, detective, and as you know, he was also in the treehouse that night."

"So it was Max Ferguson? He pinned the blame on Richard Mann for what happened?" Sauter interrupted, purposely twisting her words, bringing a scowl to Margaret's lips.

"No, detective, Max did not pin the blame on Richard. He did not tell me what happened to Michael Koenigs. Max was a loyal man, to a fault, as they say, a major understatement in this instance." Margaret started to speak rapidly, determined to get her story out without further delays. "It wasn't until his boy Nicholas was gone and he had nothing to live for, no hope, that's when he finally told me that the truth as I knew it wasn't the truth at all. Even then he wouldn't tell me what happened in the treehouse. He still wouldn't break the pact that he had made that night with Richard, Jackson Kelly, and my . . . and Tim." She could no longer bring herself to call him her husband. "Max said it was Tim's responsibility to tell me, that a husband and wife shouldn't have secrets in the first place." Her eyes misted over and her throat contracted.

"There was a secret though, isn't that right?" Sauter interjected. Margaret looked at him as if he were stupid.

"It turns out my husband is a weak, piddling man, detective, a man who lived a lie because of some sick, distorted idea of friendship, of loyalty, just like Max, just like the whole lot of them," Margaret's voice waned into weariness, "For years Tim played the victim, they all did, four innocent children forever scarred by the horror they witnessed that night in the treehouse. Ironically, that's no doubt true, but not because they watched Christopher Koenigs go crazy and kill his brother. Richard put the noose around Michael's neck and pushed him to his death, but Tim said he and Max and Jackson were as much to blame because they stood by and did nothing to stop it."

"Did he say why, Margaret?" Sauter asked. "Did your husband tell you why Richard Mann killed Michael Koenigs?"

"It was typical kid's stuff, older boys hazing younger boys, but it escalated until it got out of control, playful teasing that transformed into torment. That's how Tim described it to me." Margaret snuck a quick peek at her boys, shuddering to think that they might be capable of such cruelty. "Eventually, Richard put a rope around Michael's neck and told Christopher that the only way he could save himself was to push his brother out of the treehouse, otherwise both of them were going to die. That *is* when Christopher went crazy, apparently. He fought with Richard, got the better of him and embarrassed him in front of his friends. Tim and Max and Jackson pulled Christopher off Richard since he couldn't defend himself. That's when Richard did it. He just smiled and pushed Michael out of the treehouse with the rope still tied around his neck. Richard made up the story about Christopher being crazy, being the killer, and Tim said everybody believed it but you, detective. That's why I had to talk to you, to let you know that you were right all along. Now you know *why* Christopher Koenigs is killing our children. He's avenging his baby brother's murder. He's seeking revenge for the injustice of it all. He's here because you couldn't figure it out, detective, and he's here because you let him out, doctor."

"But he should have never been incarcerated in the first place," Devine argued, no longer able to remain silent, "Christopher Koenigs did nothing wrong! He was another victim that night along with his brother. He deserved sympathy and he got shackles, instead."

Margaret bantered back, "I said he was treated unjustly, I said he was seeking revenge because of that, but that doesn't change the fact that he's here in Broadaxe hanging the sons of the men responsible for his brother's death."

"I agree, it all sounds very logical, it all makes perfect sense," Sauter slowly let the air out of Margaret's balloon. "I'll admit that I had come to the same conclusion myself, that it had to be Christopher Koenigs, that it couldn't possibly be anyone else. It seems as though we've been duped, however, led to believe that it was Christopher Koenigs through the manipulation of the real killer . . . a killer who had a secret to protect, perhaps?"

"What do you mean? What . . . what are you saying?" Margaret stammered, unprepared to consider any other alternatives.

"Christopher Koenigs couldn't possibly be the killer, Margaret," Sauter explained. "Dr. Devine and I met with him overnight, in Canada. He's been there for nearly a week."

"That can't be," she protested feebly. "If it's not Christopher Koenigs . . ."

"Four other people, Margaret, four other people in the treehouse when Michael Koenigs died, all part of a cover-up, all part of the devil's pact you just spoke of," Sauter pitched the theory to gauge Margaret's reaction. "Your husband Tim, Jackson Kelly, Max Ferguson . . . and Richard Mann."

Stripped of the benign comfort afforded by certainty, Margaret stubbornly denied the sudden swell of vulnerability. "It has to be Christopher Koenigs!" She cinched the embrace of her boys up one more notch and glared at Sauter with desperate defiance. He shook his head slowly, burying the haunting specter of Christopher Koenigs once and for all through the fixed stare of unblinking, sympathetic eyes. Margaret averted her misty gaze and twisted her desolate face upwards, lips trembling.

"I must seem quite the fool, living with something like this festering for so long and too stupid to figure it out, too complacent to even try," she batted away incredulous tears and turned back to Sauter. "It always seemed incomprehensible to me, the way Richard Mann held such sway over three grown men, how they always deferred to him . . . always." Briefly, the focus fell from Margaret's green eyes.

Sauter didn't let her drift too far away. "You know these people better than anyone, Margaret, do you think that's what's happening now?"

"I don't know these people, detective, isn't that obvious?" She dropped her head in resignation. "I thought I did, I even loved one as a husband and one as a best friend, but I didn't really know them at all. I'm left with my two boys here, they're all I've got left, and I intend to make sure no harm comes to either one of them." Her faltering voice strengthened as she finished.

"What about your husband? What about Tim?" Sauter felt the eyes of the two young boys upon him as he asked the question.

"What about him?" Margaret reacted defensively, no longer comfortable with the marital association.

"Where has he been this past week?" Sauter prodded. "What's he been up to? I'll be blunt, Margaret. Is there any chance Tim is involved in these murders somehow? That any of them Max, Jackson, Richard – are involved?"

"It sounds like you're asking me to do your job, detective." Margaret could see she surprised Sauter with the smart ass remark.

"I'm just asking questions. That's my job," Sauter winced at the corny Sgt. Joe Friday imitation. He countered Margaret's "are you serious" expression with one of his own that said "just humor me." Margaret nodded respectfully, suddenly embarrassed by her obstinacy.

"I realize that you're only doing your job, detective, that you're trying to figure out who murdered those three little boys, and the last thing I wish to do is make that job any more difficult," she apologized. "I'll do anything I can to help." Sauter nodded once. Margaret continued, "Tim is an emasculated mess, barely functioning. He has nothing to do with it. I have no reason nor desire to protect him, so this is not the obligatory alibi of a spouse, if that's what you're thinking." She turned to her boys. "I despise the man. It sickens me to even look at him, living a lie and knowingly dragging me and his sons down with it. These killings put him over the edge – Jimmy, Nicholas, Terry – he's lost it. The last I saw him he was curled up in a fetal position on the bed. He told me there were voices in his head constantly."

"Voices?" Sauter interrupted, vividly recalling the words that had once echoed insistently inside his own skull . . . *Go to the meadow . . . Save the child . . .* "What did the voices say? Did he tell you?" he asked breathlessly.

Margaret eyed Sauter curiously, "Voices in his head, constant voices, that's all he said," she paused and reflected, "No, wait, he did say Jackson Kelly and Max Ferguson had heard voices too, right before their boys were killed . . ." her vocal cords constricted and choked off her words.

"What about Jackson and Max?" Sauter continued to push, "What can you . . ."

Margaret jumped in, "I don't know if it's true and I sincerely doubt it, but from what I've heard Jackson Kelly has been stone cold sober since his boy Jimmy was killed. Believe me, if it's true, that's saying something because next to his wife Dorothy, he was the biggest boozer in Broadaxe. Jackson's not a killer, detective, but when it came to Richard Mann, he was the biggest ass-kisser in the bunch."

"And Max?" Sauter pressed impatiently.

"Max is dead, detective. Suicide," she announced blandly. "He shot himself out in the woods by Cattail Lake, right after he admitted there was this terrible secret. I suppose he's still out there. I didn't alert the authorities. I didn't want them wasting any time on him with a killer on the loose." She realized her tone was callous, but she didn't care.

"So that only leaves . . ." The metal blinds clattered and Sauter broke off momentarily as the office door swung jarringly open. He smiled unfavorably into the beady blue eyes of the pale, slender visitor who had barged in uninvited. "Richard."

Clad in a sateen, navy blue track suit with white piping accenting the arms and legs, Richard Mann rocked nervously from one bright white tennis shoe to the other. His thin lips were curled back over tiny gray teeth that caged an obviously agitated tongue. Still relegated to the hallway, Kunick stood behind Mann with his right hand resting conspicuously atop his service revolver. Devine scurried across the office and joined Sauter near the chief's desk. Margaret remained seated on the couch, clutching her boys and glaring at Richard with unconcealed disgust.

"I typically find it flattering to be the focal point of any conversation, but I suspect that doesn't apply in this instance." Richard sauntered into the office with his distinctly feminine gait, turning to make sure that the chief and his gun were following dutifully behind. "Megs. Detective." He flashed an annoying smirk at Margaret and Sauter, then extended his lithe hand toward Devine. "And I have yet to make the pleasure of your acquaintance." Rebuffed, Richard turned to Kunick.

"Dr. Amelia Devine," the chief quickly assisted, "one of the shrinks who worked on Christopher Koenigs out in New York. She's the one responsible for his release. That's the way Dr. Perkins explained it to me, anyway."

"Dr. Perkins?" Richard abruptly lost interest in Devine, "When did you talk with Dr. Perkins, Bobby?"

"Hell, she was here in Broadaxe, Dickey. Got here early yesterday morning and just left today," Kunick explained hastily. "She was here to help solve the murders, to help find Christopher Koenigs, but she went back to New York as soon as she found out he wasn't here."

"Not here?" Richard gasped with genuine surprise. "What are you talking about, Bobby? Not here! Of course he's here! He murdered my child last night! He killed Jimmy Kelly and Nicholas Ferguson, just like he killed his own brother!"

"Liar!" Margaret leapt from the couch and snapped Richard's head around with an open palm. The sting of the hard slap resonated inside the enclosed, cement box office. "Liar!" She screamed in his reddening face a second time. "You killed Michael Koenigs, you son of a bitch! You put the rope around that boy's neck, you pushed him out of the treehouse, and you blamed it on his brother! Your life is a complete lie, Richard, and you forced others to live that lie with you!"

Richard rubbed the crimson skin of his cheek, the annoying smirk wiped away and a hint of pain in his expression. "Megs, I never understood why you always had to be such a bitch, why you never had the decency to honor my request and call me Dickey."

Richard's face collided with the vehement brunt of Margaret's palm a second time, raising an immediate raspberry welt that complemented the tender red flesh on the opposite side of his face. She retreated to the couch quickly and corralled her boys, peppering their heads with repeated kisses. Tony cowered while Billy adopted his mother's angry posture. Richard ceased massaging his cheeks and stood leaning forward, unmoving, a rat seeking the next passage in the maze. Sauter stepped in front of Margaret to deter Richard from any ill-advised thoughts of physical retaliation. He stepped back aside when she started to speak.

"Max told me there was a secret you all shared." Her voice was calm and confident. "He told me there was a secret, then he killed himself. I suppose you weren't aware of that little development, were you? *Richard.*" She emphasized the name, pleased to see that he was too shaken to notice. "He couldn't live with it anymore, but it took the loss of his only son to bring about that fatal bout of conscience. The secret didn't die with him, though, Max at least made sure of that. He knew Tim would tell me, tell me more out of weakness than any sense of responsibility. He was right. Tim told me. Now I know everything. You're a murderer, Richard, and I'm no longer referring solely to Michael Koenigs. Three other children are dead now, and I can't help but wonder how far you'd go to protect yourself, to perpetuate the myth you helped build."

Richard raised his hands and backed away until he stood adjacent to Kunick. The chief gaped at Richard, dumbfounded by the agonizing revelation of unexpected betrayal.

"Wait a minute, wait a minute," Richard tittered nervously. "This is all bullshit, crazy talk, isn't that right, Bobby?" Eyes glazed, Kunick didn't respond. "Christopher Koenigs is no myth. He's the killer, everybody knows that. Get Dr. Perkins back here. She knows. Christopher Koenigs is the killer! He's the killer! He never should have been released from the institution." He thrust an angry, accusatory finger at Devine.

"It's over, Richard. Give it up," Sauter took an aggressive step in Richard's direction, "Christopher Koenigs is not the killer. He's been nowhere near Broadaxe. The chief knows it, Dr. Perkins knows it, we all know it . . . everybody knows it but you. Your boy just died, Richard. I'd think you would be a bit more upset."

Richard deftly snatched the service revolver from Kunick's waist and waved the loaded gun wildly in front of his frail, quivering frame. He aimed the gun at Margaret initially, then frantically swung the blue steel muzzle at Devine before settling his aim directly at Sauter's forehead. The hollow barrel traced tiny circles in Richard's trembling hands and tears rolled down his cheeks, still rosy from Margaret's hostile touch.

"Shut up! Don't you dare tell me how I should feel about my dead boy!" He barked. "All brawn and no brains, Sauter. That's what people always said about you," Richard sputtered with vehemence as he caressed the trigger with his twitching index finger. "I'm sure you must have heard that, eh detective? Well, people were right. You were too thick to figure things out. You needed an uppity bitch like Megs here to finally figure it out for you." He flashed a sneering, desperate glance at Margaret. "I killed Michael Koenigs, you're goddam right I did! It was his brother's fault. Christopher asked for it. He could have kept things from turning out the way they did."

"Why Dickey? Why?" Kunick reached out for his pilfered weapon as he implored Richard for an explanation. Richard reacted reflexively, whipping the gun in Kunick's direction, rapping the chief on the side of the head with the hard metal. Fresh blood oozed from the still healing lump above his temple.

"I'm warning you, Bobby, back off! Nobody disrespects Dickey Mann, do you hear me? Nobody!" Richard's entire body shook as he issued the threatening rant. "Christopher Koenigs found that out the hard way. He learned that there's a high price to pay when you mess with me. He found out! He could have played along, he could have at least been scared." Richard sobbed heavily, then composed himself. "He *should* have showed me the respect that I deserve! Instead he decided to fight, a wise ass little kid who got too big for his britches. I put him in his place, I knocked that little bastard down a notch, and then some!"

"Please, Dickey, come to your senses and give me back my gun." Kunick's entreaty fell on deaf ears. Richard slowly backed into the doorway and trained the pistol back on Sauter, arms fully extended.

"You think I'm going to let you pin these murders on me, detective, murders I didn't commit?" He tilted his head to one side and coughed up a nervous laugh. His voice rang high-pitched and strained. "Michael Koenigs has been dead how long? Twenty-odd years? Yet here I am, a free and unfettered man to this day. I thought Christopher Koenigs was the only one I had to worry about after I killed Michael, but as it turned out, you, Sauter, you were a thorn in my side. It was easy to convince everyone else, the chief here," he waved the revolver at Kunick without looking his way, "Jackson, Max, and Tim, even the famous Dr. Sarah Perkins. All of them believed my story, followed along like sheep. But not you, Sauter, no, not you! Still, you were helpless then, just like you're helpless now. I eliminated Christopher Koenigs as a threat. I should have done the same with you! But it's never too late, is it, detective. You're a sorry son of a bitch, Sauter. I haven't forgotten how you tormented me! You deserve to die!" Richard tightened his grip on the pistol and his mouth cracked wide in a maniacal grin.

Sauter dropped to the linoleum floor at the crack of the shot, bracing for the searing burn of the bullet as the concussion echoed loudly in the cramped, concrete space. Kunick's revolver clattered to the floor and bounced to within inches of Sauter's nose. He rolled to his side and glanced up at Richard, who teetered back and forth as a dark stain spread across the chest of his navy blue track suit. Fear flickered heavily in his eyes before the panicked blue pupils rolled to white. His knees buckled, then caught, suspending Richard for a brief moment before he crumpled and came crashing down at Sauter's side, revealing Corcoran standing rigid in the hallway, weapon drawn.

Kunick dropped quickly to his knees and rolled Richard

on his back. He checked for the fading pulse, first in the wrist, then in the neck. The chief shook his head somberly and reached to close the lids of the vacant, staring eyes. Richard's limp body spasmed and the last gasp of life flickered through the waiting corpse. Richard's hand shot up and grasped Kunick's forearm, pulling the chief within earshot of his dying, whispered words.

"I . . . didn't . . . kill . . . my boy. No . . . one else . . . only . . . Michael . . ." The haunting ablution hissed through his bluing lips like air from a flat tire, and he was gone.

CHAPTER TWENTY

Margaret didn't shield her boys from the dead body. Instead, she rose deliberately from the couch and tugged the two, eyes wide and mouths agape, roughly to their feet. Richard Mann was splayed out on the worn linoleum in a posthumous pose that would leave behind the chalk outline of a slender man high-stepping his way to the grave. The stale office air closed in further as the tannic residue of Corcoran's revolver filled the cramped space.

The rubber-soled sneakers of the boys' reluctant feet chirped sharply as Margaret dragged Tony and Billy from the couch to the corpse. Kunick knelt over the body with his hand hanging above Richard's graying face, still poised to close the eyelids, yet paralyzed by the brief, startling resurrection. Sauter was up off the floor, half-sitting on the edge of the desk with his left arm draped around Devine's quaking shoulders. The chief's heisted revolver dangled at Sauter's side in the loose grip of his right hand. Corcoran maintained her rigid stance in the hallway, black boots spread wide and arms held ramrod straight, the revolver still pointed at Richard's lifeless form.

Margaret slid her hands up to the back of her boys' heads and gripped their skulls, forcing them to focus on the blank expression of death.

"I want both of you to take a good look, I want to make sure you always remember the face of this liar, this murderer," she callously nudged the shoulder of the corpse with her foot, "Never forget this face, do you hear me? This is the face of the man who killed your friends, Jimmy and Nicholas, he's the reason why Max is dead, why your father is a stranger to us now. This is what happens to a piece of filth, never forget that." Entranced by morbid curiosity, Tony and Billy stared in limp bewilderment.

Kunick rocked back on his haunches and removed a folded white handkerchief from the back pocket of his crumpled khaki trousers. Very daintily, he dabbed at the blood oozing from the reopened wound on the side of his wide, round head. Beads of perspiration glinted from his forehead and upper lip. The handkerchief fluttered open and he wiped up the sweat. His face immediately began to glisten anew as he methodically folded the soiled cloth and returned it to his pocket.

"Goddamit, Corky! At ease!" His back to the hallway, Kunick barked the command blindly, somehow sensing Corcoran's undue diligence. "The man is *dead* for chrissakes! Jesus! What the hell did you do? What in the hell were you thinking? Put your goddam gun away!" Instantly, concern creased Kunick's brow. He fingered his empty holster, replaying the unfortunate escalation of events in his mind.

"I'll tell you what the hell she did, Bobby. She saved my ass, that's what she did!" Sauter popped up from his perch on the edge of the desk and lifted his left arm from Devine's shoulder, up and over her head. "You were thinking he was going to shoot me, weren't you Corcoran?" Holstering her weapon, she looked up and tersely nodded her agreement. Sauter smiled, nodded back, a tacit thanks. "I was thinking the same thing, that he was going to shoot me, shoot me with *your* gun, Bobby!" Sauter waggled the wayward service revolver in his fingertips, taunting anger out of the embarrassed chief.

"Hand it over, detective," Kunick seethed, red-faced and sweating profusely, holding a hand out to Sauter like a beggar on his knees.

Sauter twirled the revolver in his hand and presented the wooden butt to Kunick, then just as quickly spun it back, stopping the rotation with the barrel pointed at the floor.

"Not just yet, chief," Sauter demurred, tightening his grip on the gun. "If you don't mind, I think I'd like to hold on to this for a bit. After all, there's a bullet inside that nearly had my name on it, maybe still does. Let's just say I want to make sure that bullet doesn't find its way out."

Kunick shook his head gravely and his lips parted in a thin, forced smile. Laboring to stand, he tried in vain to shake the kinks out of old knees folded beneath wide buttocks for far too long. His trousers bunched at the tops of his shin-high leather boots, refusing to fall free as he peevishly stomped his feet. The small muscles in his cheeks twitched noticeably, tiny spasms triggered by the aggravated clenching of his firmly set jaw. Sauter braced for the eruption, anticipating the final, unavoidable dissolution of his fragile friendship with the entrenched chief of police.

Kunick surprised Sauter by somehow dialing his boiling temper back to simmer. "Begging your pardon, Mrs. Schumacher, but I don't think it's proper for you to be filling those boys' heads with false information." He addressed Margaret indirectly, speaking in a controlled, calm voice incongruous with the threatening intentions he leveled at Sauter through his unrelenting stare.

"I'm sorry . . . did you just? . . . I'm not sure . . ." Caught up in the drama of the looming confrontation between Sauter and the chief, Margaret didn't anticipate being drawn back into the conversation so abruptly. "False information?" She regrouped quickly. Are you implying that Richard Mann isn't the killer?" She turned to Sauter, fear and uncertainty flashing in her green eyes. "But I thought . . ."

"You thought what?" Kunick cut Margaret short, mocking her confusion. His vengeful eyes never left Sauter. "You thought the detective here had it all figured out, is that it? All those years and you never really figured out what happened to Michael Koenigs that night in the treehouse, am I right, Henry?" His lips parted in a dopey grin. "It was that famous instinct of yours telling you something was amiss, that remarkable gut feeling. Instincts and gut feelings pale in comparison to the truth and proof, detective, and once again you appear burdened with too much of the former and not enough of the latter. Richard Mann confessed to killing Michael Koenigs with his dying words. If you choose to believe that, detective, it would seem only logical to believe that he was telling the truth when he denied killing the others."

Sauter chuckled, shook his head. "Are you actually so gullible that you're buying that last breath bullshit, Bobby? My instincts were dead nuts, this asshole lying on the floor confirmed it." He waved the revolver at Richard. "I didn't have any proof, I'll grant you that, but I always suspected that he was at least partially at fault for Michael Koenigs's death. Come to find out he was *the* killer, cold-blooded, a *genetic sociopath* if you will." Sauter spit the words out sarcastically. "It was you who defended him back then, Bobby, same as you're defending him now. Hell, you always have, and honestly, for the life of me, I never could understand why."

Kunick didn't blink. "I never thought Dickey had anything to do with the hanging of that Koenigs boy," face blank, voice monotone, "I truly believed Christopher Koenigs killed his brother."

"Couldn't have been more wrong, eh chief?" Sauter rubbed it in.

"That's what I believed. What else can I say?" Kunick shrugged his shoulders. "Believed it right up until Dickey admitted otherwise, would still believe it if I hadn't been here and heard him set things right myself."

"Set things right?" Devine stepped forward and wagged a finger in Kunick's wide, worry-free face. "When Richard Mann pushed Michael Koenigs out of that treehouse he took one life and ruined another," she turned to Margaret sympathetically, "ruined the lives of many others," then snapped quickly back to Kunick. "His confession is meaningless now. It hardly sets things right, and it's highly offensive of you to suggest that it does! What about the children who died this past week? It seems he stopped short of setting things right on their account."

"Dickey said he didn't kill the others, only Michael Koenigs, you all heard," Kunick maintained stubbornly, still refusing to take his eyes off of Sauter.

"His own child died last night!" Devine's voice clicked up an octave. "One would think he would be distraught, heartbroken, at home comforting his family. Instead he waltzes into this office and has the audacity to flirt with me like some kind of . . . like some . . ."

"Cheeseball," Margaret had no problem finishing Devine's fragmented thought, "and I agree, what I just witnessed was anything but a grieving parent. If it were one of my boys . . ." she trailed off, glassy-eyed, then refocused. "I saw a man desperate to save his own skin, a man who killed before and would have killed again if Officer Corcoran hadn't been here to stop him."

"I defended Richard Mann out of the conviction of my beliefs," Kunick refused to back down. "The women here, aside from Officer Corcoran, they may not understand that, but as a man of honor, Henry, as a man of the law, I would surely think you would. I was proud to call Dickey my friend. What happened all those years ago in that treehouse doesn't change that. Still, it's a hard thing to accept sometimes, the truth."

"From certain people," Margaret corrected, "not from everyone." She thought of Tim and for the first time wondered if she could have accepted the horrible truth from him. *Was honesty even an alternative considering the circumstances of Michael Koenigs's death and its sordid aftermath?* "For certain people the truth isn't an option." Margaret spoke the thought aloud without intending to, a revelation that dripped from her mind to her tongue. With her boys attached to her hips, she moved between Sauter and Kunick so she could look the besieged chief directly in the eye. "Maybe you're a liar, a liar just like your friend, your *dead* friend. Maybe you knew Richard killed Michael Koenigs all along, but maybe you're just like all the rest of them – Max, Jackson, Tim – for whatever reason maybe the truth wasn't an option for you either."

Beset with the calculating discomfiture of a cornered animal, Kunick's eyes narrowed and his nose twitched nervously above pursed lips. Sauter and Devine stood shoulder-to-shoulder behind Margaret, sandwiching Tony and Billy in-between. Corcoran, confused and disconcerted by the exchange, had moved just inside the doorway of the crowded office, two or three steps behind the chief. Kunick glared at his accusers over the blue-gray body at his feet. He extended his left arm, slowly, palm upturned.

"Gimme my goddam weapon," he hissed between heavy, nasal breaths. Sauter declined with a barely perceptible shake of the head. "Son of a bitch!" Kunick fumed, "Nobody comes into my station, my own goddam *office* . . ." He lunged forward and dropped one boot on the opposite side of the corpse, then froze, mid-straddle. "You've damn well gone and done it now, detective," cocking his head to one side, he peered down the barrel of his own service revolver, "You've crossed a line, you realize that, don't you? Ain't no turnin' back now, no siree!"

Reaching awkwardly around Margaret's right side and over Billy's head, Sauter leveled the gun and aimed just below the silver badge pinned to Kunick's chest, his index finger floating ahead of the trigger. Margaret shuffled to her left and fell back alongside Devine. Sauter gradually lowered the barrel until it pointed at Kunick's left kneecap.

"The killing's over, Bobby, far too many have died already, but I'm warning you straight out, one wrong move and I won't hesitate," he warned. "I'll hobble you, I shit you not!"

Kunick hovered indecisively astride Richard, face-up with his beady eyes still open in a death stare, jaw slackened. The dead man appeared mortified by the unflattering view of the chief's ample bulk looming above him. There was a collective inhalation held inside by all through the drawn out silence, as if the office had been submerged in water. Lowering his outstretched arm, Kunick once again allowed the anger to drain from his face. He retracted his forward leg with a grunt, grimacing as he watched the revolver mirror the movement.

"Corky?" The chief beckoned his trusted subordinate for back-up. Corcoran balked. Her cultivated tough cop exterior melted away, her rigid bearing eroded. She froze, slackjawed and mortified, much like the man she had just killed. Kunick saw Corcoran's inaction reflected in Sauter's face.

"Officer Corcoran, draw your weapon! Now!" Kunick growled. "That's a direct order!"

Corcoran flinched, lurched forward and flirted momentarily with the holstered weapon on her hip, but once again refused to acquiesce. Reluctantly, Kunick finally diverted his attention from Sauter and the weapon pointed at his knee. Corcoran averted her eyes when the chief looked her way. Kunick chuckled, a forced, festering laugh, dismissing his once trusted sidekick with a disgusted click of the tongue.

"Whose side are you on here, officer?" Kunick posed the question lethargically, leery that he already had the answer.

"Sides?" Indignant, Corcoran's uncharacteristic frailty fizzled. "All along I've been operating under the assumption that we're all working on the same side, chief! I understand you and the detective have your differences, a history, but we're all officers of the law, we're all supposed to be working for the common good, together!" She didn't care if her idealism sounded naïve or misguided. "Sauter said it chief, far too many people have died. It stops right here, right now!"

The suffocating tension suddenly ebbed, the water drained from the room, evoking a relieved, collective exhalation. Abandoned and alone, Kunick smiled and shrugged his shoulders, determined to blunt the impact of the incendiary accusations with a calm, confident demeanor. He once again extracted the handkerchief from his pocket and pressed it to the wound on his head, putting it away following a close inspection of the absorbed blood. Bending at the waist, he wiped a hand down Richard's forehead to his chin, closing the vacant eyes. He took the time to free the stubborn trouser legs from the tops of his boots before straightening back up.

"So, here we are, at an impasse of sorts, I suspect." His tone hinted mischief. "It seems I stand before my accusers, my jury and my judges, all conveniently wrapped up in one." He swept his hand dramatically from Corcoran to Devine, paused, moved to Margaret, then stopped at Sauter with a flourish. "It boils down to a matter of he said, she said, so often the case in these types of situations, I'm afraid." Smug, clearly amusing himself. "More importantly, in this particular instance, it's a matter of *I* said, *they* said. *I*, of course, am the chief of police of this little backwoods town, have been for many a year, long enough that the gentlefolk of Broadaxe trust and respect me . . . or fear me. Either way, when Chief Bobby Kunick speaks, people 'round these parts listen. My word's golden, always has been, always will be."

No longer guarded against the imminent threat of Kunick's hostile intent, Sauter relaxed and folded his arms across his chest, the revolver obvious and at the ready. "So tell me, Bobby, what is the golden word? Richard didn't kill those children? Is that it? *I* say he did, but you disagree. Complicity, chief, it may not be the golden word, but it seems mighty appropriate. *We* say you're guilty of it, an accusation you've yet to deny. What is it, Bobby? What's the golden word?"

Striking a thoughtful pose, hand on chin and mouth downturned, Kunick's large, round head bobbed slowly as he considered the question. A light flickered into his tired eyes, an electric current that triggered a misty, melancholy curtain of tears. His eyebrows arched and his frown fractured, fell away.

Struggling to regain his shaken composure, the chief focused on Tony and Billy, forcing an unconvincing smile as he winked at one, then the other.

"With all due respect, Mrs. Schumacher, I feel the need to point out that you got it all wrong." He raised his distant gaze from the boys and engaged Margaret. "The truth is *always* an option, always, it's just that sometimes . . . well, for some folks anyway, faced with certain circumstances . . . it's just that sometimes the truth isn't the most attractive option available." He turned to Sauter, the unconvincing smile curling into a sinister grin. "Richard Mann is our killer, sure, I'll go along with that, case closed."

Unsettled by the defiant chief's sudden, unexpected reversal, Sauter stammered, "What? . . . Wait a minute, Bobby, just what the hell are you trying to pull . . ." Kunick raised a hand and cut Sauter short.

"Listen, Henry, like I said, there's a reason I've been the chief of police here in Broadaxe for so long, and when push comes to shove, whose word is ultimately the one that's going to be believed?" The question was posed rhetorically, but Kunick was still happy to provide an answer. "That's right, mine, and I say Richard Mann is the killer! That's what you all wanted to hear, isn't it? Fine, I'm in agreement, no skin off my ass, nobody gets hurt."

"*You* don't get hurt, that's the more attractive option. Am I right?" Sauter again pointed the revolver at Kunick, confused by the chief's motives. "You don't actually believe Richard Mann is the killer, that's obvious, but you're suddenly willing to just go along with it? That's incomprehensible! Nobody gets hurt? If Richard *didn't* hang those children, Bobby, who did?"

Kunick chortled derisively. "I say Richard isn't the killer, you call me a liar, I change my mind and agree that he is the killer, and you still don't believe me! What the hell do you want from me?"

"The less attractive option, goddammit!" Sauter shouted angrily, his patience with the evasive, waffling chief worn thin. "I want the truth! You ran away from it after Michael Koenigs died and you're still running away from it to this day!

I hope it's been worth it, Bobby, the lies and the deceit, I hope you've been adequately compensated for the loss of life, for all the misery and suffering that you helped cause."

Kunick sighed heavily and dropped his eyes back down to the dead body at his feet. "The truth is I never did know exactly what happened that night in the treehouse. Let's just say I knew it was in my best interest to make sure nobody else did, either." He reluctantly raised his head and for the first time Sauter saw genuine pain and remorse reflected in the chief's eyes. "You remember the pressure I was under, Henry, you remember how anxious the folks around here were for a quick, clean resolution. Dead children hanging from trees wasn't exactly the image the locals wanted associated with their quaint little tourist town. I was strongly urged to accept the story, *the sworn testimony* provided by Richard, his account of what happened to Michael Koenigs, testimony backed by three other eyewitnesses, need I remind you. I did what I was told, plain and simple. Like I said, people 'round these parts trust me for a reason."

Corcoran stepped further into the office and positioned herself at Richard's feet, half a corpse away from Kunick. "*I trusted you, but I don't trust you anymore*," she said softly, her voice saturated with the agony of betrayal. The chief turned his head and regarded his disillusioned underling with a mixture of pity and disdain. Unfazed when she withdrew her revolver from its holster and aimed the weapon at his broad, glistening forehead, he blithely ignored the mutinous incursion.

Turning back to Sauter, "Whether you choose to believe it or not, I wasn't aware of the role Richard played in Michael Koenigs's death, I believe I've already made that quite clear. Was I surprised by his confession, by the fact that Richard was responsible? No, in retrospect I suppose not, and I do regret everything that's happened. I'm sorry Christopher Koenigs paid so dearly for a murder he didn't commit. I'm sorry that three more children are dead, that officer Seth Colins and Max Ferguson are dead. I never imagined . . ." his voice broke, trailed off. He cleared his throat and resumed defiantly, "I believed, or at least chose to believe, that Christopher Koenigs was his brother's killer, that he *had* come back to

Broadaxe to kill again. I hate to admit it, but it was actually a relief to think that we'd gotten it right all along, that he was a demented killer, a genetic sociopath." He smiled wistfully. "Needless to say, it was a hell of a shock when he was released, when I saw that treehouse again and children started turning up dead. I thought it all had been long forgotten, like a bad dream, that the sins of the past were dead and buried, just like Michael . . ."

A queer expression crossed Kunick's face and he averted his eyes. The incomplete thought hung in front of Sauter like near-ripened fruit, tempting yet too soon to pluck. Better to leave Kunick twisting precariously at the end of the branch, lips pursed as if he had just bitten into a poison apple. The chief cleared his throat and shuffled his feet. Seeking an escape route, he clumsily tried to change the subject.

"Hasn't this poor man laid on my floor long enough?" Kunick gestured at Richard, still running in place, his bloody chest drying to a dark crimson.

"Nice try, Bobby," Sauter scoffed, "but I didn't need you to remind me. I hadn't forgotten about Michael Koenigs's grave. I still intend to go out to the cemetery and take a look. I've just been passing the time here with you, patiently waiting for the court order." He glanced down at his watch and flinched when he realized that the afternoon had evaporated. "Goddammit! Why in the hell didn't . . ."

"I've got it right here," Corcoran interrupted as she hurriedly produced a folded sheet of white paper from her back pocket. "It was on the fax machine when I got back from the airport. That's why I showed up here at the chief's office when I did." She handed the court order to Sauter, glancing at Richard's dead body resentfully. "Sorry about that, but it slipped my mind, what with the shooting," she turned to the chief and her voice took on an angry edge, "what with the shooting and all."

Sauter unfolded the paper and quickly perused the court order. Satisfied, he refolded the paper and snapped it noisily against the chief's revolver.

"Richard's not going anywhere, Bobby. He'll be here when we get back." He waved the weapon at Kunick and then pointed the barrel at the door. Eyeing Sauter defiantly, the chief stubbornly ignored the signal to depart.

"Why?" Margaret broke in and delayed the standoff. "I promised that I'd take you to the grave, detective, and I'll keep that promise, but I need to know why. Why do you want to go to the cemetery? What do you expect to find there?"

"Someone asked me a favor," Sauter answered cryptically, watching Kunick intently for his reaction. Beads of perspiration once again formed on the chief's forehead, clinging to the skin like mounds of dew on a broad, blushing slope.

Still clutching her boys tightly, Margaret persisted. "You'll have to do better than that, otherwise I'm not going." She tilted her head to garner Sauter's attention. "Tell me why you're so curious about that poor child's grave, otherwise you're on your own."

Sauter stiffened, felt sweat trickling down his own spine, suddenly aware that he was uncomfortable with the impetus behind his interest, but committed nonetheless. Oddly compelled to honor the request of a man he had judged insane, Sauter realized he couldn't answer Margaret's question because he kept asking it of himself. Why? He had no idea, and he had no choice, so he plunged forward, boring back in on Kunick.

"Christopher Koenigs claimed that his brother Michael's body was never recovered, Bobby. *He* asked me a favor, he wanted *you* to show me where Michael is buried. He wanted *you* to show me Michael's remains." Sauter paused and shook the fist that held the court order, flapping the paper in Kunick's face. "So that's what *we're* going to do! All of us, right now, let's go!"

Kunick still didn't budge. He punched his hands deep into the front pockets of his khaki trousers and arched his back, holding the pose as he let loose with a forced, high-pitched laugh.

"I'm not going to any goddam cemetery!" The laughter faded to a determined frown. "This case is closed, didn't you hear me? I'm getting good and goddam tired of repeating myself, but if need be, I'll say it one more time. I'm Bobby Kunick, chief of police, and I say it's over!" He took a deep breath and softened his tone. "Jesus, Henry, you've got to let this go! This has been killing you, little by little all these years, this crazy goddam obsession of yours. Put it behind you old friend, put it behind you before it's too late."

Sauter ignored the chief's unconvincing concern. "Was the body ever recovered, Bobby?" Kunick stonewalled. "Answer me!" Sauter shouted, the veins in his neck bulging, his throat strained. The chief busted out with an execrable grin.

"My, my, my," he began slowly, "I nearly forgot! You lost a couple weeks of your life there, didn't you, detective. That night in the meadow, the dead child hanging from the treehouse, that was a little more than you could handle, wasn't it?" Kunick smiled at Devine, shook his head disapprovingly. "I imagine Henry probably never mentioned it to you, did he, doctor, the fact that he, how should I put it? Took a leave of absence?"

Sauter felt the hot burn of the blood rushing to his cheeks. "That's right, Bobby, I was a little shook up, I've got no problem owning up to that," but in truth the recollection made him cringe. "I was a rookie cop for chrissakes! It shook me up pretty bad and I had to shut down for a bit. That's how I coped, but that's got nothing to do with . . ."

"Bullshit!" Kunick exploded, "It's got everything to do with it! Poor, sensitive Sauter! Who do you think it was who dealt with the whole goddam mess while you were curled up in a little ball?"

"I was hardly . . ." Sauter tried to defend himself, but Kunick offered no breathing room.

"You were hardly any use, that's what you were!" he bellowed. "Worse yet, when you finally did snap out of it, you were a nuisance! Some things never change, detective. You're still a pain in the ass! I'm not traipsing around any cemetery, digging up graves! Michael Koenigs is dead and buried. Let the child rest in peace!"

Sauter straightened his arm and once again targeted Kunick's kneecap, clicking back the hammer of the revolver. "Move, Bobby, now, or I'll blow a hole in your leg and drag your fat ass to the cemetery! Maybe I was a nuisance, maybe I was a pain in the ass, but I was right goddammit! You knew it, and you did nothing, I don't give a shit what you say! You're the chief of police of this podunk little town? So fucking what!"

"So shoot me, go ahead, because that's the only way you're going to get me to . . ." Kunick's eyes widened and his voice caught as he instinctively raised his hands above his head.

"We're going to the cemetery chief. We're going to put an end to this once and for all." Corcoran pressed the cold steel barrel of her service revolver into the base of Kunick's skull. Her eyelids fluttered and bitter tears dripped from the thin curve of her lashes. She cocked the hammer of the gun and waited, her hand unsteady, shaking just enough so the barrel bounced subtly against the chief's neck.

Unnerved, Kunick caved. "Okay Corky, easy now, I'll go out to the cemetery, you've convinced me, no need to get crazy, let's all just calm down." Raw fear seeped through his rapid, quivering words, "but it'd be best if we waited 'til morning, it's just about dark I imagine. Let's do this right, do it in the light of day, give me a chance to get a hold of the boys out there at the cemetery, do the digging with a machine in the light of day, that only makes sense."

Corcoran didn't bite on Kunick's transparent bid to buy himself some time. "I've got a flashlight and I've got a shovel. We'll go tonight."

*   *   *

Serrated patches of muted light dappled the dirt of the narrow path that fell away into the tangle of brush cloaking the darkened hollow. Red dots of sky blinked like bloodshot eyes through the still branches of the pine trees bordering the deserted cemetery. Headstones jutted from the soft, sandy soil, row upon row of crooked, gray teeth marking the horde of bodies rotting in the earth's cold underbelly.

"I'd like to go down to the grave, take you right to it, but . . ." Margaret looked back over her shoulder at the police cruiser. She smiled and waved to Tony and Billy, sitting obediently in the back seat with the windows rolled up and the doors locked. Pitiable and forlorn, Tony cupped his fingers and waved back. Billy, frustrated by his mother's overprotective doting, scowled and turned away.

Corcoran handed a heavy black metal flashlight to Devine, "I'll stay back. I'll keep an eye on the boys. They'll be safe with me," she suggested with convincing reassurance, gun in hand. "I think I should hang back and keep a lookout, make sure nobody else shows up unannounced."

Devine took the flashlight in her right hand, clicking it on and off to check the beam. Her left arm was draped over Margaret's shoulders, providing a measure of comfort to both. Sauter waited at the head of the trail with his gun trained on Kunick, who lazed against the shaft of a shovel like a road worker on break.

"I wouldn't send you off into the dark with dead batteries," Corcoran muttered her offense at Devine's inspection of the flashlight. She holstered her weapon and folded her arms across her chest, flat and bulky from the bulletproof vest beneath her crisp uniform. "The offer still stands. I'll watch the boys and I'll watch your backs," she addressed Margaret, "otherwise you're welcome to wait here as well."

Margaret fidgeted nervously as she glanced back and forth between the trail leading to the hollow and her boys in the backseat. "It's not that I don't trust you . . ." she eyed Corcoran apologetically. Her mind raced. "Oh, this is ridiculous," she blurted self-consciously. "I *do* trust you. You've shown you can be trusted." She looked askance at Kunick, who feigned boredom. "Richard is dead. The killer is dead, right? I've got to give Tony and Billy some breathing room sooner or later, Billy especially, or I'm afraid he'll end up hating me for it." Tears pooled in her eyes. "It's no way to live, this past week, suffocated by fear."

Margaret nodded at Corcoran, a stern, determined tip of the head. Wriggling out from beneath Devine's arm, she lit out down the trail without another word, without another look back at her boys. Tony and Billy watched their mother until she dropped out of sight below the crest of the slope. Giggling, giddy with the presumption of freedom, Billy playfully punched Tony in the bicep. Devine turned on the flashlight and hugged Margaret's heels. Sauter kicked the shovel out from under Kunick's arm and prodded the chief until he grudgingly fell in line.

A dank chill rolled up the trail, a palpable gloom oozing from the elongated shadows of the hollow. Dead, twisted limbs arced above the narrow path, the skeletal framework choked by the lush, compound leaves of invasive black locust trees. Sharp, spiny branchlets groped at Margaret's head, pulling free tiny tufts of her thick red tresses, causing Devine, Kunick and Sauter to plod stoop-shouldered in her wake. The path seemed more precipitous than Margaret remembered, the hollow much deeper, a sinister catacomb in and of itself.

The misty white beam of the flashlight danced and flickered, lending a herky-jerky, silent movie aura to the steep descent. Sauter listened to the wheezing for several steps, following the raspy breathing as it circled from his right to his left. The thick, guttural inhalations began softly, then grew louder with each step closer to the bottom of the ravine. It reminded Sauter of the rattled respiration of a heavy smoker, or the labored breathing of someone seriously out of shape.

"You really need to take better care of yourself, Bobby, you sound like a heart attack waiting to happen and we're walking downhill for chrissakes." Sauter spoke into the back of Kunick's head as it bobbed down the dimming path.

"What the hell?" Kunick grunted as he turned to look back up the slope at Sauter. "I was just about to say the same thing to you."

Devine raked both of their contorted faces with a blinding flash of light before she swung the beam downhill towards Margaret. The disturbing wheeze saturated the hollow, pressing down from above like a blanket of fog, louder, more intense, the threatening hiss of an animal stalking the underbrush. It was there, upon them, about to overtake them, then dissipated, leaving behind a silence that was equally unnerving in its suddenness.

Devine placed the spotlight back on Sauter, just below his chin. He reflexively raised a hand to shield his eyes. "Is this really such a good idea, Henry?" she asked timidly. "Maybe we *should* just wait until tomorrow, when it's light. What do you think? I don't know what the heck that just was, and I don't think I want to find out."

Sauter leaned to his left and looked down the trail past Devine. "How much further, Margaret? Are we nearly there?" He revealed his intentions with his framing of the question.

Margaret backed away a step or two and moved to the side of the trail. Devine redirected the flashlight, illuminating a small opening in the brush in the flat floor of the ravine. She ran the light around the perimeter of the weed-choked glen, catching the faint reflection of the plain white tablet on her first pass, quickly jerking backward and settling on the neglected tombstone.

"I'll be a son of a bitch," Kunick mumbled the oath as he stumbled forward to the abandoned grave, stunned, the shovel dragging behind in the dirt.

"Start digging, Bobby, let's get this over with and get the hell out of here." Sauter pointed the revolver at Kunick when he issued the command, moving to the foot of the grave alongside Devine and Margaret.

Using the shovel to support his weight, Kunick dropped slowly to one knee and reached out tentatively for the head-stone. He ran his fingers across the cold white marker, deliberately tracing each of the letters and numerals chiseled into its stone face. Momentarily entranced by the long forgotten piece of the past, he had to physically shake himself to break the spell. The sharp tip of the shovel's spade dug into the soft soil atop the grave as he struggled to stand. Scratching his rib cage with his left hand, Kunick let go of the shovel and raised his right hand above his head, index finger extended.

"I'll tell you what, you want to dig this grave up? Any one of you? Well, you be my guest." He pulled the shovel from the ground and dropped it at Sauter's feet. "Not me, I'm not wasting my energy," he grimaced, "and I'm fairly certain you're not going to shoot me if I don't."

Sauter cursed, chagrined that Kunick had called his bluff. He tucked the revolver into his belt and snatched the shovel up off the ground. He stepped to the center of the grave and drove the spade into the soil with his foot, turning over a clump of fresh earth and pitching it to the side. Sauter excavated the soil with a curious fervor and the hole grew quickly. As Kunick watched the work proceed, he became more agitated with each successive shovelful of dirt.

"Hold on, hold on for chrissakes," the chief bellowed desperately, throwing his hands in the air, "You are one mule-headed pecker, Henry Sauter! Needless to say, I never did think things would get this far, but here we are, digging up Michael Koenigs's grave! Well, stop, would you? Just stop! I can tell you what you're going to find, an empty casket, that's what!"

Breathing heavily, Sauter leaned on the shovel and shook his head at Kunick in disbelief. "My god, Bobby, what do you mean you never found that child? The boy was dead!" The chief shrugged his shoulders and shuffled his feet.

"We searched and searched after Christopher Koenigs carried his brother's dead body out of the meadow that night, but Michael never did turn up, not a sign of him, nothing, like he was swallowed whole by the forest. We figured it was animals that got him, same as we suspected when Jimmy Kelly disappeared. That's the god's honest truth," Kunick raised his hand as if he were swearing an oath. "There's bear in these parts, Henry, you know that, same as wolves or coyotes. We figured something got a hold of him and dragged him off, you know, sort of like any other carrion. Like I said, we scoured those woods around the treehouse, but we never found one thing. The way that poor family suffered, we convinced Michael's folks to go on with the funeral, to go ahead and put their child to rest, proper-like, even though we never found his remains. Keep digging if you'd like, but there's nothing down there, and besides, I don't see what difference . . ."

Kunick jumped at the crisp crack of the shotgun and dropped into a defensive crouch as the blast reverberated through the hollow. Sauter pitched the shovel and pulled the revolver out of his belt, aiming the weapon blindly into the underbrush as he motioned for Margaret and Devine to join him in the freshly dug hole. A high-pitched, piercing cackle rolled downward from the highground, racing toward Michael Koenigs's grave ahead of the dry snap and crackle of breaking twigs.

Dorothy Kelly burst into the small opening toting a

shotgun in one hand and the ever-present silver flask in the other. Weaving in a wild-eyed, drunken stupor, she drank sloppily from the flask and threw her head back in maniacal laughter. She was dressed in the same clothing she wore to her boy Jimmy's funeral, the long black frock soiled and wrinkled, the fringed red leather moccasins dulled by dust and dirt. Her pale white skin shone ghost-like in the gloom and dingy strings of matted beige hair crawled from her scalp like a tangle of snakes.

"Y'all not gonna find Michael Koenigs down here, not in this grave! Never been down there, never will be." Dorothy licked her blanched lips and sipped from the flask greedily. Sticky brown liquid dripped down her chin. She wiped it away with the sleeve of her black frock and stared at her captive audience through rheumy, bloodshot eyes. "Sure 'nough though, he done been down here in this hollow many a time, seen him myself. Dare say you done seen him down here," she shook the silver flask at Margaret, "day my boy Jimmy got buried, you done seen him down here with you own boys. Suppose'n he'd done like to meet up with those boys of your'n again," she cackled, tipped the flask, and pointed the unsteady shotgun barrel in the general direction of the grave. "Now git! You all git from here now. Michael, he don't want the likes a you 'round here, and I dare say, neither do I."

Margaret's heart began to pound wildly when she recalled the little boy, the stranger with the funny eyes. She recoiled in terror when she saw Corcoran explode from the narrow path and easily seize the shotgun from Dorothy's inebriated grasp. Dorothy crumpled to her knees, head bowed and drool dripping from her gaping mouth. Margaret leapt from the hole and stumbled toward the trail in a mad, frenzied dash. Dorothy glanced up as she passed with questioning eyes, the hateful menace replaced by pain and confusion, as if she had just awoken from a trance.

"My boys!" Margaret screamed at Corcoran as she sprinted headlong into the groping thorns lining the narrow path, "Where did you leave my boys?" Corcoran tried in vain to assure Margaret that Tony and Billy were still locked safely in the backseat of the police cruiser, but the words were muted by the panic-fueled adrenalin pulsating through her veins.

The breadth of the narrow path seemed to have diminished even further. Margaret ducked into the compressing tunnel, the ascending corridor painted pitch black by the encroaching curtain of thorny underbrush. She plodded up the steep pitch on nightmarishly heavy legs, searching blindly for any sign of remnant sunlight ahead. The thorns once again snatched tufts of her disheveled red hair and sliced into the skin on the back of her hands, which she raised protectively to shield her face. The waning light on this new moon night proved too weak to penetrate the complete and utter darkness sinking into the hollow, threatening to suffocate her soul and her spirit.

Margaret slipped and fell to her knees as she neared the crest of the slope. She scratched and clawed her way out of the hollow and staggered to her feet. Tony's terror-stricken face peered out at her from the back of the police cruiser, his nose squashed flat against the window, the glass fogged by his breath and moistened by his tears. The far door of the police cruiser was peeled back like the lid from a can of sardines, a gaping hole framed by shards of twisted metal and broken glass.

"Billy!" she screamed in benumbed dread, shocked by the harrowing realization that her child was already gone.

BILLY

Billy noticed him first, the strange boy who wanted to be their friend, peering out from behind a headstone with his odd, opaque eyes. The child would jump out into the open and dance a queer little jig, grinning and waving at Billy to come join in the play, only to bounce back to his hiding place, where he would resume the game of peek-a-boo. It was torment, watching the lucky boy frolicking, unfettered and free, while he was trapped in the backseat with his chicken-livered brother.

When Tony finally caught sight of the boy and realized he was trying to tempt Billy into disobeying their mother's strict orders, he grabbed his little brother by the back of the shirt and wouldn't let go. Billy wriggled and squirmed, but he couldn't break free of his big brother's grip. Standing guard outside, the police officer heard the commotion and wagged an admonishing finger at the rambunctious boys. Tony and Billy ceased immediately and offered their cutest smiles to the officer lest she give their mother a bad report about their behavior.

The officer smiled back and turned away, retreating to her post at the crest of the hollow. As soon as she was gone, Billy elbowed Tony in the ribs and received a hard pinch on his ear lobe in return. The brothers settled into a temporary truce. Billy slid across the vinyl seat until Tony's arm was completely extended, clinging to the collar of his little brother's shirt until it pulled taut around his neck. Billy immediately tried to find the strange little boy, but he no longer peeked out from behind the headstone, no longer danced the queer little jig atop the brown bed of decaying pine needles blanketing the grave sites.

Billy finally located the boy at the far reaches of the cemetery, at the edge of the forest, and he wasn't alone. Jimmy's mother was there, the drunken, crazy woman who had chased them from this spot not long ago; the same day his friend, her son, was buried not far from where he sat. Suddenly, in unison, they both turned their heads and looked at Billy, bringing goosebumps to his skin. Frightened, Billy pointed the odd couple out to Tony, whispering that Jimmy's mom had a gun.

Jimmy's mom was scary, always had been, and the boys huddled closer together as she slowly wobbled towards them, teetering unsteadily between the field of tombstones. She trudged through the cemetery like a zombie, her vacant eyes fixed in a distant stare. When she crouched down and began to creep stealthily in the shadows of the headstones, Tony freaked out and began to pound wildly on the window of the police cruiser, screaming at the police officer for help. The alarmed officer hurried to the rescue, but by the time she arrived Jimmy's mom had disappeared.

The shotgun blast rang out from the crest of the hollow. Jimmy's mom, hoisting the shotgun above her head and laughing hysterically, now stood where the officer had just been. She turned on her heels and bolted down the narrow, bramble-lined path, prompting the police officer to follow in reflexive pursuit, luring the boys' appointed guardian away. Left alone in the dreary cemetery, the night suddenly seemed darker, the shadows more menacing, and Billy no longer struggled to free himself from his big brother's clutches.

There was a hard rap on the window, evoking a collective gasp from inside the police cruiser. The strange little boy was there, right outside the door, once again beckoning for Billy to come out and play. Billy stared at the frayed, red bandana tied tightly around the child's neck, the awful scars etched into his tender pink flesh like lightning bolts. The boy grinned pleasantly and motioned for Billy to open the door. When Billy shook his head and refused, the pleasant grin quickly faded to a malicious scowl.

The strange little boy ripped the bandana from his neck and stale, rancid air wheezed audibly from the jagged holes torn in his throat. Clumps of hair fell away from the pallid, drooping skin of his scalp and a sparse, skeletal frame emerged from beneath desiccated flesh. The window of the police cruiser screeched like a chalkboard as sharp, bony talons clawed angrily at the glass until it finally imploded into the backseat. Billy felt the searing burn of hot knives burrow into this shoulder and heard his shirt tear away from his wailing brother's grip.

Cold, hard stone slapped against his arms and legs as

Billy caromed off tombstones, his body limp and useless, incapable of fighting back. Stars pinwheeled overhead in a dizzying array, then blinked out as the blackened branches of the forest erased the night sky. Hot waves of hoarse, inhuman panting rolled across his face and malevolent, jeering laughter echoed in his ears. Constricted with pain and paralyzed by fear, Billy's vocal cords failed each time he opened his mouth and tried to yell for help. Skidding helplessly across the forest floor, roots and rocks shredded his clothing and scraped his skin raw, making the soft caress of the purple petals all the more soothing when he suddenly found himself floating in a sea of flowers. Billy saw the treehouse looming above, his final, fateful destination cradled in the crooked branches of the bur oak. Pinching shut his eyes, he wished with all his might, wished for his mother's embrace, wished that she were holding him tightly against her hip. Rising above the purple lupines, up into the blackened portal of the treehouse, he could have sworn he heard her voice, desperately calling his name . . . Billy . . .

CHAPTER TWENTY-ONE

"Billy!"

Margaret had just regained her footing after stumbling at the crest of the hollow, only to have her knees weaken and give way beneath her once again. The agonizing force of her shrill cry burned her throat and robbed her of air, but she refused to fall. She tottered onto her toes, gasping, groping for balance.

"Mommy!" Tony cried out from the backseat of the police cruiser, the ragged remnant of his little brother's shirt collar clutched tightly in his fist.

The terror in her child's eyes pulled Margaret forward. She lunged, and gravity took hold, coaxing Margaret into a wobbly trot that ended with a thud. Tony jumped back from the window just before his mother slammed into the door with her shoulder. Hitting with enough force to dimple the metal, Margaret dropped to one knee and yanked repeatedly on the unyielding door handle. Her muscles constricted and her flesh tingled as panic coursed through her body. Using the police cruiser as a crutch, she worked her way around the back of the vehicle. Perched on his knees, Tony kept his eyes glued to his mother as he bounced across the broken glass littering the seat. They met at the gaping hole where the rear passenger door had been violently torn from its hinges. Tony sprang from the opening and fell into his mother's arms.

The embrace was tender, but brief. Squatting at his level, Margaret held her son at arm's length and shook him gently, "What happened to your brother, Tony?" Her tone was calm, yet urgent, "Who took your brother? Which way did they go?" Frightened and confused, Tony hesitated. Margaret shook harder. "Tony!" she jerked him closer and shouted in his face, "Billy! What happened to Billy!"

Tony slowly raised his arm and pointed to the distant, dimly lit corner of the cemetery, his entire body heaving with heavy sobs. "The little boy, mommy, the little boy took him."

Margaret eyed the mangled police cruiser skeptically, then turned and followed Tony's trembling finger. Straining to see in the day's last light, she noticed movement in the dark lip at the edge of the woods. It was there and gone, too quick to be certain, but . . . *it could have been Billy.*

"Margaret!"

Margaret snapped her head toward the direction of the voice. Detective Sauter, on the trail leading up out of the hollow. She pulled Tony's forehead to her lips, "You run, Tony, you run to the detective as fast as you can, do you hear me?" Hard kisses slurred the words. Margaret pushed Tony in the direction of the trail. She climbed into the police cruiser through the missing door and rolled into the driver's seat. With one eye on the rearview mirror, she hit the gas and fishtailed down the cemetery's gravel road. Sauter sprinted over the crest of the slope, waving frantically, Devine and Corcoran close on his heels. As soon as Tony arrived safely at the detective's side, Margaret punched the pedal to the floor.

It was a rite of passage for children growing up in Broadaxe, the Halloween visit to the meadow where Michael Koenigs died, the stroll among the headstones at the nearby cemetery. With Tim's ardent blessing, Margaret made certain Tony and Billy never tagged along, much to their chagrin. The other children inevitably filled her sons' heads with tales of a little boy's voice beckoning from the forest, of haunted visions of a spectral treehouse floating in the gnarled branches of the bur oak. The locals tried in vain to baptize the newcomer shortly after Margaret arrived in Broadaxe as a teenager. She never gave the outlandish stories much credence, yet she never went to the meadow to find out for herself. It wasn't fear that kept her away, she was simply unwilling to disrespect and desecrate the sanctity of such places, places that brought others so much sorrow and pain.

The hazy glow of the headlights carved a finite bubble into the blackness of the night. Although Margaret had never been to the meadow, she knew exactly where it was located. Every soul in Broadaxe knew – the meadow, the treehouse, Michael and Christopher Koenigs – all woven tightly together into the stained fabric of local folklore. The white lines of the highway streaked by in a blur. There was a road just ahead on the left, a nondescript dirt road that led to the meadow, a gap in the forest wall that would be easy to miss at such a high rate of speed, but she never once thought of slowing down.

Fragments of introspective madness began to coalesce inside Margaret's head as she contemplated the incomprehensible. *How could I have been so blind!* she beat herself up one second, *How could I have known!* and consoled herself the next. The bitter sting of bile pooled in her gullet when she reflected on the shattered simplicity of her former life, a cherished life she had come to despise in the short span of one week. Yet it all seemed so distant, a faraway, forgotten dream rendered an unconscionable nightmare by the senseless parade of death.

Margaret felt like an innocent bystander trapped among the crowd on the sidewalk, forced to watch the moribund parade pass by, and it pissed her off. It didn't have to come to this, it *never* should have come to this. Four frightened little boys, scared to death of the punishment that awaited them if their role in Michael Koenigs's death were uncovered. Four frightened little boys who surely never imagined a fate far worse than the grim reaping that would be harvested from that long dormant seed of deceit.

Margaret hated them all, dead or alive. She hated Richard Mann, the self-centered son of a bitch ultimately responsible for the lives of each of the children hung from the treehouse. She hated Jackson Kelly for being such a spineless, alcoholic ass-kisser. She hated Max Ferguson for befriending her in the first place, for dragging her unwittingly into the terrible secret from the past, for bringing the others that shared that secret into her life. With a twinge of sadness and regret, she realized she hated her husband, Tim, simply because he loved her. In the end, she hated herself for loving him back, for bearing his child, a child destined to suffer for his father's sins.

Caustic tears trickled down Margaret's cheeks and she pounded the steering wheel with her fists. Dorothy Kelly's drunken lisp hammered incessantly at the back of her brain. *Y'all not gonna find Michael Koenigs down here, not in this grave! Never been down there, never will be . . . day my boy Jimmy got buried, you done seen him down here with you own boys. Suppose'n he'd done like to meet up with those boys of your'n again.* Chief Kunick's graveside confession ensued, turning the hot, angry blood pulsing through her veins to ice. *We searched and searched after Christopher Koenigs carried his dead brother out of the meadow that night, but Michael never did turn up, not a sign of him, like he was swallowed whole by the forest.*

The frenetic beating of her heart throbbed in Margaret's head and her lungs ached with breathless anguish. The exaggerated tales of impressionable children, *a little boy's voice, beckoning from the forest,* it was too surreal to believe, *a spectral vision of a treehouse floating in the gnarled branches of the bur oak.* She began to tremble uncontrollably. Each of them had been driven to distraction by unrelenting voices in their heads; Tim, Max, Richard, and Jackson, voices that slipped into the ether the minute their sons went missing. Innocents, spirited away into the night, only to be found hanging from a treehouse suspended in the branches of the bur oak.

Christopher Koenigs, sittin' in a tree, K-I-L-L-I-N-G - the chorus of snide little voices crept out of Margaret's subconscious with unsettling clarity, *First comes a shove, then comes despairage, then comes Michael in a funeral carriage.* The tiny voices faded into a haunting, mournful whistle that suddenly seemed to be coming from outside of her head, seemed to be coming from *everywhere.* Nearly too late, she caught the shadow-obscured entrance to the narrow dirt road out of the corner of her eye and cranked the wheel hard to the left without easing off the gas. The tires screamed as the police cruiser slid sideways across the pavement, spewing a shower of gravel as the wheels bit into the soft shoulder and propelled the swerving vehicle into the forest.

Margaret had seen the boy twice, the little stranger, once in her own yard the morning Jimmy Kelly was murdered, then again in the hollow following the funeral. *You done seen him down here with you own eyes.* Her mind was a blank, unable to recall anything about the child, as if his image had been erased from her memory. *He had funny eyes,* Nicholas had told her, *like telescopes, or magnifying glasses, like he could see everything or they sucked everything in.* Nicholas also told Margaret that she would likely meet the boy someday, that he promised to come back and play. Now Nicholas and Terry were as dead as Jimmy, and Margaret feared that Billy was the latest playmate selected for the fatal game.

Margaret careened down the tree-lined passage, clipping off small pine trees and bounding over jutting rocks in a frantic race toward the meadow. The police cruiser rollercoastered over a small rise and Margaret slammed on the brakes, skidding across a matted carpet of grasses and ferns before jolting to a stop against the unrelenting trunk of a centurian pine. The headlights illuminated a grassy trail that serpentined through the forest. Margaret ran through the trees, plodding on legs rendered distressingly heavy by the gnawing fear that she might be too late, that her little boy may already be hanging from a noose below the treehouse.

The swaying sea of purple lupines momentarily mesmerized Margaret when she finally reached the meadow, panting with exhausted desperation. The rigid cones of the flowers snapped angrily at the chilled night air, wickedly beautiful sentinels standing watch, warning Margaret to proceed no further. The treehouse loomed overhead, brooding and malevolent in the bur oak's protective embrace. An eerie silence settled over the meadow, quieting the animated lupines. Margaret scanned the darkness for any sign of Billy, for some indication that she wasn't alone, that she wasn't too late.

The sinister, deep-throated mirth reverberated through the trees, the same wheezing, scratchy laughter that had descended upon the hollow holding Michael Koenigs's empty grave. The lupines began to sway again, gently at first, undulating in a hypnotic dance that intensified as the unnerving laughter neared the meadow. Margaret sensed the ethereal movement in the darkness to her left. She turned, straining to discern the nebulous shadow as it crept across the forest floor.

"Billy!" she croaked out in sheer terror as she witnessed her child's limp, lifeless body disappear beneath the purple shroud. Margaret threw herself into the nefarious field of flowers, struggling to break free as the lupines lashed out at her body and tangled her legs. She gasped with repulsion at the hideous creature that emerged from the concealing purple lupines. It clambered up the massive trunk of the bur oak with one sinewy claw and clutched her little boy's bloody shoulder with the other. The creature cocked its head at Margaret and snorted derisively as Billy swung slowly in a pendulous arc, blinking at his mother with tortured, uncomprehending eyes.

Margaret broke free of the floral restraints and lunged for her son, "Billy!" she grabbed hold of his ankle and felt the queer sensation of weightlessness as she rocketed upward. The fetid air of the dank treehouse filled Margaret's lungs and burned her eyes. Billy's ankle slipped from her grasp and she tumbled across the dusty wooden planks of the treehouse floor, choked by the putrid odor, sputtering for breath. She lay on her side disabled, paralyzed and helpless, but she summoned the last of her waning strength when she saw the noose hovering like a halo above her child's head.

Margaret sprang to her feet and somehow knocked Billy free. Whimpering softly, he scampered to the rough hewn treehouse door and pressed his back against the wall, crouching in abject fear. Margaret winced with the searing pain of the hot needles puncturing her side and gagged at the stench of the hot, stale breath washing over her face. Spurred by the manic power of protective maternal instinct, she worked the coarse rope over the decaying skin of the creature's skull and tried to pull the noose taut around its slender, decaying throat. Puffs of white, misty vapor seeped from the jagged puncture holes torn in its neck, but the creature's gray, rotting flesh rippled pink and healthy each time the noose plugged the respiring gashes.

The creature flailed wildly, cracking Margaret's ribcage with a concussive blow that compressed the air from her lungs and sent her somersaulting against the back wall. Stunned by the debilitating torque of the blow, Margaret blinked to be certain that the vision before her wasn't merely an unconscious mirage.

"Hello, my name is Michael, would you like to play with me?"

The demonic imp dissolved before her disbelieving eyes and an adorable little boy melted Margaret's heart with a sweet, disarming smile. Tufts of straight, dark brown hair spiked from the child's head in an unkempt mess, his cheeks shone red and rosy, his limbs plump and fleshy with the vigor of youth. He was clad in a well-worn red tee-shirt with faded white lettering on the front, cut-off blue jeans and black high top tennis shoes. The child danced a queer little jig, clicked his heels and giggled happily, all the while holding the noose tightly against the awful scars marring the otherwise unblemished skin of his neck.

Margaret desperately wished to reach out and take the little boy in her arms, the strange little boy with . . . the funny eyes. She looked deeply into the child's opaque, inhuman orbs and suddenly realized she had been duped by the spiteful demon lurking within. Tiny fingers fidgeted with the coarse rope and the happy giggle devolved into a harsh, gurgling wheeze. White, wispy exhalations once again oozed from the unobstructed holes, saturating the treehouse with the unmistakable stench of death.

Margaret rocked forward onto her hands and knees, "Sweep, Billy, sweep!" she shouted, prodding her son with the familiar mantra of his father, wondering if he possibly had the wherewithal to respond.

Billy never hesitated. He swiveled on his hip and swung his legs forcefully under the demonic waif's sparse, bony feet. Margaret vaulted across the treehouse and shoved the tiny corpse backward with all of her might. Teetering on the precipice of the treehouse door, the decrepit ghoul raked Margaret's face with the sandpaper skin of its' open palm, slamming her violently back into the far wall. Margaret watched in impotent despair as the morbid imp reached out and snatched Billy off the floor. She cried out helplessly as both tumbled out of the treehouse into the enveloping blackness of the night.

Margaret staggered forward, dizzy and disoriented. "Billy, Billy," she stuttered in a hoarse whisper. Tiny pinpricks of light exploded before her eyes and the treehouse whirled around her in a nauseating kaleidoscope. Her knees weakened and her rubbery legs failed. The splintered floorboards crashed against her face and flattened her nose as she descended into the black, blissful depths of unconsciousness.

. . . Lingering in the limbo of a semi-lucid dream, Margaret stubbornly refused to return to the horrifying reality that awaited her in the waking world. Billy and Tony bounced up and down on the bed, while Tim snuggled into the soft, sensitive skin on the nape of her neck and whispered softly in her ear.

"Margaret."

"Yes honey," she cooed back, reveling in the comforting, familiar feel of her former life.

"Margaret!"

"I'm right here, honey, there's no need to shout."

"Mrs. Schumacher, are you up there?" The delicious dream took a decidedly different turn. "Mrs. Schumacher, can you hear me? Are you okay?"

Margaret swallowed hard and tasted the disconcerting cocktail of dust and blood that coated her tongue. She rolled onto her back with the dawning realization that there were hard wooden boards beneath her rather than the welcoming comfort of her mattress. Blinking her eyes rapidly, she tried to bring her fuzzy surroundings into focus. She caressed her nose and cheeks, gingerly probing the painful splinters embedded in her tender flesh.

"Mrs. Schumacher?" A woman's voice now, urgent and concerned, "Please would you answer us! Please let us know you're alright. We have your little boy. We have Billy here with us."

Margaret gazed at the dismal walls of the treehouse and felt them closing in upon her. "Billy," she croaked, barely audible, "Tony." Wild-eyed with sudden panic, she sat up and pushed herself across the floor until her back was against the wall. She searched the darkened corners of the treehouse for any sign of the haunted little boy, for any sign of the vengeful demon, for any sign of Michael Koenigs.

Crawling on her hands and knees, she willed herself to the treehouse door and tentatively peered out into the cold, black night. Sauter and Devine stood at the base of the bur oak, gaping back up at her from the gloomy forest floor, both of their faces twisted into question marks. Sauter cradled Billy in his arms, bruised and battered but mercifully still alive.

"Where's the dead little boy?" Margaret posed the disturbing question with solemn sincerity, "Where's Michael Koenigs?"

Sauter slowly turned to Devine, shook his head gravely and shrugged his shoulders. He looked back up at Margaret, bewildered. "We only found your boy, Mrs. Schumacher," it was a distant, faraway voice, "we only found Billy . . ." Margaret scanned the blackness below her in wild-eyed panic. She softly mumbled a distressed whisper – *Tony, oh my god, where's Tony* – but her plaintive words were drowned out by the malignant melody saturating the oppressive night.

It could have originated in the corners of her mind, a taunting figment of her imagination, but Margaret was certain that the familiar, mournful whistle emanated from the deep, dark recesses of the forest. Unbidden and unwelcome, the chorus of sinister little voices infiltrated her head as the meadow of purple lupines swayed to and fro in eerie synchronization.

Michael Koenigs, sittin' in a tree, K-I-L-L-I-N-G . . .

Made in the USA
Charleston, SC
16 November 2012